ENDORS

Naomi, the Rabbi's Wife, by Miriam Finesilver, is an amazing book and a joy to read. It's incredibly well written, and the story draws the reader in from the first page. I fell in love with the characters...from Naomi, to Daniel, to Naomi's counselor Melinda. Even the characters who aren't so lovable, like the theater producer Gary, are fascinating. I recommend *Naomi, the Rabbi's Wife* to anyone who is searching for powerful inspiring literature.

Rabbi Michael Wolf
Writer-director: *The Sound of the Spirit*
Author: *The Upper Zoo, The Linotype Operator*

Naomi, the Rabbi's Wife combines romance and biblical truth in a Jewish paradigm. Naomi, the heroine, is on a quest for fame and romance in her role as an actress in New York City. She gains a measure of recognition and success, but her relationships suffer from her wrong decisions. Her quest for fame turns into a quest for forgiveness. At that point she meets the rabbi, and her world is turned upside down. Having been an actress and a script writer, Mrs. Finesilver knows how to develop the characters and increase the tension until the surprising ending. Besides being an excellent novel, this story is made for the screen. The dialogue has depth and humor, and the plot is not predictable but unfolds at the right pace to thoroughly engage the reader. Those who seek out biblical romance novels will love this one. An added bonus is getting an education in Judaism, its biblical observance in modern-day America, and its old-world customs and Hebrew phrases. Messianic Judaism is brought into play also. I whole-heartedly recommend this book to people of every religious belief.

Nancy Petrey
Author, Musician, Bible Teacher
www.jewishrootsjourney.blogspot.com
Mizpah Tikvah Ministries on Facebook

Rabbi's WIFE

Miriam Finesilver

2nd Edition

Energion Publications
Gonzalez, Florida, USA
2021

ISBN: 978-1-63199-787-7
eISBN: 978-1-63199-788-4

Energion Publications
P. O. Box 841
Gonzalez, Florida 32560

energion.com
pubs@energion.com

Table of Contents

PART II

Y'shua, Your love would have been enough
(Dayenu—it would have been sufficient),
but You kindly gifted me with Michael—
only the Father of Lights
could have brought this man
into my life.

Michael, I love you.

PART I

Chapter 1

September 1977

*N*aomi, alone in the elevator for the final fourteen floors, once again practiced her audition piece. "Someone to watch over me ..." Hearing her voice crack, she mimed holding a gun to her head, pulled the trigger and made a popping sound.

Emerging from the elevator at the twenty-ninth floor, she squeezed past all the other actresses crowding the hallway and walked toward the sign-in desk. *Every actress in town must be here today. Great, like I'm really the one who's going to get the part.*

The woman at the desk was busy painting her fingernails a bright red. After an attention-getting cough from Naomi, the woman sighed. "Yes?"

"I'm Naomi Gold. I signed up this morning. Can you tell me how soon you might be calling my number?"

Continuing to apply the nail polish, she asked, "What's your —?"

"Sixty-eight."

Running a still-wet fingernail down a checklist, she said, "You're next."

"You're kidding? I thought—"

Immediately the door to the hallowed audition room opened and a plump bleached-blonde young woman slumped out, her mascara streaking down from her tear-filled eyes.

"Next."

Naomi moved swiftly to the all-important open door, flashing a smile at the curly-haired young man holding it open. At the same moment, a petite brunette carrying a Styrofoam cup filled with

1

coffee rushed to the sign-in desk. Naomi attempted to avoid a collision, but the other actress was running full-tilt. They collided and coffee splashed onto Naomi's expensive new cashmere sweater

"I'm sorry," the actress said. Placing the cup on the desk, she reached into her purse.

"That's okay." Naomi absentmindedly picked up the half-full cup and entered into the room.

Shutting the door behind them, the young man extended his hand, but Naomi carried the coffee cup in one hand and her portfolio in the other. Since she was trying out for a part in an improvisational group, she might as well start now.

"Hey, figured you must need some coffee by now," she adlibbed, adding a smile and an intentional shrug of the shoulders.

He peered into the cup. "It's half empty."

She pointed her chin to the area where the coffee had stained her right sleeve. "Here's the other half."

Having recently seen his picture in the *New York Times* magazine section, she knew this was Gary Ruben, the show's director. *What am I doing kibitzing with him? I'm such an idiot.* Then she heard him chuckle. *Whew.*

Struggling not to spill the coffee, she reached into her leather case for her headshot.

"Allow me," he said, taking the cup from her. "I'm Gary."

"Thank you." She found his brown eyes warming.

A statuesque raven-haired woman, impeccably dressed in an expensive business suit, rose from her seat and strolled over to receive Naomi's picture. Turning it over she scanned the resume which was imprinted on the back.

"I'm Gwen Champion, the casting director, and over there," —she paused and pointed to a corpulent bald-headed gentleman sitting with his back to all three of them—, "is our producer."

"Thank you." Spotting the piano player, Naomi retrieved her sheet music from the portfolio and handed it to him. "I'll give you a signal when to come in with the intro. Pianissimo at first," she instructed, "and when I start singing, go to mezzo piano."

He glanced at the three-panel judge and jury with a quizzical look. Maybe her tone had been too assertive. After all, to them she was merely another unknown actress.

Naomi turned toward Gary. "Too much chutzpah, huh?"

"I think I'm getting used to it with you." He turned toward the piano player. "Steve, do what the lady says." Taking his seat, he smiled and winked at her.

At that moment, she would have been thrilled to stop everything and simply enjoy spending time with this famous and apparently fun-loving man. But she needed to focus. If she did well such a time may come. She paraded herself to the center of the room, and began her monologue.

"Okay, so you see this ravishing creature, right?" She struck a fashion model's pose. "Not to shock you, but I wasn't always so beautiful. Picture this: nine years old."

She drooped her shoulders, puffed out her cheeks and spread her arms wide apart.

"Chubby would be putting it kindly—Dad called me pleasingly plump, but just between us, I don't think I really was pleasing to anyone. Then there was the matter of the hair—total frizz—and eyeglasses no less."

Reaching into the pocket of her skirt, she pulled out an oversized black pair of spectacles. "The only one in my grade who had to wear them. Now, let me tell you about my best friend, Marianne Leibowitz. You got time?"

Gary Ruben nodded, "Go on."

"Marianne. Perfect size six, hair went into a perfect flip, and to top it off her parents inherit a fortune and move into this absolute mansion. It's Marianne's big birthday party at the Leibowitz mansion. In my mind, Dad drops me off not to a party but to an execution."

Naomi paused to move a finger across her neck, symbolizing her throat being cut. "When you're fat, got frizzy hair and glasses, you're a natural shoo-in for the role of most picked-on kid in the class. It was bad enough that lately Marianne joined in with everyone

3

else picking on me, but this day Mrs. Leibowitz decides she would make fun of me, too. 'Oh look at the birthday cake—bet Naomi could eat the whole thing all by herself.'

"The reason I remember this day is not because of the being picked-on stuff—why should it be different?—it was the norm back then. I remember that day because something kinda extraordinary happened."

As Naomi talked, she crossed to another area of her performing space. "I managed to get off by myself in a nook in their gigantic kitchen, and while sitting there it was like this thought came to me: there's something more real than any of this. It was like I was treated to a momentary glimpse of reality. I had found the meaning of life."

Naomi acknowledged the musician. Taking his cue, he very softly played the song's intro.

"But, whoops, now you see it, now you don't. Like I could almost see the thought as it went flying away, I literally tried reaching out to grab it." Gesturing as though attempting to catch something, she made eye contact with Gary. "The question is this: Is there someone who watches over us?"

With the piano picking up in volume, Naomi began singing in a velvety alto voice about her longing to know if someone was watching over her. After the first verse, the pianist, following the notation on the song sheet, switched from a ballad-type tempo to an up-tempo blues beat.

Once she finished her audition piece, Naomi waited to hear the familiar "Thank you, we'll call if interested." Instead she saw a wide grin on Gary's face.

He asked, "Did you write the monologue part yourself?"

"No. I lived it."

Turning to Gwen, Gary said, "Let me see her resume." After a quick scan, he asked, "Naomi Gold? What is it really? Goldstein? Goldberg? It's never just Gold." He winked and then shifted his gaze to the others and confided, "Truth is I'm Rubenstein, not Ruben.

"Well, you're wrong," Naomi blurted, then hesitated for a well-timed pause. "It's Goldblatt."

Gary rose from his seat, took Naomi's hand and ushered her to the door. "Goldblatt, huh?

The waiter plopped the hot metal tray on their table. "Here you go, ladies. Salami pizza, extra cheese, Sicilian style. Anything else I can get for you?"

The pungent smell from the garlic combined with the sweet smell from the fresh basil elicited a loud rumbling from Naomi's stomach. Yet her taste buds called out for something else: crushed red peppers.

The cacophony of sounds distinctive of Goldberg's Pizzeria was a blend of New Yorkers who talked at their tables as if trying to be heard on a subway train, the clink of silverware and thunk of plates, and the unneeded music blasting out of the overhead speakers.

Naomi shouted, "Can I have the red pepper?"

The waiter seemed to look right through her. She screamed louder. "Crushed red pepper."

He snatched up the condiments tray off another table and plopped it in front of her.

Aah, good ole New York type rude.

Slapping a white dish towel across his arm, he flashed an intentional smile toward Anne before heading back to the kitchen.

"I saw that," Naomi said, teasing her roommate.

"Don't you dare. He doesn't like me." Anne shook out a white cloth napkin and smoothed it onto her lap. "It's simply I'm nicer than all of you New Yorkers, so he appreciates me.

"Anne, face it. He finds you cute. Especially when you show off your dimples for him."

"Stop it. You're totally embarrassing me. Besides which I want to hear more about your audition."

"The most amazing thing is Gary—"

"Gary, the director?"

"He winked at me. Twice."

Anne folded her arms across her chest and pursed her lips.

"You think I'm making this up? Well, you can wipe that smirk off your face." Naomi placed a slice of the steaming hot pizza on her plate. "Do you remember the interview they had with him in the *New York Times* about a month ago?"

"I do."

"Oooh, you do not. You're faking it. Your eyes are doing their quick blinking thing." With complete abandon, Naomi poured the red pepper onto her slice. "I caught you."

"You did." Anne blushed and lowered her head. "Sorry."

"I'm teasing. Will you please just eat your pizza?"

Anne raised her head and laughed. She cut her slice with a knife and then delicately picked up the bite-sized piece with her fork. "And will you please eat your pizza, too, before the cheese slides off and falls on your lap? Like last time."

Both laughed as they enjoyed their first bite.

"You know," Naomi said while chewing her food, "if I was a casting director and I had to find someone to be like the complete opposite of me, you'd get the part in a New York second."

"But what if I got a wig with curly red hair? Then we'd get to play twins."

"I remember when . . . oh, who was our acting teacher back then?"

"You mean Bill Hickey?"

Naomi nodded and signaled to the waiter for a refill of her diet Coke. "Remember when he assigned us to work on that scene together? At first we couldn't find a scene to work on, and then we couldn't find a place to rehearse."

"You were living in that 'hotel for young women.' It was so small we couldn't both fit in your room at the same time."

"And you lived with that aunt of yours." In a mockingly snooty voice, Naomi said, "And, you are never to bring those filthy theatre people into my house. She was one mean lady."

"Naomi, I probably never told you this, but you really helped give me confidence in myself."

"I did?"

"I was so scared when I first got here. And I didn't like people making fun of my so-called Midwestern twang. Almost every day I thought about flying back home, and if it hadn't been for you, I probably would have."

"Thank goodness you didn't. What a waste that would have been." Naomi spotted the waiter two tables from them. He carried two large pitchers and she held up her glass, dinged it with her fork, and in a loud voice said, "Excuse me."

He cocked his head to one side, smirked, and sauntered over to their table. He refilled Naomi's glass, and without even a request from Anne he topped off her iced tea.

Naomi arched her eyebrows. "Someone here doesn't seem to mind your non-city slicker ways." She bit into her pizza and quickly smacked it onto her plate. "I forgot the cheese." She shook a copious amount of parmesan cheese, covering not only the pizza but also the tablecloth surrounding her plate.

"Are you going to tell me more about the audition or not?"

"Gary's got this thick curly hair. It's sort of wild, not too long but not too short either. It fits his face and his whole personality. If you coulda seen that playful smile of his."

"Thick curly hair? You're sure you weren't just looking in a mirror?"

"His is sandy blonde." Naomi leaned forward. "Can you imagine what our kids would look like? These cute curly-haired little moppets."

"Uh, need I remind you, you were not trying out for the role of Mrs. Gary Ruben?"

"A girl can dream, can't she?"

"This is about your career, Naomi. Isn't that your real dream?"

"You're right," Naomi sighed. "Sometimes maybe I lose a little perspective, huh?"

"I told my singing coach about your audition and she told me the story. They need to replace Francine Chambers because—"

"I know. I wanted to tell you last night but you went to bed early. Francine got discovered through the Improv Asylum and now she's going to California—"

"To star in a new TV series. Naomi, one day that could be you." Anne put her hand up, signaling to wait a moment—her pizza was getting cold. After slowly chewing a small bite, she continued. "I didn't really have to go to bed that early, but I was concerned. You were getting all worked up, and I thought 'what if she doesn't get the part?' But now—"

"I understand. So, can I ask you a favor? Just in case I have a message from the answering service when we get home, *for a change*, could you just this once eat as fast as me?"

"Just this once." Anne took a large bite of her pizza and washed it down with the iced tea.

Soon after, they paid the check and stepped out of the restaurant. About a block from their four-bedroom walk-up they met with a heavy downpour of rain. They flung their coats over their heads and ran the rest of the way home.

As soon as she entered the apartment, though breathless from walking up four flights, Naomi made a beeline for the telephone.

"This is Naomi Gold. Do you have any messages for me?" Naomi waited for the operator to check and watched Anne put the leftover pizza in their refrigerator.

"Gwen Champion's office called. You have a callback tomorrow morning at 9:30."

Naomi squealed and jumped up and down before hanging up the phone. "I got a callback. Tomorrow morning . . . a callback. Anne, I gotta get this part."

"Don't you have to go to your parents tomorrow?"

"I don't have to be there until dinnertime on Saturday. You know, at sundown. It's crazy. Tomorrow night starts Yom Kippur and like usual the next night Mom and Dad want me there to break the fast with them."

"What's crazy about that?"

"You've lived with me through two Yom Kippurs already. Have I ever fasted? Yet I go home every year to basically pig out with the family pretending I'm famished because I haven't eaten in twenty-four hours."

"Then what's the purpose?"

Anne's question took Naomi off-guard. "I don't know. It's family, that's all. I gotta get to bed. Need my beauty sleep."

"Yeah, especially for tomorrow." Anne walked toward her bedroom but then turned back. "In case I don't see you in the morning, good luck."

"Thanks."

As Naomi readied for bed, Anne's question replayed itself. What was the purpose? The more she tried dismissing it, the more resentful she became. *How dare her question my traditions?*

"Naomi Gold. I'm here for a—"

"They're expecting you." This time the woman at the sign-in desk actually made eye contact. "You can go right in."

As Naomi entered the audition room, Gary rose from his chair. "Hey, Goldblatt, come on and step up to the plate."

Even with their backs to her, Naomi recognized the casting director and the unnamed producer from yesterday. A heavyset stranger with blonde hair stood in front of them.

Gwen Champion twisted in her seat to face Naomi. "Ms. Gold . . . Goldblatt . . . oh, for goodness sake, just tell me what you want to be called."

"I'd prefer Gold. That's what's on my resume. But, please, call me Naomi."

"Of course." Ms. Champion stretched her arm toward the unidentified man. "Tony is the longest-standing member of Mr. Ruben's troupe and has graciously given his time to work with you today."

"Thank you."

Tony resembled a giant teddy bear and his gracious smile spread across his broad face. "From what I've heard, seems I better get used to working with you."

Gary held out a four-page script. "Since you're so fast with your mouth, Naomi Gold, I'm figuring you'll enjoy a cold reading. Here you go."

Tony whispered, "Let's just have some fun, okay?"

"Naomi," Ms. Champion said, "this is a sketch Tony has performed for the last month with Francine Chambers. If we like you, this will be a part you will be playing. It's called 'The Taming of the Jew.'"

"Hope you're up on your Shakespeare," the producer's gravelly voice warned.

Gwen Champion stood and positioned herself to block the producer from Naomi's line of vision. "Tony will read the role of Pet Rock and you will read Kvetch."

Naomi attempted her first line, but stumbled over the fast-paced tongue-twisting words. "Sorry."

Tony put his arm around her. "Shakespearean prose. Whew, it's a beast, isn't it? Took me awhile, but now all that iambic rhythm, it comes naturally. Go ahead, try your line again."

"Let us be quick-sah and get to the bar mitzvah."

Tony laughed. "By jove, I think she's got it."

At the completion of this skit, Ms. Champion handed her a longer sketch, a spoof of a 1960s Beach Party movie. Naomi played Crabette Funicello, and Tony played Crabby Avalon.

They bantered through a couple of pages of dialog. Gary then punched the play button on a cassette recorder. Naomi easily glided into the classic bubble-gum tune.

When their duet ended, Tony smiled broadly. "All right."

Gary turned off the cassette recorder. "Time to run through some improvs."

Mr. Producer stood, pointed to his watch, and exited the audition hall.

For the next half hour, Naomi and Tony improvised scenes in front of a bus stop, at a Macy's Thanksgiving Day parade, and inside an airplane during a thunderstorm. Each scene required a different format, from soap opera, to foreign language gibberish, to musical comedy.

Abruptly in the middle of a TV sitcom parody, Tony stepped out of character. "I want to work with her. She's good."

Gary rose and gave a thumbs-up. "For you, Big Guy, anything. She's hired."

"Really? I am?"

Naomi ran up the four flights, flew into her bedroom, crawled under the bed, and brought out her suitcase. Battered a bit but still the special gift Naomi's parents gave her to say "Now you're on your own." Dad, of course, had to add, "And you better make us proud." With bright yellow, red, and orange flowers splashed on the imitation leather material, how could a girl not love it?

With the phone scrunched between her left ear and shoulder, she tossed a pair of pajamas, an extra skirt and blouse, a pair of jeans, and a change of underwear into the suitcase. "Hi, Mom. What time's service at the *shul* tonight?"

"You mean tomorrow's, don't you, sweetheart?"

"No, I don't mean tomorrow. I want to be with you and Dad tonight, and also to fast with the both of you."

She halted the frenetic packing and sat on her bed. "I was going to surprise you when I got there, but I'll tell you now—"

"Oh sugar, you met someone. Who is he?"

"No, Mom, I'm not getting married. That's not the surprise, okay? But listen. I got a part in an off-Broadway show. I'm going to be joining the union. I'll really be a working actress and I won't have to waitress any more. Anyway, I feel I should be, I don't know, thanking God, cause maybe He's really watching over me, huh?"

"I'm so proud of you. My best daughter."

"Mom, I'm your only daughter, but okay, you're my best Mom."

"I love when you tell me that. Sugar, the service tonight starts at seven."

Naomi scanned the bus schedule which rested on her nightstand. The Greyhound leaving the Port Authority at three should work perfectly. "Okay, Mom, I'll be there at six. Tell Dad to pick me up."

It only took another few minutes to finish stuffing the suitcase. Before leaving her room, Naomi's eyes were drawn to the sampler hung above her bed. Years ago, her mother had embroidered the prayer: "Now I lay me down to sleep. I pray the Lord my soul to keep. If I should die before I wake, I pray the Lord my soul to take."

Along the border, Mom had stitched pink chubby cherubs. A little girl knelt beside a bed, hands clasped in prayer.

When Naomi was a child, Mom would kneel beside her at bedtime and before they prayed, she'd asked, "What's something you can thank the Almighty for, Shug?"

According to her mom, the One honored at the *shul* needed to be thanked. Like a good girl, she would do exactly that.

Before boarding the bus, Naomi paid a visit to her favorite bookstore on the first floor of the Port Authority.

"Hi Gus, what's the newest bestseller?"

The elderly craggy-faced man called out to one of his employees. "Mike, open that box just came in." Turning back to Naomi, he asked, "You read *Love Story*, right?"

"Of course. Didn't everybody?"

"Then you're ready for the sequel. *Oliver's Story*. Selling like hot-cakes. Hadn't seen ya in a while." He accepted the check she quickly wrote out. "Don't worry about I.D. Sssh, only for you, cause you're a cutie, been one ever since first time you came in here. What were you then, all of thirteen?"

"Yup, thirteen. Thanks. Next time I see ya, I'll give you a book report."

The first passenger to board the bus, Naomi had her choice of seats. She opted for one by the window at the very back. Whether she read her new paperback or found herself distracted as she tried to absorb this exciting new chapter in her life, she craved solitude.

You've come a long way, kiddo.

Thirteen years old—her first solo Greyhound into Manhattan. It was soon after her Aunt Ida had mentioned a teen acting workshop. "It's part of the Stella Adler Acting Studio."

The name sounded impressive, though she didn't have a clue who Stella Adler was. "Dad, I wanna go. Can I, please?"

Mom had misgivings, but Dad had a hard time denying his only daughter anything she wanted.

For the next three years, each Saturday morning Dad drove her to the Sugar Bowl. The bus depot's local diner was also the place to go for breakfast on Saturdays.

The first time Naomi climbed the steps onto the bus, she heard half of Ellenville yelling at her dad. "Where's your daughter think she's going? Saul, what are you, crazy? You can't let a kid go into the city by herself. What are you, *meshugenah?*"

Expecting her dad to demand she get off the bus, Naomi turned around. She instead saw her father remove the ever-present pipe from his mouth and answer his critics. "She's gonna be a star one day. Wait, you'll see."

Now, eleven years later, her dad would have the satisfaction of seeing he was right. Saul and Helen Goldblatt's successful daughter, the pride of Ellenville.

Okay, maybe it wasn't a starring role on Broadway, but it could lead to one. Look what it did for Francine Chambers.

Two hours whizzed by. She attempted reading her new paperback, but after the fifth time reading and rereading the first paragraph, she stuffed it into her shoulder bag. Her heavy eyes shut and she occupied her thoughts with her opening night. And how she would celebrate this momentous night going out afterwards with Gary Ruben. *Well, a girl could dream, couldn't she?*

And then perhaps there would be a review from the *New York Times*. Sure, they had already reviewed the highly acclaimed Improv Asylum, but maybe they'd be interested in checking out the newest member of the comedy troupe.

"Ellenville," called the bus driver, jarring Naomi from her realer-than-real fantasy.

She disembarked from the bus and immediately saw her pear-shaped dad. The sight of him puffing away on his pipe made her want to run up and hug him. But she knew better; Dad was not an affectionate man.

"Hi, Dad."

"I'll wait for your suitcase. Mom's in the diner. Go on in."

"Good to see you, too, Dad."

"Always a kidder, aren't you? Go on in. We gotta get something quick to eat."

Naomi walked inside and saw all the familiar faces and heard all the familiar voices. Harry and Bessie Schwartz sat with Mortie and Evie Bluestein. And Mildred Shapiro yelled at Margaret, the waitress, "What do you mean bringing me soup that's cold?"

Same old, same old.

"Naomi, look at you, a sophisticated New Yorker now," boomed Bessie.

Everyone turned and stared. Naomi waved and walked toward her mom, whose eyes filled with tears. Thank God for Mom. Her southern upbringing made up for Dad's New York gruffness.

Mom cupped her hands around Naomi's face and cooed. "Oh, honey, you look beautiful."

"I've missed you, Mom." Truth was she rarely ever thought about her parents, but making her mom happy was a good thing, wasn't it?

"I ordered for you. We have to be at *shul* by seven and since you'll be fasting with us, you need to eat."

"What did you order?"

Dad slid into the booth. "The suitcase is in the car. The food's not here yet?"

"Not yet, hon. Naomi, I ordered your favorite, hot pastrami on rye and potato salad."

"And cheesecake? I won't be eating til tomorrow night, so why not?"

Forty minutes later, Dad parked their car at the bottom of a hill, along with almost every other Jewish family living in Ellenville—and they climbed the small but steep hill leading to the *shul*.

"Hey, Dad, remember when I once asked you why we didn't just drive up to synagogue?"

"And you remember what I told you? We're good Jews. We're not supposed to drive on the Sabbath. You remember?"

"And do you remember what I said? I asked you, 'Dad doesn't Rabbi Eisner know everyone's parking their car and then walking up?' I mean c'mon already—it's still silly."

"And you still have a fresh mouth."

Mom squeezed her daughter's hand, and together they laughed. Dad thought about it for a second, shook his head, and then decided to laugh with them.

As they entered Ezrath Israel, a wooden building built in 1907, Dad reached into his pocket for his *yarmulke*. He plopped it onto his shining bald spot and accepted the hairpin Mom offered him.

He hardly has any more hair to clip it to these days. Oh, Dad, I wish you'd let me hug you.

He proceeded into the main sanctuary reserved for the men only. Mom took Naomi's hand and together they made their way up the creaking stairs to the balcony reserved for the women. As usual, they sat in the front row so Mom could lean over the rail and watch the rituals performed by the Rabbi and the other men. Naomi guessed her mom probably also wanted to avoid all the petty gossiping from the other women.

Before the service began, Mom looked directly into Naomi's eyes. "How are you doing, shug? Are you lonely? Do you still get depressed?"

"Mom, stop worrying about me. I'm okay. Besides, it looks like the service is starting."

Two men ascended to the platform and pulled back the curtains of the ark. Mom's countenance softened.

She actually has goose bumps. Oh, why can't I be like my mom?

By the time one of her parents' best friends, Milt, came forward to read from the Torah scrolls, Naomi's mind had wandered to again imagining her opening night.

Mom whispered, "Naomi, these are Moses' last words to the Israelites. He knows they'll end up worshipping idols. But he tells them whenever they apologize and return to God, God will forgive them." She kissed the top of Naomi's head. "He loves us, Sugar. He'll forgive us anything, if we ask."

Naomi flinched and gently pushed her mother away.

Chapter 2

October 1977

*M*aybe another swig of that pink liquid would unknot Naomi's stomach. *Yuck? Tastes like chalk.*

Curled into a fetal position on the freezing white tile, her haunches were becoming numb. Great way to make an entrance onstage. What if she ended up tripping over herself the first time the audience got sight of her? Great. Above her head was a paper towel dispenser. She stretched her arm, grabbed a few sheets, and tucked them under her. *Yeah, like they'll keep me warm.*

Achoo. The smell from the mildew didn't help either.

Yet this antiquated moldy place served as her refuge. Maybe one day she'd make it to Broadway. *Bet backstages there have real bathrooms befitting a professional actress. In that case, I better act like a professional.*

Beyond her little sanctuary, she sensed the nervous excitement as the other cast members prepared for Friday night's performance— and for the new kid's debut. Did they trust her not to let them down? And how selfish could she be? This was the only bathroom and she was hogging it when others probably needed to use it.

She moistened toilet tissue in the sink, and carefully removed the Pepto-Bismol caked around her mouth. Her dark red lipstick needed to stay intact.

After a careful inspection in the bathroom mirror, she determined her stage makeup still looked freshly applied—despite the undertone of upset-stomach-green. *A new color for my Crayola crayon box.*

Through the thin wall, the stage manager shouted, "Places, everyone." Time for the comedy troupe to take their places before the house lights darkened and the stage lights went up.

Naomi needed to get out there. But what if her stomach wasn't ready?

Gary's panicked voice echoed in the hall outside of the bathroom. "Where's Naomi?"

"Think she's locked in the bathroom," Julie said. "I'll get her."

"No, *I'll* get her."

The feet got closer and then came the quick rapping on the door. "Goldblatt, outa there!"

"My stomach's queasy."

"Want me to give Julie your solo? You know I'll do it."

Please, God, help me. Don't let my tummy . . . She cracked open the door and broke out in uncontrollable laughter.

Dressed as an ultra-orthodox Jewish man for the first skit, Gary was wearing a long black coat over baggy black trousers. His black fedora, pinched at the top to form a triangle, had a long curled sidelock glued to each side.

"Vhat? You make fun vit me?" Gary teased in a heavy Yiddish dialect.

"I can't help it. I love especially your *peyos*."

Gary moved his head from side to side making his sidecurls dance to and fro. "Give a look." His Yiddish inflection made her laugh all the more.

"They gotta tickle your cheeks?"

The stage manager interrupted. "Places."

"Tickling's for later." Gary winked, moved into position for his entrance onstage, and motioned for Naomi to join him.

She took her station in front of Tony. "This is your night," he whispered. "All month you've had to watch Francine, and you've been great at the rehearsals. Finally it's all yours. Break a leg."

Complete blackout.

No pink goo in a bottle could calm her stomach and bring all her senses to such heightened attention as did the moment before stepping out onto a stage. She heard every murmur coming from the audience, every rustle of a Playbill, and even the quiet crackling of the overhead microphones.

This is what she lived for: the moment the show began and continued with its own momentum, a world created by sheer imagination about to unfold. She thrilled at the anticipation of carrying the audience with her on this adventure.

How many times now had she heard Steve play the music which ushered in Gary's entrance? Yet this evening each chord produced an intense surge of energy throughout her body.

With the familiar theme song to the movie *Rocky*, the first skit, *Shlocky*, opened the show. Gary danced on stage and sang, "Oy, I'm going weak now, fasting hard now, won't be long now, Yom Kippur ending soon now."

Naomi entered as Shlocky's ditzy secretary. "Shlocky, I forgot you're fasting—I brought you your usual bagels and lox." She then turned to the audience and confided her secret love for the boss. "He doesn't eat, and me—I eat my heart out."

Steve played *Close to You* and Naomi sang, "So, nu? I want to be close to you. Why do bagels suddenly appear every time you are near? Like me, they long to be close to you." Naomi ended her parody of the famous Carpenters' song and the audience's enthusiastic applause filled the theatre.

After her duet with Tony as the famous Crabby and Crabbette, the audience not only applauded, but cheered.

For the last portion of the show, which called for pure improvisation, the cast members, each took their turns as the "emcee."

Tony went first. "You've been a great audience, but, you know, folks, sometimes we run out of ideas and need your help. We know you paid a lotta money to be here, but now we're putting you to work. To start, give us an occupation. Gary, c'mon out here."

Gary raced onto the stage. Tony prompted the audience, "What would you like our friend to be? A doctor? A bus driver?" With half the audience shouting out suggestions, Tony pointed to a man near the front. "Sir, I couldn't hear you. What did you say?"

"A magician," the stout man yelled.

"Terrific." Tony turned to Gary and told him, "*Poof* you're a magician. But every Houdini needs an assistant."

Gary immediately responded. "Of course, and I pick our newest cast member, Naomi Gold."

Naomi sprinted out from the right side of the stage and Tony exited to the left.

Together the couple quickly hit their stride. Gary initiated the dialog as well as the action while Naomi aided in moving the action along. But what could she possibly contribute to give it a twist? Francine always managed to be an asset during these improvisations.

Then the inspiration came: when Gary waved his magic wand, she refused to disappear. "You owe me money. Pay me for last week and *poof* I'll disappear."

Gary paused as the audience's laughter reached its crescendo and then subsided. His back to the audience, he winked and mouthed "Good job."

When the show ended, Gary grabbed her hand so they stood next to each other for the curtain call. Once they were all backstage, he asked, "Wanna go for a drink?"

Could the evening get any better? At each Passover Seder, her family sang *Dayenu*. As a young girl, Mom told her, "Honey, it means 'it would have been sufficient.' We're thanking God because He always gives us more than would be sufficient."

Tonight, in her heart, Naomi declared, "*Dayenu*."

Julie, in a sudden mad dash for the dressing room, almost knocked Naomi over. *What's with her?*

Naomi turned to follow Julie but was interrupted by Tony. "Naomi. I want to introduce you to my wife." Tina was as chunky as Tony, but didn't seem as friendly. Cordial at best.

In the dressing room, while removing her makeup Naomi spoke to Julie's reflection. "You okay? Is something bothering you?"

"I don't want to talk about it, okay?"

"But . . . well, I just wanted to tell you how much I love watching you and Tony in the Shakespeare skit. I'm glad they gave it to you instead of me." Naomi shook her head. "I'll be honest—I stink at that stuff."

"Yeah, Tony and me, we're good together."

Naomi remained silent. At the first rehearsal, she had noticed Tony's wedding ring and observed the way he and Julie enjoyed each other's company. Naomi had foolishly thought the two of them were married to one another. Now it dawned on her—she never saw a ring on Julie's finger.

Well, who am I to judge? Sure glad Gary's available. At least I think he is.

"I'll go to the bar and get our drinks," Gary shouted in competition with the jazz band. "What can I get you?"

"Vodka martini, dry, with a lemon twist." She'd heard Natalie Wood order that in a movie once. Sounded sophisticated.

Between the dank smell of the place, the discordant sounds coming from the musicians, and a case of jitters, Naomi hoped not to end up with a headache. Better not have another stomach attack either. The bottle of pink chalk remained in her dressing room.

Gary returned with two similar-looking drinks, although one had a lemon twist and one a pearl onion. Was his a martini, too?

He edged into the leather bench next to Naomi and pressed his hip against hers. "I like an onion with mine."

She must have been on target if he ordered the same thing as her. And she was glad he misinterpreted why she was staring at his drink. Just because their glasses looked alike, she had no idea if that meant their contents were the same. For all she knew, his was a gin and tonic—that's what she remembered hearing Robert Wagner order once. *An onion, though? Huh?*

Gary clinked his glass with Naomi's. "Can't believe you've never been to Arthur's before."

"Well, I'm a country girl after all."

"You actually lived in the Catskills? All I knew were the hotels there. Whatever hotel my parents were going to, they'd *schlepp* me and my brother with them. I hated it. Barry even had his bar mitzvah at one of them. We never even thought about people living there all year round. Must have been boring."

"I couldn't wait to get to New York City. A friend and I once found a way to write out Ellenville that showed what we thought of the place." Naomi took a napkin, reached into her purse for a pen, and wrote out *E-vil.* "What'ya think?"

Gary looked at the napkin for a brief moment and then returned his intent gaze to Naomi. "Better drink up. There's a two-drink minimum here. No cover charge, but . . ." He picked up her glass and placed it in her hands.

With a stab at imitating Natalie Wood, Naomi lifted her martini glass to her lips and took her first swallow. Oh dear, Natalie never winced. Her head down, Naomi twirled the lemon rind in her fingers. A few seconds more and the bitter taste from the vile liquid should fade away.

"So, what hotel in the Catskills did you usually go to?"

"It depended on where Dad was performing. You look confused. I thought you read my *New York Times* interview."

"I did, but . . ."

"Dad's a stand-up comic. At least now he's getting better gigs than the Borscht Belt in the Catskills. Mostly Las Vegas."

"Oh, of course. Now I remember."

She felt like Anne, pretending to remember the very same interview her roommate had pretended to read. *Sure hope my eyes aren't doing that quick blinking thing like Anne's did.*

Naomi managed another sip. "We'd always get stuck going to hear the comics when we had relatives visiting from out of town. And you know what my dad would do?"

Gary jumped in before she could answer her own question. "He finished the joke with them, right?" Disgust sharpened his features. "That's what all the local yokels did."

Ouch—did he think she was a yokel, too? "What about your mom? Is she an entertainer, too?"

He scoffed. "Mom? Give me a break. Best she does is make a meal off and on. She can't even tell a joke at a party."

"My mom is a good cook, but she's incredibly shy. She grew up in—"

"I'm almost ready for my second glass. You need to catch up."

As Naomi obediently tossed back her vodka, the lemon rind swam into her mouth. She delicately covered her mouth with her hand and surreptitiously removed the nasty fruit.

"Wait here." He slid away from her. "I'm going to get us both refreshers. Be back in a minute." He disappeared into the crowd.

Naomi tried not to sulk, but she always resented being interrupted. There was an embarrassment with it—why would he want to hear about her Alabamian mom? But still, it was rude. Her mom taught her that. And every time Dad interrupted Mom, Naomi hurt for her sweet mom. But this sulking needed to stop immediately. Not only was Gary cute and extraordinarily talented, but he could be her ticket to stardom. So what if he interrupted poor little Naomi?

Get over it. One day girls will be imitating me—I'll be my own Natalie Wood.

Gary returned with two new drinks. "What were you going to say before I so rudely interrupted?"

She felt his hip again pressing against hers as she sipped from her second martini. "Rude? Who, you? No, I was probably the rude one—boring you with—"

"Your performance tonight was great. You're already better than Julie, and soon you'll be better than Francine."

"It's so much fun working with you."

"We were meant to work together. We could be the next, I don't know, I could go all the way back to Burns and Allen."

"Or how about Lucy and Ricky?" She giggled.

Gary moved in closer and slid his arm around her neck. "Lucy and Ricky, huh? Why not? You know, I've been playing around with this idea for a TV series. Why not a modern-day *I Love Lucy*?"

"*I Love Naomi*?"

"Now watch it, don't put words in my mouth." His kiss melted any last remnant of Naomi's inhibitions. "Drink up and then we'll go to my place. You like cats?"

"I grew up with dogs, never a cat."

"You'll love Zoey. There you go, we'll name our TV series, '*I Love Zoey.*' And you'll, of course, play Zoey."

A short time later they were in a subway car on their way to his Brooklyn Heights apartment. Naomi said, "I was kinda surprised when Tony introduced me to his wife. I thought him and Julie—"

"Those things happen. What if you found out I was married or involved with someone else? Or what if I found out you were? Would that really change anything? If we liked each other, why shouldn't we be together?"

Even in her inebriated state, Naomi was unsettled by this. Why couldn't she just find a way to think of this as romantic? To love someone so much that whatever the circumstances, it wouldn't matter. *I'm way too insecure, that's all. I need to get over it.*

Instead she thought about the role that would propel her to stardom. The announcer's trained voice resounded in her imagination: And now time for *I Love Zoey*, starring the irrepressible Naomi Gold.

Wonder what the name of Gary's character will be? And would she go by Naomi Gold-Ruben or simply change it to Naomi Ruben?

Two months later, Naomi scampered up the four flights and rushed into her apartment. Anne stood by the kitchen counter putting away groceries.

"I've got big news." Naomi reached into her purse and brought out a small box. "Gary gave me this last night for Chanukah." She opened the box and revealed two keys resting on a white satin cushion. "He wants me to move in with him."

Anne froze, a can of soup in one hand and a loaf of bread in the other.

"That new girl in our acting class, Cheryl, she's looking for a place." Naomi shrugged off her heavy coat. "Look, if you don't find someone right away, I've enough money—I could give you a month's rent if I need to."

"You only just started seeing him."

"Anne, this is the first time someone I'm crazy about is crazy about me."

"What are you going to tell your parents?"

"I don't know, I guess I'll just tell them. They'll probably be more accepting of it than you are." She turned her back and hung her coat in the closet. "You should see that scowl on your face."

"If he's so crazy about you, why doesn't he ask you to marry him?"

Naomi's mouth thinned and she glared at Anne.

Anne said in a soft voice, "I just don't want you to get hurt."

"I'm a big girl, ok?"

Anne sighed. "When are you moving?"

"This Thursday."

"You're giving me three-days' notice and that's it?" Anne set a can of soup on the counter. Hard. "What's the hurry?"

"I'll pay the next *two* months' rent . . . even if you find a room-mate right away. I already paid Gary my share of rent with him, but I won't leave you in the lurch. Good enough?"

"It's not about the money." Anne sat on the couch, leaving enough room for Naomi to join her. "I care about you, even if you don't care about yourself. When I first met you, you seemed like the most secure person I'd ever met. I remember thinking maybe one day I'd lose my insecurity and be as confident as you."

Naomi moved toward the couch but only straddled its arm. "Yeah, I had to convince you not to go home. That would have been such a waste. I hope you know by now what a great voice you have."

"And what about you? Do you know how pretty you are? And how talented?"

"Why are you asking me that? What are you trying to say?"

"It seems you're more insecure than I am."

Naomi swung her legs and stood. "I really need to start packing." She headed toward her bedroom, then stopped and faced Anne. "You're right. I'm not all that confident. I just put up a good front. But Gary's helping me believe in myself. I'm sorry but I gotta go pack."

Before packing, Naomi picked up the phone in her room and called Tony. "It's me, Naomi. Gary told me to call you. I'm moving in with him this Thursday. Could you help me?"

"I'll check if I'm free. But what about Gary? He's puny, I'll admit, but he's got two hands."

"Very funny. He told me you'd say something like that. But he's got a super important appointment with his agent."

"How much stuff?"

"Just some boxes—no furniture."

"Yeah, I can do it. But you sure you know what you're doing?"

"You sound like my roommate."

Once she hung up, she wandered into the kitchen. Anne glanced up while plopping a dollop of mayonnaise into a bowl. "I'm making tuna fish. Would you like a sandwich?"

"With the sweet relish?"

"Of course."

"I'd love one." Naomi grabbed napkins from the pantry and brought them to the table. "What do you want to drink?"

"My usual."

Naomi poured iced tea for both of them and sat across from Anne. "It's been my dream since I was a kid to someday live in a brownstone in Brooklyn Heights. Did I ever tell you that?"

"A brownstone?"

"I'm reading your mind. Still no elevator, that's true, but it's at least one flight less than ours . . . I mean yours. It'll be more money, but, wow, I never dreamed of getting paid as much as I am, and Gary says that's only the beginning. Maybe we'll end up in Hollywood. Maybe even married by then."

Tony lumbered into the apartment and plunked down a large cardboard box. "Last one. What's in here? Bricks?"

"Books actually," Naomi said. "Ooh, be careful," she warned as Tony bumped into a thin rectangular box leaning on the couch. "That's something Mom embroidered for me." She ripped open the box, slid the framed embroidery out and showed it to Tony.

He read, "Now I lay me down to sleep, I pray . . ." He smiled and said, "That's really sweet. My sister made something like that for her little girl. Very sweet."

"Thanks. Let me get you something to drink."

She led the way into the small kitchen. Zoey jumped onto the Formica countertop.

"What's Francine's calico doing here?" Tony scratched behind her ears and she rubbed her head against his hand.

"Zoey? No, that's Gary's cat. Boy, she really likes you. I go near her and she hisses." Naomi opened the refrigerator door. "Soda or just some water instead?"

"Give me a can of Coke if you got one. I'll take it with me." Under his breath, Naomi thought she heard him say, "Gary's cat, huh?"

"What?"

"Nothing. Listen, I'll take the Coke with me."

"You're leaving?"

"I have an audition at four today. Need to get home and freshen up. It's for a soap opera. Make sure your boyfriend helps you with the unpacking. Let him do some of the work, okay?"

"I'm sure he will."

Tony grinned. "See you later."

Before she could thank him properly, he was gone. Something about seeing Zoey seemed to rattle him.

The sampler looked too fragile sitting on the floor. Naomi reached into the thin box and found a small envelope where she had placed the nail used in her previous apartment. She soon found a tiny hole above the bedroom dresser providing the perfect place. She inserted the nail securely in the wall, carefully lifted the sampler and balanced the wire in the back of its frame onto the nail. She stepped back. This now felt like home.

Opening the closet door, she pushed Gary's clothes to one side of the rack. But even so, would there be enough room for all hers? And why hadn't he done this himself?

He must've been in one big rush and all excited about pitching his—no, our—TV show today.

Would he be put out with her scrunching all his clothes together like this? He might be. She fanned all his shirts, sweaters, slacks, and jackets back out as they were before she touched them and chose to lay her clothes on his—*no, their*—bed. He'd tell her where to hang them when he came home. *Their home.*

His—*no their*—phone rang. Weighed down with an armload of dresses, she stared at the answering machine as it clicked on.

"This is Gary Ruben. Nah, it's not me, only a machine. But go ahead, leave a message and the real Gary Ruben will call you back."

Whoever it was hung up without recording a message. Gary will now have to change the greeting to say something like "Hi, this is Gary and Naomi"? Or maybe they could record some kind of funny skit for their greeting. Oh, that would be so much fun. This also reminded her she needed to cancel her answering service, which Gary called "old fashioned."

An hour later, the clothes were stacked on the bed and she was lost in a sea of crumpled newspaper she had used for packing. A key turned in the front door.

Gary.

No time for a cursory look in the mirror. She brushed back her hair and pinched her cheeks before realizing her hands were covered with newsprint. Now her face probably was as well.

Gary walked in and laughed. "Very cute."

"I'll go wash up. Give me a minute." She ran into his—*their*—bathroom and quickly scrubbed her face and hands.

Gary followed her in. "Don't you want to hear how the pitch went?"

"Of course. I'm sorry."

"They loved it. I'll tell you more when you get dressed. Dinner out, okay?"

"Sure." She went to her stack of clothes. "I hope you don't mind. My clothes are all on the bed right now." She found her favorite pants suit.

He followed her into the bedroom, looked around the room not only at the mess on his bed, but also the stack of empty boxes. Then he noticed her sampler. "You have to be kidding. Naomi, I'm a grown man, I can't have something like this in my bedroom."

Instantly she removed it from the wall and asked, "Where should I put it?"

"I don't know. How about your favorite store? You know, the Salvation Army."

She slid it under the bed. "This okay for now?"

"Sure. C'mon, can't wait to tell you about today." Gary grabbed her hand and *whoosh* down the stairs they went.

Naomi gasped as Gary hailed a taxi. "Wow, you're kidding," slipped out of her mouth before she could stop it. Never before did he spring for anything like this. Always they took the subway.

"Not kidding, news too good for a subway." A taxi pulled to the curb and the cabdriver opened his window. Gary leaned in and said, "Junior's Restaurant. The one on Flatbush."

They slipped into the back seat and Gary asked, "How'd the move go?"

"Tony—" The car swerved frenetically to the right and Gary slammed into Naomi. "Uh, as I was saying—." This time she was stopped midsentence because both she and Gary were tossed to the left.

Gary tapped on the plastic window dividing the front from the back of the car.

The driver slid the partition open and eyed Gary's reflection in his rearview mirror. In a heavy Russian accent, he asked, "What you want?"

Gary squinted his eyes to read the name on the identity plate. "Hey, Anatoly, ya wanna take it easy? My lady friend's gonna get a concussion you keep this up."

"Yes, sir," the man nodded, sliding the partition shut once again.

"Do I have to wait till we get to the restaurant? Gary, please tell me, are they interested in our idea?"

"*Our* idea?" He arched his eyebrows. "Whoa. *Our* idea?"

"Well, I contributed."

Gary brushed his lips across her neck and breathed into her ear. She knew what he was doing, and it worked every time. For whatever reason he might have to distract her, she enjoyed it—way too much.

He again asked, "How'd the move go?"

"Good. Except I don't know where to put my clothes. I'll have to squeeze all yours over to one side to fit mine in."

"So, what's the problem with that?"

"I felt bad, you know, smushing all your—"

"It'll be fine. I'll move some of my summer stuff into the closet in the office."

"And we need my name on the mailbox."

"No problem once again. What else?"

"Your answering machine. The message. Can we record something that has my name on it, too?"

Suddenly his easy agreement to everything halted. "Hmm. Something about that doesn't seem . . ." He stroked her cheek and played with a curl dangling off her forehead. "Honey, it wouldn't be professional . . . we need to keep our personal and our professional lives separate."

"What am I supposed to do? Get my own phone number?"

He withdrew his hand from her face and snapped, "Why shouldn't you?"

Her upper body tensed and her eyes began to blink involuntarily.

"Stop looking like that, Naomi. You can still get rid of that silly answering service. Tell you what, I'll help you pick out a machine like mine. But our names need to be kept separate."

She desperately wanted to ask why, but held back. Thankfully, at that very moment the cab came to a stop in front of Junior's Restaurant.

The popular glorified diner bustled with activity. Gary put his arm around Naomi's waist and escorted her to a booth by the window. "I'll treat tonight. They make great steakburgers."

Their orders soon taken, London broil for him and a steakburger for her, Gary was ready to tell her the events of his day. "Just like Rhonda promised . . . she is such a super agent—"

"You still have to get her to see my work."

"Yeah, I'll get to that." Gary pursed his lips together and said, "When you interrupt me, I lose my train of thought."

"I'm sorry. Rhonda got the producer?"

"An *associate* producer, but not just *any* associate producer. This guy's big in Hollywood. He's found projects for Norman Lear himself. The guy's name is Sid, and he loves the idea of doing it as a soap opera parody."

"Ahem, *my* idea."

"That's not how I remember it exactly—more like a collaborative effort. But wait til you hear this. He says we'll do it without a laugh track and with a live studio audience. Outrageous, huh?"

"Why?"

"It'll look more like a soap opera that way. Okay, and one more thing: he wants to change it to *I Love Chloe*. Sid said it's catchier." He shrugged his shoulders. "Who knows?"

"As long as I still get to play Chloe, it's fine with me."

The waitress placed their food before them. "Anything else?"

"Yeah, I love your half-sour pickles," Naomi said.

31

"Better bring a big bowl of them," Gary said as he looked at Naomi and winked.

Naomi laughed. "Somebody would think I'm pregnant, huh? I love my pickles."

"Good way to keep your figure," Gary said. "The TV cameras add something like ten or fifteen pounds. Hope you know that."

She bit into a bright green crunchy pickle. "Umm. These are great. So, you're saying, yeah, I'll definitely play Zoey or Chloe or whatever we call her. Right?"

He jabbed a fork into the largest pickle he could find in the bowl and bit into it. "Naomi, who else could play the neurotic housewife? You're a natural. Look how neurotic you were about where to hang your clothes. Now since I'll be playing the oblivious husband, mine will take a stretch of the imagination." He paused. "Uh, sweetie, that was your cue, you were supposed to say something like, 'Oh, but, Gary you're such a good actor you can do it.'"

"Guess I was being the oblivious one. Sorry."

"You know what? You say 'sorry' a lot. That's good. That shows a neurotic personality. We'll use that in the script."

Their dinner arrived. Naomi reached for the salt at the same time Gary did. "Sorry," she said.

He shook his finger at her and smirked.

Both ate in relative silence until the decision for dessert. "Since I have to watch my figure, you wanna share one of their giant slices of cheesecake?"

"Depends which one."

"Could we get the brownie marble?"

"As long as you eat less than half. Think how many calories must be in it."

Soon the luscious slice was divided between the two of them. However, she did not enjoy it. Awareness of the calories overshadowed its taste.

"Sounds like a done deal the way you're talking. Gary, I can't believe it. We should be jumping up and down."

"Ain't over till the fat lady sings."

Her eyes popped open and the dessert sat in her mouth un-chewed. "What? Fat?"

"Man, you really are neurotic. The fat lady . . . it's an expression like saying 'the game's not over yet,' or even better 'don't count your chickens before they hatch.' You're not fat, so would you please chew your food?"

On their way out, she thanked him for treating her to dinner. Again, he hailed a cab. Several blocks before home, he said, "I might need to go to California to pitch this to the big guys. Hope you're prepared for my being gone for a little while. I'll divvy up my parts between Tony and even you and Julie. A girl can play some of them."

"California? But I just moved in—"

"Stop with the neuroses, okay? It shouldn't be for long, and then hopefully they'll agree to film the show here in New York. If not, we'll move to California. My lease here in Brooklyn will be up in July, so either way it'll work out. We move or we stay. Meanwhile, you'll keep our apartment warm for the both of us."

Naomi's mind buzzed, trying to grapple with all the rapid changes in her life. Since they sat in silence until reaching *their* brownstone, she assumed Gary was preoccupied as well

On their way up the stairs, Naomi said, "You know, Tony's a really great guy, carrying all my boxes up these stairs, but he got kinda weird when he saw Zoey. He said she was Francine's cat."

"It's no big deal. I told Francine I'd take care of her until she got settled in California. Don't know why Tony got weird. Probably your imagination."

Gary turned the key but before opening the door, he gave Naomi a passionate kiss.

Our new life together. He loves me.

Once inside, they threw their coats onto the sofa. Zoey grabbed onto Gary's leg and whimpered. "Better feed her."

"I'd do it, but she doesn't seem to like me."

"Give her time, she will." He walked into the kitchen, Zoey following close behind. Soon he returned to the living room, sat on the sofa and pulled Naomi onto his lap. "Speaking of Francine, you know Rhonda's the agent who got her started in L.A. I told her all about you and she wants to meet you."

"Really?"

Gary nodded. "I told her to give you maybe another few weeks, then she should catch your performance in the show."

"Aren't I good enough now?"

"Another few weeks, that's all."

Later that night, Naomi lay in bed listening to Gary's ragged breathing. It might have been ragged, but he at least was sleeping. Of all the nights she had slept over in the past, this was the first time sleep evaded her. Shouldn't it have been even more blissful now that this was her home, too?

Then why this sense of dread? When would Gary leave for California? Would she soon be sleeping alone in this big bed? Why did he think she wasn't good enough for Rhonda to see her perform? And why couldn't they have the same phone number and its answering machine? And why hadn't he mentioned the lease of her new home would be up in July?

He's right. I really am neurotic.

Chapter 3

Being Passed Over

"To My Best Daughter, Your father will not relent as much as I plead with him. I have told him you are our child, and our love can't relent either. But, darling, you were not raised to live like this. Please forgive your father for calling you that name—you are not a tramp, but to live with a man, you know this is not right. How will this end? Even if you marry him, I don't know if your father, even then, will relent. Will I ever see my little girl again? Soon it will be Passover. Will it be our first Seder without you? I think about coming to visit you, but, sweetheart, your father forbids me. Love, Your Best Mom."

Naomi dropped her half-eaten candy bar on the coffee table, slipped the handwritten letter back into its envelope and ran to the bathroom. With a handful of toilet tissue, she wiped her eyes and nose. It was now after 4:30 p.m—too close to the time Dad would be coming home from work. If she called Mom, and Dad walked in . . . Naomi hadn't the heart to do that to her mother.

Pee-eww. Zoey's litter box, ensconced behind the bathroom sink, called for cleaning again. *Why don't we ship the cat off to Francine already?*

The front door opened and Gary called out, "Naomi, where are you?"

"Coming." When she returned to the living room, Gary waved the candy bar at her.

"I told you, the camera adds up to ten pounds." She opened her mouth to object, but he interrupted. "We'll talk about this later. Right now, I need to call Gwen and set up some auditions."

"Why? What—"

Gary put his finger to his lips. "Shush." He flipped through his address book until he found what he needed, then dialed. "Gwen, it's me, Gary. We have to schedule auditions and find someone to fill in for me."

Naomi gasped.

Again Gary put his finger to his lips. "I'll be going to California in three weeks, not sure for how long."

Naomi nibbled on her candy bar as Gary gave Gwen the time and place for the casting call.

"Glad I can always count on you, Gwen. Bye." He hung up the phone. "Give me that candy bar."

With a pout, she walked over and handed it to him. Gary tossed it into a nearby garbage can, keeping his eyes fixed on Naomi. "As for the phone call with Gwen, you knew this was coming, so can we please be grown-up about it? I had another meeting today with Rhonda and Sid. He has a couple of producers already lined up in L.A. for me to meet, and he's working on getting more." He took her by her shoulders. "This is big, Naomi."

"Who? Who are the producers?"

He scoffed. "Oh, like you'd know their names."

"No, I guess not. But isn't it possible I could go with you?"

Gary sauntered into the bedroom, discarding his tie and belt on the way. "I have a lot to do, including airplane reservations."

"Why can't I go with you?" She followed, picking up his clothes along the way.

"I already told you, I need you to stay here—you're the best one in the cast now." He changed into a pair of running pants and a sweatshirt. "I need you to hold it all together while I'm gone."

"But, Gary, the show's run might be about over. Let's face it. The audiences are shrinking, especially on the weeknights. And you know Tony got a callback for that soap opera."

"Get serious, Naomi. Tony is not soap opera material. And I'll write him a new skit. That'll make him happy."

"You haven't written anything new in a while . . . for any of us."

"Oh, so now you're joining all the backstage back-stabbers."

Her heart raced and her throat muscles clenched; what if she'd been caught? Backstage last weekend she had joined the others in a complainers' klatch. Had he overheard any of it? "Gary, it's just that they asked me if I could talk you into writing some new stuff."

"And you said?"

She chuckled. "I told them they gotta be crazy if they think I can talk you into anything. But it's kinda true. I mean, they're getting restless. Why not close the show and let me—"

"I know what I'm doing. When I speak to all these big shots in Hollywood, don't you think it'll be good for them to know I still have a show running off-Broadway? And that I can keep it running even when I'm out of town? I know what I'm doing."

"I realize that. I'm sorry."

Brushing past her, he said, "I'm going into the other room and type up some notes from today's meeting."

"I'll make dinner."

After seasoning the chopped meat that had been thawing all day, Naomi molded it into a meatloaf. Earlier in the day she had planned to use the heart-shaped casserole dish she had found in a consignment shop the week before. After staring at it momentarily, she shook her head and hid the dish in the hinterlands of the pantry. Out came the plain old Teflon loaf pan.

Meat slapped into the pan, oven preheated and ready to go, she set the timer. And sat, staring at the clock.

I better do it now and get it over with. What if he never does it? Like he promised . . . I could wait and ask him over dinner. But what if . . .

She steeled herself and with determination walked into the spare bedroom Gary used for his office. "While you're still in the show, would you call Rhonda so she can see my work? You said you would and I'm sure I'm good enough by now, but she has to see me working with you."

"You're breaking my concentration. Later, okay?"

Suddenly an unpleasant feeling at the back of her throat, followed by the sense of her stomach muscles contracting, stole her attention from the current situation with Gary.

"Sure." She hurried to the bathroom and turned on the tap water before leaning over the toilet bowl. The last thing she needed right now was for him to hear her retch.

After Friday night's curtain call, Gary drew the cast together. Naomi had already shared the dreaded news with Julie, who referred to it as "the death knell for the show."

"Okay, announcement everyone. I'm leaving in two weeks for California. I've got a chance to pitch a new TV show. Can't expect me to give up something like that, right? We've been auditioning for a replacement for me. Found a guy. Don."

Don? He's picking Don?

"You're all going to have to do double duty for the next two weeks while we rehearse with him." Gary held up a stack of papers. "Here's the schedule I made up." He handed the papers to the stage manager who then dispersed them to the cast.

Boy, they're like the walking definition of disgruntled. And no wonder. The house was only half-full tonight. The show is dying. And Don? That's like the final nail in the coffin

Gary grabbed her hand. "I need a drink. Hurry up and get ready, okay?"

She nodded as she hurried off to her dressing room. Julie was already sitting in front of the mirror, slapping on the makeup remover. "Here." She slid the jar of cold cream to Naomi.

"Thanks."

"So did you audition with this Don guy?"

"Sure did. Julie, he never once made eye contact with me. It was like working with a cold fish. I even told . . . oh, never mind."

"I don't know. I really need to move on. And you know Tony's hoping to get that part on *Days of our Lives.*" Julie studied Naomi's reflection. "Gary's going to be leaving, huh? If we went ahead and closed the show, then you'd be able to go with him. Have you thought about that?"

"Umhmm."

"Sometimes it feels like it's the same audience out there every night. I mean they all come up with the same dopey suggestions. Every time they're asked, 'Give me a location,' how come all they ever come up with is 'a bus station'?"

"I know what you mean. Hey, can I ask you something? Do you celebrate Passover with your family?"

"Of course. I remember getting sloshed one time. I probably was all of seven years old. I'll tell you, that Manishewitz sure can pack a wallop." Julie knit her brows together and tilted her head. "Why on earth are you asking about Passover?"

"Been thinking—this will be the first time I won't be with my parents. Gonna be weird."

The next day during rehearsal with Don, an emergency run to the bathroom caused Naomi to vanish for a few minutes.

When she returned to the stage, Gary demanded, "Where were you?" He sat in the front row of the theatre drumming his fingers on a small table. "We need to go over the *Shlocky* bit again. Don's even put on his costume for you."

"I'm sorry." She bit her lip. Why was she always apologizing? He hated it when she did, and she hated herself for doing it. "I was feeling . . . I don't know, kinda queasy . . . I'm better now." She crossed over to Don and fed him his first line.

When performing this routine with Gary, she worked hard not to break character and laugh out loud at his antics. No such problem with Don.

"Okay, good enough for now," Gary declared. He turned around to face the back of the theatre. "Where's Tony?"

Naomi shrugged her shoulders. The backstage door slammed and she stared into the wings. "He's coming now."

She waved Tony onto the stage, trying to hurry him up. "Gary's ready for you. I think for the baseball skit."

Tony walked to the center of the stage, peered out to where he knew Gary always sat and shielded his eyes from the bright proscenium lights. "Need to talk with you." He leapt off the stage and marched over to Gary.

Oh no, I know what's coming.

Naomi and Don waited onstage. "Think you might have a few more parts coming to you," she muttered under her breath to Don.

"Why? Tony quitting?"

"I think so."

"Hope this show's not sinking. Man, my luck." Don swore.

Gary walked up to the stage and lifted his head toward Don. "Make sure you come tonight and catch our performance."

Don nodded and shed his costume as he made his way backstage.

Gary turned toward Naomi. "C'mon, let's hurry and get something to eat before the show."

She took the stairs located at stage right and joined him.

"Excuse me, what's that look?" he asked.

"Tony got the soap opera, didn't he?"

"Naomi, no one likes an 'I-told-you-so.'"

"Hmmm, but I did . . . look, why can't I come with you to California? Just close the show already."

He picked up his jacket and handed Naomi her suede coat. "I need you. I've told you that. And, you know what? I'm going to give you some of Tony's parts. The baseball one—why can't that be a female? You'll be adorable in that."

She didn't feel adorable, but knowing who would be in the audience this evening motivated her to make sure she gave an outstanding performance.

Naomi wasn't sure, but she believed the redhead sitting in the third row, left of center, had to be her. Gary had described Rhonda as a flaming fireball and all during the performance the woman was writing notes feverishly.

When the curtain call ended, Naomi hesitated. Should she mingle with the crowd and "accidentally" bump into the woman? But she had no need to make a decision since the flaming redhead from the third row stormed her way backstage as if she owned the joint.

She paraded herself directly to Naomi, while turning her head to address Gary. "Why did this young lady have to call for herself? What were you doing? Saving her for another agent?" She pinched Naomi's cheek. "Sweetie, you're adorable. Now here's the question: are you free tomorrow at two?"

Naomi nodded vigorously.

"Good." Rhonda handed Naomi a sheet of paper with an address scribbled on it. "They're auditioning for a new Mop & Glo commercial. Cinderella and her wicked stepsisters."

The entire cast gathered around the agent and the actress, unabashedly eavesdropping. The only member off to the side was Gary.

Rhonda said, "Let me hear you say 'Cinderella, mop that floor.'"

Naomi pointed to the floor and in the meanest, most strident voice she could muster, she said, "Cinderella, mop that floor. Now!"

Tony, Julie, and the stage manager applauded.

"Okay, cookie, do that tomorrow and we're set. You have a resume you can give me? I'll send it over to the casting people in the morning."

Julie squeezed Naomi's arm and smiled. "I know where you have a stack of them. I'll get one."

While waiting for the resume, Rhonda turned to Gary. "I'm really disappointed in you. Here you have a girl ready to be a moneymaker for me, and she has to call me herself."

"Well, as for this audition tomorrow," Gary said, "I need her for rehearsal tomorrow, to work with my replacement."

Julie returned with the resume and glared at Gary. "I'll fill in for Naomi."

Gary reluctantly accepted Julie's offer and grabbed Naomi's elbow. "Let's get out of here."

As Naomi and Gary headed for the subway, she scrambled to keep up with him. Finally she stopped. "Would you wait up, please?"

He turned around, never for a moment slowing down his pace, and said, "I don't like being snookered."

"Hey, I have my own problems, okay?"

With a smirk, he stopped. When she caught up with him, he asked, "What kind of problems?"

"How would you feel only being considered for the wicked stepsister and never even given a chance to play Cinderella? Huh?"

"Is that it?"

"And as for walking ten steps ahead of me, I had an uncle used to do that with his wife. It was disgusting and I never—"

"Can we please . . .?" He slipped his arm around her waist and moved her forward.

Neither spoke during their subway ride. About one block from home, she tugged at his sleeve. "I had to call Rhonda. You promised one day you would call her for me, but you didn't. And I thought I was ready, and obviously I was."

"You're right. I admit I was caught up with all the things I need to do to get ready for my trip."

"And I wanted her to see me working with you. Not with Don. He'll never replace you."

"But you're doing a great job covering for him."

Thirty minutes later, they sat on their sofa. Gary sipped some wine while Naomi declined her usual nightcap. "Not tonight. I'm not feeling . . ."

"I'm waiting." She did not finish her sentence and he reached for the tablet of yellow paper sitting on their coffee table. "Where'd my pen go?"

"I don't know. I'll get one from your office." She quickly ran into the back room and stood as still as possible. Maybe the room would stop spinning. Maybe she was coming down with something.

The dizziness continued, but Gary's impatience pressed in on her. She grabbed a pen from his desk and hurried to the living room.

"Would you stop looking so miserable? I'm only going to be away maybe a month or two. Once we get the show sold, Sid says he thinks we'll shoot it right here in New York. So, you'll keep our place for us. Did I tell you, Sid got a place for me to stay in California?"

"You said he was working on it. You mean it's set now?"

"An actor he knows who is on location is willing to let me live in his bungalow while he's not there. It's all coming together. Meantime, I've got some things to do, but you better get some sleep. You have a big audition tomorrow."

It was unusual, but this night she was able to drift into sleep almost immediately. However, Zoey's sudden leap onto the bed woke her in a flash. The cat tapped Naomi on the nose and nuzzled her fluffy head onto her pillow. Again, unusual. And the beauty of the purring stirred up unusual feelings as well.

"Come here, sweetie." Naomi tentatively stroked the shiny fur. No hissing, only more purring. "What a sweet little baby." Her hand stopped mid-motion. Never ever had she experienced this weird maternal-like ooey-gooey thing.

"I thought you told me the cat didn't like you?" Gary stood in the doorway. "I was thinking, since I'll be in LA, I can take Zoey to Francine."

"But . . . I know this'll sound crazy, but maybe I'm starting to bond with her. And besides the house is going to be empty with you gone. I want her to stay."

Gary scratched his head and smirked. "Sure, why not?"

He climbed into bed and his snoring soon joined with Zoey's purring. The only other sound was her breathing. And every car driving down the street. And the wind whistling outside. And the worst sound of all: the *what if* echoing in her mind.

First she recalled the melody, then the lyrics—was there someone watching over her?

Why had she chosen that song? Maybe Anne had suggested it. She couldn't remember. All Naomi knew was she felt like a little lamb lost in a wood. A lamb who was trapped, ensnared by her own stupidity.

Who was this man sleeping in bed next to her? Did she love him? At this moment, she didn't even like him.

But what if . . .

Naomi and Gary kissed goodbye as the cab driver threw the last of his suitcases into the trunk.

"I'll call you tonight," Gary said. "Have a good time today. This may be your first commercial but it won't be your last."

Could a day be more of an emotional roller coaster than this? Filming her first commercial and about to live alone for who knew how long.

She waited until the taxicab moved into traffic and waved her last goodbye. Better get going. With helping Gary get all his stuff downstairs and waiting with him while he hailed a cab, she was in danger of running late. Better scurry—back up to the now empty apartment.

Fifteen minutes later dressed and her hand on the doorknob, she abruptly dropped her pocketbook to the floor and ran into the bathroom. Naomi downed two Dramamine tablets, recommended by the pharmacist. Once out on the street, she made a spur-of-the moment decision: she, too, would take a taxi to the production studio.

The stars must have been smiling down upon her because a cab pulled up immediately.

Sliding into the back seat, she gave the address. "Manhattan, Fifty-fifth and Madison." Whew, the Dramamine seemed to be working.

Gary was probably almost to the airport by now. Yeah, Gary would be traveling clear across the country. Thankfully, though, today would be a big day for her as well. She was shooting her first commercial.

But still there was the eventual coming home to an empty apartment. No, wait a minute, Zoey would be there, her new best friend. And right from shooting the commercial, most likely she would grab a quick bite to eat and then get to the theatre in time for tonight's performance. A commercial shoot and then a stage performance.

Girl, everything you've always dreamed of.

Naomi smiled as she recalled how she received the news about being cast in the commercial. Rhonda called Gary, got his answering machine and left a message. "I told you, cookie, your girlfriend's going to be a real moneymaker. Had to rub it in your face. And don't waste your breath, I'll call her and tell her myself."

It still stung a little bit that she was never considered for the part of Cinderella, or perhaps even the fairy godmother, but nothing wrong with the challenge of playing a villainess. And, of course, one day she would be the comic lead in the soon-to-be TV hit of the season. Everyone would love Chloe.

Yet Naomi wondered about Rhonda's reaction the day she went into the agent's office to sign an exclusive contract. Pen in hand, Naomi told her, "You know, soon I'll be making money for you with the TV show Gary's pitching."

The way Rhonda arched one eyebrow and pursed her lips together still nagged at Naomi. Happily, she was jarred from this disturbing memory—the sudden familiar thunking and squeaking of windshield wipers snapped her back into the present. When did it start raining?

With determination, she chased away all negative memories and fears regarding the future. Naomi would choose to believe someone was watching over her.

"Hey, lady, we're here," yelled the cabdriver.

To avoid the heavy downpour, Naomi ran into the high-rise office tower. She gave her name at the security desk and was guided to an express elevator which took her straight to the thirty-first floor. Once there she entered into a beehive of activity.

A young woman holding a clipboard asked, "Are you talent?"

"Yes, I'm one of the stepsisters."

The young woman pointed to a section off to the right. "They'll get you set up."

A woman wearing an artist's smock told Naomi to prop herself up on a tall swivel chair. She did so, and instantly a man wrapped a black plastic cloak around her. A thin young man in skin-tight leather pants joined the woman and together they slathered on the makeup.

They painted her lips a garish black and stretched the black eyebrow paint halfway down the outer sides of her nose. The skinny man then glued long shiny black fingernails over her real ones. Another woman walked over with a comb and teased Naomi's hair so violently that it painfully tugged on her scalp.

When they finished, Naomi stared into the mirror. They had transformed her into a gothic nightmare.

Naomi, her wicked stepsister counterpart and their wicked stepmother all were rushed into wardrobe. A masculine-looking woman gave each of the actresses matching ball gowns to slip into.

Seemed like a split second later, Naomi was ushered onto the sound stage. Lights had already been set up around a dirty kitchen floor with a giant silver bucket receiving the brunt of the glaring light. Leaning against this bucket was a huge mop.

The director, a middle-aged man wearing an obvious toupee, called out, "Here we go, people. Get into position. Three, two, one, and action."

The only retakes were necessitated by Cinderella's flubs, but not once did Naomi cause a "cut" or a "retake." The Dramamine wore off and Naomi managed to work the nausea into amplifying her mean and evil character.

By the end of the shoot, the director approached Naomi. "I wish all my talent was as professional as you, young lady. Thank you for a good day's work."

Although the theatre was a short and easy subway ride, Naomi treated herself once again to a cab ride. *I may not be cast as a princess, but why not treat myself as one?*

The rain having let up, she asked the driver to stop a block away from the theatre. A new Korean-owned fruit and vegetable greengrocer had opened on the corner and both Naomi and Julie had discovered the salad bar was healthy and inexpensive. It offered innovative and delicious ways to enjoy tofu. Who knew bean curd could taste so good? Naomi took one of their plastic containers, filled it with a mishmash of ingredients, all the way from fresh cucumbers to the marinated tofu and noodles. Four dollars and twenty-five cents provided a decent pre-performance dinner, one she hoped would cause no digestive problems.

Almost colliding with Julie at the stage door entrance, the actresses laughed together as they saw both were carrying similar containers of a salad bar dinner.

"How'd your commercial go?"

"Oh, Julie, it was the most incredible experience."

"I think you'll have plenty more of them."

"I was born for this. Julie, you need to go visit Rhonda, too. I can try and get you set up with her."

The women went into their dressing room, ate their dinner, and then applied their makeup and got into costume. As they waited for the stage manager to give his countdown for "places," Julie asked, "You look a little pale. Everything okay?"

"Sure."

"It must be hard with Gary having left today. Just seems you haven't been feeling that well lately."

The stage manager knocked on their door and pronounced, "Places everyone."

The evening's performance turned out the most dismal in Naomi's memory. The audience was so unresponsive to the humor that the cast eventually stopped pausing after the once-predictable laugh lines. Following curtain call and before changing into her street clothes, Naomi overheard Tony speaking to Julie.

"Glad next week's my last show. I counted maybe ten people out there."

"Twelve," Julie corrected.

Don walked over to them and added, "Ten really, two were my parents."

Tony slapped the newest cast member on the back. "Well, at least you'll have something to add to your resume, right?"

The backstage door suddenly swung open and all eyes turned to see the newcomer. Naomi recognized the corpulent bald-headed man from her audition—the rude producer.

He removed the toothpick hanging out of his mouth. "Three more shows and that's it. Friday show, last show. Can't keep floating this boat." Placing the toothpick back in his mouth, he turned and walked out.

Naomi ran into the dressing room and lightning-quick changed into the pants suit she left the house in earlier that day. One video shoot and one closing notice later, she could go home . . . to her empty apartment. At least Zoey would be waiting for her.

Julie turned to Naomi with tears in her eyes. "If your boyfriend had only written new skits, this maybe—"

"Maybe it's simply time . . . call Rhonda tomorrow."

Julie nodded. "I will. I'm going to miss you."

Naomi initiated a hug and Julie gratefully responded.

"You asked about Passover the other night," Julie said. "Would you want to come with me to my parents for Seder Saturday night? They're in Brooklyn, but all the way out, about an hour from you."

"Thanks, but I don't think so. How about we meet for lunch next week though?"

"Love to. How about this coming Monday?"

"Monday it is."

Julie gave Naomi the address to her favorite Chinese restaurant. Though she'd splurged on two taxi rides today, she would not give in to such extravagance on returning home. From the commercial, Naomi would receive more money than she ever dreamed of making, and Rhonda assured her the residuals for the year would be enormous as the floor polish company planned on blasting the airwaves with this ad. However, she felt an urgent need to conserve each dollar. Gary had given her his share of the rent for next month, but after May . . . who knew? Would she be responsible for the entire rent?

When the subway plunged into the inky black tunnel leaving Manhattan on its way into Brooklyn, she cried out to the someone who might possibly be watching over her. *I get the symbolism, okay? So where does the tunnel end? Is there a light at the end somewhere?*

With all the vigor sapped out of her, Naomi trudged up the three flights, tired and nauseous once again. She used the handrail to pull herself up as if it were a tow bar helping her up a steep ski slope.

The first greeting came from Zoey. Nice, but the first thing she wanted to see was a blinking light on her answering machine.

It did blink—a message was waiting. "Zoey, be with you in a second. Let's listen to Gary's message first, okay?" She punched the play button.

Rhonda's gravelly voice informed her, "They loved you today. Good job, cookie. Now, are you sitting down? This Friday afternoon you will be auditioning for *Saturday Night Live*. Call me tomorrow. Proud of you."

"*Saturday Night Live*—wow." Zoey's whining made it clear—she wasn't impressed. "Come on, girl." Zoey trailed at Naomi's heels as she walked to the kitchen.

While opening a can of wet food, Naomi conversed with her sole companion. "Well, you know, Gary only arrived today, and he also had this long layover in Texas. Don't worry, girl, he'll call tomorrow."

With the cat totally engrossed in her smelly food, Naomi poured some cereal into a bowl and threw in a handful of raisins. She finally found the container of milk in the refrigerator, buried behind the soda and juice. One sniff of the soured milk and down the drain it went. She sat at the table, exhausted, watching Zoey dine oh so elegantly.

Why not? Naomi reached into her bowl and grabbed a handful of cereal sweetened by the raisins. It didn't taste bad. Milk? Who needs it? Just more unwanted calories. After a few more handfuls, Naomi gave in to utter exhaustion.

"See ya in bed," she told Zoey.

Nevertheless, sleep eluded her. Too much to ponder and it seemed the bed creaked more than ever before. Maybe Gary's snor-

ing simply covered up its sound. Then she remembered what lay under the bed. She brought her precious sampler out from hiding and scoured the place for a nail. About to give up for the night, her eyes caught sight of the nail; it still sat in the hole above the dresser. Once her mother's embroidery again graced her wall, Naomi slept soundly.

Gulping for air, Naomi walked through the backstage door. "Sorry I'm late. Had an audition."

The stage manager shrugged and assured her it was no problem. "It's the last show anyway."

"Thanks." Naomi dashed into her dressing room.

Julie looked up and asked, "So, how'd it go over at Rockefeller Center? Am I looking at the newest member of *Saturday Night Live?*"

"I think it went well—they kept me extra long. That's why I'm late. Even did a skit with John Belushi." Naomi pulled up the back zipper of Julie's dress. "Guess this'll be the last time I help you, huh?"

"You better hurry though," Julie warned at the same moment they heard the familiar rap on their door.

"Places."

The last performance seemed to drag on forever. With Gary gone and having to work with Don, Naomi was ready to bid a fond adieu. After the final curtain call, the cast and several crew members discussed going out for a drink together, but Naomi left before anything was decided. She would see Julie on Monday, grateful for the chance to continue their friendship. Hopefully it would help fill the void left by Anne.

During the subway ride home, Naomi bounced from anxious thoughts—*why hasn't Gary even called. . . what if . . .?*—to excitement—*I could actually be on something like Saturday Night Live. But yikes! What if Gary sells the I Love Chloe idea and I also get a spot on Saturday Night Live?*

After a brisk walk home from the subway station, Naomi opened her mailbox. Maybe Gary had at least sent a postcard. Like a "wish you were here" card. *Yeah, right.*

No such thing from Gary, but a note from her dear Mom. She tore it open with her fingernail as she climbed up the stairs and stopped at the second-floor landing to read it.

"To My Best Daughter, I begged your father to let you come for Passover, but again he would not relent. Will you celebrate Passover with your boyfriend and his family? Love, Your Best Mom."

The note shook in her hand. What were her parents going to tell all the aunts, uncles and cousins to explain her absence?

Oh Mom, I love you so much. I hate to cause you pain like this. That last performance with the group was easy compared to this.

The next evening she did her best to celebrate Passover alone. In the apartment with her new friend Zoey, she poured and drank some Manischewitz wine, dipped matzoh into a small bowl of horseradish, and asked the cat the traditional question posed every Passover. "So, why is this night different from all other nights?"

The cat jumped up onto the dining room table and went over to the horseradish, sniffed it, hissed and ran from the room. Her journal entry that evening read, "Dear Diary, now I know what it's like to feel passed over. Happy Passover to me."

Deftly maneuvering her chopsticks, Julie asked, "Are you going to finally tell me about the audition?"

Of all the cast members, the one most hurt by the show closing was Julie. Sharing the news of her successful audition seemed inconsiderate.

"Oh, who knows, Julie? It seemed to go well, but you never know. Did you call Rhonda?"

Julie poured herself another cup of tea. "I've left her three messages, Naomi. I look at it like this: she saw me in the show a couple of times, with both Francine and with you. So, if she's not calling me back, it's because she doesn't think I'm good enough. Not as good as you anyway."

"But, Julie, her perception of me is all wrong."

"In what way? Do you know how many actors would love to be in your position?"

"She sees me as this comedienne, doing standup routines in a nightclub. That's not me. I want to be a serious actress."

Kerplunk. The lo mein slipped from Naomi's clumsily-held chopsticks onto her brand-new pink denim pant suit.

"Case closed," Julie chuckled. "How's Gary doing?"

"I'm sure he's busy. I've left him a few messages . . . just like Rhonda with you, he hasn't called me back."

Julie nodded. "I wonder what's going to happen with Tony and me . . . now that he's got the soap opera job."

All the cast seemed accepting of their affair. But Naomi always found herself thinking about Tony's wife. She pulled her chair out. "I'll be right back."

Why did I think I could handle this food? Oh, please, don't let anyone be in the bathroom.

When she returned to the table, Julie studied Naomi's face and pointed to her plate. "You hardly ate anything. Seems you haven't been feeling very well lately."

"I'm fine."

After a short pause, Julie patted Naomi's hand. "You know they've come up with this home pregnancy test. You don't have to go to a doctor anymore."

For how long had Naomi evaded a certain thought? Julie simply brought it to the surface. After lunch, Naomi stopped at her neighborhood pharmacy before returning home. There it was, prominently displayed in the feminine needs aisle, in big bold letters proclaiming "the first-ever home pregnancy test."

How'd Julie know about this?

She brought the package to the cashier, grateful she knew no one in the neighborhood and no one knew her. How embarrassing would that be?

As always, upon entering the apartment Naomi's eyes went to the call light on her answering machine. It was flashing—for a change.

"Zoey, is it him? Finally?"

"Hope you believe in prayer, cookie." Rhonda's voice filled the room. "You got a callback from *Saturday Night Live*. You got a real shot at this. It's big enough *I'll* even pray! Call me back for the details . . . after you pray!"

Why did such exciting news have to come at this time? She started scribbling a note reminding herself to call Rhonda in the morning, but quickly laughed and crumpled it up. *Like I'm really going to forget something this big. Okay, let's do this stupid test already.*

Thirty minutes later she stared at the white plastic thing in her hands. So many emotions all at once. She experienced a momentary thrill—*Wow, my body really works.* But then she quickly scolded herself—she could not afford such thinking.

Naomi again called Gary, and again his answering machine picked up. "Please call me. Or else I'm flying out there. Call me already."

She fed Zoey and watered the plants.

Man, seems I can't even keep a philodendron alive. Everyone else has ferns and all kinds of beautiful hanging plants in their apartment. I water them, mist them, feed them expensive plant food .... It's like they just hate me.

Okay, what to do next? The New York Times crossword puzzle had already been done. Everyone was talking about a new movie, *Grease.* Why not treat herself? She would have to sit alone in the theatre, but it would be a distraction at least for a few hours. Julie had raved about the soundtrack from this musical and it was playing down the block.

An hour later, Naomi sat in the third row, aware of all the dating couples surrounding her. Yet once the lights went out and the previews of coming attractions began, she was drawn into the wonderful world of "let's pretend." A world where she felt most at home.

By the time John Travolta and Olivia Newton John sang a duet, she was transported right into their world, so much so that as she walked the three flights back up to her apartment, a neighbor cracked open his door to see who was singing. She nodded to Mr. Sullivan and continued to sing about her one of a kind love . . . lo-oh oh oh-ove.

Naomi did not stop singing for her neighbor, but did stop immediately when she did not see a blinking light on the all-important machine. She again called her "one of a kind" guy.

He answered on the third ring.

"I was going to call you in a few minutes. Brought home some Chinese for dinner. I'm starved. Let me at least eat the egg roll and I'll call you back."

When the phone finally rang, she snapped off the television—she had no idea what she had been watching anyway—and with quivering hands picked up the phone.

"Gary?"

"What's the matter? Sounds like you've been crying."

How could she just jump into this? "Hey, I just miss you, okay?" Ouch, that was the wrong course to take. Quickly she went into damage control mode. "Nah, I'm just bummed cause I think I killed another plant. How'd it go for you today?"

"They want me to do some more edits, but I think they like the premise with the soap opera parody, and especially doing it with a live audience. It's a completely new idea for prime time, so why shouldn't they like it, huh?"

"So, how long do you think you'll stay?"

"C'mon, don't pressure me, okay? You know how many writers would kill for this opportunity? So, what's going on there?" After receiving no reply, he pressed, "Naomi, what's the matter? I don't need you getting all weird on me."

"Gary, I'm not . . . weird . . . I'm . . ." If the word was spoken, the stark reality would be irrevocable. And if she refused to speak the word . . . no, it would not change reality. Trapped. Cornered. Reality would not change, yet perhaps the right words could shape a harsh reality into something acceptable, even desirable. "I'm going to have your baby. I'm sorry for sounding upset a minute ago. I mean we should be excited. Right?"

"Are you trying to say you're pregnant? Is that it?"

His combative tone told Naomi the attempt at coloring reality with sunshine failed. "Yes, Gary, I am. I've been nauseous and—"

"Naomi, is this all in your wacky imagination? I'm going to kill you if you're scaring me for nothing."

"No, Gary. I took a test today. I'm pregnant."

"Stop your crying. You're giving me a headache."

Choking on her tears and with labored breathing, she managed to get out a few words. "If only you were here with me."

"Well, I'm not, but it's okay. We can handle this. It's not the end of the world. Do you have an idea where to go?"

"What? You mean a doc—"

"Oh, give me a break, Naomi, you know what I'm talking about. A place to get rid of it. There's a place near Lincoln Center. Go look it up in the phone book. It's a clean place. Listen, you got enough money?"

"I ... I don't know ... I ..."

"It's probably $300 at the most. I'll put a check for $200 in the mail tonight, okay?"

Naomi doubled up almost into a fetal position on her couch, trying to endure the inconsolable pain. Zoey jumped onto the couch and rubbed her head against Naomi's ankle, while Gary's voice droned on.

Chapter 4

Autumn 1978

*Like a howling in her in-
nermost being. Plunged into a
tunnel that seems to have no end. Who knew that a moment
in time would cause the inner springs of a human soul to collapse? A choice was made. A permanent wound etched into
the heart. What was promised as the way to be free was a lie
she chose to believe.*

The latest edition of the trade paper Backstage sat on the
kitchen table. Unread. Might as well stop wasting the
forty-five cents each week. Funny, Gary had pointed out
she needed to get rid of "it" because she had her career to think
about. Now, five months since taking care of "it," her career was
the last thing she thought about.

Once upon a time there was even a "hot agent" setting her up
with auditions. And a hot TV show gave her a callback, but Naomi
never contacted Rhonda for the details. Soon Rhonda left a message
with a stern warning. "Call me, cookie, or you're getting dumped
into my dead file. I mean it."

Naomi did not call back. It was all quite appropriate anyway—
she felt like a dead woman walking.

With residuals from the Mop & Glo commercial supplemented
by part-time waitressing at the Bistro, Naomi met her rent and
other expenses each month. But for how long? Now responsible
for the entire monthly rent, cab rides were a thing of the past. Gary
never returned to pack up and ship his things but asked Naomi to
perform this task. Numbly, she complied. Not long afterward, she

learned Gary's television series had been given the green light, and Chloe, the role promised to her only a short time ago, had been given to Francine.

And who could she talk to? Shame, her constant companion, only multiplied when she thought of her parents. And what about Anne? Her good friend had the wisdom to caution her, but she had only scoffed at her. The only good decision she made in the last year was keeping her precious furry friend. Holding one of Zoey's paws each night as they lay together on Naomi's pillow, hearing the sweet purring like an engine and feeling the warm breath on her cheek—that was her sole comfort.

It seemed summer would never end. Hot, humid and grimy. Yet autumn did arrive. Riding the subway home after a short lunch shift at the Bistro, she overheard two elderly men in conversation.

"Benny," one of the men was shouting over the din of the train tracks, "You won't see me tomorrow night."

"What? You won't be there for Rosh Hashanah? What's this?"

"My family and I, we're trying out a new synagogue. Don't tell anyone."

If tomorrow's Rosh Hashanah, then it'll be Yom Kippur soon.

Echoing somewhere deep in her soul Naomi heard her mother's words. "If you ask God to forgive your sins, He will, you just have to ask."

Wasn't Yom Kippur the time set aside to ask for forgiveness?

Naomi took her usual path from the train station to her apartment, yet something was definitely not usual today. This dead woman walking suddenly had all her senses on alert. There was an exhilarating newness in the air. She stepped off a curb and took a few steps when the "Don't Walk" sign flashed. Usually she would continue to the other side of the street, ignoring the horns blaring at her.

Today, however, she turned around and leapt back to the curb. Her eyes were drawn to the concrete structure she passed with indifference every day. But today it commanded her attention. Its immensely broad steps leading up to the three heavy wooden doors made it appear like an impregnable fortress. Yet the exquisite stained-glass panels above made her eyes water with its stunning beauty. They formed an archway high into the entrance of this synagogue. The two side panels displayed glowing menorahs and the central panel was etched with the treasured Ten Commandments.

Great. Just what I need to see. I've broken every one of them.

Why did she feel like an interloper, an outsider, unwelcome in this holy place? She was Jewish after all. Despite this sense of rejection, her eyes were transfixed and her feet velcroed to this place.

One of the ancient-looking doors opened and a young man strolled out. He was about 6'1" and had an athletic build, wearing a gray sweater over a simple white T-shirt, and loafers without socks. Naomi realized he spotted her. She must have looked ridiculous standing there and staring up at this imposing building.

Slowly he approached and raised one eyebrow, managing to silently communicate, "Wanna talk?"

Her eyes were no longer riveted upon the stained glass, but upon his attractive face. His blue eyes, framed with dark brown eyebrows and lashes, were warm, exuding a special kindness even as they looked directly at her. Rather than being threatening, his directness invited her trust. It was as if he were extending a complete acceptance of who she was.

Maybe it was his hair, dark brown and worn in a boyish cut, which made her feel extremely at ease. It spiked up a bit on the right, and at the left, in the back, stood a small cowlick.

She smiled and stuttered out, "I was wondering when Yom Kippur service was?"

"Tomorrow's Rosh Hashanah. Ten days later is Yom Kippur. You have a ticket?"

"A ticket? . . . Oh, I remember, every year Dad bought them early to get them cheaper." *Do I sound like a dunderhead or what?* She gave a tiny laugh. "This is the first time I'm not going with my parents."

His mouth seemed to have a perpetual smile. "If you do me a favor, I'll get you in."

Intrigued, Naomi asked, "What's the favor?"

"Apples. I have to get them at the farmers' market—you know, for the apples and honey after the Rosh Hashanah service tomorrow. And it can't be just *any* apples. I was told they have to be Red Romes. You know how to tell the difference?"

"Sure, my mother taught me."

"We have a deal then. Let's go. My name's Daniel."

"I'm Naomi—Naomi Goldblatt."

He pantomimed tipping his hat. "Pleased to meet you, Ms. Goldblatt. I'm Daniel Cantor."

Only one minute ago she had felt like an interloper. And now this handsome—rather whimsical—young man made her feel she was welcome in this very place. No, it was more than that; she was meant to be here. Something to do with destiny. She'd contemplate this later.

They crossed the street and appeared to be heading toward the waterfront. "Where is the market? I've always seen the signs, but I've never gone. Always wanted to, but never—"

"Seems I came along in time for a few new things, huh?"

She looked at him, scratching her head.

"You said you might possibly attend *shul* without your parents for the first time, right?"

Naomi blushed. "I usually go home and spend the holidays with them. It's not like I'm a pagan or something. I've always gone—"

He reached out his hand and pulled her back onto the curb—she was about to walk into oncoming traffic. Now she blushed even more.

"Didn't want this to be the first time you got hit by a car either."

When they arrived at the market, they were confronted with an overwhelming variety of apples. "Glad you're here. How do I tell which ones are the Red Romes?"

"That's easy." Without hesitation, Naomi went to a vendor. "Which are the Red Romes?"

The man directed her to the third bin on the left. Naomi looked back at Daniel who stared at her, shaking his head in amazement.

Naomi shrugged, "Hey, my father always told me 'Naomi, never say you can't.'"

He playfully hooked his arm around hers. "C'mon, let's go buy some apples."

Daniel purchased enough fruit for an estimated 200 congregants to each have a slice or two. To Naomi's sheer embarrassment, her stomach made a loud growling sound.

Maybe he didn't hear.

He smiled and asked, "Want an apple?" He quickly added, "I'm hungry, too. Did you notice that table we passed? Looked like they had some homemade breads and stuff."

"Sounds delicious."

There was a young girl stationed behind the table displaying the breads and delicious-looking spreads and preserves. She told Naomi and Daniel, "My mom makes all this stuff." Her big smile revealed her wire braces. "My favorite is the banana bread."

Both Naomi and Daniel simultaneously said, "That sounds great." When he saw Naomi digging into her shoulder bag, he tapped her hand. "My treat this time. Next time, it'll be yours."

The girl with the braces said, "Oh, and it's especially good with Mom's fresh apple butter."

"Sold," Daniel told her. "Do you have maybe some napkins and even a spoon or a knife?"

She grinned at Naomi and Daniel, putting both a spoon and a knife into the paper sack.

Bet she thinks we're a couple.

He pointed with his chin to a bench facing the East River.

It was a perfect day for sitting on the picturesque promenade. The sun's beams warmed her face while the breeze from the river was gentle. Naomi cut two slices from the loaf and Daniel opened the Mason jar filled with the apple butter and spooned a generous portion onto both their slices.

"Oh, this is so delicious," Naomi exclaimed, grabbing a napkin and catching a large dollop of the butter before it fell onto her lap.

"Oh no, you're about to—" She hastily used her napkin to intercept the apple butter about to fall onto Daniel's lap.

"Thank you . . . so normally you go to your parents . . . where is that?"

"I'm from the Catskill Mountains. A little town in Ellenville."

"Our family used to go there for vacations. To a bungalow colony. Ellenville? The only synagogue there is an orthodox one, isn't it?"

She nodded. "I'd sit upstairs with my mom. Where are you from?"

"Rutherford, New Jersey. You know where that is?"

"No, not really."

"Its claim to fame is being the birthplace of William Carlos Williams." He paused and studied her face. "Doesn't look like you've ever heard of him."

"Should I have?"

"Well, do you think you should know the poet laureate of 1952?"

His playful smile delighted Naomi. How could she not reciprocate? When she returned his smile, it was as if the heaviness of the last five months blew away into the river they were facing.

"In one of his most famous poems, he says something like to be truly happy, we need to make others happy—and that'll make us happy." He suddenly turned away from Naomi. "This is embarrassing. I can't believe I'm sharing this."

Naomi leaned forward, trying to get him to turn back around to her. "Good grief. Believe me, I'm the one who usually embarrasses herself. It's neat having someone else do it."

He now turned back toward her and they momentarily studied each other's face. Naomi spoke first. "I'm not usually this comfortable with someone, not someone I just met."

"Are you familiar with the term '*b'sheirt*'?"

"My mom used that word once, but I never understood . . ."

"I heard someone say it described anything where you could see the fingerprints of divine providence. You remember what your mom was talking about?"

Naomi put her head down and took a big bite of the bread. She felt him waiting for an explanation from her. Finally she said, "It was when Mom was talking about how she met Dad, but I don't want to bore you."

"If she spoke of *b'sheirt*, it had to have been interesting."

"Okay, but you can stop me if it gets boring."

Daniel cut himself another slice of bread and smeared on more apple butter.

"Dad was born in New York—the lower East side. His parents came over from Russia and they stayed here in New York . . . probably like your parents, right?"

Daniel took a bite of his bread and looked out at the water. "My parents' story is a little different. Go ahead, tell me about yours."

Had she hit a raw nerve? *Here's this guy I only just met and now I'm. . . oh, never mind, he's not like Gary. He really seems interested.* "The part that's different with my mom's family is that her parents, even though they also came over here from Russia, once they went through Ellis Island, they traveled south, all the way to Alabama. So, it's like I come from this mixed marriage: Dad's a gruff New Yorker and Mom's like a sweet gentle southern belle. Did you ever hear anyone say 'shalom y'all?'"

His warm eyes crinkled with a smile. "Now I have. And you know what? I think I see both sides in you." He laughed. "See? Only a southern belle would blush at something like that. Go ahead, how'd they meet?"

"Some friend of Mom's family, I think I remember his name was Hersh Siegel, was dating my aunt Yetta. He came to Mom's house one day and told her about this Jew working at Maxwell Air Force Base. Mom told me she thought he was the first Jew to ever work on the Base."

"Yeah, they were pretty discriminatory back then, weren't they?"

"Well, it turned out he wasn't in the Air Force or anything, but was a tailor at the Base, not a soldier. So they got fixed up with each other. And then before Dad returned to New York, he promised Mom he'd write to her. And this is the part I love. With his last letter, she opened it and a paper cigar ring and a one-way airplane ticket to New York City fell out. His letter told her to put the paper ring on her finger and fly to New York, and then when she got there, he'd put a real diamond on her finger."

A young man carrying a guitar case walked in front of them and stationed himself at the edge of the sidewalk with the scenic background behind him. He took out his guitar leaving the case open for donations.

"Guess this is our cue to leave," Daniel whispered and then grimaced. "I've heard him before."

They tossed their garbage in a receptacle directly behind their bench and stood to leave.

Naomi had been so comfortable with this man. What was to happen next? *Probably only disappointment.* "I don't know about this creepy synagogue thing. . ."

"Creepy? Why?"

She had no answer, but was rescued by the guitar player's screeching. "You were right."

He grinned. "I got to get these apples back to the creepy synagogue. Would you help me carry them? And if you change your mind, I'll get you tickets for tomorrow."

"Of course," she said as he handed her two of the smallest sacks.

With the walk back accomplished in silence, Naomi blamed herself for saying the stupid "creepy synagogue" thing. Arriving back at Temple Beth Orr, she told Daniel, "I've carried them this far, it's like they're attached to me. I'll help bring them in."

Once past the dark corridor, they climbed down a flight of stairs and entered a brightly lit kitchen and social area. Several elderly women were putting out plates, folding napkins, and counting out forks. One of the women called out, "Hello, Rabbi Dan. You're just in time."

Naomi dropped her sacks. "Rabbi? Rabbi Dan?"

With a somewhat mischievous smile, he simply nodded.

"Why didn't you tell me?"

"You didn't ask."

"You let me say—"

"I'm only the Associate Rabbi, not the Senior Rabbi." He picked up her sacks of apples and gently said, "I really hope you'll accept my invitation for tomorrow. It's not creepy, Naomi."

"What time?"

"Six-thirty tomorrow night. Wait here and I'll get you a ticket."

While waiting she overheard one of the women speaking Yiddish to another lady. Pointing toward Naomi, the woman exclaimed, "*Shayna maidela.*" She had been called pretty. She considered going over to this nice woman and thanking her, but before making up her mind one way or another Daniel returned.

"You sure I shouldn't pay for this?"

Daniel shook his head. "You just better come, that's all. See you tomorrow night."

Naomi floated home.

"Zoey – check this out. Didn't know I could look so grown-up, did ya?" Naomi studied herself in the full-length mirror attached to her closet door. Clothes lay in a heap atop her bed, the aftermath of Naomi's attempts to find something acceptable for the evening's Rosh Hashanah service.

She finally chose a dark brown suede skirt with matching jacket, discovered one day several years ago at her favorite thrift store. Not only would it have cost a fortune if bought new, but it also flattered her figure.

Naomi, stop thinking about Daniel. He's not the reason your feet were like velcroed in front of the synagogue.

Inherently she knew the God her mom talked about was the One guiding her steps. How could she think about a man, especially a rabbi, before she got right with God Himself? But what was she to do, lie to herself? Since waking up this morning, the image of the handsome man with the playful smile and warm eyes seemed to dance in front of her.

Rabbi Dan . . . He introduced himself as Daniel. Why can't I call him that? No, guess I'll have to call him Rabbi Dan.

Walking to Temple Beth Orr, Naomi imagined telling Mom she would be attending a Conservative *shul* and sitting with the men. The only time Mom experienced such a thing was at her wedding.

The wide concrete steps leading into the synagogue were easy to scale, even with her rarely-worn high heels. Not wanting to look at fellow congregants fearing she was the only person there without a family, she kept her head down and dug into her pocketbook for the ticket. At the last step, she looked up and saw him standing at the front door, shaking hands with each person entering. Even with a dark suit and tie on, he still managed to appear casual. Naomi especially enjoyed seeing his cowlick poking out from behind his *yarmulke.*

He saw Naomi and his smile broadened. He leaned into her and discretely asked, "Remember where I told you to sit yesterday?" She nodded and he handed her two books. "I should have given you these yesterday. This one is your *Siddur*. It has the prayers we will be doing today, and this one is the *Chumash*."

"The what?"

"Your Bible. Relax, Naomi. I'll see you afterwards for the apples—Red Romes, of course."

With the press of people waiting to say hello to Rabbi Dan and make their way into the synagogue, she smiled and followed others into the sanctuary. The men were in suits and virtually all the women wore fancy, often large, hats. Another generation. Naomi recalled one Rosh Hashanah seeing her mother dust off a fussy-looking blue hat. She was so grateful when Mom said, "Don't worry, sugar, you don't have to wear one."

The sanctuary was roughly as high as it was long and wide, comprised of light tan brick and blond wood. On the wall behind the raised platform were large Hebrew letters. One day Dad had explained to Naomi, "See these letters—they're to help you remember your Ten Commandments."

Guess I'm going to have to deal with the Big Ten eventually.

Beneath the letters and at the top of a three-step approach to the raised platform, she recognized the Ark. All the years of Jewish Youth Group came back to her as in a flood. She remembered the day their teacher escorted the young girls into the sanctuary to see close-up the elements only the men were allowed to touch.

Fifteen years later, she could still hear Mrs. Zabrinsky's warning. "You can look, but never ever touch it. You know what's inside there, girls? The Torah."

Even if Naomi could never touch it, she could gaze upon the beauty of the ornate cabinet which held the sacred scrolls covered in its rich indigo-colored velvet fabric. It would have been lovely to touch.

Hearing people greet each other with *L'Shanah Tovah*, she tasted a sweet familiarity. They may have been reciting by rote their good year wishes to one another, but to Naomi, a newcomer amongst them yearning to feel embraced, these words evoked a time when she was accepted. She took the plunge and turned to the family sitting in front of her and wished them *L'Shanah Tovah*. They did not respond with much warmth. The husband muttered in a monotone the expected greeting back.

Soon after experiencing this sting of rejection, a man walked onto the platform wearing a blue and white prayer shawl draped over his head, the fringe delicately cascading down his frame. He stopped very deliberately at the right side of the lectern, stood perfectly still for a brief moment, giving enough time to create a dramatic profile and commanding a contagious hush throughout the sanctuary. Once the stillness filled the room, he lifted up a shofar and brought the large ram's horn to his lips. Naomi was transfixed at this tableau, her eyes especially resting on the ancient trumpet with all its unique twistings and bendings.

She lifted her moist eyes upward and silently mouthed, "Thank You." As the ancient music pulsated in the air, she understood God had created a pocket solely for her, a pocket in time and space.

A short balding man wearing a white robe and a white yarmulke came forward. "I welcome you." He turned to Daniel seated on the platform, "And Rabbi Dan welcomes you."

I guess this guy's the Senior Rabbi. Nothing like Daniel.

The Senior Rabbi asked people to turn to page five-hundred and eighty for a responsive reading. Naomi went into panic mode. Daniel intuitively glanced over at her and smiled when he saw her looking back at him. He subtly lifted up the book on his lap which was the prayer book he had given her.

She took his cue and read responsively with the others, thanking the "Lord our God and God of our fathers."

A woman, also in a white robe, seated to the right of Daniel, stood. The Rabbi gave her room to share his lectern, and her chanting began. Allowing a woman to perform the role of Cantor was as novel to Naomi as her being allowed to sit among the men. As a performer herself, Naomi saw clearly the Cantor enjoyed performing before the crowd. Perhaps because the Cantor was an attractive young woman, long blond hair perfectly draped around her shoulders, there was a twinge of jealousy. *Oy, thou shalt not covet.*

The Senior Rabbi was silently mouthing along with the Cantor. To Naomi it appeared he wanted to be the one doing the chanting, but now was not his turn to lead.

Huh, bet he's a control freak.

Sure enough once the Cantor's role was finished, the Rabbi eagerly rushed back to the central place he had temporarily abdicated, almost stepping on the hem of her robe.

It was time for the sermon. "Today is our formal beginning for the High Holy Days, the Days of Awe. We should all now embark on the solemn process of introspection and repentance for our past misdeeds."

Introspection and repentance for my past misdeeds? All of them?

"These next ten days are a time when all life on earth is subjected to God's review and judgment. This is the time to seek God's forgiveness." He folded up his glasses and walked off, exiting from a door behind the platform.

She must have been so preoccupied with the man's opening statement that she missed all the rest of his sermon.

Rabbi Dan moved up to the lectern. "*Kiddush* everyone! Please join us, especially for some apples and honey."

Following the others as they made a quick exodus from the sanctuary, Naomi arrived back in the downstairs social area. Each table had a white platter with apples cut into slices and arranged around the rim of the plate. In the center of each was a bowl glowing with honey.

Stationed inside to warmly greet everyone was a petite silver-haired lady. In a face aged with wisdom and experience was a smile displaying youthful dimples. This woman managed the unique ability to carry herself with dignity while at the same time exuding a folksy old world sense of Jewishness. *Yiddishkeit* is what Naomi's parents called it.

"Hello, I'm Sylvia, Rabbi Lehrer's wife." Introducing herself to Naomi, she extended her hand and offered a firm handshake.

"Hello, I'm N—"

Daniel walked over to the two women. "Sylvia, this is the young lady who helped me with the apples yesterday. Naomi Goldblatt."

"Oh, I was hoping to thank you." Continuing to hold Naomi's hand with a firm grip, Sylvia confided, "I had a horrible toothache and when our Daniel volunteered to get the apples instead of me, I was thrilled. But when I told him they must be Red Romes (my husband doesn't like any of the others —oy vey, don't ask), you should have seen the look on this sweet boy's face. He's thinking, 'apples, shmapples, what's the difference?'" Sylvia turned to Daniel and asked, "Am I right?"

Daniel laughed. "Sylvia, I've told you, stop reading my mind."

"I watched him walk out the door and said, '*oy veis meir*, an apple is an apple, all I ask, let them be red ones! That's all! Let the apples be red. And lo and behold, I come down here this morning and I see this beautiful collection of sparkling Red Romes."

Rabbi Lehrer joined them. "Who is our new friend?" he inquired of his wife. "Please, introduce me."

"Naomi, this is my husband, Rabbi Joseph. Joseph, this is Naomi." Sylvia put one hand on Naomi's back and gently nudged her toward her husband. "You need to thank her for getting the kind of apples you like."

Trying to modestly protest, she was interrupted by the Rabbi. "It's always good to see a new face." While shaking her hand, he turned to Daniel. "Rabbi, would you care to do the blessing over the food for us?"

Daniel thanked the Senior Rabbi, and quickly moved to the center of the room amongst a crowd of about one-hundred and fifty. All eyes turned to Rabbi Dan as he did the *Baruka* over the food. Naomi noticed the Cantor move to stand alongside Daniel. She was now in a pastel blue silk suit which clung to her shapely figure.

With his right hand, Daniel held up an apple slice for all to see. In his left hand, he held the bowl of honey. "During Rosh Hashanah it is traditional to eat apples dipped in honey. Why do we do this? Because it tastes good? Or is it simply tradition? May we instead think how we wish our Gracious God would bless us in this New Year with fruitfulness and with His sweetness. Taste the Lord and see He is good. Barukh atah Adonai, Eloheinu melekh ha'olam."

After the "amen," Naomi saw most people were already in their pre-assigned seats. Sylvia leaned in to Naomi. "Come, dear, sit with us."

The "us" included Rabbi Lehrer and Daniel, as well as the Cantor, Sharon Caseman. The Senior Rabbi sat across from Naomi, peering at her through his wire-rimmed glasses, his thin lips tightly pursed. Naomi felt as if she were being scanned—from the inside out.

Sharon sat to Naomi's right and reminded her of the girls from the "in crowd" in high school, possessing confidence which bordered on smugness.

Sylvia, on Naomi's immediate left, dipped a slice of apple into a bowl of honey and handed it to her husband. Turning to Naomi, she asked, "Where are you from, dear?"

"Ellenville."

Rabbi Lehrer wiped the honey from his chin. "Ahhh, Rabbi Eisner. He was my professor at Hebrew University."

Daniel, seated across from Naomi, gave her a warm glance. "This is the first time Naomi didn't sit separated with the women, in the balcony." To Naomi, he asked, "How was it? I looked over at you and you seemed truly moved."

"There were a few times I felt like this hush in the air. I don't know if this is right to say but it was like being Jewish meant I was to be holy . . . I'm not explaining this right. I'm sorry."

"Well, we are the chosen people, chosen to be holy," Sylvia volunteered.

Daniel was either unaware or chose to ignore the apple slice Sharon was proffering to him. "It's nice to hear someone use the word holy. I'm not sure if our people are afraid to speak of our being holy or they don't really care." He turned to the Senior Rabbi, inviting him to join the discussion. When Rabbi Lehrer did not speak, Daniel prodded with a simple, "Rabbi?"

"Ah, yes, very true," the Senior Rabbi replied distractedly. "Sorry, everyone, but we need to begin our procession to the East River." He pulled out his chair and strode to the center of the room. "Everyone, it is time for *Tashlich*. As you leave the room, on your way out by the door you will see plates filled with small pieces of bread. Take a few with you and soon we will symbolically cast our sins into the River. Once we arrive at the pier, we will gather in a large circle for some brief songs and readings, and then we will each throw our bread into the river."

While walking to the pier, Rabbi Lehrer approached Naomi and suggested a visit with him and his wife at which time they could discuss more involvement at the Temple. This helped redirect her thoughts as she watched Daniel and Sharon walking comfortably together.

Arriving at the river, Rabbi Lehrer prayed, "Who is a God like thee? . . . Thou does not retain thy anger forever."

While he prayed, she squeezed the small piece of challah in her hand and before casting it into the water, she whispered her own small prayer, "Oh God, will You forgive my sin?"

Maybe there would be forgiveness, but how could she know for sure? She wished she could ask Daniel, but the shapely blonde Cantor, was diverting his attention. *You don't deserve someone like him anyway.*

Walking back home, she wondered what the meeting with the Rabbi would entail. More scanning? More judgment? Hopefully not. Instead she would hold on to a strand of hope—perhaps embracing her religion would stop that howling in her soul and would even repair the relationship with Dad.

For the rest of the night Naomi pondered Rabbi Lehrer's message. After all the years spent in synagogue, she only vaguely remembered the teachings regarding the time between Rosh Hashanah and Yom Kippur. Was it simply because today she was not segregated from the men, or could it be Someone was opening her ears to hear as if for the first time?

Several hours later, gazing into the mirror while brushing her teeth, Rabbi Lehrer's words echoed in her mind. "While the gates of heaven are still open, our sages tell us to seek amends with all we may have offended in the last year." Naomi knew upon hearing these piercing words earlier in the evening, they pertained to her father.

However, another relationship needed mending as well. The one with Anne. The last conversation with her old roommate was in March. The occasion was Anne's first singing engagement at a club in Soho. With Gary not interested in accompanying her, Naomi went alone and sat at a table with Anne's new roommate.

Anne startled her audience when she closed her act by belting out the lyrics to "O Happy Day." In her rich mezzosoprano voice, they heard, "O happy day, o happy day, when Jesus washed my sins away. O happy day." Songs extolling the name of Jesus were uncommon and unwelcome in Naomi's world and Anne's finale created quite a stir.

After taking her bow, the singer walked across the club floor, skirting the waitresses carrying trays laden with mixed drinks. Naomi jumped up from the table to hug her friend. Anne looked expectantly to her.

When words were not forthcoming from Naomi, Anne prodded by asking, "Well?"

"Your voice—oh I wish I had your voice." Naomi sipped from her martini glass. "You need to lose the holy roller stuff though. You could be so great, but then you do something like that—it's like you have a death wish."

Since that time there had been no communication between these two friends.

Naomi dropped her toothbrush, letting it fall into the sink. She walked back into the living room, picked up the phone and dialed Anne's number. Only a year ago this was her phone number, too. One year and so much destruction.

"Anne, it's me, the one you love to hate." She did not wait for a reply. "I'm calling to say I'm sorry."

Not only was Anne forgiving, but she offered, "I'm glad to hear from you."

Naomi surprised herself by blurting out, "Anne, I think maybe you'll understand more than anyone else I know. I'm becoming religious."

Naomi waited for Anne's reply, grabbed a TV guide sitting on her coffee table and flipped through its pages. *Anne, answer me already. I hope she doesn't think I'm putting her on or something.*

"And how does Gary feel about this? Is he becoming religious, too?"

Naomi mumbled, "He's gone. It's over." Hopefully Anne would detect the finality in her voice and would not probe further.

"Oh . . . who's the new guy, the one you're becoming religious for?"

"It's not like that. There is this guy, but no I can't even let myself think like that. I mean, Anne, he's a rabbi."

"Okay, if it's not for a guy, then what happened?"

"There's this synagogue near me. I don't want to say it was God, but something was making me stand in front of it. Like it was telling me, 'What you're looking for . . . what you need . . . you'll find it here.'"

"Why can't you say God? I know we have two different gods, you and me, but still why shouldn't you believe in yours? Religion is good."

"You want to get together soon? I'd love to see you."

Before hanging up, they agreed—Goldberg's Pizzeria the following week.

One week before Yom Kippur, then the gates will close . . . all my misdeeds . . . all of them—yikes, I'm cooked.

Chapter 5

T'shuvah

Naomi arrived at the temple in the same outfit worn three days earlier, on Rosh Hashanah. If she were truly to become more religious, she would need to find some more conservative-type outfits. *Salvation Army, here I come.*

She found Rabbi Lehrer's secretary on the telephone in what sounded like a heated argument. Nodding to Naomi, she indicated a seat across from her desk.

"Look, these are the rules," the secretary stated firmly. "You have to be a member if you want the Rabbi to marry your daughter. You let your membership lapse two years ago. I sent you reminders."

The Rabbi's office door opened and after a short glance at his secretary, he noticed Naomi. "Please, Ms. Goldblatt, come in." Walking into his office, he explained, "My wife will not be able to join us. Will you be comfortable meeting only with me? Of course," he assured her, "I will leave the door open."

"That'll be fine." She had hoped Sylvia's presence would offset this meeting feeling like an interrogation.

"Good. I'm delighted you were with us on Sunday, as well as visiting us today."

"Rabbi, I'd like to—"

Daniel stuck his head in the doorway. "Rabbi . . .oh, Naomi, what a surprise."

The Senior Rabbi ignored Daniel's reaction to Naomi. "Rabbi Dan, did you need something?"

"I simply wanted to tell you I was going to lunch."

A woman's voice called from the hallway, "Dan, are you ready?"

Turning as Sharon came into view, he answered, "Yes, I'm coming."

The couple walked away while Rabbi Lehrer studied Naomi. "They make a nice couple, don't you think?"

From microscope to x-ray machine. Hah, good thing I've had all those years of acting classes." Yes, they do," she confirmed.

He continued to probe her true feelings. "Did you know Rabbi Dan's last name is Cantor?"

"No, I didn't."

"My wife enjoys saying, 'Our Cantor will one day be Mrs. Cantor.'" He paused, again studying her expression. "I suggested you visit with us today so I might ask, 'What can we do for you?' Am I wrong or do I perceive you are looking to more fully embrace your Judaism?"

"Yes. No, I mean you're not wrong. You're very perceptive."

"I owe much to my wife. I often receive credit that actually belongs to her. Sylvia told me she perceived this about you and nudged me to speak with you."

"Your wife is charming."

"I thank you and couldn't agree more."

Naomi took a deep breath, feeling at ease now to ask what was most on her heart. "Rabbi, the other day you said it was like when we threw our bread into the river, we were casting our sin into the water. But how can I know for sure my sin is forgiven?"

He peered at her over his wire-rimmed glasses. Brows furrowed and chin studiously pulled up, he answered. "Ahh, good question, Ms. Goldblatt. The sages teach we must make amends with all to whom we might have offended. Do you recall? I spoke of this in my sermon." With deliberation he removed his eyeglasses, and in a voice practiced at inviting confidentiality, he asked, "To whom do you need to make amends?"

She had been nervously rubbing the bottom button on her suit jacket and suddenly realized the thread was giving way as a result. Something else was needed to work out her agitation. Her leather purse was lying on the floor next to her right foot, with the long straps placed on the armrest of the chair. While answering the Rabbi's question, she used both hands to twist the soft leather straps.

"Because of what you said on Sunday . . ." She changed her tone to one of playful defiance. "See, I *was* listening." The old pretend-to-be confident Naomi had flown in to make a guest appearance. "Because of what you said, I talked with a friend and we are okay now."

He peered directly into her eyes. "Is there anyone else? I think perhaps there is."

"Yes. My father."

"My dear, you must do this by—"

"Yom Kippur, I know . . . I'm sorry for interrupting. It's just I know I need to do this and I will. But, Rabbi, there's something else. I have this feeling . . . I don't know how to describe it except it's like no one's holding me up anymore. I used to think I was a decent human being, not exactly a saint, but not a terrible person either. Now it's as if I need someone to help protect me from myself. Sounds crazy, huh?"

He began searching intently through his pen cup as if he had lost an expensive family heirloom. Would he ever answer her?

Finally, leaning back in his chair, he responded. "Ms. Goldblatt, it is not to do with whether you are crazy or not. We refer to it as the 'evil impulse.' This is why the yoke of the law is so beautiful. There is a word in Hebrew: *t'shuvah*. Are you familiar with this?"

"No."

"*T'shuvah* speaks of repentance—to repent from your sins and return to God"

"How do I do that? I can become more religious, to attend synagogue when I can, but I waitress Friday nights. I don't know if you approve of waitressing or not. My father doesn't." She deepened her voice in imitation of her father. "No one in our family ever slung hash." The Rabbi was not laughing. "But see, I haven't had the motivation for a while now to keep up with my career."

"Oh, and what is your career?"

"Theatre. I'm an actress."

A woman's voice was heard coming from behind Naomi. "Oh, I knew you looked familiar."

The Rabbi greeted his wife. "Come, dear, sit down. Join us."

Sylvia took the seat next to Naomi and patted her hand. "You are one of the wicked stepsisters in that Mop & Glo commercial, aren't you?"

Naomi's first reaction was of embarrassment as she looked toward the Rabbi, but was relieved when he said, "You're right, dear. Now I recognize her, too. We always laugh when that ad comes on."

Naomi stood up and mimicked her own performance. "Cinderella, mop that floor." Hearing their laughter, she confided, "Wish I coulda gotten the part of Cinderella, but, hey, that's the story of my life."

By the time Naomi reached Junior High, she knew her mom's routine: the second Thursday of each month was Mom's date with self-beautification. Like clockwork, on that Thursday, Helen colored her hair with Roux Blue Mink Rinse.

On this particular second Thursday of the month, Naomi came to surprise her parents. If she used her own set of keys, it might frighten her skittish mom. *She's probably got her hair soaking right now. I can just see the towel around her neck and big blobs of color dripping on the towel.* Naomi rang the doorbell.

"Who is it?"

Naomi answered only with another ring and soon saw the door open a crack, then swing wide open.

Helen grabbed Naomi by the shoulders. "Is everything okay? It's so good to see you, but are you okay?" Helen went to kiss her daughter, but pulled back when she saw her blue hair rinse drip into Naomi's auburn hair. "Honey, I'm so sorry." Quickly, she took the towel from around her neck and soaked up the runaway blue blobs.

The two of them looked affectionately at each other and then burst into girlish giggles.

"I came to surprise you, Mom—and Dad, too. I'm hoping it'll be okay between him and me again soon."

"Oh, sweetheart, I'm sure it will. I've been praying. And crossing my fingers, too." She made a small fist, bent down slightly to reach the credenza in their foyer. "Been knocking on wood, too."

"Speaking of knocking, I brought some knockwurst from Katz's Deli. I know how Dad loves them." She held up a brown bag.

"My sweet best daughter."

"I'm your only daughter, your only child, and Dad told me he was hoping for a son."

"No, he loves you, honey. Ever since he first saw you. You should have seen his face."

"Forget it, it's okay. Besides which your hair's gonna turn like navy blue or something in a second. It's getting kinda dark. Must be time to rinse it out."

Helen glided into the kitchen, turned on the water and adjusted its temperature.

Naomi offered, "Let me help. I'll rinse it out for you." While testing the water and doing a bit more adjusting, she added, "Besides which you are my best mom."

Once the color was washed out of her hair and swirling down the kitchen sink, Helen retreated to her bedroom. Time to put in the rollers and sit under the hair dryer.

"You know where I keep the vase, sugar. Would you get it out? Your father should be home soon."

Way back when, Dad must have figured out her mom's once-a-month ritual. As far back as Naomi could remember, the same day Mom colored her hair, Dad would arrive home with a dozen red roses. He would come through the front door of their simple cinder-block home and call out, "I'm home. What's for dinner? Smells good."

Dad always handed the long-stemmed beauties to Mom, who had already prepared a vase to receive them.

This Thursday upon entering home Naomi's father was greeted with some very distinctive aromas. "What? I smell ... what is that? ... smells like knock—"

Naomi stood there, smiling at her father while helping her mother with last minute dinner preparations.

He looked cautiously at her while with one hand Naomi quickly reached for the vase and took the flowers from him. "Yes, it's knockwurst. Not just any knockwurst though. I went all the way down to the lower east side, to Katz's deli. I know they're your favorite."

While enjoying their dinner, Naomi informed her parents she was no longer living with "that bum" and was also attending *shul*.

Dad expressed his approval. "Now I can be proud of you again. Tell you what? Let's go to Carvel for some dessert." This was Dad's way of saying "welcome home."

With some luck maybe the gates of heaven would not slam in her face this year.

The bus ride back into the city the following day became like an emotional roller coaster. One moment she was jubilant. Being accepted back into her parents' home gave her a sense of security she had been lacking. However, the fear she had expressed to Rabbi Lehrer remained. Who was holding her up? And how could she trust the gates would stay open?

As a child, after a Bible lesson with her Jewish youth group, she visualized God: He was in the clouds, wearing a big black judge's robe and held a huge gavel in his hand. *Who knows when He might whack me with that thing?*

The roller coaster went up with a childlike sense of security and then swiftly plunged downward with a crippling sense of insecurity. *If only I could have stayed with Mom and Dad a few days more . . . if only I didn't have to work at the Bistro tonight.*

The thought of quitting her waitressing job made her smile, but if she quit, how would she pay the rent? Maybe she needed to consider moving somewhere cheaper. But she'd be breaking the one-year lease which she had to sign three months ago. By the time she was on the subway from the Port Authority Bus Terminal to her apartment, her mind had been made up. She would call Rhonda.

Maybe she could get back into her agent's good graces. Maybe an acting career was still available to her. But did she deserve anything truly good? Would the God of the Ten Commandments smile down from heaven on her? Could she get back into *His* good graces? She had done what the Rabbi had said. Amends had been made with both Anne and with her father. But what if she left someone out?

Sudden and sharp came that howling deep within her soul, so painful she tightly squeezed her eyes shut, as if she could shut out the unbidden thought: the one she most needed to ask forgiveness from, she could not. Naomi herself was the reason this one was not alive to ask.

Was "it" a he or a she?

This mental whirlwind accompanied her all the way to her front door. Upon entering, Naomi noticed the red blinking light on her answering machine.

"Wow, Zoey, no one ever calls me anymore. Maybe it's for you."

The message began with a jumble of background noise. About ready to hit the stop button, Naomi heard Rhonda's distinctive husky voice.

"Darling, I hope you literally have gotten your act together by now." The agent took a dramatic pause before continuing in a booming voice, "Because Mop & Glo wants to use you again. Call me as soon as you get this message."

Naomi, as instructed, called Rhonda back immediately.

"Cookie, they are prepared to offer you almost twice what you made for the first one. They've gotten great feedback on you. People have said you're their favorite of the wicked stepsisters."

It was all set. Monday she would meet with the producers of the commercial. And now she could give her notice to the people at the Bistro.

God was smiling down from heaven on her. He was pleased with her. She tilted her head upward, hoping her words would travel above the ceiling. "Thank You. I'm not all alone. You are holding me up. I'll try . . . I'll try to be good from now on."

Seeking to keep this sacred promise, Naomi, after working into the late hours Friday night at the Bistro, arose early the next morning to attend Saturday services at the Temple. Although the entire congregation was invited after the service to partake in a full meal in the downstairs area, Naomi left the synagogue. She was exhausted and needed a few more hours of sleep before returning for her last Saturday night waitressing stint.

Whatever it took to show the One watching over her, and even now richly rewarding her, that she was worth His kindness . . . she would do it. Hopefully then she would avoid the whack on the head from His gavel.

Chapter 6

Yom Kippur

Naomi awoke craving a cup of coffee. She had been fasting since sundown last evening and had been told to abstain even from coffee. A warm bagel with lox and cream cheese would be nice, too.

Yet as the congregants left for the night, they had wished one another, "May you have an easy fast." This morning Naomi was still scratching her head over this. The Rabbi said they were to think of fasting as a sacrifice to the Lord. If it were a sacrifice, why should it be easy? An easy sacrifice—sounded like an oxymoron.

Well, no need for her to worry about it since this morning she was finding it anything but easy. *I want my coffee.*

During the evening service Naomi had jotted down a portion of Scripture read by the president of the *shul.* She thought she might look at it later. Maybe doing so this morning, while still in bed, would take her mind off of coffee, eggs, bagels, and even the bacon she smelled drifting in from the apartment below.

She jumped out of bed and closed the bedroom window. Getting back under her comfy comforter, she grabbed the Bible Daniel had given her from the nightstand. There was something about what the man had read that made her curious, even though she was now too distracted to remember what. Where was the scrap of paper from last night? Probably in her purse.

Hopping out of bed and picking up the Bible, she walked into the living room. It wasn't in her leather bag, but now the fragrance of freshly brewed coffee from the apartment below assaulted her. Loosely holding the Bible, she ran and slammed shut the living room window. From the middle of the book out flew the scrap of paper.

Leviticus 16. Thankfully the Bible contained a Table of Contents. She found chapter sixteen. "Thus shall Aaron come into the holy place: with a young bullock for a sin offering, and a ram for a burnt offering. He shall put on the holy linen coat . . ."

Huh? Maybe Orthodox Judaism has it right—women are better kept separated from the men—let the men read from the Torah and let the women just sit by themselves and do their gossip. Though shalt not be sarcastic, Naomi!

She persevered and continued reading. Certain words seemed to stand out: ". . . offer . . . make atonement . . ." The question of what exactly "offer" meant was like a candle flickering in the darkness of her consciousness. Did this speak of animal sacrifice? No, she would not even consider such a thought.

However, her eyes were unwilling to move past ". . . kill the bull as a sin offering . . . blood . . . on the mercy seat . . . mercy . . ." Mercy—maybe she could simply wrap her mind around that one word—she most certainly needed it.

All this talk of the animals being a burnt offering somehow made her think of charbroiled meat, which only made her aware of how hungry she was. Surely she needed mercy to make it until the evening when she would enjoy breaking the fast with her new temple family.

Last night upon leaving, Daniel had asked, "Will I see you tomorrow night? I can put you down for our congregational dinner. Will that be all right?"

He probably asked all the others the same question. Besides, I have to think of him as Rabbi Dan. But he introduced himself to me as Daniel. I feel something special when I think of him as Daniel. Naomi, stop it!

Time to return to the world more familiar to her and look at the new Mop & Glo script. She needed to be ready for filming in less than a week. She had left the script in the back bedroom—Gary's office. *Oops, my office now.* Naomi lifted herself up from the couch and left the Bible open on the coffee table. Zoey made her cute little "chirping" sound and pawed the pages.

"Bad cat - stop it. I'll feed you in a minute."

Yet the pages uncovered by the mischievous cat compelled Naomi to give them her full attention. She read, "The eternal God is a dwelling-place, and underneath are the everlasting arms . . ."

The everlasting arms— the eternal God, He is holding me up. I'm not out here alone.

Tears poured forth from some inner wellspring. This sudden emotion did not surprise her, but simply expressed what had always been inexpressible. God actually cared enough to speak to her, and He was willing to do so using her cat.

She was transported back to the kitchen inside the Leibowitz mansion on the day when the elusive thought had floated past her—the thought which contained the promise that there was a meaning to life. The yearning to know if there was Someone watching over her could no longer be treated simply as material for an audition piece.

Audition piece . . . focus, Naomi, focus. you gotta work on your script. You only have an hour before you need to be back at the shul.

All through the service, Naomi's mind wandered. She could not control her renegade imagination—whether it centered on the issue of animal sacrifice or on how nice Daniel looked sitting on the podium. The blast of the shofar, signifying the end of the Yom Kippur service, startled her.

Naomi saw everyone suddenly rise and she followed suit. They began reciting something from their prayer book. Naomi quickly opened hers to nowhere in particular and feigned reading the closing prayer with the congregation.

Rabbi Dan then came to the microphone and invited all those with dinner tickets to join him and Rabbi Lehrer downstairs. "Let us enjoy breaking our fast together."

Sylvia had finagled the seating arrangements so Naomi once again was seated next to her at the Rabbi's table and across from Daniel. After twenty-four hours of abstaining from food, out from the kitchen came platters of brisket with roasted potatoes. It was a beautiful sight and its savory aroma made Naomi's mouth water. And lo and behold what group was served first? The Rabbi's table, of course. The food arrived and all talking ceased. The only sound heard was the hollow rumblings from Naomi's stomach.

The older Jewish woman setting the platter on their table turned to Naomi and smiled. "Good to see a young woman with a healthy appetite. Enjoy it, honey."

Daniel also smiled. "Last time I heard that sound, it was an excuse to enjoy apple butter and zucchini bread."

"You mean banana bread."

"I stand corrected." Daniel replied. With his whimsical display of humility, Naomi again saw the smile she found so endearing.

Rabbi Lehrer looked over at Sharon and then turned to Naomi. "Tell me, Miss Goldblatt, any thoughts on our Yom Kippur service?"

"Joseph, don't put her on the spot like that," Sylvia gently scolded her husband.

Sharon interjected, "I'm sure your husband wasn't trying to do that." Turning to the Rabbi, she continued, "Were you, Rabbi? I'd enjoy hearing her observations, too." She looked across the table at Naomi. "After all, this was probably your first time to really observe Yom Kippur, or even Rosh Hashanah, too. Isn't that right?"

Naomi swallowed her brisket and quickly washed it down with water. "I'll be honest with you. All during service today my mind was wandering. I mean, I was honestly in awe of last night's service. I'd have loved it if it went on for another couple of hours."

Sylvia reached across the table with her fork and clinked her husband's drinking glass. "And how long have you waited for someone to tell you that, dear?" Still looking at her husband, she directed the next words to Naomi. "Dear, you have made the Rabbi's day. Hasn't she, Joseph?"

While attempting to go along with the lighter tone of the conversation, he prodded, "Yet today your mind wandered. Were you just too hungry to concentrate?"

Naomi took the plunge. "No, that's not it at all. At last night's service Leviticus Sixteen was mentioned."

Sharon was passing the brisket to Daniel, but was left holding the platter because his attention was riveted on Naomi.

Daniel nodded. "Yes, a passage from Leviticus was read." His eyes still on Naomi, he received the platter. "Thank you, Sharon."

"This morning I read it for myself, and that's why my mind wandered. I'm trying to learn more about our religion. I need to understand what . . . please don't think I'm being presumptuous or anything, but I need to know what God would want from me."

Daniel leaned in toward her, holding his fork in midair. "That's not at all presumptuous. Most people, I'd say, are more interested in thinking what *they* want from *Him*." Turning to his senior rabbi, the young associate added, "Would you agree, Rabbi?"

Rabbi Lehrer gave a slight nod, and immediately turned to Naomi. "Tell me, were you able to follow through with what we spoke of at our meeting? Making amends, particularly with your father?"

"Yes. Thank you for guiding me in that direction." Her voice grew in excitement as she told about the sweet reconciliation with her father. "That would have been enough, on its own, but—"

Sylvia chimed in, "*Dayenu.*"

"Oh, yes, exactly." Naomi expressed her enormous gratitude. Not only was the relationship restored with her parents, but also, "I got a job doing a sequel to my Mop & Glo commercial."

"*Mazel Tov*," offered Rabbi Lehrer and Sylvia.

Simultaneously Daniel exclaimed, "You're an actress? Why didn't you tell me you were an actress?"

Before she knew it, the words tumbled out. "Why didn't you tell me you were a rabbi?"

Sylvia seemed to have an uncanny ability to know when to jump in. "Don't you recognize our pretty young friend from the Mop & Glo commercial, the one with Cinderella? It's on TV all the time."

"I don't watch television, Sylvia," Daniel admitted. "But if Mop & Glo has a Jewish girl playing Cinderella, I'll go out and buy the stuff tonight."

"Don't waste your money, I'm not Cinderella, just a wicked stepsister."

"Good," Daniel announced to the whole table. "All my floors are carpeted anyway."

All laughed and finally dug in to eat the hearty meal put before them. And then came the large platter of assorted rugelach.

"Thank you, Beatrice. They look delicious," Rabbi Lehrer complimented the heavyset middle-aged woman who had served their table all evening. "Ah, you made my wife's favorite, apricot. Thank you for all your hard work and please tell all the other women in the Sisterhood how much we appreciate them."

"I hope you enjoy them. We gave you a few extra of the chocolate ones. We know they are your favorite, Rabbi." Putting her hands inside the pockets of her apron, the woman walked back to the kitchen.

Sylvia handed her husband two of the chocolate pieces and turned to Naomi. "And what are your favorite ones, dear? I bet you like chocolate, too?"

"No, actually, I really like the raisin ones. Do the women who are serving us do all the cooking, too?"

"No, of course not," Sharon said sharply. "The dinner was catered. It was on your program, thanking Kaufman's Deli for providing this meal to the Temple."

Naomi hesitated for a brief moment. "Rabbi, I'd like to help, too. Anything I could do, you just tell me. I mean my Mom taught me to make rugelach—and challah, too. I mean what could I do to help here?"

The Rabbi removed his glasses and began cleaning them with an unused cloth napkin. He signaled his wife not to answer Naomi. "My dear, this is very admirable of you. Sylvia and I can see you are a responsible young adult. However, I'm sure you will be in agreement with this: you must first become a member of Temple

Beth Orr. Rabbi Dan, when do you begin your next cycle of new member classes?"

"The current one will finish at Chanukah. I planned to start a new class right at the first of the year." Smiling towards Naomi, he invited, "Can I sign you up?

"Yes. Definitely."

Daniel bit into his apricot rugelach and smiled toward Naomi. "You'll be the first on the list." Turning toward Rabbi Lehrer, he inquired, "Would you agree, even though not a member yet, Naomi could still work on building our Sukkah?"

Daniel received a nod from the Rabbi and turned back to Naomi. "Would you like to help build the booth we will use to observe Sukkot? Tomorrow I need to go buy some palm fronds, citrons . . . well, you get the idea. Sounds like a trip to the farmers' market. Are you free to help me? We can get some whatever bread it was."

Savoring her raisin rugelach, Naomi chewed on the word *b'sheirt*. Daniel told her it was "where you could see the fingerprints of divine providence." Banana bread, zucchini bread, who cared?

I'll even eat broccoli bread.

Unable to sleep that evening, Naomi slid off her bed onto the floor. She bent her knees and leaned over her bed, and made prayer hands as her mother had taught her. As if still praying with her mother, she began, "Now I lay me down to sleep. I pray the Lord my soul to keep. If I should die before . . ."

Abruptly switching from her childhood prayer, she cried out, "Are You there? Can You hear me? Please, I need Your help. I am so scared. I can't stop thinking about Daniel."

Not only was there fear of how heartbroken she would be at his rejection, but also condemnation for even imagining such a "holy man" would be at all interested in someone like her. "And here I am thinking about a guy when I should be thinking about You. I stink. Can you ever forgive me?"

It was as if a gentle yet firm hand cupped her chin and lifted her head upward. Someone *was* watching over her. She eased her way back into the bed and found Zoey resting on the side of her pillow. Naomi stroked her furry friend as she closed her eyes to sleep the sleep of a child who knew she was loved and secure. The purring of the cat was a sweet lullaby.

Too bad not enough time to run to Barnes & Noble—maybe they'd have a book on Sukkot for Dummies. Probably not. She would at least arrive at the Farmer's Market ahead of Daniel, look around and hopefully get a feel for the holiday by seeing what the vendors had on display. Although most of the proprietors were not Jewish, Naomi figured they were keenly aware of their local clientele and would know the items in demand for Sukkot.

Arriving at the Market, she was greeted with the sight of the Chasidic men, dressed in their black coats and hats. Images flashed through her mind of Gary mocking their attire when they performed with the improv company.

That stupid schlocky skit—get out of my head—I don't have time to think about you. Any minute now Daniel will be here and I'm going to look totally ignorant.

Naomi made a decision. She would ask one of the vendors to tell her what most people bought for Sukkot. She took a step toward the same man who had helped her with the Red Romes when from behind she heard someone say, "Caught you!"

It was almost as if she could detect his presence by a fragrance. He did not use any cologne yet Naomi sensed with enjoyment a warm vanilla-like aroma. She turned around and saw Daniel. His brown eyes danced with delight. "I know you. You were about to ask them what to buy, weren't you?"

He was wearing blue jeans and a plain white t-shirt with a tweed suit jacket, hands casually resting in the pockets of his jeans. When her eyes caught sight of his brown leather cowboy boots, she blurted out. "You know, you could at least dress like a rabbi."

Reaching into a jacket pocket, he produced a yarmulke. "Will this help?" His countenance then changed to one of concern. "You look cold. You want my jacket?"

She declined his offer but he quickly noticed a booth selling hot apple cider. He returned the yarmulke to the jacket pocket and pulled out his wallet. "C'mon, let me buy you something warm to drink."

Soon they were seated on a bench enjoying the hot cider with a generous portion of banana bread. "Naomi, I enjoy being with you. You are refreshingly honest."

"No. I'm not," she mumbled, never raising her head to meet his eyes.

"You're so honest you're about to tell me why you're not honest, right?"

"Oh, Daniel—I'm so sorry, I should call you Rabbi Dan—"

"I introduced myself to you as Daniel. Please, feel free to continue calling me that." With a gentle touch, he placed two fingers under her chin, encouraging her to look up and into his smiling face.

Her eyes made contact with his and she confessed, "I don't have a clue about Sukkot. I only said 'yes' because I wanted to be with you."

"Okay, you made your confession, now it's my turn. I asked you because I wanted to be with you." He saw the unabashed happy surprise light up her face and playfully jabbed her arm. "How about them apples, kid?"

For a moment laughter relieved her nervousness. However, soon she had a sobering thought. "What about Sharon?"

"Naomi, religion is not . . . well, it's not a business to me and it's not a stage either, you know, a place to perform. I know you're an actress, but that's separate from what I'm talking about. And I don't mean to talk unkindly about anyone."

Daniel finished his bread and took another swallow of cider. "Sharon seems interested in me. I don't want to hurt her feelings and sometimes I worry that I'm needlessly encouraging her." Daniel scowled, and with a shake of his head suggested, "Let's change the subject. I want to talk to you about this actress thing. The Temple will be doing a Chanukah play."

She had been trying to hide how chilled she was, but then a strong wind blew toward them from the East River. Daniel removed his jacket and placed it on Naomi's shoulders. "I've been given the job of writing, producing, and directing—and I'm way over my head. Naomi, I could use some professional help."

"Sounds like fun. I'd love to."

"Okay. Now that Chanukah's taken care of—"

"It is?"

Daniel playfully cleared his throat and shook his head, imitating a teacher chastising his student. "Do you want to learn about Sukkot or not?"

"Sorry."

"Let's start with this—you grew up in an orthodox home, so what did you do back then?"

"We weren't . . . we went to an orthodox synagogue because it was the only one in Ellenville. Mom was the religious one. She lit the candles every Friday night, but Dad wasn't like Mom. In fact, I remember him once saying to Mom on a Friday night, 'Helen, you don't need to do this, we're Americans now. That was in the old country we had to do that stuff.'"

Daniel gently brushed a rebellious wisp of hair away from Naomi's face. "Your parents were first generation Americans, right?"

Naomi nodded. "But I don't remember doing anything for Sukkot. And what about you? What did your family do?"

"We didn't either."

"Were yours first generation, also?"

Daniel appeared uncomfortable. "No. I'll tell you about them some other time. But for now, I need to teach you about my favorite festival."

92

"Sukkot?"

"I hope if I do a good job telling you why it's special to me, you'll be excited to celebrate it, too. And, then, of course, we are here to do some shopping."

Another brisk gust of wind coaxed Daniel's cowlick to stand up and take a bow. Following Naomi's eyes and her chuckles, Daniel lifted his hand to his scalp and quickly found the stubborn tuft of hair. "I've had this thing since forever. The girls used to tease me. Said I looked like Dennis the Menace." Reaching into his jacket pocket he again brought out his yarmulke and fastened it to his head with a small silver clip. "Now you know why I became a rabbi."

Naomi tucked the still-showing cowlick under his headpiece. "Hope you don't mind – it was still sticking up. I like it though. It helps make you less intimidating."

"Do you find Rabbi Lehrer intimidating?"

"Yes, but his wife Sylvia, she helps—you know what I mean?"

"Yes, I do. When I first started working under the Rabbi . . ." Daniel stopped abruptly and fanned both hands away from his body. "Whoa. I don't need to go there. Let's talk about Sukkot. Think of it as a time set aside to give thanks. Moses commanded us that we were to live in booths or tabernacles for seven days, so we might remember the Lord's goodness during the years of wandering in the wilderness."

Naomi put her hand on his for a brief moment, fighting back tears. "Daniel, I think that was me. I feel like I have been wandering in some wilderness, but now it's beginning to change."

He held her hand in both of his. "Naomi, let me tell you about the menorah. It's not only for Chanukah. See, God told Moses they were to make a beautiful gold lampstand, a menorah, for the tabernacle where He would dwell with them. Try to picture this menorah because God's instructions about His design . . . well, they amaze me."

"I'll close my eyes," which she readily did. "Paint me a picture."

"One piece, the shaft, the branches and the bowls, all one piece of pure gold. And on the almond branches, again all one piece, picture the almond buds and almond blossoms. Did you ever see almond blossoms?"

With her eyes still closed, she shook her head no.

"Picture a small white delicate flower. But here's what I get excited about. There's one main shaft, or trunk, and coming out of it are six almond branches. What does that make you think of?"

Although afraid to give the wrong answer, she ventured, "I think I see a tree." Opening her eyes, she quickly apologized, "I'm sorry. What did you want me to see?"

He grasped both her shoulders. "Exactly what you saw. I had a professor at the Hebrew University. When he drew the menorah on a chalkboard, I yelled out, 'It's the tree of life.' That was not a cool thing to do in Dr. Bronstein's class. He reprimanded me and half the class gave me dirty looks. That night I couldn't sleep . . . Oh, Naomi, I'm talking your ear off."

Now she grasped his shoulders. "The tree of life?"

He took both her hands and clasped them tenderly in his. "That night I kept wondering if God could have instructed Moses to make it that way so it would remind us of the tree of life, and what if it was God's way of telling the Jewish people *He* would dwell with *us* at the present time until one day *we* will dwell with *Him*. And in the meantime, we do what Rabbi Lehrer talks about—we embrace the yoke of the law. I believe Rabbi Lehrer learned that from your rabbi, Rabbi Eisner."

"You're nothing like Rabbi Eisner, thank God." Catching herself, her hand went up to her mouth. "I'm sorry. That was like the old me. Stupid."

"You're not stupid, but we should get down to business. My fault. Let's talk about what we'll be doing at the Temple to celebrate Sukkot."

"Yes, please."

"The festival is for seven days. The *shul* will celebrate the first night and the last together, eat dinner, sing some songs, read some prayers and the Rabbi will read from Leviticus."

"Leviticus?" In a panicked voice, she asked, "Is he going to talk about killing animals?"

"Oh, so that's it. I remember at the table you started to say something about reading Leviticus, but you were interrupted."

"I don't understand why there's all that stuff about killing and blood?"

"I'm sorry, I can tell it really upset you, but we need to save this for another time. Soon we'll start the new members' class and we can talk about it there. Okay?"

"Sure. Besides which," Naomi pointed her finger toward the river, "our favorite singer is back."

Daniel took her hand and helped her off the bench. "Time to decorate our tabernacle. Let's find ourselves the perfect *etrog*."

"Huh?"

Daniel continued holding her hand. "C'mon—I'll show you. It's a citron."

Naomi watched as Daniel painstakingly sought out the most exquisite specimen and inspected its furrowed leathery rind. Holding one of these oblong lemon-like fruits, he pointed out, "The shape is good, but it doesn't have the fragrance I'm looking for."

The nonchalant Daniel was gone and in his place was a man diligently searching for the sublime. Finally he chose the *etrog*. "Now to make our *lulav*."

First they hunted for the perfect date palm frond, which Daniel tested meticulously to ensure that it was both sturdy and straight. It had to have whole leaves that lay closely together and were not broken at the top.

Next they scoured the market for branches from a myrtle tree. Each potential candidate received the sniff test from Daniel. "They must be aromatic." Lastly were the branches from a willow tree, lined with long and narrow leaves. This shopping expedition finished in less than forty-five minutes.

Naomi complained, "I was perfectly useless. I learned a lot, but I wish I could have helped."

"You will. Now it's your turn. The Sukkah booth has to be decorated. I'm counting on you to not only make it pretty, but also fun."

A six-foot-long garland made up of plastic citrons had already caught Naomi's eye. "Can we go back to the table over by where we got the bread?"

"Sure."

Displayed next to this garland was a lifelike grape vine with bunches of leaves surrounding small plastic grape clusters. Naomi insisted they had to have one vine showing off green grapes and a second one with red grapes. "Of course," Naomi insisted, "this means we need at least two of the citron garlands."

When several lanterns were also packaged up for them by the vendor, Daniel asked, "We're done, right?"

But Naomi ran toward another table. "Daniel, look." She held up another garland of plastic apples, lemons, oranges, pears, and even a pineapple.

"Okay, but don't forget, I can't go over the budget they gave me."

However, as they trudged out of the marketplace with all their bags, a large laminated poster shouted her name. It was a collage of photographs taken at the Wailing Wall in Jerusalem.

Naomi implored, "I'll buy it for the Temple with my money. Please."

Daniel shrugged his shoulders and smiled. Naomi took off and before Daniel caught up with her, she had already removed the poster from its picture hook.

She told Daniel, "It'll be like when we're sitting in the sukkah, we can pretend we're in Israel. Have you ever gone there?"

"No. What about you?"

"No, but my mother—it's her dream to go there someday."

"It's my dream, too."

The vendor cleared his throat, reminding them he was waiting. Daniel pushed her wallet out of the way. "I'll get it with the Temple's money. Don't worry." He took out his own wallet and tore out a check.

"No, if I pay for it then after the holiday I can take it home. I'll put it up in my apartment and it'll remind me—"

"Forgive us," Daniel told the vendor, "give us a second." His solution: the Temple would buy the Wailing Wall poster and after Sukkot, it would be given to her as a gift, thanking Naomi for all her work.

Enjoying their walk back to the Temple, Naomi asked, "Do you think the *shul* will ever have a trip to Israel?"

"I was told they tried once, but couldn't get enough people to sign up." Daniel abruptly put his bags down, stopped walking and turned to Naomi. "Let's pray—we'll ask the Almighty to make it happen one day."

"Wow, now it's not only my mom's dream, but mine, too."

Chapter 7

Feasts of Rejoicing

ecause of Mop & Glo I went to the ball. Mop & Glo . . . oops . . ." Bringing the container of floor polish to her face, it slipped right out of Cinderella's hands.

"Cut," sighed the director. "From the top—everyone, places again. Stepsister number two, give Cinderella her line again."

Naomi moved back to full front camera position and with perfect delivery spoke her line. "What were you doing dancing with the prince? Why weren't you home mopping the floor?"

It was now close to five p.m., with the shoot having started promptly at eight a.m. Under the hot lights, the actresses' makeup had streaked several times and demanded touchups. Never once did Naomi cause a "cut" to be called. Always it was Cinderella, who must have required at least thirty takes for one line. The stepsisters might have been wicked, but they were professional.

Stepsister number one walked over to Naomi, rolling her eyes in the direction of Cinderella. "Guess that's what happens when you rely on your looks, huh?"

Naomi chortled. "Like I would know. And I have somewhere really special to be soon."

"Where?"

"It's the first night of Sukkot."

The woman appeared baffled. After Naomi gave a short explanation of the Jewish Festival, the actress rolled her eyes once more. "I'm going to get another cup of coffee. Want me to get you one?"

99

Naomi shook her head and the actress walked toward the coffee pot sitting in the corner of the studio. *She must think I'm like a religious nut or something.*

While Cinderella's lipstick was being touched up, Naomi enjoyed stoking sweet memories of time spent with Daniel. When others complimented her for decorating the Sukkah booth, Daniel stood to the side beaming his approval. Even Rabbi Lehrer commented, "Lovely touch," when he saw the poster of Jerusalem's Wailing Wall.

She had to be there tonight. *If Cinderella doesn't get her act together, I'm going to just tell them I have to go. Yikes, I can't do that—Rhonda will kill me.*

But she was saved from career suicide when the producer announced to cast and crew, "Everyone, go home. This is going to take another day to wrap up."

Naomi arrived at the temple about forty-five minutes late. As she entered the synagogue's main corridor she could hear the festive sounds of Israeli folk music which increased in volume as she made her way to the courtyard.

In front of the prefabricated hut used as a sukkah booth eight women performed an Israeli dance. They were perfectly synchronized and exuberant, the older women as radiant and joyous as their younger counterparts.

Off to one side was the cassette recorder playing the music and directly at the center of the booth was Sharon singing. "This is a time of rejoicing. Hallelu—hallelujah."

As the tempo of the music and the singing picked up, the dancers let go of each other's hands and moved into the center. They clapped their hands, fanned back out, and repeated this movement several times, until once again they grabbed hands and moved as if they were one body. A time of rejoicing.

Feeling like a complete outsider, Naomi retreated to sitting on a concrete bench several yards away from the others. Once the music faded and everyone had applauded the breathless women dancers, Sylvia approached Naomi.

"I was so afraid you weren't coming. I kept looking for you. You worked so hard making this the most beautiful sukkah ever, how could you not come and enjoy it with us?"

Rabbi Lehrer's wife led Naomi to the others seated at tables inside the ornate hut. Once again the kind woman had placed Naomi at the table where she, her husband, Daniel and Sharon were seated.

Daniel rose to pull out Naomi's chair at the same moment Beatrice came serving two huge platters, one with stuffed cabbage and the other with small fried dumplings filled with ground meat and mashed potatoes, known as *kreplach*.

Naomi smiled. "Beatrice, it all looks delicious. Do you have more food to bring out? Let me help." She rose from her seat and headed for the kitchen.

She passed where Sharon sat, who grabbed Naomi's hands and shrieked, "What's on your fingers?"

With all eyes now on her hands, Naomi looked, too. "Oh," she said with a grimace, "these are the wicked stepsister's fingernails. I'm sorry."

Beatrice lifted Naomi's hands to her eyes, and saw the absurdly long shiny black fake nails, filed to a dangerous point. "Not with those nails, honey. Of course, you could probably slice the bread for us. Our knives are dull compared to these."

Sylvia reached over and put a generous portion of the *kreplach* on Naomi's plate. "Sit, sweetheart. Sit."

She sat back down and thanked Sylvia. "Guess I better explain, huh?" Naomi gave them a synopsis of her day filming the television commercial. She concluded by explaining, "So, since Cinderella kept flubbing her lines, I'll need these fingernails for tomorrow morning. Could be a whole day more of shooting."

Daniel announced to the table, "And Naomi has rescued me. She's going to help with the Chanukah play."

Oh dear, she hadn't given this much thought; her mind was most definitely preoccupied with Daniel, but not with the Chanukah play. Suddenly one came to mind—a performance done with the youth from her *shul* in Ellenville. She leaned over to Daniel. "I have the perfect play for us to do."

More and more of the families were now arriving in the synagogue playroom in anticipation of seeing the children perform. An excited buzz was in the air.

This year Chanukah uniquely fell on December 24. While so many celebrated Christmas Eve, at Temple Beth Orr they were enjoying the first night of the Feast of Dedication.

Naomi gathered the children who were in the play together, but noticed Mindy was missing. "Steven, where's your sister?"

Eight-year-old Steven lisped, "Mindy afwaid, Mith Goldblatt." He cupped his hand to his mouth, making it clear he had a secret. Naomi stooped down, her ear to his lips. Steven whispered, "Mindy locked herthelf in the bathroom."

Daniel walked over to Naomi. "Nervous?"

Naomi stood back up. "Got a little problem here, but believe me I know how to handle it."

Daniel put an arm around Naomi and pointed toward the first row of folding chairs. "See those people over there? That's my parents." And when a young woman walked in the door, he exclaimed, "I don't believe it. My sister came."

"What's so unbelievable about that?"

"Tell you later."

"I gotta go take care of the little problem we have—Mindy." About to walk their separate ways, Naomi spied her parents walking through the door. She grabbed Daniel's arm and said, "My parents are here, too. They've surprised me. Okay, talk later."

Naomi walked into the girls' bathroom and knocked on the door to the closed stall. "Mindy, it's going to be okay. Come on out."

The young girl opened the door and stuck her head out. "Miss Goldblatt, I'm scared. You know how I start giggling? I'll mess everything up."

Mindy listened intently as Naomi recounted her own days of stage fright. "And tomorrow, I have an audition for a big TV show, and am I nervous? Of course I am. But that doesn't mean I won't go. Mindy, you've been doing a great job and everyone's going to love you tonight. Do you trust me?"

Mindy looked at Naomi and smiled. "I trust you, Miss Goldblatt." She grabbed hold of Naomi's hand and together they walked out of the little girls' room.

Naomi did indeed have a big audition coming up—*Saturday Night Live* was giving her another chance. Although she had been overjoyed when she received this news from Rhonda, Naomi now experienced something much more gratifying—a joy that penetrated into her soul. Little Mindy trusted her.

Together Naomi and Daniel gathered the cast of children and gave them last minute instructions. Daniel promised them, "You'll be great. And afterwards, all the latkes you can eat."

Before Naomi could walk away, Daniel squeezed her shoulder. "You're gonna be great, too—no, you *are* great. See you afterwards."

Rabbi Lehrer carried a handheld microphone and walked to the center of the room. "Welcome everyone. What a wonderful turnout we have tonight. You are in for a special treat. Our new friend, Naomi Goldblatt, has directed what she informs me is called 'story theatre' and Rabbi Dan has worked tirelessly on this as well." He turned to Mr. and Mrs. Cantor. "You should be very proud of your son. And now, Rabbi Dan, if you would introduce our wonderful cast."

Taking the microphone from Rabbi Lehrer, Daniel smiled at the audience. "Let me first introduce you to our writer, director and narrator. Naomi Goldblatt."

Naomi had already taken her position over to the corner of the room, sitting on a piano bench. She stood up and waved to everyone.

"Now, here's our cast." Daniel turned to the children fidgeting restlessly behind him and instructed, "Remember, when I call your name, step forward. Ready? First, Mindy Kaplan."

He beckoned the bashful girl to step forward, "Come on Mindy. Ahh, good girl. Mindy will be playing Rachel Levine. It's okay, honey, you can step back now. Now for our three latkes, we have Steven Kaplan, Doug Berkowitz, and Barbara Stein." Three children dressed in brown burlap sacks, representing potato pancakes, came forward.

Daniel waited until they moved back to their place. "And guess who's playing the rabbi? Rabbi Lehrer's and Sylvia's grandson, of course, Barry Lehrer, and for our music teacher, Judith Cohen." Judith, an extremely outgoing girl, came forward and twirled around and curtseyed before returning to her place with the others.

"Now for the mayor, Jonathan Berman." Jonathan came forward wearing a large hat with the label "Mayor" boldly imprinted on it. Daniel then finished by introducing seven other children who would be acting as somewhat of a chorus in the story. Walking over to Naomi, he handed her the microphone.

Naomi addressed the audience. "It was the first night of Chanukah. Rachel was at the *shul* making potato latkes. Everyone agreed she made the most delicious latkes in town. She dropped each latke into the sizzling oil."

With a little coaxing from Naomi, Mindy finally stepped forward, wearing an apron and holding a frying pan and a spatula. The young girl flipped a piece of brown paper in the pan as if it were a latke. Unfortunately she flipped it too high and could not catch it back into the pan. Mindy's brother ran to pick it up and handed it back to his sister. The other children snickered.

Rabbi Dan, standing in the corner opposite Naomi, shushed the children, even though he himself chuckled.

Naomi told the audience, "While frying up her latkes, Rachel began to sing."

Mindy, in a surprisingly loud and confident voice, sang, "I make latkes nice and round. Everyone tells me my latkes are the best ever found."

As narrator, Naomi continued. "Then three latkes jumped right out of the oil and went plop onto the floor. They started singing."

"Bet you can't catch us." The children pranced around the stage, not exactly coordinated with one another, but trying their hardest.

"Then Rachel exclaimed . . ." Naomi waited for Mindy to say her line, but when none was forthcoming, she cued her by whispering, "Stop, we . . ."

Immediately Mindy said, "Stop, we need you tonight."

While Naomi narrated, the children carried out the action. "Rachel ran after the latkes. The latkes rolled past the rabbi's study and when the rabbi saw them, he called out . . ."

Barry Lehrer, wearing a prayer shawl and yarmulke, ran to the latkes and yelled, "Stop latkes, stop."

The boy also wore wire-rimmed glasses in imitation of his grandfather. He had been directed to take on some of Rabbi Lehrer's mannerisms, such as peering over his glasses. However, Barry seemed to be enjoying this way too much. Naomi hoped his grandfather would not be offended and blame her.

She continued the narration. "So now the rabbi chased the latkes and Rachel chased the rabbi. Now the bad little latkes rolled past the room where the music teacher was practicing her tune. When she saw the latkes, she trilled in a sweet voice. . ."

The young girl playing the music teacher sang, "Stop. We need you for tonight."

In a panicked voice, Naomi told the audience, "But the latkes continued running and singing. So the teacher chased the latkes, the rabbi chased the teacher and Rachel chased the rabbi. The latkes rolled out the door and in front of the *shul* where two boys were playing ball.

Two boys mimed throwing a ball to each other until the latkes walked in front of them. Together they screamed, "Stop, we need you for tonight."

Naomi increased the panic in her voice. "But the latkes did not stop and they all chased the latkes through the town until they reached the mayor's office."

The boy wearing the mayor's hat stepped out and demanded, "Stop latkes, by the order of the mayor."

Naomi walked to the center of the stage and leaned in to the audience. She worriedly told them, "The latkes didn't stop and now everyone, including the mayor, was chasing them. But after all this rolling, the latkes were hot, even hotter than when they were in Rachel Levine's frying pan. Just at the edge of town was the river. The latkes rolled straight toward it, but everyone yelled . . ." Naomi crossed back to the piano bench.

The children yelled, "Stop latkes stop."

Naomi had directed them to speak as a chorus, but they never did grasp this concept. Hearing their individual voices overlapping one another, Naomi laughed. "The latkes hadn't listened before and they didn't listen now, but as they plopped into the river, kerplunk."

The latkes were now supposed to mime dropping into a river, but instead they started a shoving match with each other. In a louder voice, speaking directly to the little latkes, Naomi repeated, "As they plopped into the river . . ."

The latkes finally went kerplunk, and Naomi continued. "A miracle happened in front of everyone's eyes. The water turned into chunky applesauce. Rachel blinked, then one, two, three, she grabbed the latkes right out of the river and put them on her tray. There were enough latkes and enough applesauce for everyone to have a bite."

Naomi stood, grabbed the hand of the child nearest to her, and they all bowed. The crowd rose from their seats, cheered and applauded the little actors. Families grabbed the children and enthusiastically scooped them up in their arms. But little Mindy, not forgetting her friend, Miss Goldblatt, squirmed out of her mother's arms, ran to Naomi and hugged her waist.

Daniel called to her. "Naomi, please, I want you to meet my parents."

"Okay, but let me get mine first. Then we can all meet."

Saul was so proud of his daughter he even gave her a bear hug, a rare occurrence. Before she brought her parents to meet Daniel and his family, he came over to her.

"Naomi, this is my mom, Zofia, my dad, Stefan, and my sister, Dana."

She shook each of their hands and introduced her mom and dad. Daniel reminded them there would be food served in the social hall.

"Yes, I smell. Delicious," said Stefan, speaking with a thick Polish accent.

Dana stood apart from everyone and had none of the warmth found in Daniel. In shaking her hand, Naomi actually became embarrassed as Dana did not even move her hand in the slightest.

Stefan was a thin man with thick salt and pepper hair. He had clear blue eyes, eyes that seemed to have seen a lot of pain. And there was a softness about him, like one who knew life was fragile. His wife, also with a thick Polish accent, seemed more hardened than her husband. Her hair was more white than silver, and with a face which seemed too young for such white hair.

Rabbi Lehrer and Sylvia joined them. The Rabbi congratulated Naomi on doing an excellent job, and told Saul Goldblatt, "You should be very proud of your daughter."

As they all followed the smell into the social hall, Sylvia leaned in to Naomi. "Next is Purim, you know. You would make a wonderful Queen Esther."

Dana abruptly announced, "I'm leaving. I'm going with Ed and his family to midnight mass." She turned around and was gone. Stefan shook his head and put his arm around his wife, appearing to soothe her. Naomi could not help but notice the tightening of Daniel's jaw. She never saw him this upset.

Once they were all seated, Beatrice came and placed a platter overflowing with latkes, while another woman brought two bowls, one with sour cream and the other with applesauce. Daniel's mother reached for the sour cream and Naomi caught sight of the numbers tattooed on her arm. Zofia must have instinctively known they were seen because she quickly took the sleeve of her sweater and pulled it down to cover the hideous mark.

Toward the end of the evening, Daniel explained he would drive home with his parents and spend a few days with them in New Jersey. "What about your parents, Naomi? It's a long drive for them to go back tonight. Do you have enough room in your place?"

Although it was a two bedroom apartment, she had only one bed. Saul and Helen could stay at Naomi's Aunt Ida's on Flatbush Avenue, but it was snowing out. Also, it was Christmas Eve which meant the subway system would be running on a shortened holiday schedule.

Daniel offered, "They can stay at my place tonight. Here's the keys. I'll write down the address."

Even though affection continued to grow between her and Daniel, she had never been to his home and he never to hers. Watching Daniel write his address on a napkin brought an unexpected warm glow deep within her soul. She felt . . . ? Cherished? Was this possible?

Maybe this is a sign God has forgiven me.

Nevertheless, an ache gnawed at her when she looked across the room at Mindy and her mother.

Chapter 8

Dayenu

*Y*ou did good, cookie. They liked you, but they said they already have Gilda Radner, so they don't need you. It's a compliment if you think about it."

"Thanks, Rhonda." Naomi tried catching her breath. "I appreciate you're letting me know."

Now Naomi could get back to her exercises. Twenty-five more jumping jacks to go and then the sit-ups. At one time losing out on a job with a blockbuster TV show would have devastated her. Yet she seemed actually relieved. All she wanted was to dream about Daniel—anything else would have been a distraction. For the last six days, he had been staying with his family in New Jersey and calling her every day, each phone call ending with confessions of missing each other.

Towards evening, he called. "How'd it go? Did you get any news on your audition?"

"They said I'm too much like someone already on their show. But that's cool. How about you? What'd you do today?"

"Same old thing . . . helped Dad at the furniture store. He's really having a hard time moving his inventory these days. I'm glad I've had the time to help him some, but I'll be leaving in the morning. Can't wait til tomorrow night. I'll pick you up at six, okay?"

"I can't wait."

Tomorrow would mark their first official date. New Year's Eve. Both admitted they had never gone to Times Square where crowds gathered each year to see the ball drop at midnight.

Daniel suggested, "Let's go. First I'll take you to Luchow's for dinner."

Naomi would finally eat at the legendary German restaurant near Union Square. Growing up, Dad had mentioned the name Luchow's many times, and always with a tone of reverence.

With the date set, Naomi had instituted her new exercise regimen. She already knew the dress to wear—a blue velvet form-fitting cocktail dress which had been sitting in her closet for at least two years. Another thrift store eye-catcher, worth buying and holding onto until the right occasion presented itself.

Oh boy, I have four days to lose five pounds. And what if I eat too much at dinner? Then my dress just rips. Charming., Excited as she was, the adrenaline alone might burn off a few pounds.

Sit-ups finished, she couldn't resist trying on the dress once again. The scale hadn't shown any change as of yet, but after all the exercising, maybe a few inches had miraculously vanished.

On the way to the bedroom, her eyes caught sight of the time. Meeting Anne for lunch in less than one hour, there would be no time to even shower.

They chose a new vegetarian restaurant in the downtown Wall Street area. Getting there on time was more doable than going further into midtown. Anne was starting her new year's resolution early; no more meat for her.

One way to not gain weight—tofu and sprouts. Yuck.

Happy to the point of giddy, Naomi stepped into the train imagining Anne's delight in hearing about Daniel. The door was about to close when a mother and her three-year-old daughter boarded the train and found the only remaining seats.

The little girl wore the cutest mittens, and reminded Naomi of Mindy Kaplan. She then experienced a quick and sharp stab into her soul. *Was mine a girl? Was "it" a she?*

Naomi wanted to avert her eyes, but couldn't ignore the fact the mother looked utterly confused as she studied a subway map which she kept folding and unfolding. No one else on the crowded train seemed to notice the woman's distress.

Naomi rose from her seat, grabbed a pole to hold onto as she stood in front of the woman. "Can I help? You must be new to the city?"

The mother, about Naomi's age, eagerly and gratefully looked up. "Yes. My husband's parents live here and they're sending us on a shopping expedition." She hugged her little girl as she explained, "We need to get to Fifth Avenue and . . . I forgot, the street . . . it's FAO Schwartz, if that helps."

The toddler excitedly told Naomi, "It's the biggest toy store in the whole world."

The internal howling returned and was now deafening. *Was "it" a she—a cute little girl?*

Quickly, without being rude, she would give the woman directions and walk away. "You need to get to East Sixtieth Street and Fifth Avenue. Get off at the Fifty-Ninth Street Station. Have a good time."

Fleeing, she moved to the other end of the subway car. Nevertheless, her eyes kept moving back to the little girl.

I don't deserve someone as good as Daniel. How could I have ever even entertained such a thought?

During her walk from the subway station to Reade Street, she worked on numbing the pain. She would not talk about Daniel and instead put her attention on Anne. After all, she talked too much about herself anyway.

Naomi spotted Anne from a block away. She was always so punctual. The restaurant was jam-packed, but Anne pointed to a company of three gathering up their things.

Once seated, Naomi studied the menu, her brows furrowed. "Okay, what's tempeh?"

"It's from fermented soybeans."

"I don't think so." Eyes moving to the other side of her menu, Naomi asked, "Soba noodles?"

"It's made with buckwheat flour. There's a salad bar behind you. If you get the salad bar you'll see what everything looks like before you get stuck with a whole plate of it."

111

"What are you getting?"

"The salad bar."

After a third trip to refill their plates, they were ready to go beyond small talk and do some serious catching up. Naomi kept the promise made to herself and fixed her full attention on Anne. "Tell me all the new and wonderful things happening with you."

Anne hesitated for a moment. "I guess you were right in a way. Ever since I sang that religious song, no one's letting me on their stage anymore."

"You're kidding? That's not fair."

"The song I sang that night, I used to sing it with our youth choir. There were a lot of different ones, but I especially loved that song and thought if I did my own arrangement, others would love it, too. Naomi, I didn't even really think about the words."

Jesus—that was the only word Naomi recalled—that one always seems to offend everyone. What that name had to do with "Oh Happy Day" puzzled her, but right now all that mattered was her friend. "What are you doing for work? You still doing my shift at the Bistro?"

"No, I actually signed up with a temp agency. They're getting me secretary and receptionist jobs." Anne squeezed some lemon into her water. "What was that expression you used to use? Oh give all?"

"You mean *oy gevalt*?" Anne nodded. "I only used it when things were really bad. What's really bad?"

"The lease on our apartment . . ." Anne corrected herself, "*My* apartment is up middle of January and the new roommate's leaving." Anne reached across the table for Naomi's hand. "This town's hard."

Naomi put her hand on top of Anne's. "I've missed you so much. Who knew coming to New York City, I'd find my best friend? I thought it was to become rich and famous, but maybe more to learn what being a friend is all about." Abruptly she grabbed her bowl and stood. "I'm going to get some more of those noodles."

Naomi returned and asked, "Would you consider moving in with me?"

Anne's face brightened. "I've always wanted to live in Brooklyn Heights, and in a brownstone, too."

"And it's quick and easy getting into Manhattan."

"How much would rent be?"

"Only a little more than we both paid in Manhattan. Gary got a good deal and it was passed on to me."

An agreement was soon made. Anne would move in toward the end of January, giving Naomi time to clear out the second bedroom. The bill divided in half, they walked toward the subway station together.

Since Anne would soon be living with her, she better tell her about Daniel now—just in case this relationship continued into the new year.

Learning about Daniel, Anne's jaw dropped and her eyes widened. "I don't get it. How come you waited until now to tell me? The old Naomi would have been bubbling over with this news. He sounds wonderful."

Naomi lowered her head and mumbled, "I don't deserve him."

"You don't deserve to be happy? That's silly. You do like him, don't you?"

"Like him? I more than like him. That's just it. I'm scared. I don't want to be hurt. Once he sees me for who I really am . . ."

"So you're saying he's not too bright, is that it? You've hoodwinked him? Naomi, he probably sees you the same way I do. You're someone who is easy to love."

Walking down the stairs into the station, Anne advised, "If he's interested in you, you should be enjoying it. And since it seems you've turned over this new leaf, maybe God is rewarding you."

They hugged goodbye before Anne made her way to the uptown platform and Naomi to the other side.

How come I feel like I hoodwinked God?

In anticipation of Daniel entering her home, for the last week Naomi had given her apartment a face lift. She had the parquet floors polyurethaned, engaged a maid service to add a special sparkle, making the mirrors and windows glisten, and Mop & Glo helped the vinyl tile in her kitchen look brand new. Naomi had considered purchasing several hanging ferns, but the thought of killing another plant made her cringe. Instead the living room had three vases filled with Birds of Paradise and daisy mums.

When the doorbell rang, her heart fluttered—she was more nervous than on any opening night. One quick spritz with vanilla-scented Glade, and then she opened the door. Daniel was dressed in a charcoal gray striped suit with a teal-colored shirt and tie. "Hi, come on in."

"Naomi, you look beautiful . . . but I don't think I should . . ." His voice trailed off, and then he saw Zoey who had walked right up to the door's threshold. He stooped down and petted the little calico fuzzball.

Zoey stepped back into the living room, as if inviting Daniel to step inside. Nonetheless, he remained standing at the front door. After an awkward moment, Naomi walked to where her coat lay over the sofa's armrest. Daniel stepped inside, picked up the coat and stood behind her, holding it open.

Her camelhair coat now on, she turned to face him. "Thank you."

His flushed face bent towards her, but then he cleared his throat. "We have a dinner reservation for seven." He put his arm around her waist and led her out the door.

During their walk to the subway, Daniel said, "Naomi, I hope you understand . . . You know in our parents' time, a gentleman . . ."

For the first time, she saw him at a loss for words. She jumped in, "You know, I've seen movies, old movies, where they'd talk about courting—and I always thought it was beautiful. Silly of me, huh?"

Standing on the subway platform, they waited for their train and suffered through an uncomfortable silence. Finally they looked at each other and began to laugh at their bashfulness.

Naomi confessed, "I think I'm more nervous now than I was at my first prom."

At that moment the train pulled in to the station. Holding Naomi's hand, Daniel walked her into the almost empty car. Once seated, he continued holding her hand. "Tell me about your first prom."

"It was totally weird. My mom knew Ira Jacobs' mom, so they worked it out that Ira would ask me to the prom. When he asked me out, I was really flattered cause I didn't know about the mom stuff. So, we get to the dance and before I know it, he's disappeared with my best friend Marianne. Dad came and picked me up at the school, and then he tells me about the two moms and their conspiracy." *Brilliant, Naomi, letting him know what a loser you were.* "What about your first prom?"

In a serious deadpan voice, he answered, "I only went to one prom, and I only went because Mom asked me to take her friend's daughter. . . That was a joke—a stupid one perhaps." He lifted her hand to his lips and softly kissed it. "The truth is, I never fit in. People made fun of me saying I was too serious."

"Daniel, if you're so serious, and I can tell you are, then why me? I'm like this silly little Jewish girl."

"Is that how you see yourself?" She nodded her assent. "How can you be so wrong? I see you better than you see yourself."

Before she could absorb these tender words, they arrived at their station. Walking to the restaurant, he put his arm around her waist. "And I like your fun side—not silly, but fun. Enough said?"

With delight, she agreed. "Enough said."

The old world interior of the restaurant promised an elegant dining experience. Luchow's had seven separate dining rooms. Their table was in a room with potted palms, elaborately carved columns, chandeliers offering a soft diffused glow, and oak wall paneling.

Above the paneling the walls were lined with moose heads. When Daniel noticed Naomi fixated on the heads of these animals, he whispered, "Look good? That was last week's special."

A large menu in her hand, Naomi used it to hit her date over the head. They chose to share an appetizer of flambéed thin pancakes with lingonberry sauce. Daniel's main course would be sauerbraten and Naomi took his suggestion and ordered the roast goose with chestnut puree.

Naomi commented, "You're really familiar with this place, aren't you?"

"Since I was a kid, whenever we came through the tunnel into Manhattan, Dad would want us to go here. My mother would object. 'Stefan, they're German.' My father would say, 'Yes, but where else can we get good roast goose, Zofia?' So half the time we'd come here and the other half we'd get a hot dog from one of the vendors on the street. Saved us enough money that they could send me to college."

"You know what I loved from those vendors? Their pretzels. Those big soft ones with all that kosher salt."

"You mean I could have gotten away with dinner at some street corner, a pretzel for you and a hot dog for me?"

He must be paying a fortune for this dinner. "Daniel, I love being here. Truthfully, going out with you on a date, well, you know, *dayenu*, but to be here in probably the fanciest place I've ever—"

Cupping her cheek with his hand, he quietly told her, "*Dayenu* for me, too, Naomi."

They were interrupted from this intimate moment by a loud "ahem." The waiter smiled as they turned to him. "Would you be ready to order? If not, please do not hurry."

Once the order was taken, Daniel began, "Let me tell you about my sister."

"Daniel, what was she so upset about the other night?"

"It wasn't just that night. Let me explain Dana to you. Naomi, both my parents were in the camps."

"I saw the numbers on your Mom. Your Dad also?"

"Auschwitz." He uttered the name of this death camp as though he were forced to drink a glass filled with acid. "I'll tell you more about that another time . . . if you want me to."

"I want to know more, more about you and your family, but only if you're okay telling me."

"I am. But right now: Dana. I'd say it's pretty much my mother's fault. Dana's five years younger than me. I watched as Mom never let her go through the normal teenage woe-is-me stage. Here's a perfect example: our favorite subject, the Prom. To begin with, Dana's upset because she thinks she won't have a date, so she's sulking around the house. As her big brother, I'm trying to comfort her, telling her not to worry. And Mom, you know what she offers for comfort?"

With a thick Polish accent, Daniel continued, "You don't know real problems. After all me and your father have gone through, you feel sorry for yourself because no one asks you to a crazy dance? Vhat *mishigas*!" Speaking in his own voice again, Daniel said, "Anyway, Dana did finally get a date." Motioning Naomi to lean toward him, he confidentially whispered into her ear, "I asked my friend Barry to ask her out."

"Wish I had a sweet brother like you."

"You're an only child, right?"

"How'd you know?"

"It shows. You're a spoiled brat."

The waiter now arrived with their thin pancakes, covered in the red lingonberry sauce. With flare, he poured a thin stream of cognac over the dish, produced a small torch and ignited it. The result was a beautiful blue-tinged flame. This partial combustion left behind an additional sweet aroma. Dividing the one serving into two separate plates for the couple, he said, "Please, enjoy."

"Miss Only Child, you should have my plate since he gave me the biggest portion."

In between "oohs and aahs" as they were enjoying their appetizer, Daniel continued talking about his sister. "So, Dad makes sure his daughter has a beautiful frock—that's what he calls it—and by the way, yours is gorgeous."

"Truth is I'm scared to death I'm going to get red sauce or something else on it. Can velvet be dry-cleaned?"

"My only advice: try not to."

"Anyway, back to Dana."

"She has the frock, she has the date, and then the night before the prom she gets a pimple and begins carrying on, and again Mom says 'Vhat? A little pimple? You don't know vhat real suffering is.' And this kind of thing kept happening."

"But, Daniel, your Mother was right."

"Yes, of course, she was. But it wasn't fair to a young girl. It was like she could never get any sympathy. And it loaded her up with all this unbearable guilt, then the guilt, I think, fueled this anger. So, what does she do to jab at Mom, and unfortunately to Dad and me? First she tells us she's gay and brings her girlfriend Nina over for Thanksgiving. Nina was a psychologist so every time any of us said anything at the table, she'd begin analyzing it. Dad, who's the more calm one, he was cutting the turkey with the new electric knife Mom and I bought him. He held the knife out toward Dana's friend and said, 'Leave. You vill now leave my house, please.' When Dana threatened to leave with Nina, I got up, opened the door, and asked if they wanted to take a drumstick or a wing with them."

Daniel then explained about Dana's newest relationship, another opportunity to jab at her family. "Ed's African-American. Naomi, my family's not a bunch of racists, but because with the persecution they went through, the fear of Dana having to experience the same has been like a knife into their heart. And it's not like Dana loves Ed. I mean she might, but it appears more like it's just another way to get back at my family. And I hate to see her hurt Ed. He's a nice guy."

From the adjoining dining room, waltz music came floating through the air, romantically played by a string ensemble. Their appetizer finished, Daniel asked, "Will you dance with me?"

Naomi's smiling eyes conveyed a definite yes, and Daniel stood up, pulled out her chair, and led her to the dance floor.

"This makes up for my first prom," she told Daniel.

By ten o'clock, they had finished their dinner. Daniel attempted to hail a taxi, but had no success—it was New Year's Eve. With it being unseasonably warm for December, Naomi asked, "Couldn't we walk? It would be fun."

The atmosphere walking the twenty-eight city blocks to Times Square was a world apart from the refined surroundings at dinner. Boisterous crowds filled the streets. Although these revelers were in sharp contrast to Daniel and Naomi, they walked hand in hand, not at all bothered by the rowdiness surrounding them.

Daniel, as if to accentuate this contrast, asked, "So, Naomi, read any good books lately?"

"Good of you to ask, Rabbi Dan," she answered, going along with his playfully studious voice. "I'm reading *The World According to Garp.*" Going back to her normal voice, she confided, "I don't think I like it, it's kinda creepy."

"Oh, like the synagogue, huh?"

"Are you ever going to forget that?"

"Probably not."

"So, what are you reading, Rabbi Dan?"

"Stop with the Rabbi Dan stuff already. Actually I'm reading a book I really love. It's called *The Snow Leopard.* The author, Peter Matthiessen, had gone to Nepal to study these Himalayan blue sheep, which is amazing all by itself, but he went hoping he'd also see a snow leopard. They are supposed to be absolutely beautiful, Naomi, and very rare. The book is all about his five-week adventure climbing through the winter snow. He writes it in a way I can really see it, and even feel the cold, too." She had stopped walking. "Why are you looking at me like that?"

"You are one very interesting man, that's why. I love that you love a book like that."

"Not creepy?"

"Now stop it already."

Arriving at Times Square, they joined all the other celebrants. A stage had been erected for the occasion and Dick Clark was introducing different singers and musicians. When the countdown began, Daniel and Naomi shouted with the chorus of about one million people, watching the famous ball, adorned with hundreds of light bulbs, make its descent from the flagpole.

Sharing a kiss at midnight: *DAYENU.*

Chapter 9

January 1979

New Year's Resolution #1: So far so good. Jogging one mile for the third day in a row. From her home to the Brooklyn Heights Promenade Naomi figured to be about one-third a mile, jogging around the promenade itself was known to be one-third a mile, home another one-third, and, voilà, one mile. And then there was the walk back up the stairs. Much more pleasant than the jumping jacks and sit-ups in her living room. The promenade much more scenic. And a wonderful excuse to charge up her credit card at Bloomingdales, after all a girl needs her pink jogging gear.

Opening the door, Zoey immediately began whining to be fed. In a breathless voice, she scolded, "Girl, hush. Give me a second." Kicking off her running shoes, she noticed the blinking light on her answering machine. "Oooh, three messages, you're really gonna have to wait now, girl."

The first was from Anne. "Hi, Naomi. Happy New Year. I was wondering if we could work out a time for me to see my new living quarters. Thanks."

Naomi scribbled a note to call Anne and played her second message. "Hey cookie, you ready for this? Campbell Soup wants you for their next commercial. No audition, you already have the part."

Hurriedly she scribbled a note to call Rhonda and listened to her third message. Hearing Daniel's voice, she moved closer to the phone. "Naomi, I'm looking forward to seeing you tonight. But for now I need to tell you there won't be any new member classes. Rabbi Lehrer said you were the only one signed up. Last fall I had only two and one all of a sudden dropped out. You think I'm doing something wrong? Anyway, all you have to do is fill out an application form and then the Membership Committee will interview you. See you tonight."

Both Rhonda and Anne would have to wait, as would the starving cat. "Hi, can I talk to Rabbi Dan, please?"

Daniel was soon on the line. "You're freaking out, aren't you?"

"Interview me? Who? How many?" Naomi pictured a roomful of people all like Rabbi Lehrer, with all scrutinizing her as they peered through their identical eyeglasses. More like an interrogation than an interview.

"There's about five on the committee right now. Relax, Myomi." Hearing his new pet name for her, Naomi's heartbeat went thump thump. Continuing to calm her fears, he added, "One of them is Beatrice, who can't wait for you to be a member knowing you want to volunteer in the kitchen with her. Except I told her hands off, you're reserved for the youth." From thump thump, the heartbeat went thud.

"Daniel, I don't know about working with the youth, I don't think—"

"After the Chanukah play, you have to . . . the kids love you. If you want, of course, you can also work the kitchen. When I see you tonight at *shul* for *Shabbos*, I'll give you the form to fill out."

After finally feeding the cat, Naomi called her agent and learned the same producers who did the Mop & Glo commercials had now created a recurring character for another company. They wanted Naomi for "the Campbell Soup lady," pushing a cart and calling out, "Hot Soup, get your hot soup right here."

"First thing Monday, you'll stop by my office and pick up a script. I'll give you the time and place for the shoot then. Next year this time, you're going to be walking down the street and little kids will be telling their mommies, 'Look, there's the Campbell Soup lady.' Told you you'd be a moneymaker, didn't I?"

Well, better than "Look, Mommy, there's that wicked stepsister."

Zoey pulled back her lips, flattened her ears against her head, and gave out a loud hissing noise. For a moment Naomi feared she would swat at Anne—thankfully, instead the cat ran out of the living room, into Naomi's bedroom, and whoosh under Naomi's bed.

"Good, stay under there," Naomi yelled at the cat. "Anne, I'm so sorry. You just gotta give her time to warm up to you. The stupid cat used to do that to me, but now she's my best friend—at least when I feed her."

Anne smiled. "Don't worry. I probably was too aggressive with her. I'm going to love living here, and the view from my bedroom even—I mean, wow, trees to look at."

Both women laughed as Naomi passed a tray of cheese and crackers toward Anne. "You really like it then?"

Anne's grin widened. "This'll be a nice way to start off the new year. Now, tell me about your new commercial. I'm dying to hear how it went."

"They're already talking about a sequel to it. Can you believe it? It was the same director from the two Mop & Glo ads and he told me at the end of the shoot, 'I like working with you. You're very professional.' I was so flattered. Course, the only thing is I always imagined the kids who picked on me growing up, when they one day saw me on the big screen, they'd eat their words. You know what I mean?"

Anne scrunched her forehead and tilted her head. "I don't get where there's a problem here."

"I wanted to be like the new Natalie Wood and instead I'm like this frumpy Campbell Soup lady. Oh, forgive me, Anne. I'm such a jerk. Dad would yell 'you ingrate you.'"

"It's true, you do have a lot to be thankful for. I can't wait to meet your rabbi friend."

Naomi's eyes went to several sheets of paper sitting in the middle of her coffee table. "Yikes. I have to fill out the new membership form by tonight. I've been kinda putting it off."

Anne stood and grabbed her down jacket. "Okay, I better go and let you do it." Naomi walked her to the door. Slipping her gloves on, Anne pointed to the papers on Naomi's table. "Why were you putting it off?"

'It's kinda intimidating."

"You just did your third commercial—if you can do that—"

After laughing together and waving goodbye to Anne, Naomi went to the application form she had been trying to ignore.

The preliminary questions were already filled out; she had answered them the very night she came home with the form. It was toward the bottom of the first sheet where she had stopped. With a grimace, she picked up the phone and dialed the synagogue.

Daniel himself answered the phone. "Tribe? Daniel, they're asking what tribe I'm from."

"You're joking? You're just now filling out the application? Naomi, you have the interview in less than two hours. Leave it blank. A lot of people do. It's not a big deal. I'll see you tonight."

She hung up and plunged into the five-page form. HOW DID YOU HEAR ABOUT US? *My feet were simply velcroed to the cement in front of your place! How am I supposed to answer this? I write God led me here, and they'll lock me away.*

She rushed past the next block of questions. NAMES OF THE APPLICANT'S CHILDREN AND THEIR BIRTHDATES. Naomi scrawled NA.

PREVIOUS SYNAGOGUE AFFILIATION. Did it count where she went with her parents? Moving right along, she came to DO YOU WANT TO PURCHASE PLOTS IN OUR CEMETERY AT THIS TIME? *Yikes, no!*

Finally, she made it all the way to Attachment B, a list of synagogue activities. PLEASE MARK THOSE AREAS YOU ARE INTERESTED IN. She checked Kitchen Support. In the next column was Youth Activities. Daniel wanted her to check this, and she thought of little Mindy Kaplan. She blinked away the tears and ran into the shower.

Moments before, Naomi had bitten into a jelly doughnut and a gob of jelly oozed out. She now returned from the kitchen after having quickly wiped her white blouse with a wet rag.

"I think I got it all off. You know, Anne, it's weird. You'd think I'd be doing cartwheels because of things going so good with my career and all, but I'm more excited that the Temple accepted me as a member."

For Naomi it was also weird being in her old apartment. Daniel would soon arrive with the truck he rented to help with Anne's move. She never asked, but he simply offered. His goodness took her breath away.

Leaning over the back of the couch with her knees resting on its pillows, Anne peered out the window. "Is that him? There's a truck, it must be him."

Naomi ran and leaned over the couch with Anne. "That's him. And can you believe it? He found a parking space right in front."

Grabbing Naomi's shoulders, Anne exclaimed, "He's so cute. You didn't tell me."

"I can't wait to introduce you."

Anne ran to the door and flung it open while Daniel was still making his way up the stairs. As soon as introductions were made, Anne told him, "It's so nice of you to do this for me. I really appreciate it."

With a wide grin, he said, "I'm glad to do it." His eyes scanned the apartment. "All this?"

"Don't worry about the furniture. Anne sold it to the couple who'll be moving in here. The only thing we have to worry about is the boxes."

Being a Sunday, traffic was light. However, Daniel did not have the same luck with parking in front of the brownstone in Brooklyn Heights. He took his chances and double-parked while they unloaded the boxes in front of the building.

He instructed them, "The truck rental place is only a block away. You both wait here while I return it." He shook his finger at both women, chiding them, "Don't start lifting them by yourselves, okay? Wait for me."

One hour later, all twenty-two of Anne's boxes were safely transported to her new apartment. Both the old apartment and the new were walk-ups, and the threesome was ready to collapse.

Naomi now shook her finger at Daniel. "We're buying you dinner. No arguments, okay? You pick the place."

"You don't have to do that. I enjoyed helping. Reminded me of my school days when I worked for Dad delivering furniture."

But Anne insisted. "Please, I'll feel better if I can do something to thank you."

He smiled. "Okay. Teresa's Restaurant. You know, Naomi, the one on Montague Street."

"No, we want to take you somewhere nice," Naomi whined. "That place is more like a diner or something."

Looking at Anne, Daniel asked, "Didn't she say '*you* pick the place'?"

"But why *that* place?" Naomi demanded.

"Look, lady, it's the best Polish food in town. Better than my Mom's."

Naomi shrugged. "Then let's go."

Since Teresa's was mostly known for their brunches, this Sunday evening they found the place pretty much all theirs. Menus were brought almost immediately upon being seated, but they largely ignored them—this was the first real opportunity for Daniel and Anne to get acquainted.

Daniel smiled toward Anne. "I can't wait to hear you sing. Naomi has told me what a beautiful voice you have."

Anne demurred, "She's just being nice. I don't think anyone else in this town feels that way. What I want to hear is more about Naomi and her career." She turned to Naomi. "I'm sure your agent is sending you on more auditions. I can't believe you haven't told us anything about what's going on."

"I'm working on talking about myself less. I have such a huge ego."

"Been meaning to talk to you about that," Daniel said, "but haven't been able to get a word in edgewise, because you're always talking—about yourself."

After the second time the waitress came by their table and was told they weren't ready to order, Anne suggested, "Let's look at our menus for a minute. You have any suggestions, Rabbi?"

"Just call me Daniel. I really like their stuffed cabbage."

"Anne's a vegetarian, Daniel."

"Perfect." Leaning across the table, he showed Anne, on his menu, where there was a vegetarian platter. And you can get their blintzes as well. Potato or cheese." Turning to Naomi, he asked, "And you?"

"Broiled kielbasa. I could absolutely never be a vegetarian, I need my meat."

After their orders were taken, Anne inquired, "You don't keep kosher, I gather."

"No," he acknowledged with a smile. "As of now I haven't been, but I'm pondering it."

"Really?" Naomi asked.

Rather than going further into this subject, Daniel explained to Anne, "You know I don't have a television. If your friend over here keeps getting her face on it, I might have to buy one."

Naomi protested, "No, I think it's kinda cool that you don't watch television."

Anne's potato blintzes arrived before the other food. When asked if they would like to share this golden crepe-like pancake with her, they declined. "It smells delicious," she told Daniel.

"*Es gezunterheyt*. That's Yiddish for eat in good health," he told her. "Would you like some sour cream with it? That's the way we always ate it at our house."

Anne eagerly nodded and Daniel signaled for the waitress. "Could we please have some sour cream?" Turning back to Anne, he said, "Naomi has told me how you both met, but can I ask you something I'm curious about?"

"Yes, of course."

"Alright, here's what I was wondering. Why did you decide to come to New York City? Naomi told me you were from a small town in Ohio. So, had you visited here first? Or the first time you came here was when you moved here? What compelled you?"

Naomi looked at Anne. "Isn't he amazing? That is such a great question. I never even asked you that myself."

When Anne blushed, Daniel instantly apologized. "You don't have to answer if I'm embarrassing you."

"It's ironic, here I am trying to make it as an entertainer but when I get a lot of attention, I feel awkward." She took a quick breath. "I came here on vacation with my parents and my older brother when I was thirteen. We went to see a Broadway musical and right then I knew what I wanted. It was magical, all these people dancing and singing together. I had always been told my singing voice was good and even did a few solos in our church's choir."

The waitress arrived with the sour cream, as well as carrying Daniel's stuffed cabbage and Naomi's kielbasa. With steam engulfing their table, Anne gave a quick conclusion to her story. "After two years of college at Ohio State, I couldn't wait—I was restless to move to the Big Apple and against my parents' wishes, I did." She inhaled deeply the meaty smell coming from Naomi's dish. "I'm about to break my New Year's resolution."

Naomi laughed, cut a generous piece from her sausage and placed it on Anne's plate.

In return, Anne plopped a potato blintz on Naomi's plate. "Daniel, is it okay if I ask you a question?"

"Of course."

"Naomi told me about your parents . . ."

"You mean being in a concentration camp?" Anne nodded and Daniel gently told her, "Please, feel free to ask."

"I just wondered where they met. Did they meet in the camps? I mean, of course, there's a lot of questions about all this, but I thought maybe you could tell me, you know, how they met."

"My parents' story is rather incredible. Not completely a good kind of incredible, but I choose to believe I see God's hand in it.

128

They grew up in Poland, in a *shtetl*—that's like a ghetto for Jewish people. Their little village was called Debica. Mom and Dad's parents arranged for them to be married on Mom's twentieth birthday. So, Mom's birthday also became her wedding day. I have pictures of her from back then, and she was beautiful. I was told all of Debica turned out to celebrate."

Daniel turned his face away from the women and toward the window. His face averted from theirs, he reached for his water glass. When Naomi put her hand on his shoulder, he patted it, turned back to them and smiled.

"Mom's birthday and wedding day also became the day the Nazis destroyed Debica. Some were killed on the spot and others were shipped off in trains to Auschwitz. Mom and Dad spent their wedding night in one of those trains. The next day, after the train stopped, they were separated, the men herded into one camp and the women into another. Five years later they were both released. Mom had given up hope Dad was still alive, but my dad, well he's a man who clings to hope. I love that about him."

Naomi and Anne, with all their attention on Daniel, had not touched their food. He playfully scolded, "Eat your food. *Essen!*"

Naomi explained to Anne, "That means eat." To Daniel she insisted, "You haven't touched your food either. We'll all eat, but please tell us how they got back together. I can't believe I never asked you about this."

"You didn't ask because you probably felt it was too sensitive a subject. That's the way most people are. It's a sweet story in its own way. Dad went from one refugee camp to another, and finally found Mom in Austria."

Naomi was ready to hear more. "What about the rest of their family—well, actually *your* family?"

"The only one that seems to have survived is my Aunt Luba. Can't wait for you to meet her. You'll love her. And she'll love you, too."

Daniel finally dug into his stuffed cabbage. "This is delicious. Almost as good as my Mom's."

Anne bit into the meat Naomi had given her, rolled her eyes, and exclaimed, "Oh, this is delicious, too."

Halfway through their meal, Anne looked over at Daniel. "Your parents must be so proud of your being a rabbi."

"Dad is. Mom, I'm afraid, is too bitter." Daniel laid his fork down on his plate and leaned in to Anne. "It's complicated. So many times people have tried to wipe out our people, and too many of the Jewish people our age, they just don't treasure our Judaism. Mom says after all she saw, how can she believe in God? And Dad says even if there is no God, still it's good to affirm 'I am a Jew.'"

"And Daniel," Naomi told Anne, "makes it mean something. He really does."

"No, My-omi, don't give me credit for what God Himself is doing in your life. God is the One gives meaning. Not me."

The One watching over me—yes, He is giving meaning to my life— and even bringing my life and Daniel's together. Naomi watched and listened as Daniel and her new roommate became acquainted.

What's next? Hmmm, think I need to get to know Dana?

"How long ago did your sister move to Staten Island?"

"About three months ago—a little before you met her. Ed's got a job there as a pharmacist. You sure you're up to dealing with Dana? I mean Ed's nice, but Dana . . ."

After having followed the twists and turns of the walkway, Daniel and Naomi reached the front of the crowd. While forced to move swiftly, Daniel managed to ask, "Are you enjoying having a roommate?"

"It's an adjustment, of course, after living alone for . . . awhile. But, yeah, she's great."

They finally descended the ramp and stepped onto the ferry as Daniel put his arm around Naomi's waist. "Is this your first time on the ferry?"

"Years ago we used to go to visit Dad's brother who lives in Staten Island. Been a long time since we visited them though."

Once inside, Daniel indicated the rows of long wooden benches. "We can sit here if you want, or we can go stand out on the deck. It's cold and a little windy, but the view of the Statue of Liberty, I think, is worth it."

Wrapping her scarf tighter around her neck and putting her gloves back on, she said, "I choose the view." They walked past the benches and stepped out onto the bow.

Soon the horn was blasting and they were departing. The wind definitely kicked up a few notches as they stood together, but they held to their decision, as well as to each other.

"So, let's talk about the Purim play. First of all, Sylvia is demanding you play Queen Esther. And I agree.

"But what about the kids?"

"No, this won't involve them, except they'll be in the audience with their groggers and booing Haman. That's the fun part for them, and for us we get to be the actors."

"Then that's perfect actually, because I did have an idea. I just didn't see how I could use the kids in it."

"Tell me."

"Did you ever see *Annie Hall?*"

"Didn't everyone? But what's this to do with Purim?"

She was relieved that although Daniel did not watch television, he did go to the movies. Seeing her expression, he chuckled. "What? I'm not supposed to go to the movies?"

"No, but—"

"With television, people sit in front of the thing with their faces glued to it. I didn't want that to be me. We'll have to go on a date to a movie soon, huh? Now back to Purim."

While enjoying the view of the lower Manhattan skyline and the close-up view of the Statue of Liberty, Naomi explained her concept. Woody Allen would be Mordecai and, as in the movie, he would narrate part of the story, and Queen Esther would be based on Diane Keaton's character. Wacky, nervous, and somewhat of an airhead.

"I love it," he assured her. "And, of course, you're perfect for the wacky Queen."

"Then you gotta be the King."

"No, Naomi, I don't act."

"You will this time."

During the remaining ride, they bantered back and forth about his participation in the performance and spoke of other people at the Temple who could play some of the various roles. Soon they were sitting inside the St. George Tunnel, waiting for Dana and Ed to pick them up. After thirty minutes, Daniel asked for change from a worker, went to the phone booth and called his sister's home. No answer. He also tried Ed's work number, but was told this was his day off.

Naomi suggested, "What about where Dana works?"

"She doesn't. Once in a while she'll sell one of her paintings, but that's about it."

After an additional fifteen minutes of waiting, Daniel looked at Naomi. "C'mon. The ferry's about to leave. We'll go back to Brooklyn and see a movie! What d'ya say?"

"I love it," she told him as they reboarded the ferry for a return trip. "You know I've decided I'm very shallow."

With no apparent provocation for this confession, he raised one eyebrow and silently communicated, "What's going on? Wanna talk?" It reminded her of the first time they met—the day she had been velcroed to the sidewalk in front of the synagogue.

Today he chose to be more deliberate and eventually gave voice to his question. "Naomi, are you having an insecurity attack?"

"Probably. I was amazed though when Anne asked you a question and I ended up hearing more about you than I ever heard before. Daniel, I wish I knew the right questions to ask you because I want to know you better."

"You sure about that? What if I were to tell you about my rebellious years?"

Her eyes popped wide open.

"The rebellion didn't actually start until I went to seminary— sad, isn't it? I guess I went with too many expectations. I had a passion to study, to learn about the God of our ancestors. Somehow I'd finally be able to make sense out of why the horrible things happened to my parents . . . and to all my other family I never got to meet. But what I found was this passionless study and it had nothing really to do with faith at all."

They were both being pummeled by the cold damp wind. Daniel wrapped his arms around her and led them into the more sheltered area. This time they would take advantage of the wooden benches.

Once seated, he told her, "In high school I had somehow found these two books—they were both by the same author. I think you will understand this, these books stirred up this longing inside me—I wanted to really know God."

It was as if all time came to a halt, her heart held its breath, and all her senses were riveted to this moment. "What were the books?"

"*God in Search of Man* and *Man in Search of God.*" He nodded as he watched Naomi's enthusiastic reaction to this title. "We were meant to talk about this, weren't we? The author believed Judaism should not be a set of rules you had to force yourself to believe, or some mold you had to squeeze yourself into. I remember this one sentence of his—'an irresistible presence inviting us to experience Him.'"

He cupped her chin in his hands. "In seminary, they ridiculed me, both classmates and professors, but still I refused to go along with this lifeless body of facts they wanted us to study and then regurgitate back to them in our tests. My grades went down, of course, and I became angry. And cynical. I had no idea anymore why I was studying to be a rabbi, but I didn't know what I wanted to do instead. I began taking drugs, and doing a few other things I shouldn't have."

After a slight pause, he continued, "After about a year of this, I was on the subway and I met a young guy, his name was Irwin. We started talking and he told me about this *havurah* he had at his house. It was this informal Jewish fellowship and I started going. It was a wonderful time. And because of this group, I went back to seminary. Knowing there were Jews like me out there, I didn't let the ridicule get to me." He playfully warned, "I can be stubborn, you know."

"And now? Are you happy being at our *shul?*

"I am, but it took a while. Last year when I first got there I was still unrealistic. I was looking forward to helping people more with their issues on faith and morality, but all they were concerned with was more everyday problems. Seemed so mundane at first, but probably about two months before I met you, I discovered I really liked helping people with their everyday problems."

Clanking made it impossible to be heard for a few minutes as the ferry maneuvered to the dock. The ramps were lowered to the ferry deck and they walked off the vessel and emerged into Lower Manhattan.

"What movie are we going to see?" she asked Daniel.

He seemed preoccupied. Instead of answering her question, he asked one of his own. "Could you ever be happy if you didn't live in New York City? Actually, I guess, that would mean giving up your career? How would My-omi feel about that?"

Chapter 10

For Such a Time as This

*N*aomi, could you ever be happy if. . ." The more appropriate question right now had to be "Naomi, could you ever be happier?" Although Daniel had asked her not to give him credit for what God Himself was doing, in her heart they were intertwined. God had to be the Giver of such a wondrous gift as Daniel. For the last six weeks, her feet were barely touching earth itself.

On this particular night, Daniel and Naomi ate an early dinner, sharing a bowl of *bigos*, a stew of sauerkraut and kielbasa, their favorite dish at Teresa's. The couple were dressed in their Purim costumes as King Ahasuerus and Queen Esther. They had no reason to be uncomfortable walking on the streets of Brooklyn in such attire—most of the neighborhood was dressed in similar fashion.

Having hurriedly finished their meal, they rushed to the synagogue for the Festival. Climbing up the wide stairs to the Temple, Daniel's crown began to totter and fell with the sound of light metallic plinks.

"Don't wait for me. You better go in," he yelled to Naomi.

The downstairs social area had been turned into a large carnival, in great part due to Naomi's contribution and Beatrice's willingness to allow her kitchen area to be co-opted for this event. Not only would they perform the short play Naomi had written, *Plotz and Edicts*, but she and Daniel had thought up some fun activities.

The first booth upon entering was the "Dig for Treasure in the Negev." Hidden in a tub of sand were prizes, all set for players to dig them up. Another booth, especially set up for the girls, was the Shushan Salon, which boasted a beauty parlor offering wild hair colors and face painting.

Rabbi Lehrer's and Sylvia's son Isaac volunteered to man the "Pop Haman" booth. Earlier Isaac and his son Barry blew up balloons and drew Haman faces on them. They then attached the balloons to a backboard of thick Styrofoam. With a carnival barker's voice and holding out a handful of darts, Isaac was already drawing people. "Step up, everybody. Who wants to be the first to pop Haman?"

Next to her son and grandson was Sylvia at the Decorating Crowns craft booth. Here children decorated cardboard crowns with glitter, plastic gems and stickers. It was then theirs to wear for the rest of the evening.

The activity most dear to both Daniel and Naomi was the Trip Thru Israel. It had required the most work and filled half the space in the downstairs area. They had constructed a mini-golf course which traveled around a giant map of Israel. Daniel's father, Stefan, persuaded the owner of an actual miniature golf course in his city to donate clubs and balls for this event. Since Stefan had pledged to keep his eyes on these items, he manned this area, along with Naomi's father, Saul.

Naomi's mom, Helen, worked with Sylvia and helped the children decorate their crowns. Because of Sylvia's and Helen's winsomeness, Daniel's stoic mother Zofia was helping as well.

Almost all arrived in costume, whether dressed as a Purim character or simply wearing a Mardi-Gras type mask. Rabbi Lehrer, soon to play Mordecai, came dressed as a Chasidic Jew, reminding Naomi once again of her improv days with Gary.

Out of the corner of her eye, Naomi saw Daniel run to greet a woman in her mid-fifties. She heard him call out "Aunt Luba," to this attractive woman probably wearing the most sparkly Queen

Esther outfit in the room. He hooked his arm around his aunt and led her to Naomi.

"Ah, Danielek, as handsome as ever. And, so this is your sweetheart?" With a twinkle in her eye, Aunt Luba pointed a finger toward Naomi. "I've heard about you, young lady. Danielek, why haven't you brought her over for dinner, shame on you." Again, with her finger pointing at Naomi, she said, "Make sure he brings you. But now, children, go, go, I can see you're busy. Danielek, take me to my sister. Where is she? "

Daniel escorted her to Zofia while Naomi continued buzzing around the room, checking on all those in her cast. Daniel, of course, would be King to her Queen Esther. Haman would be played by the President of the *shul*, Morris Berger. Although Naomi had very little if any dealings with this man, she was told after the fact that she had done an excellent job on typecasting; it seemed many considered Mr. Berger to be quite the villain.

While moving about the room, Naomi saw Daniel taking her father aside. They walked into the hallway where they appeared to be having a private conversation. *What's that all about?* She was tempted to go into the hallway and eavesdrop, yet resisted.

An hour into the evening, Rabbi Lehrer stood on the raised platform rented especially for the occasion. "Are you ready to hear the whole *Megillah*?" All affirmed they were looking forward to hearing the public recitation from the Scroll of Esther.

The Rabbi whispered into the microphone, "You are in for something special tonight. Our Cantor could not make it, and I believe you will all be surprised when you hear our very own Rabbi Dan chanting the *Megillah* for us."

Daniel can chant?

He walked up onto the platform, took the microphone from Rabbi Lehrer and began the traditional Hebrew chant which told the story of Esther. His voice was as lyrical and with as wide a range as Sharon's, yet with a poignant sincerity to his delivery.

After completion, Daniel handed the microphone back to Rabbi Lehrer, who prayed, "Blessed are You, our God, King of the Universe. You take up all our grievances and judge accordingly. You bring just retribution upon all enemies of our soul for we are Your people, the apple of Your eye."

All present cried out, "Amen," and Rabbi Lehrer jubilantly asked, "Are you now ready for the Purim *Spiel*?" The crowd responded enthusiastically—they were indeed ready.

Daniel reminded everyone, "Don't forget—take out your groggers." Not only did the children take out their noisemakers, but holding the wooden handle, they twirled the revolving metal piece. Talking over the clamor, Daniel said, "Now that's what you do every time you see Haman or hear his name. Okay?"

Barry Lehrer jumped in, "We can also yell 'boo.'"

Daniel laughed. "Of course. And why do we do this?"

Again the Rabbi's grandson jumped in. "To blot out Haman's name."

"Right you are, Barry. Now, it's showtime." Daniel stepped down from the platform.

Rabbi Lehrer, as Mordecai, climbed up and took center stage, rubbing his chin. "What am I doing in Persia? I'm a Jew. If you don't believe me, just read the book of Esther—it's there in black and white, 'Mordecai the Jew.' I mean it's one thing to be a bagel growing up in a bagel factory . . . but being a bagel growing up in a Persian donut shop, that's something else. And when these Persians wanna dunk you, they dunk you."

Despite Rabbi Lehrer's misgivings about Naomi's writing, his people were enjoying it. Their joviality proved infectious, waves of laughter rippling through the crowd. The Rabbi waited for the laughter to fade and beamed toward Naomi.

After giving in to a chuckle of his own, Mordecai continued, "The captivity has been fifty years already. So, what am I doing in Persia—shopping for rugs? I miss the land, I miss the gefilite fish . . . but here I sit, in the land ruled by King Ahasuerus. Ah, here he comes now."

Daniel entered while plopping an Alka Seltzer into a glass of water. He turned to his Servant, played by Barry Lehrer. "*Oy*, too much wine last night. So where's Vashti?"

In an overly loud voice, Barry delivered his line. "Don't you remember? The Queen's been deported. Uh, as per your orders, sir."

"My orders . . .?!" Naomi loved the wonderful job Daniel was doing as the ditzy king.

The Servant recapped yesterday's events. "Last night you asked Vashti, your queen, to display her beauty before your guests at the banquet. She refused."

"She did? How dare her! Then what happened?"

"As you recall, oh great and lucid King, we had no choice. After she disgraced both you and the whole kingdom, you gave her the royal heave-ho."

Soon the Servant planted an idea in the King's mind. A beauty contest would be held to replace the Queen. They walked off the platform as Mordecai stepped back up, this time with Naomi following close behind.

At this time Naomi wore a dark smock over her beautiful queen's costume. "Hi, cousin Mordecai the Jew. Wanna hear my new poem?"

His attempt to dissuade her was unsuccessful. While Naomi recited her silly poem, Mordecai reached for a roll of paper towels set on the stage. He unrolled it as if it were a large scroll. "Kid, I'm going to enter you in a contest I heard about. Let's look at the rules."

The silliness continued until finally the contest was over and the results were announced. "Cousin Mordecai, I won!" Naomi threw off the drab smock and tossed it to the side, and in all her resplendence took her place as Queen Esther.

The King was happy and declared, "Not only is my new queen beautiful and graceful, but . . ." Esther deliberately tripped her way across the stage. ". . . Fetch the Royal Crown!"

Beatrice stepped up and handed Daniel a large bottle of RC Cola. Naomi exclaimed, "Oooh, No-cal!"

This was Haman's cue to enter. With his first step onto the platform, the children engaged their noisemakers and added a generous helping of loud booing.

In the next scene, the Queen informed the King, "There is a plot which has been hatched by a wicked man. All because one man wouldn't bow to him. Haman is a very wicked man."

This prompted the children's school administrator to lead the children in singing. "O once there was a wicked, wicked man, and Haman was his name, sir."

The Purim *Spiel* came to an end when Esther saw the Servant walking away and asked him where he was going.

Barry answered, "To the dairy, Queen." Unable to contain himself, the boy chortled right along with the audience. For a moment, Naomi feared he would forget his next line, but Barry came through. "Would you like a burger, King?"

"Sure. I deserve a break today."

They took their bows—no boos but only cheers. Naomi grabbed the microphone and said, "I know it was a bit corny, but what d'ya expect? I'm from the Borscht Belt." She looked over at her father. He beamed with pride.

Beatrice brought out the *hamantashen*, a triangular-shaped pastry, some filled with prunes, some with apricots, and others with poppy seeds. Naomi was ready to walk toward where both hers and Daniel's family were seated when Daniel came running over to her.

His face flushed with excitement, he told her how well the play had gone, but she interrupted him. "Daniel, your chanting—it was beautiful. I didn't know . . ."

It was his turn to interrupt. "Before going to our parents, would you walk out into the foyer with me?"

In an alcove off to the side, near the library, Daniel took her hand as he bent down on one knee. In his other hand, he held a small box. "My-omi, will you be my Queen?"

When they reentered the festive carnival area, the *hamantashen* took a backseat to the diamond ring glistening on Naomi's finger. Helen unabashedly shed joyous tears and Saul had his own way of showing his happiness: he simply kept smiling and nodding his approval.

Unlike her father, Daniel's appeared unafraid to express tender affection. Stefan, his face crinkling into a wide grin, locked his arms around his son. Zofia, although not showing the same gaiety as the others at the table, walked over to Naomi and pinched her cheek.

"*Bubbeleh*, you make my *boychik* happy."

With this first interchange between them, Naomi could not hold back the tears. "I'll try to, Mrs. Cantor."

Aunt Luba sprung up from her chair and inserted herself between Naomi and Zofia. Being shorter than Naomi, Luba stretched her neck to look into Naomi's eyes. "You not worry. I see—I see Danielek happy."

Being a weeknight, the festivities ended early. The Cantors would drive back to New Jersey and the Goldblatts would stay overnight at a nice hotel in Manhattan—a special treat for Helen.

As was now his custom, Daniel walked Naomi back to her apartment. "You'll have to tell Anne. She might not be as happy as everyone else. I know we still need to set a date and all, but we'll make sure to give her enough time to find a roommate."

Yes, there was much planning to do, yet tonight she would simply soak in the splendor of the entire evening. With all the excitement, from the diamond on her finger to her new extended family, the most prevalent memory for her was her future husband's chanting. "Daniel, I can still hear you chanting the *Megillah*. I had no idea . . ."

"It's different doing it in public."

She tilted her head to one side. "I don't understand. When else would you do it?" They were now in front of the steps leading up to her brownstone. The streetlight shone on Daniel's face where Naomi believed she detected a blush.

"Hmm, I better explain. I try to start almost every morning this way, whatever text I'm reading in the Scriptures."

"Really? That's . . . beautiful," her voice had suddenly faltered. She would be embarking more and more into a world alien to her. How could she not ultimately disappoint Daniel?

After studying her worried expression, he took her hand up to his lips. "Why do I get the impression you're thinking I'm like some kind of spiritual giant? My-omi, I'm not Moses, okay? Let me tell you about something that happened to me last week. First of all, the reason I chant is because I found it easier to remember the text that way. The melody is like a language all by itself and that way the text becomes a part of me. I can walk down the street and a passage I've sung can end up relating to a situation I'm in and it'll pop into my mind."

"That sorta reminds me of how I've memorized scripts for myself." Wow, she could actually relate.

"So, last week I'm really upset about a member of our Temple. He had been particularly disrespectful to me the day before. I mean this guy, I think, loves to humiliate me. " Daniel stopped and teasingly shook his finger at her. "Now I know you and your curiosity, but forget it, I'm not telling you who."

"Sorry."

"I'm in the shower and I can't stop thinking what this guy said to me the day before. Obviously it was eating away at me. Then part of the *Megillah*—about Haman—came to my mind, and, bam, I realized I was becoming just like Haman."

"You gotta be kidding me. You? No way."

"The truth is when any of us get caught up with our ego or our position, it can happen. Even me, your knight in shining armor. Think about it—pretty much everyone else at the Temple shows me respect except this one guy, and I'm getting all bent out of shape because he doesn't bow down to me."

"Oh, what a relief," Naomi exclaimed, "you're human. I feel much more comfortable now."

"I love you, My-omi."

"I have no special name for you. Can I call you Danielek, too?"

"Only if you can do it with a Polish accent."

"I'll work on it."

Naomi charged into her apartment—she would burst apart if she didn't share the excitement with Anne right away. However, Anne's bedroom door was closed and Naomi heard her rehearsing for an audition piece. The temptation to interrupt was tantalizing, but she resisted.

It's not all about me. Besides, the thought of going straight to her own room actually seemed much more appropriate. Time alone to imagine her glorious future and to also convince herself her past had been redeemed.

Her costume tucked away in a plastic garment bag, the former Queen Esther sat cross-legged on her bed in her flannel PJs staring at her radiant diamond ring. The most beautiful facet of this diamond? The man who placed it on her finger.

Ready for what she believed would be the most amazing rapturous sleep, she snuggled up inside her fluffy comforter and sank her head into a brand-new marshmallow pillow. The glimmering beams from the winter-white moon fell perfectly onto her pillow. Naomi was prepared for the sleep of the innocent. She was mistaken.

Suddenly an onslaught of doubts flooded her mind. *He doesn't really know who I am. . . what I did. What he likes is the person I'm pretending to be. . . .*

Eventually sleep did come, but with it came the nightmare. Naomi walked alongside a peaceful lake listening to the sound of a young girl's childish laughter. She followed after this sweet sound, the laughter becoming louder the closer she approached its source. Abruptly, however, the lake turned into a turbulent waterfall and the young girl's laughter turned into a scream.

At the top of the waterfall was a child being pushed by a detached hand. In an instant the face of the child was clear: it was Mindy Kaplan. Naomi flew to where Mindy and her attacker stood. Her attempt to rescue the girl failed as the same detached hand pushed Naomi backwards.

Now lying on the ground, Naomi saw her father standing over her as if through a fisheye lens. He told her. "You should be ashamed of yourself. You disgust me."

A flash and the image changed. Naomi sat huddled in the corner of her childhood bedroom. In the background she heard Mom's plaintive voice. "Saul, please, we need to take her to the hospital. Maybe her baby can still be saved."

Naomi awoke, her heart pounding. Lying at the foot of the bed, the cat looked up, stretched her back, and meowed.

The next morning Naomi walked into the kitchen for her routine cup of coffee. Seeing Anne at the table with her routine cup of tea, Naomi placed her left hand in front of Anne and said, "Daniel gave this to me last night."

Anne's glee was contagious and helped Naomi chase away the images from last night's horrific dream which still sought to disturb her.

The hugging and jumping up and down finished, Naomi poured a cup of coffee. "He actually got down on his knee. But, Anne, don't worry, please, I won't leave you high and dry—like I did before. We haven't picked a date yet or anything."

"I'll ask around. I could even put an ad in the *Village Voice* for a roommate." Anne rose from her chair, opened the refrigerator and turned to Naomi. "I'm going to have some yogurt. Want one, too?"

Naomi nodded and went to the silverware drawer. "I got the spoons. As for the furniture, I know, here I go again, but this is all Gary's stuff. He just left it here. You can keep it all or sell it." Naomi took hold of Anne's elbow and looked directly into her eyes. "This stuff can't go with me into my new world."

Anne smiled and with both hands holding a yogurt container asked, "You want the strawberry one?"

"Sure." Sitting back at the table, both women stirred their yogurt. "Daniel has no idea about Gary or anything, and I don't want him to know."

"Things really must have been awful with Gary—more than you're telling me. Is there something I don't know about?" She waited, but when Naomi appeared all the more distant, Anne assured her, "You don't have to tell me, but you also don't have to pretend with me."

"It's not like I don't completely love Daniel . . ."

"And he completely loves you, too. I've seen it."

"But not the real me," Naomi cried out.

"Do you remember we had this conversation once before? And I asked you if he was so stupid you could have hoodwinked him? Now that I've met Daniel, I can see he's not stupid."

While cleaning up from their miniscule breakfast, Anne said, "You've talked about the Rabbi's wife—what was her name?"

"Sylvia." Naomi, about to put her coffee mug into the cupboard, stopped in mid-motion. "You realize that's what they're going to call me one day? The rabbi's wife. No casting director in their right mind would ever cast me in that part."

Anne turned off the water, took the cup from Naomi's hand and gently placed it into the cupboard. "Let's go sit back down."

Once seated, Anne explained, "What I was going to say is maybe you could talk with Sylvia."

Panicked, Naomi exclaimed, "I can't tell her everything."

"What's everything?"

"I'm sorry, forget I said that."

Everything? It's only one thing—it's not everything.

Chapter 11

B'sheirt – Soul Mates

F or the next week, Naomi went from. I should call Sylvia to No, I'd feel weird. After all, Sylvia probably was always a "good girl." She would never understand Naomi's fears of being unworthy to be the wife of a rabbi. And not just any rabbi—Daniel deserved the best of the best. Yet he loved her—and she was beginning to believe the woman he loved was actually the real Naomi. The soul buried inside, longing to be set free and to flourish.

Nevertheless each night dreams persisted with the disembodied voices, the accusing finger pointing toward her, and always Mindy Kaplan's innocent face.

Daniel, sweet amazing Daniel . . . as Anne had said, he was not stupid. One evening they were jogging together along the promenade when he turned toward her. "It must be intimidating, huh? One day you join a synagogue, the next day you're engaged to the Rabbi."

His insight caused her to gasp for air, more than the fast pace of their run. He placed a hand around her shoulders and led them to stand near the railing where they gazed upon a beautiful sunset with the backdrop of the Manhattan skyline.

"I was so scared you'd start thinking the way I've been acting was because I had changed my mind or something."

"I'm not stupid, Naomi."

She turned away from the view across the river and looked full front into Daniel's eyes. "Wow, that's what Anne said." When she saw his furrowed brow, she knew an explanation was in order. "I told her basically that maybe I'd hoodwinked you—don't you love that expression? I mean, what if I'm not all you think I am?" She now averted his gaze, her head down peering into the murky East River. "If you ever discovered you didn't actually love me, I'd . . ."

Daniel gently put his fingers to her quivering lips. "Hush. You're My-omi. I know who you are." He drew her into his chest and cradled her in his arms. "Somehow you have this idea that to be religious, you have to become perfect."

Naomi pulled away from Daniel. "Don't you?"

Daniel drew her back into his chest. "You know what the prophet Jeremiah wrote? He said it's only because of the Lord's mercies that we are not consumed. We try to do our best, My-omi, my bride-to-be, but, please, never forget God's mercy."

The next morning Sylvia telephoned Naomi. "Dear, would you like to come over for lunch today? It will be just the two of us. It would be nice to have some time alone."

Walking to Sylvia's home, Naomi contemplated how this invitation came about. She wasn't stupid either—she felt assured it came from Daniel's instigation. And she was grateful—it felt right.

It was a brisk end-of-March day, the sun shining through the row of oak trees. Within a few blocks from home, she entered into the neighborhood of Carroll Gardens. When given the address, she had assumed it would still be in the Heights, but as she moved into this more residential area, its homey character seemed much more fitting for Sylvia - *and her husband, too, I guess. Remember, Naomi, mercy—even with Rabbi Lehrer.*

Naomi found the address she had jotted down on a scrap of paper. Climbing up the stoop to the stately two-story duplex brownstone, she heard Sylvia call to her from the second floor window. "There you are. I'll be right down."

Sylvia ushered Naomi into the first floor living room. The interior showed obvious contributions from both the Rabbi and his wife. The furniture, appearing austere and uncomfortable, was offset by the family pictures framed in dark wood on the soft rose-colored walls.

"Something smells wonderful," Naomi told Sylvia.

"It's my day to cook Italian. Hope you like chicken parmesan." She ushered Naomi into the dining room area. "I also have spaghetti and garlic bread. Ooh, you better not be seeing Daniel after all the garlic."

"I am. I'm meeting him for dinner at his Aunt Luba's tonight. Right now he's at the hospital visiting some of the members of the *shul.*"

Sylvia pulled out a chair for Naomi at the dining table and then walked toward her kitchen. "I'll be right back."

The dining room walls were painted a muted green. The fireplace had a large mirror trimmed in mahogany wood over its mantle, with the dining room table and chairs all made from a rich mahogany as well—the same mahogany in appearance as was found in the Goldblatts' home.

The conversation during lunch consisted of small talk . . . how delicious Sylvia's cooking was . . . how nice her home was . . . By the time Sylvia brought out a platter of cookies, Naomi was beyond full but imagined she'd hurt the woman's feelings if she declined.

"Come, dear, let's enjoy these in the living room."

Once they were settled together on the stiff-backed Victorian-style couch, Sylvia said, "I remember when Joseph proposed to me—no, it was even before that—when I *knew* he would be proposing to me. I was so grateful to have Joseph's mother to talk to. You see, Joseph's father was a rabbi, too, and so his mother understood my nervousness—my fears actually."

When Sylvia paused at this point, Naomi assumed it was to coax her to now speak of her own fears. Not ready to do so, Naomi bit into one of the flaky cookies. Crumbs fell all over the couch and onto the parquet floor. Sylvia deftly swept the crumbs into a small napkin and the mess was gone.

"Sylvia, I am nervous. You're right. It's like this: I call Daniel 'Daniel' because it's hard for me to call him Rabbi Dan. He's Daniel to me, and when I think of him as Rabbi Dan I get all queasy inside."

"He is Daniel to you. And the boy—I mean man—needs someone who will see him as Daniel. Of course, you must see him as a rabbi, too. After all, that's the calling on his life."

"But how does he see me? I mean can he see me as a rabbi's wife?"

"Naomi, I will ask you what Joseph's mother asked me. Can you be a rabbi's wife or would you simply be the wife of a rabbi?"

"I hope I can be a rabbi's wife. I believe I understand the difference." Naomi sat back on the sofa while at the same time leaning in toward Sylvia. "Daniel is so wonderful. It doesn't seem like religion to him, it's more like he has this relationship with God and I want that, too."

Sylvia placed her half-eaten cookie on her plate. In a soft yet firm voice, she advised, "Darling, don't be too idealistic. You will need to be prepared instead by being realistic. Maybe your future husband has a relationship with the Almighty, but relationships with people will also be a large part of his work—and yours, too."

"Sylvia, I've thought about that. I mean he's right now at the hospital visiting people. And I know you do things like that, too, but I'm not sure that's something I'll be—"

With a broad smile, Sylvia chided her. "Nonsense, my dear. I've watched you. You can. And Daniel wouldn't have asked you to be his wife unless he was confident you would be an asset to him."

"An asset?"

"And you thought you were a deficit. Shame on you. But as I said you must be realistic. Some people are more challenging than others." Sylvia suddenly sat up straight, craned her neck, and appeared to have a mischievous twinkle in her eyes. "I have an idea. Have you met Daniel's sister since our Chanukah party?"

Naomi shook her head. "No, why?"

Her eyes still twinkling, Sylvia told her, "She could be good practice for you." Sylvia giggled girlishly. "Didn't expect that, did you?

Sylvia lifted up the platter of cookies and brought it to Naomi. "I'll tell you a secret. Joseph's mother gave me all the practice I needed. Whew, she was a handful. Now, this is to be kept between us girls."

"Your secret's safe with me."

Sylvia returned the platter back to the coffee table after Naomi indicated she was too full for more. "You will need practice in dealing with difficult people. They are most certainly out there. Let me ask you, for starters, how many brothers or sisters do you have?"

"I'm an only child."

Sylvia clucked her tongue. "Oh my, you definitely need practice. I could introduce you to a few people from the Temple." After contemplating this idea for a moment, she jokingly reassured, "No, I don't have the heart to do that to you, not yet anyway."

Naomi now reached over for one of the cookies as she peered into Sylvia's face. "You're scaring me."

The older woman's face crinkled up with a wide grin. "Start with Daniel's sister. Intuition tells me you'll do fine with her. And it'll be a *mitzvah*, a good deed, for Daniel and for . . . what's her name?"

"Dana."

"Yes, for Dana. She must be very unhappy. Only hurt people hurt people. That's your first lesson: hurt people hurt people. Repeat that after me, dear?"

Naomi was thrilled—she was not alone but had a mentor. She gladly repeated, "Hurt people hurt people," and then asked, "Can I meet with you regularly?"

It was agreed they would meet once a week for these luncheons and Naomi had her first homework assignment: Dana.

In parting, Sylvia hugged her new student. "Who knows, maybe Daniel's Aunt will sharpen your skills, too."

"The hardest part, I think, will be to convince her I'm hungry. I'm going to be eating dinner in about one hour. And I'm stuffed. Your chicken parmesan was delicious and I ate too much."

Travelling to Aunt Luba's apartment took Naomi deeper into the heart of Brooklyn—Flatbush Avenue. "I hope I'm not late," Naomi told Daniel when he opened the door for her.

With one hand he held up a finger and with the other pointed to his mouth which was obviously full of food. His head turned to show her a large platter of antipasto.

Looking around the room, Naomi felt she was back at Sylvia's. Rose colored walls, mahogany wood tables, and the smell of—could it be?—chicken parmesan?

Naomi did notice one major difference in Luba's home. Rather than family portraits gracing the walls, one wall showcased Marc Chagall prints and another wall displayed what appeared to be original artwork. Naomi's impression was that these were works in progress.

After a large swallow, Daniel said, "A little bit late, but don't worry." Daniel kissed her cheek. "My aunt is *potchking* around the kitchen. You're her special guest. She's probably been in the kitchen since yesterday getting this dinner together. You better be good and hungry."

He bent down over the platter of antipasto, picked up a large chunk of cheese and put it in front of Naomi's mouth. "Here have some cheese. There's also some artichoke hearts. They're my personal favorite."

She opened her mouth and accepted the provolone cheese. *I better make a personal note—keep artichoke hearts stocked in my future kitchen.*

While *potchking* in her kitchen, Naomi and Daniel could hear Luba singing. *Beltz, Mayn Shtetle.*

"Sounds almost like Klezmer music," Naomi observed. Since a child, Naomi had always been drawn to this distinctive musical style. Something about the sounds made her feel a part of the old Eastern European world of her ancestors.

"You like Klezmer?"

"It's a fun sound."

"We got a date! There's a Klezmer band playing in the city next week." After another artichoke heart, Daniel commented, "You're not eating. You want something else. I can ask—"

Naomi jumped in quickly. "No, I'm fine." *How am I going to eat any more today?* She sniffed the air and asked, "Daniel, do I smell chicken parmesan?"

"How'd you know? With spaghetti and . . . ? C'mon guess. What else do you smell?"

"Garlic?"

He nodded. "Garlic bread. My aunt has a new Italian boyfriend she wants to impress. So, how was your time with Sylvia?"

"She's wonderful, Daniel. Thank you."

"For what?"

"Well, just in case you kinda prompted her to call me, I'm glad you did." On her train ride to Flatbush, Naomi had contemplated the woman's advice, and now plunged in. "Daniel, why don't we ask Dana and Ed to join us at the Klezmer concert?"

"Are you—"

Luba came waltzing out of the kitchen and asked, "Smell gut? Come, children."

Daniel and Naomi followed her into the dining room and were surprised by the formality of the table setting. Two lit candles sat in an elegant pair of crystal holders, a vase filled with pink roses was between the candles, and the table had been set with the finest Wedgewood formal dinnerware.

Daniel hugged his aunt. "You didn't need to do all this for us."

"Danielek, not for you, for Berto." Staring longingly at the fourth table setting, she told them, "Maybe he still come. Later. Ve see."

Naomi recognized heartbreak when she saw it. "The table is beautiful. And if Berto doesn't come, it's his loss."

Luba pinched Naomi's cheek. "Danielek, you do gut." She then asked Naomi, "You hungry?"

"Starving." She glanced into the kitchen and noticed all the pots and pans piled up on the countertop and on the stove. *Oh, please, if You can hear me, forgive me for lying and make me hungry.*

Over dinner Naomi asked about the half-finished canvases on the living room wall. Luba looked at Daniel and asked, "You vant I tell her? Or you?"

"I'll explain, you eat." Smiling Daniel said, "They're Dana's. It's typical of her, never finishing anything. Aunt Luba keeps them hung up on her wall to remind my sister every time she comes here. See, actually what happened is one time the whole family was over at Dana's old place, before she moved to Staten Island, and we noticed a bunch of canvases piled up next to where the garbage was. None of us said anything—no one but my aunt."

With a broad smile, Luba empathetically stated, "Art—not garbage." Dinner was finishing up and her eyes landed on Naomi's half-eaten piece of chicken. "Vhat? My chicken not gut?" Therefore, by the time their dinner was finished, Naomi's plate was clean. Yet when Luba told them to wait while she got out the dessert, Naomi protested. "I can't, Aunt Luba."

With actual tears pooling in her eyes, Aunt Luba said, "Ah, you must. I make Italian vedding cake." She stepped into the kitchen leaving orders with Daniel. "Tell her, she must eat."

When Luba proudly brought out her fancy confection, Naomi oohed and aahed, and then forced herself to eat. She also observed Luba's eyes staring at her front door. Thinking the woman still hoped her boyfriend would show up, Naomi wanted to distract her. "Daniel told me the story of your life is fascinating. He wanted you to tell me. Would you?"

Luba nodded. "I only one of family not go to camps. Know vhy?"

"Please, tell me."

She rested the palms of her hands under her chin. "My face. Face like a *shiksa*, no? My face save me."

Daniel cleared his throat. "Naomi, she always tells the story this way. And always I tell her it's not nice to use that word. But it's so ingrained in her. Aunt Luba, next time just tell people you looked like a Gentile with your blonde hair and blue eyes—don't say *shiksa*."

"Danielek, this name all my life I hear." She then turned back to Naomi. "Last time I see Papa, he is behind fence. He vhisper to me, 'Lubomira, run.' Then Papa point to my face, 'But, Lubomira, never forget you are a *Yid*.' And never do I forget." She wiped the tears trickling down her face. "Tell story a hundred times—every time, I cry."

Daniel explained, "It wasn't until about ten years after the war when she found my mother."

"Zofia, my sister, she only one. Rest of family vere no more."

Although not sure what would be appropriate to say, Naomi nonetheless felt Luba was waiting expectantly for her reaction. "It amazes me, Aunt Luba, after going through all this, you don't seem bitter. You seem even happy, or at least upbeat."

Luba looked at her nephew and pointed to Naomi. "She thinking vhy your mother bitter and me not." She then turned to Naomi. "Yes?"

"Well . . . in a way, yes."

"Zofia see all killed. Our mother, precious *Mamala*, die in her arms." She cut another slice of cake and placed it on Naomi's plate. "Eat."

"I'll have the baked ziti," Daniel told the waitress. "Naomi, did you make up your mind what you're having?"

Naomi looked up at the waitress with a smile. "Just a small house salad, please."

Naomi folded up her menu and explained to the others at her table, "I've been eating way too much lately. I'm trying to diet."

Ed laughed and nudged Dana with his elbow. "What is with you women? Dana's always saying the same thing." Then looking at Dana, he asked, "What are you having, babe?"

"Chicken parmesan and spaghetti."

Café Figaro had filled to capacity. Naomi noted that the Greenwich Village restaurant was now turning away people at the door. "Boy, I'm glad we got here when we did."

The waitress gathered up the menus and walked away. With the food ordered, it seemed the awkward silence returned. Naomi squeezed Daniel's hand and leaned across the table to Dana and Ed. "I can't wait to hear the Bohemian Nights play."

She received only a polite nod from Ed. Dana sat stony-faced. Daniel squeezed Naomi's hand back and whispered, "I warned you."

Naomi spied a couple at a nearby table playing backgammon. "Let's play. We can ask the waitress for a game."

Both Ed and Daniel were receptive to the idea, but Dana told them, "You can only have two players."

"We can play as teams, boys against the girls," Naomi coaxed. She reached across the small rickety wooden table to Dana. "I'll come sit next to you and Ed can sit where I'm sitting." No response. For an extra incentive, she added, "And you know we'll win."

"I'm outnumbered." Dana rose from her seat and said, "I'll even go get a game for us."

By the time the food arrived, they were on their second game, and true to Naomi's word, the girls had won the first and were winning the second. Ed and Naomi switched back to their original seats, as their plates were set before them.

All but Naomi complained that their food was bland and over-cooked. Naomi's iceberg lettuce was fine as was the French dressing. Daniel reminded them they were not here for the food. The place was more a coffee house than it was a restaurant—but tonight for the first time Café Figaro featured a Klezmer band.

As the musicians began setting up, Daniel got the attention of the waitress and asked for some espresso. "It's the only way I'm going to stay up."

"I'll keep poking you," Naomi teased. Why hadn't she been more sensitive? Friday night and all day Saturday were the busiest time in a rabbi's life, and by Saturday night her fiancé was exhausted. "From now on, we won't make plans for Saturday nights, okay?"

Taking her hand and looking tenderly at her engagement ring, he kissed his future bride.

Dana commented, "Ed and I don't need a piece of paper. And I'd rather we gave the money it would cost for the diamond and for the wedding to some charity."

Ed put his hand up to his forehead, covering one eye, and shook his head. "Daniel, I'm sorry, man. I don't know why she's including me in this. I'm happy for you and Naomi. I mean, hey, marriage was good enough for our parents."

Naomi was grateful the waitress arrived at that moment. She brought coffee just as the band picked up their instruments, ready to begin. The first sounds heard were from the accordion and flute, followed by the cornet, and soon the hammered dulcimer, the snare drum, and lastly the fiddle and the cello.

With a splash, the cafe was filled with lively ethnic sounds. Even Dana smiled and bobbed up and down with the music.

When an especially upbeat song began Naomi rose from her seat and walked over to Dana. "Would you do the *hora* with me?"

To the surprise of both her brother and her boyfriend, Dana bounced up in a flash and the two ladies were on the dance floor. Naomi and Dana took each other's hands and spun in a circle, with three steps forward and one step back. Typical of Klezmer music, the music increased in speed, eventually reaching a frenetic pace.

They returned to the table, breathless and flushed, and explained to the men they needed to use the ladies' room. Once alone, Naomi took the risk and said, "I'm really hoping you'll come to our wedding. It'd mean a lot to Daniel."

The noise from the music made it impossible to carry on a conversation and Dana motioned Naomi to follow her. Standing outside the café, under the awning, Naomi repeated her request.

"Daniel doesn't need my coming," Dana answered. "He's in his own little world with his religion. Religion is the opiate of the masses—you've heard that before, right?"

"Maybe, but what's rudeness? The drug of choice for the rest of you?"

"I've seen what religion has done to Ed's family. It's made them act like doormats to the white people." Dana stared at her future sister-in-law, as if sizing her up. "Are you a vegetarian?"

"No, why?"

"I saw the way you wrinkled up your nose when I was eating my chicken parmesan. Actually, you know what? *That* was rude."

Naomi explained how she recently had to eat two such dishes in one day. "Both with spaghetti and garlic bread and dessert. I was so stuffed." Naomi puffed out her cheeks and did her fat girl waddle. She was delighted to hear Dana's laughter. "Can I tell you a secret?"

With her eyes unblinking and fixed on Naomi, she nodded her head.

"I lied to your Aunt Luba. I told her I was hungry even though I was forcing myself to eat her food. I was praying . . . see religion is necessary . . . anyway, I was praying I wouldn't get sick."

With girlish laughter, they returned into the café and back to their table. Daniel rose and hugged Naomi. As he pulled out her seat, he said, "What a gift you are to me. I love you."

I can do this, Sylvia, I can do this.

The band now transitioned into the poignant and slower rhythm of "Jerusalem of Gold."

Daniel pulled Naomi to him and asked, "Would you like to go to Israel for our honeymoon?"

Chapter 12

"A person may plan his path, but. . ."
Proverbs. 16:9

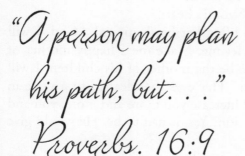

*A*fter five nights free from any nightmares, the chasm of empty shadows returned. Naomi was jarred out of her sleep with the piercing screams of babies reverberating in her head. She cupped her hands over her ears and squeezed her eyes shut. She forced herself back to sleep, but soon came the vision of Stefan's face looming over her.

"You killed one of our babies," Daniel's father cried. In a flash, the vision morphed into Daniel's face, which was wrought in agony.

Naomi awoke trembling. For the next hour, she tossed and turned. Eventually giving up on further sleep, she turned on her lamp and looked on her nightstand. Perhaps whatever current novel she was reading would pull her out from this deep pit.

Instead she found the Jewish Scriptures placed there, the result of a New Year's resolution to read them daily. Here it was catching dust. What if there would be more about killing some animal and sprinkling the blood . . . ?

Desperate times call for desperate measures. Only God can help me. Please, God, no blood . . . no killing.

Last evening at the Passover meal, Naomi joined Daniel and his family as they read from the Psalms. The Bible now on her lap, she quickly found the Psalms. But what Psalm should she turn to? With a deep sigh, she shrugged. It was no use—this book didn't speak to her.

Yet somehow her eyes landed on the first verse in Psalm 113. "He settles the childless woman in her home as a happy mother of children." Tears formed in Naomi's heart.

She closed her eyes and lifted her head upward. "God, I will make it up to You, if You let me. Make me a happy mother of children; for Daniel, let me be the mother of his children. I will thank You forever and ever." Her eyes then leaped to a verse in Psalm 115, "The Lord shall increase you more and more, you and your children." A confirmation? Yes, it had to be. He would give her children.

Those tears in her heart now spilled from her eyes gently down her cheeks, washing away the voices that had broken into her sleep.

A blissful yawn signaled she was now ready for sleep. She placed the Bible back on her nightstand, deliberately leaving it open to where she last read. A few more hours of sleep and she awoke, the distant remnants from the nightmare now shadows, nevertheless still there. And in an instant she understood what had provoked those ghastly visions.

At the *Seder* meal the day before, they had been reading from their *Haggadah* which recounted the Exodus narrative. All was fine until they came to the place where they read about Pharaoh ordering the death of all Hebrew males.

The Passover liturgy was abruptly halted by Zofia's sudden wailing. Stefan, sitting at the head of the table, stood up and explained, "We saw so many of our babies killed in the camps. My wife read something the other day about this horrible thing—abortion—being allowed in this country."

Naomi watched as Daniel put his arms around his mother. "Mom, it will never happen again. Every Jewish baby will be born and protected from now on. And one day Naomi and I will even bless you with a baby."

Stefan then lovingly boasted, "Our Danny, see Zofia, look what a gift God has given us."

Naomi had excused herself. Although wanting to run, she managed to restrain herself and calmly walked into the bathroom, running water from the sink to cover up the noise of her own wailing. *Will there always be something to remind me?*

But recalling the words Daniel had spoken only a few moments before provided Naomi the hope and courage to step back out and join everyone at the family table. One day she and Daniel would bless his mother with a child.

It was clear: the events of the day before inspired the nightmare, but thankfully this was a new day. She would pray hard and one day she would give Daniel a son. *Wow, this'll be Zofia and Stefan's first grandchild.*

Still in her bathrobe, Naomi walked into the kitchen. Preoccupied with imagining the time when she tells Daniel, "I'm pregnant," she made her way towards the coffee pot. She was oblivious to Anne standing right in front of her.

"Naomi, open your eyes," Anne warned, preventing coffee grinds from spilling all over their white tile floor.

While waiting together for the coffee to brew. Anne asked, "How was the *Seder*?"

"Daniel and his father, it was so sweet to see how they love each other. I don't think I've ever seen a father and a son get along so well. He calls him Danny, and he says it in such a loving way."

"What about his mother?"

"Hopefully over time . . . Maybe next Passover."

The coffee ready, Anne poured for both of them as Naomi reflected, "It's kinda wild. Last Passover was my loneliest Passover ever and one year later, I have one I . . . I don't deserve this."

Anne knitted her brows together. Naomi recognized the concerned look. *I'm about to get her stop-putting-yourself-down speech. If she only knew . . .*

She owed her friend an explanation. "Anne, less than a year ago, I . . ." But the words would not come out.

"A person may plan his path, but. . ." Proverbs. 16:9

"What? What were you going to say?"

"Nothing, I'm sorry." Naomi stared into her coffee cup until she could think of something else to say, "I don't know if I ever told you, but what you said about Daniel being too bright for me to hoodwink him . . ."

Laughing, Anne said, "Yes, I remember."

"The Rabbi's wife, Sylvia, she basically told me the same thing."

After a small breakfast, Naomi excused herself. She would be meeting Daniel in about two hours at a travel agency to discuss their honeymoon. Both had seen an advertisement in the New York Times: Come to the LAND OF MILK AND HONEYMOON. How could they resist?

About to step into the shower she heard the phone ring. She hesitated until she heard Anne answer. By the time she stepped out of the shower, she heard Anne's whimpering. Naomi wrapped a towel around herself and ran into the living room. She found Anne curled into a ball, her hand clamped over her mouth.

Through her sobs, Anne explained her mother had called. Anne's father had fallen from a ladder while cleaning their home's roof gutters and had been rushed to the hospital by ambulance. The doctors told Mrs. Holloway they were concerned he might end up paralyzed.

"I've got to fly out there right away. Mom says she's trying to reach my brother, but he probably can't come home from Germany. I doubt the military will let him."

"What can I do to help? Anne, I'll make your airline reservations while you pack?"

Anne thanked Naomi for her help. Daniel understood when Naomi called to explain why she might be a little late for their appointment. He wanted to give Anne money for a cab ride to the airport, but she told him, "That'd be way too expensive." She also declined Naomi's offer to accompany her to the airport.

Added to the worry for Anne's father, both Daniel and Naomi were now facing "sticker shock." The couple sat on a bench on the promenade, Naomi eating a large soft pretzel and Daniel having an Italian ice from the street vendor.

They stared at the setting sun as it bounced off the glass skyscrapers across the river in lower Manhattan and pondered whether they needed to change their plans.

Naomi broke the silence. "Did you have any idea it was going to be that much?"

"Naomi, I'm sorry to say this . . . I don't want to disappoint you, but it is more than we can afford right now."

"Daniel, I'm really not someone you have to worry about with money. I don't like spending a lot. I'm little Miss Thrift Shop. You know that."

He ruffled her hair affectionately. "Have you figured out yet how much the wedding is going to cost? I'm sure your Dad is anxious to know."

"It's going to cost a fortune—more money than Dad has ever paid for anything probably." She winced, realizing this had to be the stupidest thing for a bride to say to her fiancé. "I'm sorry. I shouldn't have said that."

He reached behind them to the garbage can and deposited what was left of his messy cherry-flavored ice. Naomi dug into her pocketbook and found some Kleenex for him.

"My fingers are too sticky. I'll be right back." He walked to the nearest water fountain and washed his hands.

While he was gone, Naomi contemplated the plans for this big wedding. Flowers, photographers, caterers, fancy invitations . . . not her style and she didn't think it Daniel's either.

Returning to the bench, he announced, "This isn't our style, Naomi. Can we get out of it?"

Jumping up from the bench, she hugged him. "Yes, please, let's get out of it." Yikes—what was she agreeing to? "Get out of what? Getting married?"

His hands again ruffled her hair. "No, silly. Never that. But this big wedding. How do you think we can . . . I don't know . . . streamline it?"

"As long as I get a nice dress I'm happy. You, God's blessings, and a nice dress, that's all I want."

"Uh, honey," Daniel gently but firmly corrected her, "you got that in the wrong order. We need God's blessings at the top of that list."

Once they came up with some downsizing ideas for what would be the most important day in their life, Daniel brought up the subject of the honeymoon. "Maybe this way we can still go to Israel. We could consider going with a group. There are different synagogues that go as a group, and that way you get a discount. We could try that."

"But then we'd be going with all these people we don't know."

This was also a reservation of his, and he had only presented the idea for her benefit. "My-omi, this is our dream, to go to Israel. I'll make sure we can afford it, okay?"

"Daniel, I have money, too, you know. I'm still getting a few checks from the Mop & Glo commercials and a lot more from the Campbell Soup one."

He studied her face. "Do you miss all that?"

"You mean the acting?"

"Of course."

"Of course, I don't. I like playing the role of bride, and soon the role of wife." In a shaky voice, she added, "And, Daniel, one day, mother, too."

Later that night she sat in her kitchen eating a peanut butter and jelly sandwich for dinner, trying unsuccessfully to reel in her thoughts. How could she not fantasize about her wedding night? The physical attraction she and Daniel experienced for one another was palpable, and his restraint with her was thrilling. More romantic than she could have ever imagined.

Why didn't anyone ever tell me this before? This feeling of being cherished took her breath away. *And if he can restrain himself, then why can't I restrain my thoughts?*

Unable to stop her naughty mind from wandering, she ran into the living room and played the cassette tape of Klezmer music Daniel had given her as a present. With the buoyant sound of Bohemian Nights, she finished her sandwich while dancing solo.

When her phone rang, she quickly turned off the music and grabbed the glass of milk still sitting on her kitchen table. The glob of peanut butter had to be washed down before speaking.

On the other end was Anne. The prognosis from the doctors was that her father would be paralyzed for life. "I don't know when I'll be getting back to New York. Mom's falling apart. I have to be with her."

It's not fair. Anne is such a better person than me. I don't deserve . . . Then it was as if she heard her dear friend's voice scolding her for such thoughts. She called Daniel with the sad news, and after listening, he said, "I'll pray for him, Naomi. What's his name?"

"Mr. Holloway, that's all I know."

"That's fine. Mr. Holloway." After a moment's hesitation, he continued, "Naomi, I might have some interesting news for us. I'll know more maybe tomorrow."

"What? What news? What is it?"

"Calm down, honey. You'll know when you need to know. I should have waited before I said anything. Now you probably won't sleep all night, will you?"

If he only knew how fearful I am of sleep . . . what happens if I have nightmares after we're married?

Once in her pajamas, she warmed up some milk and added some honey. She had vague memories as a child of her mother making this concoction for her whenever she had trouble sleeping. She brought the steaming cup into her bedroom and called for Zoey. "C'mon, girl, keep me company."

"A person may plan his path, but. . ." Proverbs. 16:9

While sipping the milk and with the cat snuggled up in the bed with her, Naomi reached for the Bible which had brought her solace the night before. She read, "When hard pressed, I cried to the Lord; He brought me into a spacious place." Naomi set the cup back on its saucer and rose from her bed to kneel beside it.

"Thank You—You have brought me into a spacious place." About to climb into the bed again, an afterthought brought her back to her knees. "God, please, help me to be a good wife and one day a mother, too. I love Daniel so much."

"Dad, it's $600, but it's the perfect wedding dress. Please." *How could he say no?*

He didn't. Naomi ran out of the phone booth and back into David's Bridal Studio. The dress needed no alterations. She gave the saleslady a deposit and told her she would also purchase the matching cathedral veil.

"Can I try it on again? Please." The lady couldn't say no either.

Stepping out of the dressing room and seeing her image reflected in the three-way mirror, the experience was the same as it had been only one hour before. This pure white gown brought tears to her eyes while at the same time uncontrollable giddiness.

The saleslady told her, "Honey, don't be embarrassed. All you girls react like this."

A few minutes later, back in her everyday clothes, she passed the same phone booth. She called the synagogue. "Daniel, I found the dress . . . it's got the longest train . . . I hope I won't trip . . . I'll have to practice walking in it . . . it's satin and . . ."

"Whoa, girl. Listen, I'm glad you called. Can you come over to the *shul* this afternoon? There's something we need to talk about."

"Is everything okay?"

He assured her there was nothing to worry about, and perhaps he had good news to share with her. She decided to treat herself to a taxicab ride. Riding a subway would take too long for this curious young lady. *Why did he say perhaps?*

Naomi stepped into the *shul* and was greeted by Sylvia who had just walked out of the library. She literally pulled Naomi towards the library. "Come, dear. We have a surprise for you."

Naomi saw Daniel waiting by the library's double wooden doors. Rabbi Lehrer then emerged from the room, shaking Daniel's hand and patting him on the shoulder. He then walked over to Sylvia. "Come, dear, we need to leave them alone." He acknowledged Naomi's presence with a nod of his head.

Once alone, Naomi and Daniel sat on the overstuffed leather sofa in the library. Daniel ruffled her hair. "You look beautiful. The radiant bride, isn't that what people say?"

"The bride is nervous, Daniel. What's going on?"

"Once you hear, you can tell me if you don't want to. It's your decision."

In the most impatient voice Naomi could muster, she growled, "Daniel!"

Taking her hand, he began explaining, "Honey, Sylvia's brother . . ." He sprung to his feet. "He's a rabbi, and he's going to be retiring." He now paced in front of her. "The Lehrers believe I would be a good candidate to take over his position as Senior Rabbi."

Catching Daniel's excitement, Naomi jumped to her feet and hugged him. "Oh, Daniel, how wonderful. Where? And when?"

"Boca Raton, Florida, Tell me, what do you think? Want to live in Florida?"

She lowered herself to sit on the edge of the sofa now. "Aren't we Jews only supposed to go there after we retire? You and me, we're too young." His pacing began again. "I'm sorry, I was only trying to be funny. Didn't work, huh?" He continued pacing. "Boca Raton sounds beautiful, Daniel. Glamorous actually." The pacing did not stop. "Daniel, when? When would this happen?"

He walked back to Naomi and sat on the large arm of the sofa. Bending down towards her, he gave her the news. "Sylvia's brother, Rabbi Moscowitz, is leaving in August and they want whoever replaces him to come a month or so early, so the new rabbi could work with the old one. They think that'd help make a nice transition."

"But we're not getting married til August. How . . .?"

Daniel now slid off of the sofa arm and positioned himself to place one arm around her neck and with his other raised her downturned chin. "My-omi, stay with me on this. Rabbi Lehrer and Sylvia both believe it would be best if I were married before I was interviewed by the *shul*. And they would want to interview me by June.

"What?"

"Oh, and actually they would want to meet my wife, too." Her wide-eyed stare was returned by him, until their unblinking stares erupted into a ripple of nervous laughter.

"So, you're saying . . ." Trying to piece this together left her tongue-tied.

"Yes, I'm saying we'd have to move our wedding up two months." In a hushed tone, he attempted to coax. "It's one way to get out of the big wedding we don't want. And you have your dress now."

"Daniel, do you think this is like a sign? That we have God's blessings? Remember, that's what I wanted, the dress, you, and God's blessings?"

He took her in his arms. "Yes, I believe it is." After a tender kiss, he reluctantly said, "You know this makes going to Israel for our honeymoon a bit harder to do."

"Daniel, I can tell how much you want this. And I can't wait to see you as the head rabbi. You'll be amazing. And don't a lot of people go to Florida for their honeymoon—so why can't we?"

"You're the one that's amazing." Standing up, he grabbed Naomi's hand pulling her to her feet. "Dinner at Teresa's?"

Her smile said yes. Walking down the steps of the synagogue, he vowed, "We will go to Israel one day, I promise."

Chapter 13

Holy Matrimony

"Naomi, you don't need to go to the mikveh. Only the Orthodox require that." Daniel had only now discovered his bride would be taking the ritual bath the following morning. Having minutes ago finished the rehearsal for their wedding and about to leave for the restaurant with the wedding party, this news blindsided him.

"Sylvia told me she had done it before she got married. She said it was a way to symbolize being made clean before your wedding. Daniel, I've never told you about my past."

Affectionately putting his finger to her lips, he said, "Shush. We both have pasts, My-omi. The Talmud says when a man and a woman marry, they become a complete human being. They enter into a new existence and the old gets erased. The sages say—you're going to love this—when a person gets married, his sins are corked." Laughing at Naomi's startled expression, he added, "Our wedding will be like our own personal Yom Kippur."

Catching the couple in an embrace as she was leaving the synagogue, Aunt Luba teased them, "All right, you two. Soon, but not yet." Holding on to her date's arm, she asked, "Danielek, where's the restaurant? Give Berto the address."

"135 Essex Street. Berto, do you need directions?"

Berto shook his head no and Naomi added "It's called Schmulka Bernstein's. Is that cool or what?"

Naomi's father, walking out with his wife, stopped to tell everyone, "Schmulka's, been years since I've been there." He then told Helen, "The best kosher Chinese food anywhere." Starting to

169

leave, he turned back to his daughter. "You've made your mother and me very proud."

Soon all had left the *shul* and were on their way to the restaurant, Daniel and Naomi in the back seat of Rabbi Lehrer's car. While driving, the Rabbi remarked that the rehearsal went very well.

Sylvia pivoted her body from the front seat to address Naomi. "Did you see how happy your future mother-in-law was tonight? Asking Dana to be your maid of honor was so sweet of you, dear."

"Well, my best friend is still in Ohio and couldn't be here. But I'll tell you, when Dana said yes . . . wow, was I surprised or what?" Naomi looked at Daniel and said, "And asking Ed to be the best man, that didn't hurt either. But seeing your Mom's face, that's the best of all."

Daniel asked Sylvia, "How'd the shower go for Naomi? She won't tell me a thing."

Sylvia did not answer but instead rolled her eyes over to Naomi. After no answer came forth from her, Daniel pressed, "Okay, girls, what's up?"

Finally Sylvia told him, "You'll have to wait until your wedding night. Especially to see your Aunt's present."

Rabbi Lehrer looked through his rearview mirror and saw the embarrassment on both Daniel's and Naomi's faces. "Sylvia, turn around, dear. You're making me nervous while I'm driving."

With her head still facing the couple, she told her husband, "But, dear, I haven't told them yet about my brother."

At the same time both Daniel and Naomi uttered an anxious "What?" Rabbi Lehrer also asked, "What? You haven't told them yet?"

Taking hold of Naomi's hand, Daniel asked Sylvia to please explain. "We both want to know."

"Of course you do. Forgive me. With all the plans for your wedding. . . Gabe called me this morning. It's a last minute thing, but he'll be coming into New York tomorrow with his wife. Their grandson graduates from Columbia next week and he thought why not come early and maybe he could meet the both of you, tell you a little about his Temple in Florida. Would you have time to talk with him? "

"Sylvia," Rabbi Lehrer scolded, "you're not being very fair." Again looking into his rearview mirror, he addressed the shell-shocked couple. "Don't feel you have to be pressured into agreeing to this."

As the Rabbi pulled into a parking space, Daniel asked, "Would you give Naomi and me a moment alone to talk? Tell everyone we'll be right in."

When it was just the two of them, Naomi asked, "What do you want?"

And he asked, "What do you want?"

"It might be nice to meet him. Get an idea about the synagogue."

"I agree. What about your *mikveh* tomorrow morning? Are you still going?"

"As long as you don't think I need to, I won't."

"Mom's in the kitchen making breakfast for Dad and her. Anne, our kitchen never smelled so good and seemed so homey."

From the kitchen, Helen Goldblatt told Naomi, "Thank her for letting us use her bedroom."

"I'm going to miss you being here so much, but I better go. Looks like Mom's making breakfast for me, too, even though I told her I'm going out for breakfast. I better tell her again."

Overhearing his daughter's phone conversation, Saul relayed the message. "Helen, she's not eating with us. She told us last night, got a big meeting with the rabbi from Florida."

"Give us a call after your breakfast. Let us know how it goes," her mother asked.

"Mom, I told you, it's no big deal. Daniel's been talking to the search committee at the synagogue and even to one of the Directors on their Board."

"Go ahead," Saul said as he shooed his daughter out of the house. "Don't be late."

Since Daniel and Naomi had discovered their favorite restaurant had a unique breakfast menu, plans were made to meet Rabbi Moskowitz and his wife at Teresa's.

Gabe Moskowitz was a barrel-chested man in his early seventies. His thick dark brown hair was salted in silver with his face sporting a completely silver beard. He exuded a comfortable warmth, not unlike his sister Sylvia. A delightful characteristic of Gabe's was the sense that at any moment he would be breaking out in a good-natured chuckle. His wife Barbara was a petite perky pixie, with hair that was completely white and eyes that were large and brown.

On Daniel's recommendation, Barbara ordered the challah French toast with fresh fruit and both Gabe and Daniel ordered a kielbasa omelet. When Naomi demurely ordered only a small bowl of fresh fruit Barbara nudged her husband and said, "Isn't that sweet, honey, she's too nervous to eat. It might have been a long time ago, but I remember. Before our wedding, my stomach was doing flip-flops, too."

Detecting a southern accent with Barbara, Naomi asked, "Where are you from?"

Exaggerating her drawl, she informed her, "Georgia, dahling. Didn't know there were any Jews in Dixie, did you?"

Doing a perfect imitation of her mother's voice, Naomi countered, "Bless your heart, shuga, I sure 'nuf do."

Daniel explained, "Naomi's Mom is from Alabama."

While enjoying their meal, Gabe asked, "So, what can I tell you about Beth Shalom?"

Daniel held his hand up indicating he needed to swallow his food before answering. After a sip of orange juice, he said, "Everything."

Barbara suggested, "Gabe, why don't you start with telling them the age of the members?"

Looking comically at his wife, he asked, "What? You looking to scare them off already?"

Barbara countered his comic performance by pursing her lips and saying, "Shame on you, Gabe. Stop trying to be funny and let them know."

Daniel jumped in and told them he was aware that the average age of the Jewish population in Boca Raton was about 75.

"I'm excited for the congregation," Barbara now told them. "They need some young people to come in and, I don't know, what would you say, Gabe? Revitalize them?"

"Yeah, you could say that," Gabe replied drolly.

"Please forgive him," Barbara said. "It's not always easy and he is more than ripe for retirement."

Remembering the advice she received from Sylvia, Naomi said, "I've found hurt people tend to hurt people."

Gabe laughed. "Sounds like my sister."

Barbara smiled. "Sylvia has been a treasure to her husband. Naomi, you are lucky to have her as a mentor."

Gabe nodded. "My wife's right. Barbara is my treasure, and Naomi I'm sure will be yours, Daniel. I'm sorry if I got this conversation off on the wrong foot. You two need some serious answers." Reaching his hand across the table toward Naomi, he told her, "And I admire you, young lady. Getting married today and willing to leap right into being the rabbi's wife."

"Thank you."

"I'll be honest with you," Gabe said. "The congregation has been dwindling. The Board is optimistic at the thought of getting a young rabbi and his wife, hoping you can, as my wife so aptly put it, revitalize the *shul*."

Naomi, squeezing Daniel's arm, told Gabe and Barbara, "My husband is amazing. He will do it."

Observing Daniel's reaction, Barbara said, "Now, now, the bride is supposed to be the blushing one."

Gabe smiled and told them, "You're a beautiful couple. Who knows? Maybe you can bring the dead to life again. There are some special people there. Both Barbara and I have come to love some of them. Others . . . well, tell you what, if you take the position, I'll write out a road map of who's who. Now I understand your best man is Negro. Is that right?"

"She's my sister's boyfriend."

Gabe assured him, "You don't have to get defensive with us. Believe me, we don't have a problem with that. Yet you need to know the members of Beth Shalom, they're not so tolerant." He shrugged his shoulders and said, "Hey, don't shoot the messenger, I'm just delivering the message."

As the men were arguing over who would be paying the tab, both wanting to treat, Barbara shared her thoughts with Naomi. "I understand you are very good with the children. Sylvia told me about your Chanukah play—sounds like it was fun. But, honey, don't expect to see any children in Beth Shalom. But, of course, soon you'll have your own."

Dana upon entering the bride's changing room caught Naomi off-guard. Her first impulse was to ask Dana, "Where's the dress I picked out for you?" However, she had been making inroads with Daniel's sister and protective walls were slowly coming down.

Masking her real feelings, she said, "Dana, don't know what I would've done without you, not only for taking Zoey. . ."

"Ed loves cats and yours will grow on me—I hope."

"But also for your friend doing the photos today. That's saving Daniel and me a lot of money."

Looking into the three-panel mirror Dana began applying lipstick while at the same time studying Naomi's reaction to her attire. "I returned the dress you wanted me to wear."

Instead of the soft pink floral dress, she was wearing a deep purple tight-fitting floor length gown, which was fashioned to bare one shoulder.

"I'm sorry, but I need to ask you . . ."

Enjoying a good laugh, Dana reached into her pocketbook and pulled out a purple velvet wrap. Slipping it on over her head, she informed Naomi, "Ed insisted I had to wear this with it. You're a bad influence on him, you know that? Now he's talking about marriage."

Naomi was coming to love this wounded woman. "Dana, I wouldn't ever want to push you into something you didn't want."

Standing back to look at her future sister-in-law, Dana remarked, "You look beautiful. Can I help you with anything?"

"Give me a hug, that's all."

"You nervous?"

Before Naomi could answer, there was a knock on the door and they were told the processional was about to begin.

The traditional Jewish wedding music began: *Ani L'Dodi Li*. Oh, how Naomi rejoiced when Daniel told her it meant "I am my beloved . . . my beloved is mine."

Almost every seat was filled in the synagogue this day. Many eyes would be on Naomi as she floated down the aisle strewn with white lilies. Her eyes, however, were fixed on the beautiful beaded canopy where Daniel stood waiting for his bride. The four poles of the *Chuppah* were draped in rows of sparkling crystal beads falling from the top of the canopy. The light passing through the crystals brought about a visible spectrum of colors dancing before her eyes.

And with each step, she was closer to the man who had treated her with honor, elegant in his sapphire-colored tuxedo. Holding her bridal bouquet of white lilies, she shyly raised her head to look into his eyes. There was his precious cowlick peeking out from the edge of his white yarmulke.

Rabbi Lehrer opened in prayer. "He who is supremely mighty, He who is supremely blessed, He who is supremely sublime, May He bless the groom and the bride."

At the very centerpiece of this traditional Jewish wedding was the bestowal of a ring by the groom on his bride. Daniel placed the gold band on Naomi as he told her, "Thou art sanctified unto me with this ring, in the tradition of Moses and Israel." Then, at her request, he chanted these words in Hebrew.

Placing the ring on Daniel, she told him, "I am my beloved's and my beloved is mine."

Rabbi Lehrer now handed a parchment scroll to Daniel. After opening it, Daniel read to Naomi. "On the 5th day of the week of the month of June, in the year 1979, I consecrate you to me as my wife according to the laws of Moses and the traditions of our people. I shall treasure you, nourish you, and respect you as the sons of Israel have devoted themselves to their wives with love and integrity throughout their generations. I will be your loving friend as you are mine. I will respect you and the divine image within you. I take you to be mine in love and tenderness."

Naomi then read, "I consecrate you to me as my husband according to the laws of Moses and the traditions of our people. I shall treasure you, nourish you, and respect you as the daughters of Israel have devoted themselves to their husbands with love and integrity throughout the generations. I vow to establish a home based on love, understanding, and the traditions of our heritage. May we live each day as the first, the last, the only day we will have with each other."

Then together they recited from memory, "May our hearts beat as one in times of gladness, as in times of sadness. Let our home be built on Torah and loving-kindness. May our home be rich with wisdom and reverence."

Daniel walked toward his bride and delicately lifted her veil. There was a loud chorus of Mazel Tov's from the crowd, but Daniel and Naomi heard none of it as they celebrated their first kiss as husband and wife.

Once Rabbi Lehrer pronounced the priestly benediction over the new couple, he had them turn to face the congregation. "Ladies and gentlemen, may I present to you Rabbi and Mrs. Cantor." He then placed a wine glass on the floor, where Daniel shattered it with his foot.

Rabbi Lehrer couldn't resist telling everyone, "Some say this is the last time the groom gets to 'put his foot down.'"

The guests were then invited to partake of a festive meal down-stairs in the social area, catered by Schmulka Bernstein's. All the kosher spareribs, eggrolls, chow mein one could eat. Saul Goldblatt was especially pleased.

Daniel and Naomi were going around to each table, thanking people for sharing this event with them, when Daniel noticed someone at a distant table and called out, "Irwin."

A sandy-haired man, wearing a goatee, in his early-thirties got up from his table as Daniel took Naomi's hand and together they walked toward Irwin. Excitedly he told Naomi, "This is the man I told you about, who had the *havurah* in his house." Now looking at Irwin, he said, "I thought you said you weren't going to be able to make it."

Irwin explained, "I didn't think I would, but I was able to trade shifts with someone at the hospital. I'm glad I'm here. But I'm afraid my wife couldn't be."

"Naomi, Irwin's an internist. He's doing his residency at Mount Sinai—when he's not playing his guitar." Turning to Irwin, Daniel asked, "You are still playing, aren't you?"

It was not hard to see why these two men were friends. Both were easygoing and affable. Yet the bride and groom had many more people waiting to congratulate them. Irwin understood and in parting told them, "We'll have to get together soon, the four of us."

In the midst of doing all that was expected of her as the bride, Dana walked over to Naomi and whispered, "Bet you and my brother would like to just be alone right now. I can't imagine waiting til you're married, but, you know, it's kinda romantic."

Zofia, seeing her daughter giggling like a schoolgirl with Naomi, was astonished. She walked over to where Daniel and Stefan were talking together. "Stefan, our daughter, look."

Putting one arm around his wife and the other around his son, Stefan looked over at Naomi. "Our Danny has done good."

A moment later Daniel took Naomi aside and asked, "What were you and Dana giggling about?"

Rather than answer, Naomi told him, "Oh, so, I'm not the only who gets curious sometimes. Remember what you told me, curiosity . . ."

"My-omi, all I know is I want to be alone with you, right now if we could."

Soon their wish would come true. The festivities were drawing to a close. Rabbi Lehrer announced it was time to recite the wedding blessings and Daniel gave the honor to Irwin. Accepting a prayer shawl from Rabbi Lehrer, Irwin walked to the center of the room and in a worshipful voice proclaimed, "Blessed art thou, O Lord, King of the universe, who makest the groom rejoice with the bride."

Finally alone in what had been Daniel's apartment, and now was theirs, Naomi told her beloved, "When I was walking down the aisle and saw you up there waiting for me . . . you looked so handsome . . . I thought I'd explode with tears, grateful ones, because you waited for tonight. You showed me such honor. I never thought I could feel so cherished. And, Daniel, when you lifted my veil, I thought I'd explode . . . and not with tears."

"We both have waited until tonight, my bride. We don't have to wait any longer."

Several times that night, an accusing voice awakened Naomi. Each time, she reminded herself, "It's okay. We're married. He's my husband. It's okay.

Chapter 14

Accepting the Challenge

F The bellhop received his tip and closed their door before Naomi exclaimed, "We can't afford this—can we?"

"You gave up Israel. I had to make it up to you. You like it?"

This expensive suite was Daniel's impulsive splurge. Until this moment he had only seen a few pictures in a brochure; the photos did not do the place justice. The travel agent had assured him any room in the famed Fontainbleau Hotel in Miami would never disappoint.

Naomi ran to the sliding glass doors and gazed out at the furnished balcony. "Daniel, there's the beach. It's right here." The doors easily glided open at her touch and she walked out onto the balcony. She turned back to her handsome husband, who was walking out to join her. "I can't wait to see the sunset from here."

He scooped her up in his arms and said, "I can't wait to watch you watching the sunset."

A few hours later the sun did begin to set and like their first wedded embrace, it brought with it a blaze of colors. Vibrant purples, pearly pinks, iridescent oranges all veiled in a golden glow. And all being reflected on the ocean water.

When Naomi's stomach growled, Daniel chuckled. "Ah, I know that sound. How about a nice dinner?"

The concierge at the front desk recommended a seafood restaurant with a waterfront view. A good recommendation indeed.

Dining on shrimp and lobster, Naomi questioned that which had been nagging at her for a while now. "Are we going to be keeping kosher?"

Daniel put down his small ramekin filled with drawn butter and arched one eyebrow. With a smirk, he replied, "Uh, good timing, Mrs. Cantor."

"Well, yeah, it actually is." She took one of the lemon wedges resting in a small plate between them. "It's too fishy for me." With her eyes on Daniel, she squeezed the juicy lemon; a large squirt of lemon juice flew directly into his eye.

Once that momentary crisis was resolved, he picked up on her question. "Naomi, I didn't grow up in a kosher home, and neither did you. I think about it and would like to dedicate myself more to God's law. Rabbi Lehrer taught that as Jews we are to take upon ourselves the yoke of the law. It's our obligation—and our privilege. So I need to be setting an example for others, but I don't want to sound like I'm better than everyone else. If anything, what I would like to do is inspire others."

This time, being much more careful as she squeezed another lemon, she simply said, "Wait a second." Once all the juice was out of the fruit, she looked up and told him, "You inspire *me*. I don't want be too gushy or anything, but it's true. And I want more from you. This morning I heard you when I was showering, you were chanting. Or would you say praying? I don't know what to call it, but I can tell you it sounded so wonderful. Would you teach me?"

Tears formed in his eyes—this time not from the lemon. He sidled his chair closer to hers. "I'd love to. Together we'll start our morning before our Maker." He brushed his lips across her neck and then onto her cheek. "You truly are My-omi. I'm so blessed by you."

Sensing the presence of someone standing over them, they looked up and saw the waiter holding out a dessert menu toward them.

Two larges wedges of cheesecake later, they were strolling hand in hand back to their hotel, walking alongside the ocean.

Daniel picked up again on the unresolved kosher issue. "So, here's the thing: neither of us grew up being kosher, and I don't want it to be a strain on us. Or something artificial."

Daniel came to a sudden halt and turned toward Naomi. "And if I do it because as a rabbi people expect me to, then couldn't I just end up making them feel guilty?"

Although he was facing Naomi, the moonlight revealed his eyes dancing to and fro.

"Daniel, look at me." His eyes turned to her and seemed to plead for help—help for this quandary he found himself in. When Naomi saw him biting his lower lip, she suggested, "Honey, let's take our shoes off—we can walk on the beach." For the first time she felt needed—what a delightful feeling.

And he instantly agreed. The warm sand was just the right medicine to ease a confused mind. They slowly made their way to the water and allowed the saltwater to wash over their feet, and eventually continued on the shoreline, making their way back to the hotel.

Then they spotted two beach chairs left sitting in the sand. Naomi asked, "Wanna sit for a few minutes?"

"It's like they have our names on it."

Naomi brushed the sand from her feet. "Did you wanna go back to the big question: whether to be kosher or not?" With dramatic flair, she said, "To be or not to be."

After shaking his head in amusement, he declared, "You're too much. But, yes, let's go back over it. The thing about making the members of my congregation feel guilty, a lot of my professors taught that's exactly what we were supposed to do. Basically it was our job to beat them into submission."

"And you don't want to do that. I mean, you're not Rabbi Lehrer."

Rising out of their chairs, they made their way the few more steps to the hotel. With the sound of the ocean behind them, Daniel said, "I've actually asked God about this, Naomi—whether He wants us to have a kosher home or not, but so far He's been silent."

"Daniel, maybe we could pray about it together?" She was amazed hearing these words coming from her own lips—this was the new and improved Naomi—the Rabbi's Wife.

That night they left the balcony doors open. The gentle wind blew into their room making the white curtains sway rhythmically and completed a perfect picture of peace and joy.

Only once did Naomi awaken with the voice of the accuser. She effectively silenced him by breathing in the beauty of the room and the beauty of her husband's face lit by the moonlight as he peacefully slept. *He is my husband. We are married. It is okay.*

The next morning, Daniel took out his prayer book, leaned over onto the bed, and kissed his wife. "Good morning, honey. Time to begin our morning blessings."

With an effort, she was able to open one of her eyes and get out her all-important question. "Coffee?"

Not a coffee drinker himself, he had forgotten Naomi basically needed to smell it before getting out of bed. "I'll go down to the lobby and get you a cup, a strong cup. Be right back."

Thirty minutes later, she turned to him and announced, "I'm ready."

Eagerly he opened his book as he explained, "*Modeh Ani*—that's the blessing we recite upon arising." The curtains still danced in the ocean breeze. "Let's go out to the balcony and begin."

Seated on the bamboo chairs, he continued his teaching. "The *Modeh Ani* is one of the first blessings a Jewish child is taught. It expresses gratitude to God for the gift of a new day of life."

"How can I not be grateful?"

Not looking at the vista beyond their balcony, but looking at her, he said, "I know what you mean." He cleared his throat and resumed the role of teacher. "So, when we arise each morning, we recite . . ." Daniel pointed to the open page. "Now, say it with me

. . . Oh, how stupid of me. You don't read Hebrew. I'll teach you, but for now, we can do it in English."

He showed Naomi the translation into English next to the Hebrew. Daniel reached for his *tallit* and placed the prayer shawl over both their heads. She then followed him in thanking the Living and Eternal King for His great compassion and faithfulness.

With their bodies leaning against one another, feeling one another's breath, and intimately sharing the *tallit*, their thoughts moved away from the purely spiritual. Suddenly breathless, their lips parted, they turned to each other and acknowledged the change of mood.

Daniel laughed and shook his finger at her. "You're a bad influence on me, you know that?"

She fled from the balcony and back into their room. Daniel ran after her, calling out, "Naomi, relax, you know I'm only joking."

Daniel's words unearthed her fear: she was not good enough for him and would only interfere with God's plans for his life. She *had* hoodwinked him—the deed was done and now she must justify her place by his side. She sat on the edge of the bed and promised, "Daniel, I want to give you beautiful babies one day."

He stood above her scratching his head. "That's a sweet promise, honey, but . . ." He shrugged his shoulders, sat down beside her and whispered in her ear, "Let's start now."

Her fears were dispelled and in its place came a buoyant feeling of acceptance.

About one hour later, they decided to rent a car and drive into the Everglades. The concierge had told them about an airboat ride offered by one of the Indian Reservations in the area. They would get up close and personal with the alligators.

They were given a bronze-colored Chevrolet Malibu and Naomi loved it. "Daniel," she excitedly told him, "We will have to buy a car won't we? I mean if you get the job down here."

"So you're already thinking what kind of fancy car to buy, huh?"

That evening he had a surprise waiting for Naomi. When getting her coffee, he had asked the front desk where they might go to hear

Klezmer music. Not only was he told of a place near the hotel, but was given a coupon which would save them on the admission price. Naomi was thrilled.

There first full day in Miami turned out to be a fun-filled adventure.

"Tomorrow, we'll try again to recite our blessing together," Daniel assured her.

Afraid of more night terrors, she asked, "Isn't there something we could say together before going to sleep?"

He reached for his *Siddur* which he had placed on the nightstand by the bed. "Let's simply say the *Shema* together. It's beautiful to say anytime. I'll do it in English with you."

"One day, when you teach me Hebrew, will I be able to chant it like you do?"

"We'll see. Don't rush things, honey. You seem to put a lot of pressure on yourself. Why do you do that?"

Her eyes cast down, she told him, "I don't want to be taking you away from your time alone with God. Maybe it's like you simply need to get me started. Then I'll do my own thing in the morning, and you'll do yours."

"My-omi, stop worrying, okay?"

"Okay."

He opened to the appropriate page and they read, "Hear, O Israel, the Lord our God is one Lord: and thou shalt love the Lord thy God with all thine heart, and with all thy soul, and with all thy might."

Daniel asked, "Do you have bad dreams?"

Why is he asking that? What if he asked the nature of her dreams? She couldn't tell him. No, never. In answer to his question, she shook her head.

"Can you believe we might be living here? Everything's so beautiful. I can't believe it. Look at that house over there."

"Honey, I'm driving. I can't look."

"You can at least look at the ocean for a second. It's over to your right?"

"The people here don't drive like they do in New Jersey. I have to concentrate."

She apologized and tried to stop saying, "Ooh, look," every five seconds. But it was not easy. The palatial estates with their opulent landscaping took her breath away. Some of them even overlooked the ocean.

For the last three days, each time she saw a home which reflected the area's Spanish heritage, she spun her fantasies. Their home in Boca Raton would have a terra cotta roof, arched windows on all three floors, and a huge balcony coming out of their bedroom and facing out onto the ocean, where she would serve her husband breakfast. To complete her fantasy, she needed to see the interior of one of these homes.

It has to have large heavy dark wood furniture, and the floors, I guess, would be Mexican tile. And maybe some kind of mosaic—the staircase will have mosaic tile on the front face of the steps. But what about the bathrooms? I can't picture them.

"Daniel, stop, there's an open house sign. We could go in."

"Naomi, I'm driving. There's cars behind me. I can't just stop." A few blocks later, he conceded, "If you really want, I can turn around and we can go see the place."

Soon they were walking around an estate that was on the market for over one million dollars. After the realtor had looked them up and down, she told them, "Go ahead, look around for yourselves. I have paperwork to do."

After surveying the first floor, they walked to the back which offered a view of the ocean. "Naomi, I think it's time we talk about what to expect for a salary if—and I mean if—I get this position."

"Daniel, I know we can't buy something like this. It's just fun to look." After a short pause, she asked, "Can we just look at the bathrooms?"

A quick nod of his head was enough—she charged up the stairs. The tile work in the master bathroom was dazzling, but she couldn't help but notice Daniel retreating inside himself. She walked over to where he sat, on the ledge of the gigantic bathtub. "What's the matter? What'd I do?"

"It's not you. It's me."

Back in their rented Chevrolet, they agreed to park the car and walk alongside the beach. As he drove, Naomi chided herself for how insensitive she had been. Tomorrow was his interview with the selection committee of Temple Beth Shalom. She was so infatuated with Daniel that the thought of anyone rejecting him was unfathomable to her—but obviously not to him.

Their shoes off and walking in the sand, she apologized. "I'll live in a tent as long as it's with you. As for the interview, I'm sure they'll want you. Sylvia's brother said they were already. . ."

"My-omi, listen, it's not whether I get the position or not. It's more about if I get the position, will I do well? Will I please God? And will I help people to not just say the *Shema*, but to mean it and live it?"

He had already gone into the lobby and retrieved a cup of coffee. Now he could awaken her.

"Oh, Daniel, thank you."

"Let's read from the *Siddur* again this morning. Together."

"You sure you can trust me? I don't want to be a distraction."

"I already did some time alone, honey. I especially needed to this morning. But I want you on the same page with me, literally I guess."

She was thrilled to feel his need for her. The only concern she had was having enough time to fix herself up before they left for his interview.

He took her hand and led her out to the balcony. "No sharing of the *tallit* this time, okay?"

Laughing, she told him, "Of course."

Studying his facial expression as he turned pages in his *Siddur*, she placed her hand on his. "Don't be nervous. You told me yesterday all you wanted was . . ."

"His Divine Providence. That's why I thought we could start by reading from here." He pointed to where he wanted her to read. "Please, would you read it for us?"

"The fear of the Lord is the beginning of knowledge." She looked up at him. "Would you chant this for us? In Hebrew?"

Once finished, he told her, "Irwin had taught all of us in his *havurah* that after we recite our prayer thanking God for His blessings, we should ask 'Who am I?' and more importantly ask God, 'Who are You?'" Naomi's face beamed. "I knew you'd like that. We'll reflect on that in the car. We need to get moving."

The drive was eye-popping scenic. The houses seemed to get more extravagant the further north they travelled. Once in the city limits of Boca, she was doing all she could to suppress her oohs and aaahs.

Fifteen minutes before his scheduled appointment, they arrived at a white-washed limestone building, appearing twice the size of the *shul* in Brooklyn Heights. It exuded the tropical air one would expect, tall royal palm trees spaced with precision all along the front. Under the extremely high-arched entrance was latticework of more limestone with a shimmering Jewish star consisting of inlaid glass mosaic tiles.

Daniel said, "Let's drive around the neighborhood for a few minutes. I don't want to be early."

She relished the idea—this opulent neighborhood might soon be theirs. Yet for his sake she suppressed her enthusiasm and drolly answered, "Oh, if you insist."

Her humor seemed to help bring him back to his usual casual and confident manner. The homes were quite lovely, a bit less expensive than what she had been ogling the last few days.

"My-omi, this is great. They almost look affordable. And we'll need to live in walking distance of the Temple—we're not orthodox, but I still think . . ."

She told him how the congregants in Ellenville would all park their cars at the bottom of the hill and pretend to have *schlepped* all the way from their homes for service. "I'm not making fun of them, Daniel . . . well, I guess I was. I'm sorry."

"I don't blame you. And I don't want to invite that kind of hypocrisy here, or wherever we end up." He reached across the car seat and took hold of her hand. "You're going to help me with this. If ever you see me guilt-tripping people, or anything that's not sincere, you're going to tell me. Okay?"

Daniel began pulling into the first parking space he saw, but Naomi alerted him. "Daniel, it says 'reserved for rabbi.' You're not there yet, Rabbi Cantor."

He pulled their rented car into an appropriate guest parking space, and they followed the small sign which led them to the office. The receptionist, a chunky middle-aged woman, after inspecting both of them from every angle, directed them to go down the hall and look for the second door on the right. Naomi's intuition told her the middle-aged woman liked what she saw in Daniel, way too much.

The door to the conference room was open and immediately upon seeing the couple, a gentleman in his late 70s or possibly early 80s, walked up to them.

"Thank you for coming, Rabbi Cantor." Suddenly realizing he had neglected Naomi, he extended his hand to her. "Forgive me, Mrs. Cantor—thank you, as well." With his hand he indicated for them to take a seat. "My name is Marvin Berman. I'm the Chair for our committee."

Daniel smiled at the four people gathered around the table and pulled out a chair for Naomi. "My wife and I appreciate your taking time to meet with us."

A frail woman sitting to the right of Marvin, in a loud voice told Daniel, "You're going to have to talk up. Marvin's hearing aid never works right." She glared at Marvin. "We keep telling him—"

A barrel-chested man stood up and demanded, "Doris, enough." Doris fumed and sulked while he turned to Daniel and Naomi. He chuckled and said, "You two must be thinking, *oy vey*, we must've walked into the wrong place." His chuckle now turned into a loud guffaw.

Doris scolded back, "Jerry, sit down and shut up."

Daniel grabbed Naomi's hand under the table and gave it a playful yet desperate squeeze. He then stood and addressed the Temple's selection committee. "We met with your current rabbi, Rabbi Moskowitz, last week. He gave us a little background." Looking at Marvin, he said, "Rabbi Moskowitz praised your faithful service to the *shul*."

Naomi tugged on Daniel's arm and whispered, "I don't think he can hear you."

Raising his voice, Daniel repeated. He then smiled toward Doris. "And Doris, the Rabbi spoke of your . . . well, let me see if I remember correctly . . . I believe it was your delicious honey cake?"

Doris gushed, "Rabbi Cantor, I'll have to make some for you and your lovely wife." Like a bashful schoolgirl, she dropped her eyes and grinned. "It's a recipe from my mother's mother."

Jerry lowered himself back into his chair. "He's hired. I like him already. So, let's go get something to eat."

"Excuse me," Marvin shouted while trying to lift himself up from his chair. Pressing down hard on the table, he came to a semi-standing position. "I'm still the Chairman of this Committee."

Jerry muttered an apology.

Marvin shakily sank back down into his seat. "Rabbi Cantor, we have some questions to ask you and then we want you to feel free to ask us any questions you have." He turned to Naomi. "Feel free, Mrs. Cantor, to ask us any questions you may have as well."

Jerry jumped right in. "I'll ask the first question. Tell us a little about yourself."

Another gentleman, with red hair and in his 40s, had been silent until now. He confronted Jerry, "We're not supposed to ask questions like that, too open-ended. How many times you've been told that?"

Doris waved several sheets of paper at the men. "We were given these for a reason. All of you hush, and I'll begin with the first question." She held the paper in front of her, almost touching her nose. "What led you to choose the rabbinate as a career?" She shook her head in disgust at the men and asked, "Now, what was so hard about doing that?"

Daniel's mouth was open ready to answer Doris' question when the red-headed gentleman broke in, turning to Daniel and Naomi. "Rabbi and Mrs. Cantor, it's a pleasure to meet you. I'm Jay, Jay Marcus. I'll be surprised if you don't want to turn tail and run, but just in case you don't, I would be glad to hear your answer."

"Thank you, Jay. This is an important . . ." Daniel stopped and asked Marvin, "Please, let me know if I'm speaking loud enough for you." Marvin nodded and smiled in gratitude, waving his hand in a motion to continue. "This is an important question, the most important one, I think."

Daniel recounted his parents' history of surviving the Holocaust, and his ensuing passion to keep their Jewish heritage alive. "And we owe devotion to the One who sustained us as a people—do we not? The Germans tried to wipe us out, but now I worry that we will finish the job ourselves. If we don't preserve the religion we were given on Mt. Sinai, then will we not fade into a mere mention in the history books? We have been given the yoke of the law as an honor and it is my hope to inspire others to love the Lord with all their heart."

Marvin glanced toward Doris, pulled out a handkerchief from his pocket and gave it to her. She, however, was not the only one at the table moved to tears by Daniel's words. Only Jerry was dry-eyed.

Jerry demanded, "Doris, what's the next question on your sheet? Let's get on with it."

The paper shook in Doris' hands. "What have been some of your most positive experiences as a rabbi?"

"Excuse me, Doris," Marvin interjected. "Let's amend this as our friend is still so young." He turned to Daniel. "Please tell us what was the most positive experience you have had as a rabbinical student, or perhaps as an associate rabbi?"

"During my time in seminary, being part of a *havurah*, I'd have to say was the most positive for me. We would meet in a man's home and there would be praying together, reading from the Torah portion and then we would have free and open discussion. It was—"

"You realize that's not something Temple Beth Shalom would go for, don't you?"

"Jerry, he's simply answering the question, all right?"

"I'm stating the obvious, Jay?"

Daniel cleared his throat which effectively stopped the bickering as the eyes were again turned toward him. "Even if it were not in the home, why couldn't that kind of informal back and forth discussion still be welcomed? I believe it could."

Doris turned to Marvin and nudged his arm. "I like this young man. I'll ask the next question." Marvin gestured his approval with a simple nod. Holding the paper with less shaking now, she asked, "What, Rabbi, is your approach to working with interfaith couples?"

"Excellent question. Again, my first thought, or I should say my first priority, is to preserve us as Jews. The more tolerant we become about intermarrying, the more we lose our distinction as a unique people. If a member of Temple Beth Shalom wanted to marry a Gentile, I would ask that the non-Jew consider conversion. This would add to our race, not diminish it. And I would want to be careful we were not so tolerant that we ended up encouraging conversion in the other direction, if you know what I mean. We do not want ever to be tolerant of a Jew converting to their religion."

Naomi realized she had never heard him quite so intense about anything in the past. She was not sure what this was stirring up in her, but could see the others were quite impressed with his conviction and ability to articulate it.

Jerry suddenly turned his attention onto the candidate's wife. "Mrs. Cantor," he asked, "what are your feelings about what your husband just stated?"

With this first opportunity to address the committee, she chose to fall back on her acting skills. "My father always told me," with her father's gruff voice she continued, "if you make friends with a Gentile, don't ever forget all they want to do is convert you."

Seemed it worked—they found her entertaining. Even Daniel was laughing. Again, the odd man out was Jerry, who broke up the levity of the moment. "You know Jay here married a *shiksa*."

Jay pulled his chair out, making a sharp scraping sound on the floor. His fists clenched and his arms cocked into a combative stance, he moved toward Jerry. The others held their breath and sat straight up in their chairs.

Jay, as if policing himself, relaxed his body, sat down and pulled his chair back in. "I'm not giving him the satisfaction." He looked directly at Daniel. "Rabbi, I am proud . . . never mind what he just said . . . but I'm proud to tell you my wife Sandy is now a Jew. She went through the classes, took the *mikveh*, and today she's a better Jew than I am."

Daniel reached across the table and shook Jay's hand. "She must make you very proud. I hope one day I'll meet her."

After learning the couple would be catching a flight back to New York tomorrow morning, Jay suggested the committee consider giving a stipend to the couple. This would allow them to change their airplane reservations and stay an extra day, or perhaps two. After all, they were taking time away from their honeymoon to meet with them. If they stayed tomorrow and into Sunday, they would be able to attend *Shabbat* at their temple tomorrow.

In an unexpected show of generosity, Jerry said, "Let's put them up here in Boca, at that fancy resort."

Once the committee agreed to Jay's suggestion, he turned to Daniel and Naomi. "Rabbi Moskowitz and Barbara are flying in today. This way you'll get to see each other."

Before accepting their offer, Daniel turned toward Naomi. With a smile and a nod, she gave her go-ahead. He told the committee, "Thank you. We'll see you tomorrow."

On their way out, Marvin promised to contact them at their hotel in Miami and give them the address of the one in Boca where they would be staying. "And maybe before you leave we would have an answer for you."

About to walk into the parking lot, Doris ran after them. "You're both darling. I hope you'll be our rabbi soon. We need someone like you."

Daniel bit his upper lip as he scanned the parking lot. "It does start at 9:15, doesn't it? Isn't that what they told us?"

Naomi looked all around, confirming they were in the main parking area. "The sign in the front, when you pulled in, it said service at 9:15."

Daniel parked the car, yet left the engine running. "There are only four cars . . ."

"And one is in the Rabbi's parking space." She pulled the rear-view mirror toward her and asked, "You don't mind, do you?"

"Your lipstick looks fine, but I don't know who besides me is going to see it anyway. The place is empty."

"C'mon, it's my wifely duty to encourage you." She held up an imaginary magic wand and told him, "Poof, be encouraged."

"Funny, Naomi, very funny."

"No, seriously, c'mon, let's go in. You know how at the *shul* in Brooklyn people wander in when they're good and ready. No one hardly ever comes when the service is supposed to start."

He turned off the motor and pulled the key out of the ignition. With one last tug on his tie, he came around to her side and opened the door. While doing so, they noticed two cars pull into the parking lot.

Daniel stopped a few feet from the front door of the sanctuary and opened a dark blue velvet pouch. He pulled out his prayer shawl as well as a blue satin yarmulke. Once both were in place, he took out a *tallit* clip which held in place his shawl.

Naomi held back the urge to hug him and smother him with kisses. *Totally not kosher.*

Inside the sanctuary they noticed Rabbi Moskowitz seated in the front row. They were about to walk over to him when a woman walked up to the *bimah* and began the service. *She must be the cantor.*

People slowly sauntered in, greeting each other in normal conversational voices. They made no effort to lower their volume and the Cantor seemed unfazed, continuing to perform in a nasal monotone. Many times her chanting faded away, as if she were simply bored and had no motivation to press on. Then the momentum would pick back up as she persevered with her droning.

Naomi pressed her lips to Daniel's ears. "You're going to have to be the Cantor along with being the Rabbi."

He reached into his pocket for a pen, scribbled something on the bulletin handed to them when they entered, and passed the note on to her. She read, "What do you mean me? I'm going to teach you to be the Cantor."

She grabbed his shoulders and forced him to face her full front. She mocked a look of shock. Thankfully they were able to restrain themselves from roaring with laughter—only a few quiet giggles escaped.

About forty minutes into the three-hour service less than a third of the seats in the sanctuary were filled. And all that were seated were silver-haired, many of them having entered with the aid of their walkers.

Rabbi Moskowitz seemed somewhat enlivened by their presence as he would often look towards them and smile. Both Daniel and Naomi had the impression if they were not there, he would have appeared as bored as the Cantor and the congregants.

When the service finished, all were invited to walk across the hall to where lunch was being served. Rabbi Moskowitz walked over to the couple and asked, "Please be my guest, sit at my table. Unfortunately, Barbara was too exhausted after our trip to be here."

Once seated, the Rabbi told them, "I hear they're giving you two nights at the Boca Raton Resort & Club. I hope you know they're not usually this generous. They never did anything like that for Barb and I." Making sure no one was in earshot, he then asked Daniel, "Would you take the position? Because sure sounds like they want you to."

Daniel turned to Naomi and arched one eyebrow. Her turn to write a note. She reached into his pocket, took out his pen and wrote on a napkin, "Do you want this?"

He wrote back, "Mrs. Cantor, I'm asking you. Can you handle this?"

She crumpled the napkin and threw it into her purse, smiled, and nodded.

A short time later, alone in their car, she said, "I grew up with parents older than everyone else's. People would make fun of me and say 'What are they? Your grandparents?' I think it's given me a special fondness for older people, but most of all, Rabbi Dan, you can do something exciting here."

"It's going to be a challenge."

She nodded vigorously.

"But you're saying we should go for it?"

Nodding even more vigorously, she added, "But get rid of that Cantor. Please."

It was now his time to nod vigorously.

PART II

Chapter 15

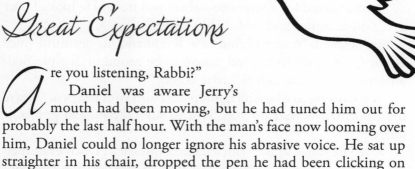

Great Expectations

*A*re you listening, Rabbi?"

Daniel was aware Jerry's mouth had been moving, but he had tuned him out for probably the last half hour. With the man's face now looming over him, Daniel could no longer ignore his abrasive voice. He sat up straighter in his chair, dropped the pen he had been clicking on and off and looked directly into Jerry's eyes.

"It's been a year, Rabbi, and still no new members."

Doris's shrill voice interrupted Jerry's tirade. "And we've lost more members, too."

"We took you on knowing you were young and inexperienced," Jerry continued. "We had hoped maybe you'd have some new ideas." He sat back in his chair and folded his arms across his chest. "Yet everything is still the same and our congregation is dwindling away."

Doris again chimed in. "And to top it off, you're getting the highest salary this Temple ever paid a rabbi."

Daniel stood up. "My salary was raised when it was agreed that I would be your Cantor as well as your Rabbi."

Jay, seated across from Daniel at this long conference table, got up from his chair. He walked halfway around the room and stood beside Daniel. "You know what this sounds like, don't you?" He waited momentarily for a reply, but received none. "It reminds me of how the Israelites treated Moses. Complain, complain, complain. We want results and we want them now. No more of this manna garbage."

Mildred, a dark-haired woman in her early fifties, the newest member of the Temple's Board, took a sip of her coffee. She then spoke for the first time since the meeting began two hours ago. "Maybe it's somewhat up to us to get new members. I admit I haven't made any effort to invite anyone to our *shul*. Have any of you?"

Daniel waited for a response—there was none. He looked over at Mildred, smiled and said, "Thank you."

She beamed. "And with our new Rabbi and his beautiful voice as our Cantor, we have good reason to be proud of Temple Beth Shalom—proud enough to invite others."

Doris, sitting to Marvin's right, poked him with her pen. "You're the chairman—what do you have to say? What—cat got your tongue?"

When he stared at her with a dazed expression, Doris examined his left ear. She shook her head at him in exasperation and told everyone, "Hold your horses." She reached straight up into Marvin's ear and turned his hearing device on.

Marvin jumped up and cried out, "What? What's going on?"

"I make a motion to elect a new chairman," Doris shouted.

Jerry's hand shot up. "I second it."

Daniel turned to Jay, still standing alongside him. "Help me here. I don't want to lose my temper the way Moses did, but I'm tempted, very tempted."

Reminding himself Moses never made it into the promised land, Daniel took a deep breath and walked over to Marvin. With a firm hand, he patted him on the shoulder and spoke in a loud voice. "From what I can see, Marvin has done an admirable job. He's served as your Chairman for a very long time."

Daniel bent down and spoke directly into the elderly man's ear. "We want to thank you for your service to the Temple."

His courtesy seemed to shame all gathered, even Jerry. Their faces were now bent down, staring at their reflection on the highly polished wooden table.

Grateful for the apparent change in tenor among the group, Daniel walked back to his seat. "I understand your disappointment, but may I suggest, hiring a new rabbi and having all these wonderful expectations, it's somewhat like a marriage."

Jerry lifted his left hand to his face, making a big show of checking his wrist watch and rolling his eyes. "*Oy vey*, the Rabbi's giving us a sermon now."

Mildred, sitting to Jerry's right, reached over and pushed his hand down. "Jerry, please, I want to hear what Rabbi Cantor has to say."

Daniel continued. "It's all about expectations. And commitment as well. So when the bumps in the road happen, whether with a marriage or with breaking in a new rabbi, I believe we need to work through the problems." He reached for the pitcher sitting in the middle of the table and poured himself a glass of water.

Mildred smiled toward Daniel and fluttered her eyelids. "I would have gotten that for you, Rabbi."

"Thank you, Mildred. You remind me of my wife. She's always looking to see how she can help others. Now as for membership, I know you are all concerned, as am I."

"Ticket sales for the High Holidays are way down from last year," Jerry informed him.

At this point, all were anxious to finish up with this meeting. A final resolution was agreed upon quickly. All would make an effort to spread the word about Temple Beth Shalom's vibrant young rabbi and a committee would be formed to brainstorm ways to promote the High Holidays, possibly offering a discount for all who purchase their tickets up until a week before Rosh Hashanah.

Jay added a final suggestion. "And how about if they can buy for a group, maybe twelve or more, then they get a special group price?"

"Fine, fine," they all mumbled as they gathered together their belongings and rushed out.

This is what I went to seminary for? Help me, O Mighty One, to please You.

Daniel drove his 1975 Volkswagen into the parking space along-side Naomi's bronze Chevrolet Malibu. He shook his head. *Why can't she park straight? Two white lines, all she has to do is line her car up between them.*

He turned the ignition off and threw the keys into his pocket. He was about to tug on the door handle when he hesitated and slammed his hands over his forehead. He must get control of his feelings before walking in the door. *I can't take this out on her.*

Halfway up the stairs to their second-floor apartment, he remembered the Chinese food he had picked up along the way. He trudged back down the stairs and retrieved the bag filled with take-out containers.

"Hello Rabbi."

"Oh, hi, Charlie. How you doing?"

"Rabbi, would you tell your wife to stay inside her own space when she parks? It's hard when I park next to her, to park my van so it's straight. You know what I mean?"

"Yes, of course. Good night, Charlie."

"Hey, Rabbi, I didn't mean to upset you."

"You didn't. Have a good night." Back up the stairs, trying to keep the paper containers upright, he recalled Naomi's sheer delight when he surprised her with the shiny new Malibu, exactly the same model and color she had cooed over during their honeymoon.

Immediately after receiving the bump up in his salary for performing cantorial duty, he had driven to the car dealership. When he presented her with it, she jumped up and down, hugging him over and over again—just like he knew she would.

He turned and looked back down at her crookedly parked car. He shook his head once again, but this time he did so with laughter. Only his free-spirited wife could park like this.

At least she hasn't crashed it.

Standing in front of their apartment, he fiddled with the keys while still trying to keep the food containers balanced. Daniel was the perfect height to look through the front door window. There was Naomi standing in front of the open refrigerator door.

He knew what that picture represented. Poor baby, she hadn't a clue what to make for dinner. "Nothing jumped out at me," she would tell him. The Chinese food was meant to be a sweet surprise, but now it would quickly turn into a rescue mission—all the sweeter. His keys tapped on the window.

Naomi immediately turned around, quickly ran to the door and flung it open. She reached out for his paper sack. "I'll take that." She ran to the kitchen countertop and placed the bag down. "Chinese?"

"Thought it would be a treat for us." He loosened his tie and threw off his jacket. "Be back after I change."

To Naomi it was like poof and he was gone. She blinked away the tears starting to form. *He knew where I went today—did he just forget?* Maybe he was simply getting tired of her running to the doctor almost every month. Nausea in the morning—wasn't that what they meant by morning sickness? Okay, maybe she wasn't nauseous every morning, but once or twice she had felt queasy.

And each time, she returned with the same answer: negative. But maybe next time . . .

Daniel reappeared. Barefoot, in his faded jeans and Bohemian Nights T-shirt, he stifled a yawn. "I'm so sorry, honey. I've had a rough day and forgot—how'd it go today?"

"Negative again."

He opened the silverware drawer and took out forks and spoons. "Well, maybe next time." Reaching into the pantry, he took out two glasses. "What do you want to drink?"

Could he be any less caring? She bit her lip and turned away from him. While removing the containers from the paper bag, she said, "Why don't you admit it? You want it to be negative each time." When sauce from one of the food containers leaked onto her hands, she cried, "Oh, great."

"It's only been a year, Naomi. Most couples don't have a baby right away, especially when the husband has a new job—especially a stressful one."

She walked over to the sink and ran water over her hands, then stormed out of the kitchen and into the dining and living room combo.

He remained in the kitchen, the drinking glasses in his hands, and stared at her from the pass-through. Maybe another day he could deal with her irrational behavior, but not tonight. This was the last thing he needed. "Can you knock off with the dramatics? I'm tired, Naomi. Can we just sit out on the terrace and enjoy the food I went out of my way to bring home?"

She walked up to the pass-through from her side and stared back at him. "You said we were going to keep kosher. I thought you were—"

"What?"

"Daniel, we need God's blessings if I'm going to get pregnant. Maybe you don't care, but I do."

He wrinkled his forehead and shook his head in confusion. "So, you figure if we keep kosher, then we—"

"Yes, yes I do, Daniel." *Tell him the truth, Naomi. It's because you're being punished—it has nothing to do with him. God will never ...*

He could no longer suppress the frustration that had built throughout his day. He held out his hands, the fingers and palms vertically indicating a barrier. "Stop—stop with all the pressure. Why are you pushing so hard about this baby thing? Stop already."

Her hands went up over her ears. "No, you stop—stop yelling at me." Walking toward their bedroom, her eyes landed on Aunt Luba's wedding present hanging up on their wall. Naomi grabbed the framed picture, yanked it off the wall and smashed it on the dining room table. She fled into the bedroom and locked the door.

After a few stunned moments, Daniel walked over to the picture. It had been their favorite of all the wedding gifts. His Aunt had lovingly framed a beautiful Marc Chagall print of a bride and groom in a loving embrace set in a rich blue background, with the words "I am my beloved and my beloved is mine" written in calligraphy and superimposed over the print.

Daniel went into their laundry room, brought out a broom and swept away the pieces of glass. Once certain the print itself had no shards of glass, he rolled it up as if it were a scroll, wrapped a plastic bag around it, and hid it in the closet.

While he cleaned the remnants from what she shamefully considered her temper tantrum, Naomi sat on the floor in a corner of the bedroom. He would never know the pain she experienced going to the gynecologist. Having to fill out the form which asked how many pregnancies, how many deliveries, how many miscarriages, and how many abortions. Since it was none of their business, she felt no compunction in lying.

Lying. That's the real sin—not whether we keep kosher or not. Who am I trying to kid? I'll never be good enough. And now she was driving away the man she loved so much, and who was so good to her. The isolation was suffocating; the hideous secret from her past was effectively killing any hope for her future.

Like a lifeline came the tapping on the door, along with Daniel's soft voice. "Naomi?"

She scooted up off the floor and unlocked the door. He opened wide his arms and she gratefully accepted their shelter. "Daniel, I'm sorry."

Soon they were sitting out on their terrace eating the Chinese food, a little cold by now, but still tasty.

"I never asked about your day, Daniel. How'd it go with the Board?"

Whether it was to protect her or simply because he was not ready to relive the day for himself, he told her, "Fine."

That night both lay in the same bed, but in their separate spheres of isolation.

Naomi awakened to the annoying sound of the alarm clock. She waited, and waited some more. A pillow folded over her ears might drown out the noise, but why wasn't Daniel turning it off already?

Squinting over to his side, she discovered he wasn't there. She let go of the pillow and sat up in the bed—in time to hear Daniel calling from the living room.

"Naomi, please turn it off."

She climbed across the bed, reached over to his nightstand, and turned the clock this way and that. *How do you shut this thing off?* Early in their marriage they had agreed, since he was definitely the more responsible party in the morning, the clock would always be placed on his nightstand.

"I'm sorry, I can't find—oh never mind, I found it."

Daniel finally heard the screeching stop and yelled, "Thank you—." No need to yell, for there she stood in her oversized T-shirt and bare feet, staring at him.

"Why are you up so early?" Her hand flew up to her mouth as she caught sight of her husband. Sitting on the couch, he appeared swallowed up by a mound of crumpled yellow paper.

He explained, "Sermon for *Shabbat.*"

"But, Daniel, it's Friday already."

"Thanks, Naomi, like I really needed you to tell me." He smirked, but when he saw her turn to walk away, he quickly said, "Honey, I'm really sorry."

"It's just usually you have it all written out by Thursday at the latest."

"Haven't you noticed, for the last month it's never before Thursday? And it's been getting later and later on Thursday."

Not only was the paper crumpled up, but her dear husband also appeared crumpled. She sat beside him and pushed the balls of discarded notes out of the way.

Kissing him, she suggested, "Maybe you could get away with telling the congregation the dog ate your homework." He was not laughing. "I'm only saying that because you look like such a sad little boy right now."

"Naomi, it's becoming harder and harder to find the inspiration."

"We haven't done any prayers together in a while either."

"I know. But look, I have to get back to this."

She could take a hint. She stood up and stepped toward the kitchen. "Can I make you breakfast?"

"Sure."

Soon she proudly brought out a breakfast tray with one of his favorites, a combination of matzoh and eggs.

He had no appetite, but how could he hurt her feelings? "*Matzoh brei*, my favorite.*"* He forced himself to eat while he scribbled, crumpled and tossed. "What about you? Where's yours?"

She stepped back into the kitchen. "Oh, I'm just going to have some cereal."

"Would you mind getting my appointment book? There's something I think I'm supposed to do today, but I'm not sure what."

She quickly found it on his nightstand and opened it on her way back to Daniel. "It's a hospital visit with Mrs. Rabinowitz."

"Oh, no, that's all the way out in Palm Beach somewhere."

"Daniel, I'll go. I'd be glad to."

An hour later, she was dressed and ready to go. Daniel walked to the door and hugged her goodbye. "Thank you, honey."

"What's tonight's sermon going to be on?"

She would have to ask, wouldn't she? "Okay, here it is—the Torah portions for this week speak about not worshipping the sun, the moon and the hosts of heaven. I'm tempted to do a sermon on why people should not be reading their horoscope."

Naomi took a few steps back from him. "Why do I feel a finger pointing at me?"

He held her hands and gently told her, "Reading your horoscope is wrong, Naomi."

"Then why haven't you told me this before?" She pulled her hands away. "Every morning you see me reading mine and you've never said anything."

"You're right, I should have told you. And this convinces me, this will be part of my sermon tonight." Daniel walked back toward the couch with determination.

Naomi followed after him. "You gotta be kidding? The women especially will kill you."

"If I hold back saying everything that could offend these people, then there won't be anything left I can say. Is this why I chose to be a rabbi? To put people to sleep?"

He turned back around to face her and again took her hands in his. "Go. I need to work on this. Drive carefully."

She was about to close the door behind her when she heard, "My-omi, you'll be a delight to Mrs. Rabinowitz . Thank you for going."

She hung the strap from her pocketbook on the doorknob, ran back into the house and flung herself into Daniel's arms. "Oooh, *matzoh brei* mouth. Yum."

The walks to and from Temple Beth Shalom had become a special time for both Daniel and Naomi. For Daniel, the walk to the Temple gave him time to discuss with his wife the sermon he had prepared. He relished her input. And the walk back home, that was a time to let down.

The walk to the *shul* this particular evening gave Naomi the first opportunity to report on her hospital visit. "You know what she told me? When she saw me walk into her room, she said, 'Mrs. Cantor, how nice, you came with your husband. I'm so glad.' Then she looks behind me, cranes her neck to see out the door and down the hallway. 'Where's the Rabbi?' When she heard I came by myself, you should have seen the look on her face. I'm telling you, Daniel, I know what she was thinking."

Always enjoying Naomi's comedic performance, he willingly played the straight man. "And what, Mrs. Cantor, was she thinking?"

"She was thinking 'what am I, chopped liver? He sends only his wife.'"

"My-omi, you're the best." He picked her up in his arms and swung her around."

"Daniel, put me down," she yelled while being flung about. "What if someone sees us?"

He put her down and affectionately ruffled her hair. "So, what happened after that? Mrs. Rabinowitz kick you out?"

"No, it actually went okay after that. I saw she had a deck of cards on . . . what do you call that adjustable hospital thing on wheels . . . they bring over to your bed so you can eat on it?"

"The adjustable hospital thing on wheels they br—"

"Very funny. I've told you, I'm the one tells the jokes. Anyway, she was thrilled when I offered to play cards with her."

"What game?"

"Gin rummy. It's a good thing we didn't play for money. The woman may be on heavy sedation, but she's one mean card player." Without a beat, she changed the subject. "You still haven't told me about how it went working on your message?"

"I went to the swimming pool after you left. It always seems to clear my head, and then I was able to finish it."

"But are you happy with it?"

With a mischievous grin, he said, "Yes. Can't say anyone else will be, but I am."

Approaching the *shul's* front entrance, she stretched her hand up to his head, grabbed a tuft of his hair and yanked it out from under his yarmulke.

"Naomi, what are you doing?"

"I like your cowlick—it suits your personality."

Taking his *tallit* out from its velvet pouch, he informed her, "You're a brat, you know that? One I'm wildly in love with."

The first to arrive was Mildred. "*Shabbat Shalom*, Rabbi."

She was immediately followed by Marvin and his wife. "*Shabbat Shalom*, Rabbi."

Daniel and Naomi now separated to individually greet each of the faithful few. "*Shabbat Shalom.*"

Throughout the Friday evening service, Naomi perceived something different in Daniel. Tonight, when performing his cantorial segments of the liturgy, he almost sounded like the Daniel of a year ago. His deep melodic voice was carried aloft by a reverence for the words he chanted and passion for those listening to also be sincerely worshipful.

He should go swimming more often.

Then it was time for the message. As Daniel had mentioned earlier in the day to Naomi, the evening's Torah portion included scripture from Deuteronomy—the Israelites were not to worship the sun, moon or the hosts of heaven.

"I find myself wondering," Daniel began, "why, when Moses made it so clear to us not to do this, do we simply say 'no' to God. I will not embarrass you by asking how many of you read your horoscope—dare I say religiously every day."

Naomi looked around aware of the people who now squirmed in their seats, while she heard others clearing their throats. And Daniel, standing in front of his congregation, was keenly aware of how many chose to avert their eyes from his.

He was hitting home; he was doing his job. The biggest reward at this time was seeing his wife's smile. She understood what his job truly was; after all, she was a rabbi's wife. The look which transpired between them at that moment confirmed it.

"I know some of you are upset at my . . . well, upsetting your apple cart. But, please, think about this: When you recite the Shema, when you say we are to love the Lord with all our heart, shouldn't you show it by obeying what He tells you? I mean, wives, you don't want your husbands to tell you they love you, and then not obey you." A well-timed smirk made it clear this was to be taken as a joke.

Naomi surveyed the crowd. *Good job, Daniel.* Not only did he get a few chuckles from them, but it seemed they lost their irritation with their brash young rabbi.

In closing, Daniel invited the congregation to join him for *oneg*. "We have some wonderful brisket tonight. Our very own Goldie

Rosen brought it for us. Thank you, Goldie." He stepped off the *bimah*, casually mentioning, "I'm starving."

Once seated at a table, Daniel was about to bite into Goldie's wonderful brisket when Jerry approached his table. "Rabbi, several of us were talking, and we don't think it's your business. A small thing like people reading what the stars say for them, some people need that kind of thing. In case you haven't noticed Rabbi, we're old. You can't expect us to change now."

Naomi asked, "Daniel, would you mind if I answered Mr. Cooper?"

"No, honey, of course not." He was intrigued—what was his wife up to?

"Mr. Cooper, I'm glad my husband said what he did tonight. I've been guilty of reading my horoscope with my coffee every morning. But having the Rabbi point out that this is wrong, that God doesn't want us to do this, I'm going to stop. We should all want to be good people, the best Jews we can be. Shouldn't we?"

Jerry Cooper had no comeback. With everyone listening, Daniel told him, "She'd make a pretty good rabbi herself, wouldn't she?"

On their walk home that night, he asked, "Did I surprise you? I know you said not to tackle the horoscope business, but, Naomi, I had to. I'm telling others to obey the Lord, so if I feel He's telling me to do something, like deliver a certain message, then I'd be disobedient if I basically chickened out. I can't and I won't do that."

"Stop getting all worked up. I was on your side. Couldn't you see that?"

He pulled her close to his side and gave her a deep kiss. One of the members of the *shul* drove by and shouted out, "Now stop it, you lovebirds."

Walking up the stairs to their apartment, Daniel asked, "Were you serious? Will you really give up reading the horoscope?"

"I . . ." She paused as they entered their apartment. "You want some iced tea? I have some of that raspberry kind you like."

"I'd love it. Give me a minute to change."

"Me, too."

Soon they were in their denim shorts and T-shirts, sitting out on the terrace and sipping tea. Time for her to answer Daniel's question.

"Here's the thing. People do things for a reason. I want to know what to expect before the day starts, so I turn to this silly horoscope in the newspaper."

Daniel's feet had been resting on an ottoman. He now brought them back down to the floor and leaned forward, resting his elbows on his knees. "Go ahead?"

Naomi put her drink down on the round glass table and assumed the same posture as her husband's. "If I'm not to do something, then it helps if I understand why—you know, why I'm not supposed to do it."

"Go on."

"I remember when you had the interview for here—you said, even if you didn't have a *havurah* in the home, you could still have a kind of informal back and forth discussion at the *shul* itself."

"I remember."

She placed her hands on his knees. "Discussion, Daniel. Asking maybe why they think God would tell them not to . . . what was it? . . . worship the stars. Stuff like that. People need to know why—I need to know why."

The following day, morning *Shabbat* service followed its traditional order, but to Naomi it was clear. Did anyone else feel it? Temple Beth Shalom's Rabbi was exceptionally energized.

When the time came for the sermon, rather than standing behind the podium, Daniel walked down the steps of the *bimah*. He made eye contact with each of the people gathered in the sanctuary, smiled, and greeted them by name.

"So," he laughed, "how many of you read your horoscope before coming this morning? I'll tell you, this was the first morning, I think, since we've been married that my wife hasn't looked at her horoscope before looking at me."

Daniel paused while laughter filled the sanctuary. "I'm not making fun of my wife—it's actually because of her we're going to do something different. She's a very smart lady, just in case any of you haven't noticed. She basically suggested we have a discussion—so I'm going to ask why you think God would, through Moses, tell us not to look to the stars for our future. Why do you think?"

When Naomi heard only some nervous titters, she stepped up to the plate. "I'm not sure. I figure if He tells me not to do it, it's for my good. But I'd like to know why. Can you tell us?"

He explained, "I believe the Lord wants us to trust in Him alone. We are to have no other God before Him, correct?"

Having apparently warmed up to this new open environment in their sanctuary, a handful of people voiced their agreement.

Daniel felt a rush of electricity—a *havurah* was taking place right here in the Temple. "God forbid, literally, we worship an idol, such as our astrological sign and from there get into our horoscope, or whatever other *mishegas*."

He then went back to the traditional close for service, again finishing by wishing everyone *Shabbat Shalom*.

It was unmistakable—Daniel and Naomi sensed a new enthusiasm among the congregants as they said their goodbyes. Daniel interrupted their walk home by suggesting, "Let's celebrate. I'd love a banana split. How about you?"

"Hot fudge peanut butter sundae for me."

They changed directions and headed toward Boca Raton's favorite ice cream parlor as Daniel wrapped his arm around Naomi's waist. "So, Mrs. Cantor, any other suggestions?"

"Yes."

Surprised by her empathetic tone, he stopped in his tracks and arched his eyebrow.

"Israel. We organize a trip to Israel with the synagogue."

Two hours and two thousand calories later, they returned to their apartment, still strategizing about a possible Israel trip.

He changed into his non-rabbi clothes, continuing to voice his excitement. "This can really bring a vitality to our membership. And, My-omi, imagine all of us, as a congregation observing *Shabbat* together in Jerusalem."

He had assumed she followed him into the bedroom, but when he did not hear a response to his remark, he turned to discover she was not there. He found her staring at the empty place on the wall where his Aunt's wedding present had been ever since they moved into this one-bedroom apartment a year ago.

He came from behind and enveloped his wife in his arms, kissing her neck. "We've got an exciting future ahead of us. Let's thank the Lord and pray the *Kedusha* together."

With wide-eyed delight, she turned around to him. "I've missed our doing this so much."

They walked out to their terrace and he placed his *tallit* over both their heads. Together they recited, "We sanctify Your Name in the world, just as Your Name is sanctified in the heavens. Your prophets wrote, 'And they called one to the other and said, Holy, holy, holy, Lord of hosts, the whole world is filled with your glory. Blessed is the glory of our God from His place. God shall reign forever, from generation to generation.' May God be praised."

Great expectations flooded their souls.

Naomi rejoiced knowing that soon would be Rosh Hashanah followed by Yom Kippur—the time to atone for her sin. If she could receive assurance of His forgiveness, then the past would be put to rest and a horoscope would not be needed to tell her future. It would be glorious. She didn't need a horoscope to tell her soon she would be pregnant.

Daniel rejoiced as he received confirmation in his heart. He was where God wanted him and the Almighty was pleased with Him. Daniel would be used to bring the Jewish people back to faithfulness in their God. There was a reason his parents had survived the Holocaust: God had a purpose for Stefan and Zofia's son.

Chapter 16

A Cord (Chord?) of Three Strands

N aomi found Daniel sitting on their sofa, once again lost in a sea of crumpled yellow paper. "Before breakfast, can we recite our blessing? It's been over a month."

He did not glance up but continued chewing his thumbnail. "You don't have to remind me. I know how long it's been."

"Ever since Yom Kippur—"

He still did not look up at her. "I said you don't have to remind me, Naomi."

Whining, I'm always whining these days. She went to the hall closet and grabbed her denim jacket. "I'm going out for a walk. Get your own breakfast." She reached for the keys dangling from a hook by the front door.

"Glad you're so understanding," he yelled as she slammed the door. *Yelling, I'm always yelling at her these days.*

There was a secluded area to the back of their apartment complex—a discovery she made when in a similar situation several months ago. A small lake provided a refuge, not only for her but also for white egrets, flocks of white ibises, a host of Muscovy ducks, and on a rare occasion a great blue heron.

Relieved to find she had her favorite spot all to herself, she leaned against a large banyan tree. As if having no will to remain standing, she slid downward until sitting on a small patch of grass.

What happened to her great expectations? Rosh Hashanah and Yom Kippur came and went, and still she had no assurance God had forgiven her sin.

And poor Daniel—it was like he had been thrown into the lion's den. The Board had been so cruel with Jerry coming up to him and announcing, "Congratulations, Rabbi, we set a new record for our High Holy Day services—this was the lowest attendance in our history."

And Naomi had to admit, no matter how hard she tried to be an encouragement, instead she whined and complained, filling him with discouragement. Daniel had continued his informal open discussion format, and she did her best to cheer him on, even when it seemed to generate very little dialog among the congregation.

The only real interest shown in the Temple's new Rabbi came from some of the women as they ogled him, especially Mildred. When Naomi warned her husband, he shrugged off her concern. "Naomi, she's old enough to be my mother."

She did get his attention, however, when she told him, "She came up to me, Daniel, and said, 'I hear your marriage is in trouble'." Daniel had been baffled until Naomi explained, "She said something about my not living up to your expectations. She said you told the Board this at one of their meetings."

He then put the pieces together. "Good grief, Naomi. She deliberately misconstrued what I said. I was comparing their expectations with having a new rabbi with the expectations one has with a new marriage."

Mildred's name topped off a new list the couple decided to compile: the "beware of" list.

Do I have to add my own name to that list? Did Daniel need to beware of his own wife? With a heavy sigh, she raised her head up to the heavens.

A stately heron flew above her and then chose to land right there at the edge of the lake. She watched as the bird stood motionless scanning for prey. With its majestic yet subtle blue-gray plumage, the bird made her heaviness vanish.

The sound of a twig crackling broke the stillness. Naomi turned around and found Daniel standing behind her.

Smiling, one finger to his lips, he pointed to the heron now beginning to wade belly-deep with long and deliberate steps. It may have been moving slowly, but in a split second it struck like lightning to grab a fish.

Naomi averted her eyes as the fish flailed about in the mouth of the bird. This reminded Daniel of how troubled Naomi became whenever the Torah readings described the animal sacrifices commanded of the Israelites.

He stooped down in front of her and opened wide his arms. Once she was resting in his protective embrace, he softly suggested, "Wanna go out for breakfast?"

They walked back to the apartment, arms wrapped around each other's waist. Naomi asked, "How's the message coming for tonight?"

He couldn't resist. "What do you think about something on Jonah and the whale?" Fending off her fists pummeling his chest, he laughed, "Will you stop?"

The pummeling stopped only because she was now pointing toward their front door. "Isn't it too early for the postman?"

"Definitely."

They quickened their steps and were able to make it in time to sign for an express mail delivery.

Daniel patiently placed the small box on the dining table; in contrast Naomi rushed to cut it open with a large steak knife.

"You're dangerous, girl." He picked up the box and clutched it to his chest, guarding it from his overly curious wife. "Let's wait—we'll bring it with us—how about brunch at Marti's Deli?"

He knew how to fight fire with fire, or in this case curiosity with curiosity. "Ooh, everybody's always talking about that place. They say their brunches are awesome. I've been dying to try it."

I could tell her they make a whale of an omelet.

From the outside the restaurant appeared to simply be a common storefront deli. Naomi insisted they try it anyway. Daniel parked the car with the caveat, "If it looks on the inside like it does on the outside, we're outta there."

His fears were dispelled. They had clearly found their Teresa's of Brooklyn Heights, right here in Boca Raton. The moment they entered, the owner and his staff welcomed them and placed them at a table by the window as they had requested. Drinks were brought to them almost immediately, coffee for her and raspberry iced tea for him.

"Cinnamon Almond French Toast for the lady and Challah French Toast for me," he soon told the waitress.

Before he was done handing the menus back to the waitress, Naomi grabbed a butter knife and reached for the box Daniel had placed on the table.

"Go ahead, honey. Have at it."

"Do you have any idea what it is?"

"How about you start with looking at the return address on the box?"

"Wow, I can't believe I hadn't thought of that."

"I'll save you the trouble. It's from Irwin." Chuckling at her look of astonishment, he said, "I was a little curious, too."

"But why would Irwin send us something?"

"Now curiosity is getting the best of me, too. Will you open it already?"

In a matter of moments, she was peering inside, with the box facing her and its open flap blocking his view. "It looks like photos," she told him.

By the time their food arrived, they were no longer sitting across from each other, but were sharing the same padded bench, sifting through the contents of the box: photos from the time Daniel enjoyed attending Irwin's *havurah*.

Pouring syrup on his French toast, he mused, "Wonder why Irwin would be mailing it to us now."

Naomi reached back into the box. "There was a note . . . here it is."

Reading it together they learned his friend had been cleaning out his basement in Long Island in preparation for a move to New Jersey.

One photo in particular caught Naomi's eye. "You never told me you play the guitar."

"Play*ed* . . . once upon a time."

"Was this your own guitar?" When he nodded, she asked, "Where'd it go?"

"I gave it to Ed. One day he was over at my apartment with Dana. He saw it over in a corner, gathering dust I might add. I couldn't help but notice, he couldn't stop staring at it, so I asked him if he wanted to play it. Naomi, he was good. He made better music with it than I ever did." Daniel shrugged his shoulder. "So I gave it to him."

"Do you miss it?"

"It was from a different time in my life. I can't allow myself to miss it."

For the rest of their breakfast, Naomi chewed on something more than her French Toast.

Naomi wanted to weep. All during Saturday's *Shabbat* service, she thought of the first service she and Daniel had sat through at Temple Beth Shalom. She recalled the lackluster performance of the Cantor, done as if by rote. She never would have believed her husband could sound so much the same.

Now the time came for him to step down from the *bimah* and invite an open dialog with those in attendance. *Oh, please, God, this time let the members start talking. Have mercy on my husband.*

"I am sure you read in the papers about the incident of anti-Semitism in Wisconsin this week," Daniel began. "This man hoped to kill as many of our people as he could. He went into a Jewish retirement home and somehow ended up shooting and killing five Gentiles and no Jews. How are we to process this? What are we to learn from it?"

Daniel paused briefly. "Are we too comfortable here in America? I think about what my parents went through . . . most of you know, I believe, they are Holocaust survivors. Do we ever consider that it could happen here? When my sister and I each turned ten, our birthday present from our parents was a passport. That's right. Their feeling was we should always be prepared. This would be a good lesson for Passover, wouldn't it? Yet at any time, we might be asked to make a quick exodus, just like the Jews had to do in Egypt. Think about it—are we too comfortable?"

When Jerry's hand shot up, Daniel and Naomi shared a quick surprised look with one another. "You know what I think?" Jerry stood up and told everyone, "Those Gentiles that were killed this week, that was God's intervention."

Daniel furrowed his eyebrows. "Excuse me?"

Naomi could not miss, even sitting several rows back, the clenching in Daniel's jaw.

"We're God's chosen people. He's not going to let anything happen to us," Jerry explained. "He protected the Jews at that nursing home and let the Gentiles get it instead."

The clenching became more pronounced and Naomi feared Daniel might say something he would later regret. She now stood to address the group. "I think it's dangerous to use that line of reasoning. Because if we did, then how would we explain about the Holocaust? My in-laws may have made it out, but what about the other six million?"

All eyes were on Naomi, the Rabbi's wife.

Now it was Daniel's turn. After all, he was the one stirred it all up—and he had to admit, it was somewhat exhilarating. "She's right, Jerry. Now, I'd love to continue this discussion and maybe we will another time, but the clock is staring me in the face."

Daniel stepped back on the platform. "As most of you know, Marvin is in need of your prayers for his failing health. He has served this Temple faithfully for many years, and deserves not only your prayers, but your time. I'm saddened to learn none of you have visited him in the hospital, nor called to comfort Mrs. Berman. Are we not admonished to care for one another?" After looking over at Naomi, he added, "Forgive me. I promised never to guilt-trip any of you. *Shabbat Shalom.*"

Naomi shouted above the clamor of the congregation scurrying to leave, "Don't forget, everyone, we have the meeting for the trip to Israel this Monday evening."

It took another hour before Daniel and Naomi were able to start their walk home. However, they made it no further than the parking lot before Jerry accosted them. "You know this new-fangled thing you're doing, this discussion format . . . first of all, if you want us to 'share our thoughts' like you told us once, then why," he now turned angrily toward Naomi, "shoot us down when we say something you don't like?"

Daniel put his arm around Naomi and pulled her close to himself. "My wife is a congregant as well, so why shouldn't she share her thoughts, too? Jerry, was there more you wanted to say? When someone says 'first of all' it usually means there's a second and a third and a—"

"Yeah, I don't like this whole new thing. I mean what do you think . . . you're teaching a class at the University or something?"

Daniel smiled. "Thank you for sharing your thoughts." In parting he added, "Have a good weekend."

The couple walked in silence until, approaching their apartment, Naomi asked, "Why did you forget mentioning the Israel meeting?" When he did not answer, she pressed, "Why do I have the feeling it's not that you forgot, but you simply didn't want to bring it up?" Still with no reply from Daniel, she asked, "Am I right or not?"

"No one's going to show up anyway. That's why."

Later than afternoon, Daniel was doing his laps in the swimming pool. Naomi sat poolside, baking in the sun and thinking about the photos Irwin had sent. The pictures seemed to capture an exuberant spirit among all those participating in Irwin's home fellowship. And Daniel appeared in animated conversation in almost all the photos she had seen of him.

"You're going to get burnt," Daniel warned as he came out of the water and dried himself off. "C'mon, let's go under the canopy."

Her hand over her forehead to shield herself from the blinding sunlight, she asked, "How many laps did you do today?"

"Twenty," he answered a bit breathlessly. "All I had to do was think about Jerry making that University remark, it made me mad enough to kick my feet as hard as I could and knife my way through the water."

She grabbed up her towel and sandals, and together they sat under the canopy. "Daniel, I was thinking about what he said, and also I can't get those pictures Irwin sent out of my mind. What's the name of the University Jerry was referring to? The one here in Boca?"

"FAU, Florida Atlantic University. Why?"

"Didn't you tell me Irwin used the college campuses to kinda recruit for his *havurah*?"

"If you're suggesting what I think you are, forget it. I have enough to do, Naomi. I just couldn't . . . no, I don't see how. . ."

"What if I try going over to FAU by myself then?"

"I'm going back in the house. You can stay out here if you like." He picked up his towel and left.

Thankfully, her thoughts quickly moved from nursing her hurt to thinking about why he might have behaved as he did. She put herself into Daniel's place and it became clear: her husband was afraid to get his hopes up again. Too many high expectations had plummeted into disappointments. It was safer to simply not try anymore.

While climbing the steps to their apartment, an idea was born, she believed inspired by God Himself. It brought with it a spark of hope.

It was her first solo expedition into the Fort Lauderdale area. Having made a firm decision to buy Daniel a guitar, the name Sam Ash popped into her mind. When living in Manhattan, she had passed this music store chain many times.

Immediately after Daniel left for the synagogue to prepare for the evening's meeting, she frantically made a few phone calls. The closest store was in Margate, Florida, a bit south of Boca. The voice on the phone was very nice and gave her good directions.

The store was empty when she walked in and Naomi received the undivided attention of the store manager, Steve.

"It's for my husband. The first real gift I've ever given him." She reached into her purse and brought out a handful of photos from the batch Irwin had sent. Each showed Daniel holding or playing the guitar he once owned. "I'd like the same one as that," she explained.

"I think it's a Yamaha. Wait just a sec." Steve reached into a drawer behind the sales counter. "It's here somewhere. . . " He now brought out a magnifying glass and used it to study her photos. He concluded, "Yup, it's a Yamaha. Nylon string. We have some nice Yamahas here. Let's go look."

"Do you have the same exact Yamaha as in these pictures?"

He walked over to a nearby shelf and took down a hand-some-looking guitar. "Not sure if this is the one, but this is a good one. And like your husband's old one, it has the same spruce wood. Want to hold it?"

"No, I'm afraid to, but how much?"

"This one's $199."

"That's all?" *Oh great bargaining, Naomi—Dad would kill me.*

"Well this is a good one for a beginner. How long since your husband played?"

"Not sure. Couple of years I guess. But I don't want a beginner's. I want something nicer, as long as I can afford it."

"Sure, C'mon over here. I have one I think you'll like."

She followed him to an area displaying more expensive-looking guitars and this time accepted the proffered instrument. "It's beautiful."

"Also a Yamaha. It's still good for beginners, in case your husband needs to relearn, but it's also excellent for seasoned players."

"What kind of wood is this?"

"The top is spruce, then look here." He pointed to the neck of the guitar and explained, "The bridge over here and the fretboard, they're rosewood. Elegant looking, huh?"

Naomi wondered if this Steve guy could tell how excited she was. A thrill ran through her body as she imagined Daniel holding the instrument. And one day he would lovingly play it. This felt so incredibly right.

Steve told her, "Got a great sound. It's ideal for finger-picking, which I saw your husband was doing in the pictures, and good for the more intimate chord progressions, too."

She yearned to bring this home for Daniel, but figured it had to be way out of her price range. Okay, maybe now she could go into negotiating mode. In as neutral a voice as she could manage, she asked, "How much?"

"Important question, lady. Special price if someone brings in photos. How do you like that? It's three hundred and fifty."

"Really? I'll take it." *Guess I flunked at negotiating—but who cares?*

"You need a case for it?"

"Yeah, or, well, I think so. How much?"

"I got a nice one sitting in the back. You can have it. Who knows? Maybe your husband will need a lesson or two. I teach both rock and classical." He took her money and handed her his card.

She spent the entire drive home devising the perfect plan for how to surprise Daniel with this extraordinary gift. *Okay, I got it. I'll leave it in the car until after the meeting tonight, then when we come back home, I'll make up some dumb excuse why I have to go back out to the car, and I'll get it then.*

Of course, with all this plotting, she missed her exit off the Interstate. As long as it didn't make her late for tonight's all-important meeting, she wasn't concerned. *Wow, tonight's a big night.*

Daniel carried an urn filled with hot water into the meeting area. He looked over at Naomi who was sorting out the packets of instant coffee and tea bags. "How many you think will show up?"

"Relax, honey, maybe you'll be surprised—in many ways." Up went his one eyebrow.

Daniel surveyed the library. His new secretary had done an excellent job setting up chairs in neat rows. "One, two, three. . ." After arriving at a count of thirty seats, he scoffed. "Denise hasn't been here long enough to know, has she?"

"Hey, maybe it's a sign. Maybe we'll have more than the two of us show up."

Daniel pointed to the portraits lined up on one of the walls. "Did you ever notice? They have all these paintings of their past presidents, but not one of their rabbis."

Hearing noises in the hallway, Naomi warned, "Shush."

The first to arrive were Jay and his wife Sandy. The Cantors, having found this couple to be congenial, were grateful to see them. Sandy, a convert to Judaism, seemed to appreciate Naomi's warm

223

acceptance of her; she did not receive this acceptance from many others in the *shul*.

Accepting a cake platter, Naomi asked, "Sandy, what did you bring?"

"It's this new recipe my sister gave me. It's called Red Velvet Cake." She rolled her eyes. "It is sooo incredibly rich."

Daniel looked at Jay and suggested, "Why wait til everyone else gets here?"

Naomi quickly volunteered to bring out some paper plates and plastic knives and forks. "I don't know why I didn't bring any out."

Returning from the kitchen and back into the library, Naomi spied Mildred, who had just arrived and was already inching her way toward Daniel. Naomi inserted herself between the two, held out a plate to her husband and said, "Here, honey. Let's get a piece of cake."

Fifteen minutes after the meeting was called to begin, twenty-three people were sitting and ready to learn more about this proposed trip to Israel. Definitely exceeding Daniel's expectations.

Daniel assured the group, "The tour company we've spoken with will provide transportation, an experienced guide, and everything else that's necessary."

Enough of the everyday details—he hoped that would suffice for now. Daniel wanted to get to what he deemed beyond the everyday. "Think of how blessed you will be spiritually. This is the dimension of our trip we should all be excited about."

The first question was from Florence Greenberg, a flashy-looking sixty-year-old, who prided herself on staying fit and managing a successful real estate agency. "How observant are you expecting us to be?"

Mike, one of the few who could still boast of having hair beneath his yarmulke, rose from his chair. "Florence has a good point. I mean, most of us don't keep kosher, and unlike you and your wife, Rabbi, we drive on *Shabbos*. So what if I want some bacon for breakfast when we're over there? How's that going to work? You're always yakking about this 'yoke of the law.' What if we don't want to be saddled with some yoke around our necks?"

This generated quite a stir. Jay tried to bring some levity into the situation by saying, "Yak, yoke, very funny, Mike." But this did not stop the carping.

After allowing a few moments for his people to voice their worries, Daniel addressed the group. "I understand your concerns. I'm glad you're expressing them at the outset. And we will have plenty of time to work out these issues. I don't ever want you to think I'm trying to 'saddle' you with anything. Think of it this way: aren't we all seeking some sort of an inner life? Some way to make sense out of our lives? I believe it's my job to help you see that your lives can be transformed by Judaism. But, I don't want to force it upon you."

Naomi was so proud of her husband. She was grinning ear to ear as she watched him subdue this cantankerous congregation. And soon she would be surprising him with a special gift.

Thirty minutes later they were in their car driving home. "Thirteen, My-omi, thirteen signed up tonight, do you believe it? And another eight said they'd consider it."

Two seconds after both were home, she went into performance mode. "Oh dear, I forgot something in the car. I'll be right back."

When she returned, there he stood holding out a large gift-wrapped package for her. And her gift wrapping was a large bow the nice man at Sam Ash put around the guitar case for her.

"A guitar?" Daniel exclaimed seeing the guitar case. "You got me a guitar?"

"And what's that in your hand, Rabbi Cantor?"

"Open it."

She tore through the wrapping in a split second and found Aunt Luba's wedding present beautifully reframed. She clutched it to her chest, tasting the tears as they cascaded from her eyes and touched her lips. God must have forgiven her, for only He could bring such a pure and perfect gift to love her. Precious Daniel, it seemed his eyes were moist as well.

He walked over to the coffee table and picked up the box of tissues. After wiping his own eyes, he extended the box to her.

She said, "First you have to take your present." The swap was made—the box of tissues for the guitar. "You better love it."

Although he spoke of how impressed he was with the quality of the guitar, Naomi knew the smile was not genuine. She had literally hugged the gift he had given her, yet he was holding the present she gave him as if trying to avoid any personal connection to it.

"What's wrong with it? Maybe they'll take it back if I got the wrong kind."

He walked over to the couch and carefully placed the guitar down "I know what you're doing."

Having followed him over to the couch, she asked, "What? What am I doing?"

"It feels like you're pushing, Naomi." He took her hand to sit down on the couch with him. Once they were snuggled up close, he gently stroked her cheek. "You're trying to get me to go to FAU, pushing to start a *havurah*. Isn't that right?"

She pulled back from him. "No, it's not right."

Wagging his finger at her, he said, "Hey, if you get mad, I'm going to have to take that picture away from you before you break it again."

Okay, he got her on that one. She playfully bit his finger, and then explained, "Daniel, you looked so happy when I saw you in those photos, so I thought you must have loved playing the guitar?"

He pressed his lips together, looked at her from the corner of his eyes, and finally held both of his arms above his head. "I surrender. You're right, I did love it." He inched away from Naomi and lifted up the guitar, placing it on his lap. After a few moments of strumming, his mouth surrendered to a wide grin. "It doesn't even need tuning. Got a good sound, don't you think?"

"It looks good, too. Especially when you're holding it."

Walking into their bedroom, she playfully said, "Of course, the FAU thing isn't a bad idea."

Soon their gifts were put aside and the only thing they were holding was each other. As their intimacy became more intense, she felt compelled to tell him, "You know what I heard the other day? Acupuncture has helped some women to get pregnant. What do you think?"

He froze. "Where'd you hear that?"

"From Anne. I was talking to her on the phone. She's still in Ohio. I don't think she's ever going to make it back to New York."

"That's too bad . . . but about this acupuncture thing, Naomi, why are you pushing so much? Can't you be content?" Seeing her crushed expression, he sighed, "Honey, I love you, but I'm tired. Let's just go to sleep. Tomorrow morning we can say our morning blessing together, okay?"

She had come to envy her husband's ability to always slip easily into a deep slumber as he lay with his back toward her. While her body lay motionless next to his, Naomi's thoughts took her tumbling into her familiar pit of isolation. *Pushing I'm pushing him. I'm going to push him away.*

Eventually sleep did claim a hold on Naomi, but with it came the garish images. She was strapped to a table. Coming towards her was a grotesquely large hose, as if from a vacuum. It made a sucking noise, loud enough to be the sound of a roaring jet engine. Then a scream drowned out everything else, coming from the one strapped down. The hose, like a monster with a life of its own, was sucking out her very insides—a life she will never know.

The unexpected ring of their telephone served to pull her out from her nightmarish abyss.

In a groggy voice, Daniel answered, "Hello? . . . Oh, I'm so sorry, Mrs. Berman. Do you need me to come over now? . . . All right. My wife and I will see you tomorrow. Again, I'm so sorry . . . See you tomorrow."

"Marvin?"

"Yes, honey. Looks like I'll be doing my first funeral."

"Merciful God in heaven, grant a peaceful rest to the soul of Marvin Berman who has passed into his eternal home, may he come under Your divine wings and find a place of rest in Your paradise. We know You punish and reward us according to Your strict account. Therefore, I beseech You to allow Marvin Berman to rest in peace."

Daniel concluded the service, closed his prayer book and walked over to Marvin's widow.

"Rabbi, thank you. You hardly even knew my Marvin, yet you captured his personality so well." With a tight grip on his hand, she brought him over to meet her children, her grandchildren, and even one great grandchild.

After the necessary pleasantries were accomplished, Daniel and Naomi were on their way home. While driving, Daniel remarked, "Looked like you got cornered by a couple of people, Jerry and Doris among them."

"You know the only thing they care about? Who's going to be the new Chairman of the Board."

"I know it was rude of them to bring it up right there at the graveside, but, I'll be honest with you, I've been wondering the same thing. I mean the Temple needs to continue having a life." Stopping at a red light, he turned to Naomi. "You seem distracted. Something bothering you?"

"I'm trying to figure something out."

"Can I help?"

The light was no longer red but Daniel still had his foot on the brake. Naomi observed, "I'm not the only one with something—"

The blaring of the car horns managed to get Daniel's attention and he quickly stepped on the gas pedal. He admitted, "Yeah. I have a few things on my mind. But I'll talk to you later about them. But for now, tell me what's on your mind."

"Daniel, Marvin was a good man. A good Jew. Probably every year he confessed his sins, threw his bread into the water, fasted on Yom Kippur, and we've been told gave a lot of money to the *shul*."

"So? What's the problem?"

"It's like you were begging God to let him into heaven. I know you had to do what's prescribed, and you did a really touching service."

"Okay, enough with the flattery. Get to the point."

"I'm just wondering, if we can't be sure someone like Marvin will get into heaven, then what kind of hope is there for me?"

Removing one hand away from the wheel, he took Naomi's left hand and brought it to his lips. "I sure wish I could answer your question. What we're taught in seminary is that as Jews we are not to concern ourselves with the hereafter. We do good here, you know, *tikkun olam*, our command to repair the earth, without looking for some reward. No motive but to please God and make this world a better place. How else will the Messiah finally come?"

Something bothered Daniel. It was the way he sounded—he hated hearing his voice coming across like one of his phony baloney professors. *How do I convince anyone, even my own wife, when I can't seem to convince myself?*

He pulled into their parking space and turned off the motor. His wife wore such a worried expression. "My-omi, you needn't worry. God's got a special place reserved for rabbis' wives. None for their husbands, only for the wives."

Halfway up the steps, Naomi stopped and announced, "We need groceries. I'm going to go back out and get a few things, okay?"

"Sure. I'm going to do a few laps in the pool."

An hour later she returned carrying a bag from the local supermarket. Naomi not only heard Daniel on the terrace playing *Adon Olam* on the guitar but also his voice singing its beautiful lyrics, "And He is my God, my living God. . ."

So engrossed was Daniel that when suddenly Naomi stood in front of him, he was startled. Now it was his turn to startle her, as he asked, "When do you want to start going to FAU?"

"Huh?"

"We need new people. Young people that will live a few more years than even us. Otherwise, if we keep losing people at the

Temple and no new ones come along, then we might as well . . . anyway, let's go to FAU."

Chapter 17

Lord, Bless this Union

"hat was a good discussion. I enjoyed it. What about all of you?" Daniel did not have to wait long for an answer.

It seemed every one of the sixteen students gathered this evening in the Marcus' home were eager to share their feelings. And all were expressing that they, too, enjoyed it.

One young man wearing a sweatshirt with the insignia from FAU, sneakers that were falling apart, and pants splattered with paint, had the loudest voice of all. He hugged his knees to his chest as he sat on the floor and said, "Rabbi Dan, this is so cool. Who would have ever thought we could tell a rabbi why we don't believe all that stuff we were taught as a kid."

Daniel cut his eyes toward Naomi. "A wise woman once told me if you're going to tell people not to do something, then it helps if they understand why."

An attractive young woman said, "Gee, wonder who that woman is?" She laughed and elbowed Naomi, with whom she was sharing the couch.

Daniel waited until the laughter died down, and then announced, "This gives me an idea." He pointed to the boy sitting on the floor. "And, Mark, you basically were the impetus for it."

"Cool man." Mark stood and took a mock bow before his classmates.

"Yeah, very cool, "Daniel said. "Starting next week, we'll go through the Ten Commandments and each week we'll discuss why

God said 'thou shalt not.' It's time we discussed why not, don't you think?"

Daniel picked up his guitar lying next to him on the floor. While giving it a quick tuning, he told the group, "You know, I remember when I had to wait forever for anyone to speak up in this group. You were all so shy, but now five months later . . . I'm proud of you guys." He strummed the first few chords and announced the last song for the evening. "Everyone, *Hineh Ma Tov.*"

This was Naomi's signal to pick up her tambourine and stand next to her husband. Together they led in the singing, "*Hineh ma tov uma na'im, Shevet achim gam yachad. Hineh ma tov uma na'im, Shevet achim gam yachad.* How good and pleasant it is for brothers and sisters to be together."

The buoyant tune was a perfect outlet for the young people to express their enthusiasm. Naomi smiled and told Daniel, "Perfect choice."

With one eyebrow arched, he looked at her. "Finally you're admitting I was right about something?"

His turn to be elbowed. Yes, she had been mistaken. She thought a more serious, more devout song would have been appropriate. *I really need to trust him more.* Oh, how she loved to look at him, so handsome in his comfortable blue jeans and loafers, and holding a guitar in his lap.

Naomi prompted the students, "Let's thank Jay and Sandy for letting us use their house once again."

The students, along with Daniel and Naomi, turned toward their hosts and gave them a round of applause. People then gathered their belongings, with a few students helping themselves to one last bite of Sandy's brownies.

Naomi shook her tambourine to get their attention for one last announcement. "And don't forget, next week the synagogue will be doing the Purim play. As a matter of fact half our cast is right here, so you better not forget." She turned toward the pretty young lady who was sitting with her on the couch. "Right, Queen Esther? Your royal highness will be very upset if you are not in the audience."

Daniel and Naomi stayed behind, Daniel to help place the living room furniture back in its everyday order and Naomi to help Sandy put away leftovers, throw out plastic cups, and get the dishes in the dishwasher.

Finally standing at the front door ready to say their goodbyes, Jay asked, "How's your house hunting going? Before you answer, here's the thing. Rabbi, I took your suggestion. I've been asking some people at the *shul* if they wanted to start having their own *havurah*. Believe it or not, there are about five couples who said yes. They're all about our age . . . ones, thanks to you, who have just joined the Temple."

"Wow," Naomi exclaimed, "That's wonderful."

"Now, if I'm correct, you said if we had an adult one, I could lead it myself. Is that right, Rabbi?" Daniel nodded. "Well, if we continue hosting the one for the students here on Monday nights, and then Sandy and I have another one here—"

Daniel jumped in. "Jay, don't worry. I completely understand. I wouldn't ask you to host twice in one week. I know Naomi and I don't have a place big enough right now, but we'll find another place for the youth to meet—don't worry about it."

Sandy laughed. "As for our son, Jake, he loves your group, and actually he'll probably love going somewhere other than Mom and Dad's, if you know what I mean."

"Great," Daniel said. "Jake's one of the best contributors in the discussions. As far as the house hunting, nothing's on the horizon as of yet. We've been working with Florence Greenberg. At the last Israel planning meeting she cornered Naomi—"

Naomi put her pocketbook on the floor. Looked like they were staying a little while longer. "I made the mistake of telling her we were looking . . . I'd forgotten she was a realtor. She's kinda aggressive." Everyone laughed in agreement. "But she hasn't shown us anything like what we told her we wanted."

Sandy walked back into the living room, waving them to follow. Once all were seated, she said, "Jay and I had another reason we brought up the whole house hunting thing."

Jay squeezed his wife's hand. "Tell them, sweetie."

"I think you know Jake works part-time cleaning swimming pools. There's a house where he cleaned the pool the other day. Jake was telling us about it. The owners want to sell it by themselves . . . without a realtor. I understand it's really nice, and without a realtor it should be a good price. It's in the Camino Real development."

Naomi shared a glance with Daniel and squeezed his hand. "Camino Real . . . you're kidding? It's gorgeous there."

Naomi was squeezing so hard, Daniel thought he better do something quick, before she cut off his circulation. "Jay, if you want to get the address from Jake, we'll check it out." Ahhh, she loosened her grip.

They finally said their goodbyes, all the while Daniel aware Naomi was about to jump out of her skin. Car doors closed and key in the ignition, he turned to her. "I know My-omi, and the answer is no, not tonight."

"But, Daniel—"

"It's too dark right now to see anything. First thing tomorrow, before I go to work, we'll drive by and look at it. If we like it, I'll call. Good enough?"

She sprung out of her seat and threw herself into his arms, "You're the greatest. How'd I get so lucky?"

The next day they encountered a problem. Because Camino Real was a gated community, they were not allowed entrance. "Daniel, I hate to say it, but maybe we should call Florence. She could probably get us in."

He shrugged. "Well, I was thinking we really don't want to antagonize her . . . she's signed up for the Israel trip and as of now we have just enough people to get the discount. Besides which, I think we signed a contract with her that even if we found something on our own, I think we're still tied in to pay her a fee."

Between the threat of breaking a contract and antagonizing an Israel trip signee, both agreed they'd call Florence. Hopefully she could get them in to see the house later that day.

While giving her business card to the guard at the front gate, Florence warned, "Now, Rabbi, I know you and your wife walk to *shul* on *Shabbos*. This'll be a bit more of a *schlep* from here. Are you prepared for that?"

Naomi sat in the front seat and answered for her husband. "We've already discussed that and decided we could use the exercise."

With the grandeur of the homes, the exquisitely manicured lawns, even the expensive cars sitting in the driveways, how could they possibly afford this place? She turned to face Daniel sitting in the back seat. He was busy scribbling a note and she was unable to get his attention.

Florence reached over to Naomi, and effectively pulled her back around. "I spoke with the owners. It needs a little updating. Nothing too major, but enough that we can negotiate a good price."

Daniel tapped his wife on the shoulder and handed her a note. It read, "Didn't get a chance to tell you, but I talked to my dad. They're giving us a gift for the down payment."

From the moment Florence turned into the driveway, they knew if they could afford it, they wanted it. The driveway was quite long and fully landscaped, with tall royal palms evenly spaced in front of the limestone ledge which afforded a degree of privacy.

The owners, Mr. and Mrs. Granger, had been called and asked to make themselves scarce while the prospective buyers walked through their home. Since the property had not been listed through a realtor, there was no lockbox hanging from the doorknob. Instead the Grangers had left a key under the cushion of a charming front porch swing.

Upon stepping inside, they stood in a spacious great room with high ceilings. Most impressive was the clear view straight into the back of the house. A combination of floor to ceiling windows and glass sliding doors showcased the Florida room off the living area.

And beyond the relaxing sunroom, they were awed by the inviting swimming pool.

Once oriented to what was more immediately in front of them, they realized they were standing in a huge living room, and to one side of this airy space was a sunken conversation pit.

Stepping down into this pit, Daniel asked, "Is this a fireplace I'm seeing?"

"Most certainly," Florence answered.

Naomi walked down to join her husband. "In Florida?"

Florence explained, "It's gas. A few homes have them down here. *Meshugganah*, isn't it?"

After inspecting the kitchen, in need of updating, they walked into the bedrooms and from there the bathrooms. Daniel took Naomi aside, and said, "Maybe we can find someone to put down that Spanish tile you like so much. Have that done in the bathrooms, if you like."

After leaving the property, they went with Florence to her office where she worked up the numbers. With Daniel's parents' gift, it was feasible they had found their first home.

Naomi was convinced somehow she had made it into God's good graces. Her life was beyond her wildest expectations. There was the present reality of a good man who loved her, the belief she was helping this man to fulfill his calling, and now possibly a beautiful new home. With all this favor the Lord was showing her, any day now she should be able to bear him his first child.

Denise, Daniel's secretary, answered, "Temple Beth Shalom, can I help you?"

"Yes," Naomi said breathlessly into the telephone. "It's me. Is my husband available?"

While waiting for him to pick up, she leafed through several home decorating magazines. Turning the pages frenetically, she tore one page halfway down the middle. Finally, Daniel said, "Hi, honey. What's up?"

She shouted into the phone, "They accepted our offer. It's ours."

"That's terrific. When do we—?"

"Daniel, I got a call waiting. You wanna hold on?"

"No, call me back, okay?"

Naomi discovered Daniel's father. Stefan, was on the other line. He told her, "Our Dana is getting married. You and Danny must come."

After Naomi expressed happy disbelief at the news, Stefan said, "When see her, you will know. She's pregnant. Big already."

The wedding would be happening in three weeks. Not only did Ed and Dana want Daniel to perform the ceremony, but Dana wanted Naomi to be the maid of honor.

"She call you soon," Stefan added. "And, please, ask Danny call me."

Naomi, doing her best to sound happy, told her father-in-law, "Of course."

Daniel arrived home that evening and instantly filled Naomi in on the conversation he had with his dad. "The problem is my mom. She says she won't even go to the wedding. I don't know what part bothers her the most. Her daughter, the bride, pregnant, or probably more the groom being black. I'll call her tonight and try to talk to her. Meanwhile, we need to make plane reservations. The sooner the better."

Usually upon arriving home, Naomi poured him a nice cold glass of raspberry tea and a glass of iced coffee for herself. They would then sit out on their terrace and catch up on the day's events. Tonight Naomi simply sat on a dining room chair, hardly even making eye contact with him as he stood near her.

He lowered himself into the chair next to her, brought it close enough that their knees touched, and asked, "What's the matter?"

Quietly she admitted, "I wanted to be the one to tell your Mom she'd be a grandmother."

He rose from his chair, walked into the kitchen and poured himself a glass of iced tea. He had a choice: show his exasperation or make a valiant attempt to change the direction this evening was heading.

With resolve, he poured her a glass of iced coffee and carried it to her. "It'll be fun. We'll stay at a nice hotel in Manhattan. I mean we need to have a vacation anyway. You can find some Broadway shows for us to go to."

He waited but received no response. He shook his head. "When are you ever going to be satisfied? We just learned we're getting a beautiful new home, and I didn't even get to tell you yet, but Dad says he can get us furniture at wholesale prices."

With that, she looked up. "Really?"

No longer shaking his head, but instead nodding, he affection-

ately assured her, "Yes, really." And then he added, "Let's go out for dinner tonight. You choose where."

Daniel and Naomi flew out of West Palm Beach the day after the Purim celebration, arriving in New York three days before Ed and Dana's wedding. They picked up a rental car at the airport and drove to the Plaza Hotel in Manhattan.

"They told me our room would be overlooking Central Park. Is it okay, Daniel? You said for me to splurge."

He gave the car key to the valet and explained, "We'll be checking in and then coming right back out. Need to drive to New Jersey."

Another staff member took their suitcases from the trunk and placed them on a luggage cart. "Your name, sir?"

"Rabbi and Mrs. Cantor."

As soon as they were released from the glass revolving doors, Naomi grabbed Daniel's arm. "Do we have to go out to New Jersey right away?"

He nudged her a few feet away from the doors and from the heavy pedestrian traffic. "Naomi, I feel compelled to talk to my mom right away. Dad's tried talking with her, and now he's looking to me for help. If Mom doesn't come to the wedding, it'll . . . we'll have time alone here later. I promise you."

During the ride into Rutherford, Dana's pregnancy weighed heavily on Naomi's mind. Daniel drove while Naomi entered a world of her own, filled with jealousy—what was Dana feeling right now? And soon a precious little voice would be calling her "Mommy." And Dana would bless her husband, making him a father.

Because of my hideous past, God will never bless my marriage. It will never be a true union.

Naomi eventually forced herself out of seclusion and asked, "What made you agree to perform the wedding? I thought—"

"I figured a Unitarian Church in a way is no big deal. It's not a real church. I mean, we won't have to worry about seeing some cross or anything like that."

Naomi waited as he paid the toll for the Manhattan Tunnel. Once they were moving again, she continued. "But you said you wouldn't ever marry an interfaith couple unless the Gentile converted." Tentatively, she added, "You said something like that, didn't you?"

With an uncharacteristic snicker, Daniel commented, "They're not interfaith anything . . . they're both pagans."

Shocked by her husband's harshness, Naomi again withdrew into her own cocoon, staring out her window, while Daniel, disappointed with his own behavior, shut himself off as well. He tuned the car radio to a station he remembered from his high school days.

He tapped the steering wheel to the beat as he sang, "And you're stayin' alive, stayin' alive, ah, ah, ah, ah, stayin' alive, stayin—"

Was she hearing this from her husband—her husband the Cantor? He sounded so cute. As if on cue, they turned to face each other, and broke out in harmonious laughter.

Still laughing, they pulled into his family's garage.

Zofia ran out to meet them and almost appeared joyful. She hugged Daniel, then Naomi, then back to Daniel—pinching his cheek, smothering him with her kisses, then pinching his cheek again. Stefan stood to the side, beaming.

And Naomi received a pleasant surprise. She had always called her mother-in-law Mrs. Cantor, but today Zofia corrected her. "Call me Momma."

Zofia had made a delicious dinner of *bigos*. "I remember, your favorite."

After dinner, Daniel walked over to his mother and pulled up an extra dining room chair which had been moved out of the way while they were eating. "Mom, why won't you come to the wedding?"

His mother looked over at her husband and said, "Stefan, you tell him I not go." To make clear this was an ironclad resolution the woman placed her cup of tea in its saucer and folded her arms across her chest. She repeated, "I not go."

Daniel bent his head down to his mother's level. "Mom, is it because she's pregnant or because you don't like Ed?" Seeing tears streaming down his mother's face, Daniel reached for a napkin.

As he wiped her tears, Zofia unclasped her arms and peered into her son's eyes. "My boy. My beautiful boy. You not know about hate. You not see . . . people do evil."

Stefan put his arm on his wife's shoulder. "Zofia, tell Danny what you told me." When he was met only with silence, Stefan told Naomi, "In Polish, it's easier for her to say." He turned back to Zofia and said, "My wife, tell what you afraid of."

In her broken English, she expressed her fear—a multiracial couple would not be accepted anywhere by anyone. "And now, vith baby . . . I know vhat hate can do . . ."

Stefan was now kneeling beside his wife and rubbing her neck, while Daniel said, "Mom, listen to me. How do we stop hate?"

When she turned her head away, he asked, "Mom, look at me. There are bullies out there. Evil people. I know that. Remember when I came home and told you about kids throwing things at me and calling me a kike and a Christ-killer? You told me to stand up to them. Well, Mom, people like Dana and Ed, they love each other and no one has a right to bully them and stop them from being together."

Zofia became quiet, her eyes moving from side to side. Eventually she put her index finger up to her lips and took a moment to make eye contact with all three individually. Finally they heard the words, "I come to vedding."

Once alone in their car, driving back into Manhattan, Daniel turned to Naomi. "My-omi, I've not been fair to you. I've tried ignoring how much you want to have a baby. Forgive me for being so selfish. I've been thinking, what if you haven't been able to get pregnant because we weren't both wanting it? Maybe God was waiting until I wanted this blessing as much as you do." With a shrug and a smile, he said, "Let's see what happens."

They returned to their hotel room, and Daniel took his *tallit* and covered himself and Naomi. He petitioned their God. "Master of the Universe, we stand before You as one, beseeching You to grant us the desire of our heart. Bring forth a child out of this union."

The plane ride back to Boca allowed time not only to reminisce about the events of the wedding, but also to map out what needed to be done to make the trip to Israel a successful event. Yet every once in a while, Daniel did say, "Hello, earth to My-omi." Her vacant stare gave it away: her mind was wondering.

A few times her mind was recalling Dana's obvious pregnancy even with her flouncy bohemian wedding dress. Her mind also wandered off to the announcement her parents had made—they soon could be retiring to South Florida. The thoughts about Dana soon having a baby filled her with resentment and remorse—thoughts of her parents living near her filled her with joy.

But the most enticing distraction was wondering how soon she could go back to the doctor to have another pregnancy test. Over and over again, she played the scene in her head. "Daniel, we're pregnant." And over and over again she envisioned his excitement.

Then, of course, there was that beautiful house in Camino Real soon to be their home. And with Stefan's getting them wholesale prices, in Naomi's mind the sky was going to be the limit when furnishing and decorating –especially the nursery. Would it be blue or pink?

Chapter 18

Before they call ...

Daniel squeezed his wife's waist and nuzzled his chin on her neck. "C'mon, honey, I'll help you clean up in the morning."

She dropped her handful of paper plates and napkins back onto the coffee table and giggled. "Sounds good."

He now steered her into their newly furnished sunroom. Oh, so inviting.

"Give me a second," she told him. "Let me get some matches."

"The candles are already lit," he whispered.

Once seated on the rattan loveseat, he stretched his legs out on the ottoman and hers went across his lap. In perfect synchrony they let out a contented sigh.

"I think the only *havurah* more exciting than tonight's was the first one," Daniel said. "You agree?"

She shook her head. "Nope, tonight's was way more exciting. I mean what could be more exciting than this? The very first one in our new home."

He tickled her feet. "Nope, you're wrong. Couldn't have had this one if we didn't have the first one."

Naomi yanked the pillow out from behind Daniel's head to wallop him with it, but he intercepted the hit. This precipitated a playful round of wrestling, ending with Daniel carrying his wife piggyback into their bedroom.

The evening ritual, since the time in Manhattan, was again performed this night. Under his tallit, they petitioned the Master of the Universe to bring forth a child through their union.

Once they had said their goodnights, Naomi added her own secret petition: *Lord, please let the gynecologist tomorrow tell me, "Yes, Mrs. Cantor, you are pregnant."* Why had she kept tomorrow morning's appointment a secret from Daniel? She really couldn't come up with an answer.

Daniel turned over in bed and told her, "Honey, the furniture you picked out and even the way you arranged it, it works terrific. I'm so proud of you."

"And I love your idea to have a barbecue for our next meeting."

They said goodnight one more time, leaving Naomi with new fodder for her fanciful world. The students, in all their exuberance, would be so happy for their Rabbi and his wife when she became pregnant. And Naomi could even be an inspiration to the young people to wait until they were married to enjoy this kind of bliss. Had she waited, there would then be no ghosts seeking always to invade her peace.

The doctor did not even make an appearance. The nurse took Naomi's sample, had her wait while the test was run, and in a very short while came back with the results.

"I'm sorry, Mrs. Cantor. It's negative again."

Wordless and expressionless, Naomi stood up, placed her purse strap around her shoulder and proceeded out of the room.

The nurse caught up with her in the hallway. "Dr. Morris wanted me to ask you if you would like a referral. He has a colleague who specializes in fertility problems. Wait right here and I'll get you his card."

Naomi did not wait for the nurse to return.

With five hours until she was needed at the Temple to help with the Friday night service, she wandered around the Town Center Mall. Only yesterday she had looked forward to having the time to browse the many home décor boutiques. Today, however, her eyes were unable to focus on anything in particular. Into one store and then into another, hoping for absolutely no human contact

Finally close enough to the time for arriving at the Temple, Naomi went to Cohen's Bakery and picked up the challah to be used for the evening's service. She had to make it home, park the car, and then walk to the *shul*. Living in their new neighborhood, the walk required an extra thirty minutes, and here she had spent the day dawdling around as if time were there to be wasted.

Driving a good ten to fifteen miles over the speed limit and even racing through a red light, she pulled into the driveway and hurriedly ran in and changed her clothes. Having made it on foot almost to the guardhouse, carrying the challah, she remembered—Daniel told her they were running low on the wine needed for *Kiddush*, the ritual performed at the end of Friday night's service. He expected her to have picked up another bottle at the store.

High heels on, she raced back to their home and reached into the pantry. Thankfully she found an unopened bottle of kosher wine, found a burlap sack to carry it in, and started on her hike again.

She arrived at the Temple, wiping the sweat off her face with a tissue. She found Daniel in the social area engaged in conversation with an elderly couple, Mr. and Mrs. Bagliebter. The wife had a tendency to corner either Daniel or Naomi and then talk nonstop. Seeing his wife enter, he waved her over.

Daniel kissed Naomi on the cheek. "Norm and Ida are telling me how excited they are. They just learned they're going to be great grandparents. Can you imagine?"

Ida shoved a picture into Naomi's face. "You know what this is? It's called a sonogram. A picture of the baby inside my granddaughter. Do you believe it? He's less than one month old but, look, you can see the little feet already."

"Excuse me." Naomi pushed the sonogram away, "I have to take the challah and the wine . . ." Rather than finishing her sentence, she simply walked away.

When the time arrived for his sermon, Daniel announced, "I had something all written out to talk about tonight, but I hope you'll forgive me if I've changed my mind."

His congregation was now comfortable with the casual environment their Rabbi had created, and now with many more young people in attendance, this free-flowing dialog seemed all the more appropriate.

He stepped off the *bimah* and addressed the congregation. "I was privileged this evening to see a glimpse of the Bagliebters' great grandchild. Modern technology is an amazing thing. They showed me a picture, a sonogram, that was taken inside the womb of the mother. I can't get it out of my mind."

Daniel leaped back up the steps to his pulpit and picked up his Bible. Turning the pages while stepping back down, he explained, "Before there was such a thing as a sonogram, King David was inspired to write Psalm 139." Daniel read from his Bible, "For thou hast possessed my reins: thou hast covered me in my mother's womb. I will praise thee; for I am fearfully and wonderfully made: marvelous are thy works; and that my soul knoweth right well."

Daniel closed his Bible, walked back up to his pulpit, and smiled toward his wife. He believed Naomi was shedding tears only because she, too, was touched by the beauty and truth of the Psalm.

Daniel's exhaustion after a hectic week dulled his sensibilities and he did not see behind Naomi's everything-is-fine facade. Usually she could fool others with this, but her husband was not so easily guiled.

If he had known what she truly was experiencing, he would not have told her as they arrived home, "Honey, I'm too tired to do our prayer tonight. I'm going right off to sleep. But I want to tell you, My-omi, since we started praying, I'm now wanting a baby as much as you do. Good night, honey."

Was this to be the remainder of her life? Rude messengers always there to taunt? The howling always there to keep her deaf to all other sounds. Forevermore the shameful ache—this was her penance.

Words like bricks piled heavily upon her breaking heart. "You will never be good enough. God will never give you another baby. Because of you, your husband will not be blessed. You have brought curses with you into this marriage, not blessings."

Those thoughts dragged her into the pit of another horrific nightmare. Grotesque images . . . ovens . . . babies screaming . . . Zofia's words echoing throughout—"People do evil."

Her muffled cries and restless movements in their bed awakened Daniel, "Honey, wake up." Once her eyes were open and staring at him, he asked, "Are you okay?"

"I did evil, Daniel. I'm so sorry."

"Honey, it's just a bad dream. Go back to sleep, okay?"

Soon she heard his rhythmic breathing again, glad she had not disturbed his much-needed sleep. She tiptoed out of the bedroom and into their den. She switched on the television and huddled up on the couch.

On the screen she saw a young forlorn-looking woman, walking listlessly in a secluded area. The camera moved to a tight close-up of the woman who now sat on a bench. Tears streamed down her face as an announcer asked, "Are you hurting from an abortion? You're not alone. Call the number on your screen for free confidential help."

Chapter 19

... I will answer

It must have been someone's home at one time. White brick and green shutters. Thankfully warm and inviting, but what was this place?

Mustering up the kind of courage it once took to enter an audition hall, Naomi parked and got out of her car. Once inside, she approached a woman stationed behind a small desk.

"I called earlier. They told me I could come in at 9:30."

The middle-aged woman removed her tortoise-shell eyeglasses and smiled warmly. "Do you know who you talked to, love?"

"Melinda."

The receptionist's finger moved toward the intercom button while at the same time an attractive redhead stepped out from a narrow hallway. The receptionist turned toward the redhead and said, "Oh, Melinda, I was about to call you." She pointed her eyeglasses toward Naomi and said, "This young lady is here to see you."

Melinda extended her hand to Naomi and said, "I have an office, we can talk in there."

Naomi nodded and followed. Expecting to find a cold sterile-type office, she instead found a space designed to feel like you were in a friend's living room. Naomi walked over to a floral print sofa. "Okay for me to sit here?"

"Please, make yourself comfortable. Would you like coffee or something else . . . soda or some water?"

"No, thank you."

Melinda then sat on a matching print chair in front of Naomi. "Do you want to give me your name?"

"No, not yet."

"When you're ready." Melinda went on to assure Naomi of the strict confidentiality adhered to at this center.

"And what is this center?"

"Like I explained on the phone, we're a women's center. Run by women for women. Some women come here because they've found they're pregnant—some people would say they were in a crisis pregnancy—and some women, like myself," she put her hand to her chest and peered into Naomi's eyes, "have needed to talk with someone about the abortion they had. Maybe they're feeling guilt . . . maybe grieving over their choice. For me, I was experiencing a spiritual crisis. And one thing most of us have had in common, we've kept all these feelings to ourselves. The shame made us feel we couldn't ever talk to anyone about all of this. For me, it was the loneliest, most isolating time in my life."

Playing with the strap from her shoulder bag, Naomi asked, "And how are you able to help? I mean, are you a psychiatrist?"

"None of us here are psychologists or psychiatrists. A few of us get paid but most of us are volunteers. Truth is you couldn't pay us enough to equal the joy we feel in doing what we do." She paused for a moment. "I'm sorry, but I want to address you by name. It seems so cold not to. Otherwise, I'll end up like Maggie, the woman you met in the front. She calls everyone love—which is fine for her, but I'd rather . . . Would you mind giving me your first name?"

"Amy. I'm Amy."

"Amy, as I mentioned many of us, after having had an abortion, we find ourselves in a spiritual crisis. Therefore, what we do here is use the Bible. There's a Bible study we would do together, Amy, to repair your relationship with God."

Naomi sensed Melinda did not believe Amy was her real name, but was gracious enough to use it nonetheless.

Melinda leaned forward. "I don't know how familiar you are with the Bible, but the Hebrew prophet Isaiah promises that God will heal the brokenhearted and that He will console those who mourn. He'll give us beauty for ashes and the oil of joy for our mourning. Who wouldn't want that?"

Who offered anything this good without a price? "The ad said this is free."

"It is. The Bible study we would go through, if you can pay it, is eight dollars, but if you can't, we'll give you a free copy."

"I can pay you."

"Okay." Melinda swiveled her chair around to face the bookshelves behind her. She quickly grabbed a book and swiveled back to Naomi. "Here, Amy, this is for you."

Naomi unzipped her purse, but was told, "You can give the money to Maggie on your way out. Let's talk a little more first."

Closing her purse back up, Naomi looked expectantly at the woman who sat across from her, albeit with a modicum of skepticism.

"First question: would you like to do this one-on-one, just you and me, or would you like to do this with a group? We have a group starting next Thursday night."

"Can I do it only with you? Besides, I couldn't come at night."

"Of course. You can take your workbook, do the homework, and we could meet next Saturday if you want."

Naomi's heart fluttered. "No, I can't usually do Saturdays." The frightening realization struck her: it was the Sabbath and she had driven her car. Where was her head? Since Daniel left earlier on Saturdays to officiate the men's prayer time, Naomi had managed to slip away. Earlier this morning, filled with anxiety about visiting this strange place, she had jumped into her car and never even stopped to think about what day it was.

"I only came today because I saw the ad last night and when I called this morning, you told me to come right in—and I didn't want to chicken out."

For the first time, Melinda laughed. "I understand completely."

"But Saturdays are definitely not usually good."

"Amy, don't worry, my schedule is flexible. We simply need to give you time to do your homework. We could meet next Friday morning, if that's good."

"Okay. Ten a.m.?"

Again swiveling back toward the bookshelves, Melinda found her appointment book and immediately began writing. "Amy, Friday ten a.m. Amy, what's your last name?"

"Winston."

Having looked at Naomi's wedding ring, she asked, "Mrs. Winston, would you be able to give me your phone number?"

"No, I can't. But I could call you if you want me to."

"That'll be good. Maybe the day before to make sure there's been no change in our appointment. One more question: Do you have a Bible?" When Naomi quickly nodded, Melinda said, "Good. May I pray for you before you leave?"

"Okay."

Melinda reached over to take Naomi's hands, but Naomi flinched. "Amy, I like to hold hands when I pray for someone, but we don't have to."

Naomi pursed her lips together for a moment and then held her hands out. "No, it's okay."

Melinda asked God to bless Amy as she sought healing for her trauma. And then the prayer was closed, "In Jesus' Name."

Withdrawing her hands, Naomi grabbed her purse and the workbook. She had already agreed to pay for the book and to avoid any confrontation she would give them her ten dollar bill and leave as quickly as possible. Later she would call and cancel her appointment.

As she was hastily making her way out, Melinda called to her, "See you Friday, and call me if you need to talk before then."

Daniel's probably at this very minute thinking "where is she?" If he only knew. And why did that woman have to say "in Jesus name?"

Okay, I'll drive back home, hide this creepy workbook thing, and then I'll have to walk to the shul. More like run.

After racing home and throwing the workbook in the trunk of her car, Naomi started her twenty-five minute trek to the Temple. This meant she would be arriving just only as a few stragglers were saying their goodbyes.

As she had predicted, by the time she approached the Temple people were getting into their cars and driving away. Only one other couple, Jay and Sandy Marcus, would be walking home.

"Naomi, are you okay? Everyone was asking about you," Sandy said.

Trying to catch her breath, Naomi said, "I wasn't feeling that well."

And now she saw Daniel standing in the doorway and shaking hands with those who were still making their way out.

At the first glimpse of his wife, Daniel excused himself and hurried to her. "I was worried about you. Are you—?"

"I'm sorry, but I wasn't feeling that well this morning."

His eyes lit up. "Morning sickness, you think?"

"No, it's not."

"Then what's the matter? Why don't you feel well?"

"I'm feeling fine now. Please, don't worry."

"Okay. Then Jason's Deli on the way home?"

"Sure."

The next day was spent with Jay and Sandy. Never having used a grill before, Daniel needed the practice, and they, along with their son Jake, were eager to volunteer their taste buds.

Sandy and Naomi were preparing the hamburgers and chicken breasts together in the kitchen while the men prepared the charcoal. Yet Naomi's mind was elsewhere. If she had been alone, she would have gone into Daniel's office and taken a look at his Bible, the one with the concordance in the back. She would have looked up the words Melinda had told her were in Isaiah.

The words kept resonating in her mind. If she could prove they were not from the Hebrew Bible but only misquoted by this "Christian lady," then she could put the whole thing to rest. She would cancel her appointment with Melinda and burn the book she had taken home.

But that would mean her hope for any possible healing was gone. The nightmares would never end, her sin would never be forgiven and the curses she brought upon Daniel would take away his hope, too.

The following morning Daniel kissed her goodbye and once his car was no longer in sight, she accomplished that which she had waited all day yesterday to do. Finding her husband's Bible sitting on his desk, she picked it up and hugged it to her chest. Yes, it was a holy book, but it was also her Daniel's Bible. She thought how much he enjoyed poring over the Scriptures and praying over what he read.

Finding the word "ashes" in the concordance, she noted it had a reference to Isaiah 61, to which she turned. There she read almost verbatim the words Melinda had spoken to her.

You are the God I've been looking for.

She delicately placed the Bible back exactly where she had found it, fondly stroking its cover. Maybe she could just take a peek into the workbook—what could it hurt? Since she had buried it deep inside her car trunk, she decided to go for a ride. Then in seclusion she would dig it out and . . . just a little look, that's all.

Driving aimlessly for about thirty minutes, she finally made the decision to drive to Delray Beach. Much less chance of running into anyone who might know her there. She easily found a parking place across from the water. Naomi pulled out a large towel also kept in her car trunk, and brought out the workbook hidden under the spare tire.

Her divergent emotions were at war within her: dread and hope. The first words she read chased away the dread and buoyed her with hope. "What a wonderful God we have, He is the Father of our Lord Jesus Christ . . ." Nonetheless, dread made a thunderous return, attempting to shove hope out of the way. Yet something was tugging at her to continue reading. "Blessed be God, even the Father of our Lord Jesus Christ, the Father of mercies, and the God of all comfort. 2 Corinthians 1:3."

Am I crazy? I can't do this. I'll ruin my marriage.

She slammed this frightening book shut before it could contaminate her any further. Naomi stood up and shook out the sand from the towel, and proceeded back to her car. There was a garbage can right next to where she had parked and she would toss this dangerous thing right where it belonged.

Yet she found herself unwilling to carry out her plan. For one thing, the garbage can had flies buzzing all around it, and the smell of something rotting came from the area. Melinda was so nice, and the words she had read from these pages . . . She carried the book back to the car, opened the trunk, and hid the contraband material under the towel.

The rest of the day was spent shopping for groceries, meeting with the contractor who would be doing their bathroom renovation, and visiting Marvin Berman's widow.

The poor woman seemed overwhelmed trying to deal with her financial affairs and other day-to-day necessities. It seemed Marvin had taken care of everything leaving Mrs. Berman to feel pampered, at least until he was gone.

Whether in visiting with Mrs. Berman, shopping, or picking out ceramic tile, never for a moment did Naomi forget the object lying under the beach towel. Like a smoldering coal locked away, any minute to erupt into a huge fire.

That evening she surprised Daniel with a gourmet meal. The biggest feat she pulled off with the dinner was duplicating a part of their dinner at Luchow's. Daniel walked in the door, found the table set with their finest dinnerware, lit candles, and sounds reminiscent of the waltz music they danced to on their first real date. Then Naomi came out wheeling a cart. On this cart was a platter of thin pancakes with bright red lingonberry sauce poured over them.

"Sit," she commanded her husband, as she poured cognac over the platter and then quickly ignited the food with a small torch.

Over dinner, Daniel told her, "I know why you're doing all this. Tonight's the Emmy Awards, isn't it?"

"Well, yeah, but. . ."

He remembered the year before how disappointed she was when he told her he was not interested in watching something that silly. Now he smiled and said, "If you want to watch it, we'll watch it."

Two hours later they were in the den, cuddled up on the couch and watching the award show while sipping from the cognac left over from dinner. Toward the end of the show it was time to give an award for the best comedy series.

Naomi no longer kept up with show business news, so was oblivious to the fact that Gary Ruben had been nominated for his new television series. When she heard his name as a nominee, it felt as though a fist had been pounded into her stomach.

As for Daniel, his attention was no longer on the television, but now on his wife. One minute she had been relaxed, but now her warm body, which had been molded around his, had become cold and stiff.

"And the winner is Gary Ruben."

With the cameras focused on him, Gary quickly stood up, leaned down to kiss the woman next to him, and then sprinted to the stage.

"I would like to thank my beautiful wife and mother of my little baby boy." Holding his award aloft, he said, "Francine, this is for you." Blowing a kiss toward her, he disappeared amidst much applause.

Naomi gasped for air. Daniel was staring at her as her lips refused to stop their quivering.

"Naomi, what is it?"

It looked like fire blazing from her eyes. She would not let him hold her, but pulled away and leapt off the couch. Locked inside the bathroom, she tried to ignore Daniel's insistent knocking and his pleas. He deserved an explanation—she could give none—she was trapped.

Not receiving any cogent answer from his wife, Daniel was left to come up with his own explanation for her erratic behavior. "You want to go back to New York. You miss your acting," he said as he confronted the closed door. "You see all those actors up there, and think it should have been you, right?"

Naomi opened the door. "Daniel, no, no, I don't miss acting. I don't."

His body now against the bathroom's doorframe, he asked, "Then why are you so unhappy, Naomi? Don't you think I can tell? I hear you at night getting up like you had a bad dream or something. What do you expect me to think? "

"I love you. I don't want to go back to New York. I don't want to ever leave you." She must find something to tell him. However lame it may be.

Naomi reached out for Daniel's hand, at which point their eyes met. "Daniel, I guess watching that stupid Emmy show, it just reminded me how empty my world used to be. It's not anymore . . . and . . . well, the bad dreams and all, well, sometimes I guess I think about all the years I wasted and I want to like beat myself up for them. I know that probably doesn't make sense to you, but . . ."

He pulled her toward him, kissing her on the top of her head. "Jay and I were talking the other day—we try to understand you women, but you have emotions that we can't even come up with a name for."

Together they laughed and embraced, the firestorm had been averted.

That night, however, she was unable to sleep. So, Gary and Francine had a little boy—how could she not turn that around in her head? How could it not crush her heart?

Since she now knew Daniel heard when she got out of bed, she chose to try to imitate a rhythmic breathing—let him think she was asleep—while actually praying for peaceful sleep to come.

What was she to do? If she pursued meeting with Melinda and reading this Christian literature, she could ruin her marriage, but if she did nothing she would most certainly ruin her marriage.

The next morning, Naomi poured a second cup of coffee while stifling a yawn. Seemed important to continue the charade—let him think she slept soundly the night before.

Daniel scraped the remnants of omelet from his plate into the garbage disposal and smiled toward his wife. "Are you excited about today?" When Naomi stared blankly at him, he reminded her, "The bathroom guy is coming. Should be here any minute as a matter of fact."

"Oh that's right."

At that moment Camino Real's guard called to announce, "Someone from Henry Tile Company's here."

Daniel apologized, "Should have called you ahead of time. Sorry, Laverne."

Naomi, still in her pajamas, ran to the bedroom. "Daniel, I'm so sorry, I should have moved all the stuff out of the bathroom, but I—"

"Don't worry, honey. Go change. I'll do it."

Once Henry had arrived and was all set to begin his work, Daniel kissed his wife goodbye. "Call me if there's any problem, okay?" Two steps out the door, he turned back. "He comes with good references. You should be okay, but if you don't want to be alone, maybe you could call Sandy."

For a good part of the morning, Naomi kept herself busy, cleaning, baking, and talking on the phone with Sandy. However, she could not dismiss from her mind the book still hiding in her car.

She popped her head into the bathroom. "Would it be okay if I went out for an hour?"

Stooped over and scraping off the old tile, he assured her, "Of course, Mrs. Cantor."

Naomi drove to Delray Beach and found the same identical spot where she sat before. Today she would move beyond that opening page which had the New Testament scripture. She would turn the page as rapidly as possible, hoping its incendiary words would not poison her.

On the next page Naomi found a list of questions she was to ask herself, determining how affected she might be from her abortion. Question number five: "Have you ever had nightmares? Shaken by how profoundly her heart answered "yes," she skipped to the sixth question: "If you do not have children, do you fear you will never be able to have them?" *Of course I do. And how are you going to help me with this? You're just a dumb book, what can you do?*

She chose to skip the rest of these diagnostic questions and instead skimmed the introduction. Some words were as if written with neon ink. She read "abortion ended the unborn baby's life . . . the woman tries to deny that the abortion killed her child."

Like a splash of cold water thrown in her face, she acknowledged what she had tried so desperately to deny. She lifted her eyes up toward the blinding sun and cried out for mercy. When her eyes looked again at the book, she read "The final step in healing is learning to accept God's forgiveness."

"Hi, Amy, glad you came back."

"Me, too."

After a few minutes of pleasantries, Melinda said, "Amy, I'm going to start a sentence, and I want you to complete it for me. Ready?"

Naomi aka Amy nodded.

"One area of my life that has been affected by abortion is . . ."

Melinda allowed time for Naomi to ponder this question. Tracing the footprints that led to where she was today, brought Naomi a newfound awareness. If she had not had the abortion, there would be no Daniel today. It all began with the need for forgiveness—it had caused her feet to be velcroed to the sidewalk in front of the synagogue. That's when out walked the love of her life.

Naomi tried voicing this revelation to Melinda. "Because of my abortion I decided to go back to syn . . ."

"Yes?"

"Synagogue. I'm Jewish."

"Well, Amy, I grew up Catholic. It's interesting how God works. After I had my abortion and was looking for relief from my nightmares and the horrible guilt I was feeling, I went back to the Catholic Church. But I couldn't bring myself to confess my sins to a man . . . you know, to the priest. Eventually I found a place like this center here."

The remainder of their hour together served to build a bond of friendship and trust. Naomi had no problem committing to meeting again the following Friday—she actually looked forward to it.

Melinda said, "The lesson you will be working on for next week will be on the character of God. Since God is the one you'll be trusting to help you, it's important to learn more about His character—especially that He is trustworthy. Makes sense, doesn't it?"

Naomi calmly nodded while inside feeling a rush of excitement.

"Amy, do you have a New Testament?" Naomi gave an almost imperceptible shake of her head. "Wait here. I'll get you one."

Waiting for Melinda to return, Naomi's head was swimming. Now she would have another book to hide. Thinking about Daniel's reaction if he knew caused her to shudder.

Melinda reappeared with a hardbound book and handed it to Naomi, whose hands were shaking. "I understand you are Jewish. But, please, it won't bite you. That's the way you're feeling, isn't it?"

"Yes."

Melinda walked Naomi to the front door. "Two more things: number one, you can call me any time you need to, and number two, there's a table of contents in the Bible I gave you. It'll help you .Your workbook is going to have you look up a lot of different passages in the Bible. Okay?"

"Your Bible or my Jewish one?"

Smiling, Melinda answered, "They're the same, Amy."

Naomi laid the Bible on the front seat next to her, along with the workbook, but as soon as she found a parking lot a block or two away, she pulled in and hurriedly snatched up the alarming material and in the car trunk under the beach towel it went.

For some inexplicable reason she felt compelled to drive to the synagogue and say hello to her husband. When she walked into Daniel's office, he furrowed his brow. "Where have you been?"

"Oh, I—"

"Henry called me. He needed to ask you something about the arrangement of the tiles, but you had gone." Shaking his head in disbelief, he asked, "Why would you leave the house with a stranger inside? I had assumed you were home all week when he was there. Was I wrong?"

"I had a few errands. You had said he had good references."

"Okay. I'm just surprised. I mean you're the one usually more cautious than me. It's okay, My-omi. I didn't mean to get you so defensive."

Poor Daniel. I'm always getting him to apologize when I should be apologizing like mad to him.

It was noon on Monday when Henry came out to the living room to speak to Naomi. She had been staring out the window debating with herself. Should she leave the man alone in the house again or should she go into her car trunk for her hidden books and risk reading them at home?

"Mrs. Cantor, you want to look at your bathroom?"

It was beyond beautiful. More spectacular than all the tilework she had seen in all the open houses she had dragged Daniel to visit with her. Rich royal blues mixed with bright yellow and burnt oranges, set in a design worthy of display in a gallery.

She called her husband to ask if he wanted to give his final approval, but he told her "I trust you. You're probably the severest critic of them all. You like it, then I like it."

Indeed she was excited by Henry's completed work, but all the more excited that he was pulling out of their driveway now, and she would have the rest of the day to visit her secret library.

Curled up on the den sofa, she opened her workbook. The first thing it asked was for her to read a chapter in Genesis, and then a portion from Exodus. *So strange. These Gentiles read our Bible more than we do.*

She was then directed to read from their Bible—the New Testament. With her hands shaking, she looked in the Table of Contents. She found Matthew and read the genealogy of Jesus Christ: "The Son of David, the Son of Abraham." From there, she was directed to something called First John. She then read that Jesus Christ was the atoning sacrifice for our sins.

Naomi became indignant and began pacing from the den to the living room and back. *How dare them, trying to say their God is supposed to be my atoning sacrifice. I just don't think so.*

No wavering this time. These books belonged in a garbage can. With resolve she snatched up these poisonous books. She would take them to an anonymous garbage can somewhere—why not back to the one over at Delray Beach—the one with all the flies.

She drove back to the beach, the books tossed into the back-seat—it wasn't safe to have them near her. Yet a feeling of dejection swept over her. Ever since seeing the ad on television, there had been a small kernel of hope.

It wasn't fair. Why can't we have a God like theirs? I can see that Jesus started out as one of us, but He's their God now, not ours. So what am I supposed to do? Convert if I want to have my sins forgiven?

The car seemed to drive itself. Next thing she knew, she was back on Delray Beach with the car parked and the motor still running. Naomi wept, choking on her tears. She turned her body around and stretched her arms into the back seat, and picked up the books intended to be thrown into the trash heap.

With the books sitting on her lap, she thought of her new friend Melinda. These books were special to her. Sacred. Naomi had left a pen nestled in the pages where she had last read and opened back to that place. Hot tears splashed onto the pages.

And there was that word again: atoning. It stood out as if illuminated by a hundred brilliant lights. She recalled the first time she read about animal sacrifice being commanded in their Bible. Moses had said it was for atonement of their sins. When seated around the table at the Temple in Brooklyn, she had asked about this, but no one had an answer. But here was the word atoning in the Bible for the Christians.

They get atonement, but we have to fast once a year, and even then no one can tell me if my sin is forgiven.

With a degree of defiance, Naomi turned off the motor. Continuing to sit in the car, she went forward with the next question in the homework. To answer this she would need to read the actual words spoken by Jesus Christ. Letting out a deep sigh, she turned to the Gospel of John. The words surprised her by their tenderness. The Gentiles' God was reassuring his disciples that he would always be with them. He sounded so kind.

For the rest of that week, until her Friday appointment with Melinda, each and every day Naomi took advantage of any time she could to sneak away and finish her homework. By Thursday, the first week's assignment was completed.

Having fallen in love with what was written toward the end of John, she tried reading John from its beginning. "In the beginning was the Word, and the Word was with God." It sounded poetic, but what did it mean?

She then read, "He came unto His own, and His own received Him not." Her eyes widened and her mouth gaped open. This she understood perfectly.

Friday came and Naomi, fifteen minutes before her appointment, was standing at the receptionist's desk.

Maggie told her, "Melinda can see you right away."

The counseling session began with Melinda's opening question. "This one has two parts, Amy. Part one, finish this sentence for me: When I was a child, I pictured God to be . . ."

Surprising herself by how rapidly she answered, Naomi told her, "A judge. I remember one day in JYO, Jewish Youth Organization, they must have been talking about God or something, and I saw him. He had on a big black judge's robe, he was up in the clouds, and he had this giant-sized gavel. And I was sure He was just looking to wallop me on the head."

Maybe it was Naomi's imagination, but it seemed Melinda was about to cry. Her eyes had definitely moistened. "Part two of the question is to complete this sentence: Now that I have finished the chapter on the character of God I have learned God is . . ."

Naomi leaned forward, putting her hands on Melinda's." I want your God. Can I have your God? All my life I was warned a Gentile would try to convert me, but the truth is, I'm ready. Your God is so . . . I need Him. Go ahead, convert me."

A joyful laugh burst out of Melinda. "Amy, please, forgive me. I'm not laughing at you. It's just not like that. The God you've fallen in love with is your God. The God of Israel. Jesus is your Messiah. If you've come to believe in Him, you wouldn't be converting—you'd still be Jewish."

After dispelling other misconceptions and myths Naomi had believed all her life, Melinda explained, "Amy, He died for your sins, not just your abortion, but all your sins. And because He was resurrected, He lives today, and He wants to live inside of you through His Holy Spirit. You can receive Him as your Messiah today and be born again."

"And I'd still be Jewish?"

"Of course. I could lead you in a prayer."

This time Naomi was the first to stretch out her hands. Repeating her counselor's words, Naomi confessed to God that she was a sinner, that she believed Jesus had died for her sins, and was then raised from the dead. With heartfelt sincerity she asked Jesus to be Lord of her life and to give her the gift of His Spirit.

She was almost out the door, when she turned around and told Melinda, "What do I do now? My husband is a rabbi."

Chapter 20

A Time to Speak

With all the Rosh Hashanahs and Yom Kippurs, Naomi never knew if she had been forgiven. Weeping the tears of one now grateful to be forgiven and set free, Naomi sat in her car breathing in this precious moment—the moment of her release.

She needed somewhere to sit and reflect. The beach? The dark clouds answered no. She was aware of a cozy-looking coffee shop on the way toward home—yeah, that would work.

Soon she was drinking an iced coffee while gazing out the window onto the busy street and reflecting on what had taken place in the last hour—the hour she knew changed everything.

When learning Naomi's husband was a rabbi, Melinda was not too proud to say, "Uh, please, sit down. I need a minute to think this through." Twirling her long red hair around her finger, Melinda had confessed, "I've never dealt with a situation like this before."

Naomi then watched as Melinda bit her lip and arched her eyebrow, so similar to how Daniel expressed himself when in a quandary. Melinda had reached for Naomi's hands and said, "Amy, we better pray. I need God's wisdom."

This was when Naomi swallowed hard and made her confession. "My name's not Amy. It's Naomi—Naomi Cantor."

"You mean your husband is Rabbi Cantor?"

Bolting upright, Naomi had withdrawn her hands and exclaimed, "You sound like you know my husband."

"Well, I don't know him personally, but I have heard about him. There's a woman who volunteers here at the Center. Jeanine. She not only talks about Rabbi Cantor but she prays for him."

"She prays for my husband?"

"It has to do with her daughter Sandy—Sandy married a Jewish man and converted, so she now goes to your husband's congregation."

"Are you talking about Sandy Marcus?"

Melinda had rubbed her chin. "Yes, I think that's her married name—Marcus. Anyway, Jeanine, just last week was telling us about how this new rabbi at her daughter's *shul*—is that what you call it? Did I say it right?"

Naomi nodded, her mouth agape.

"She told us how your husband basically took a dying *shul* and now it's actually been growing, and he's even been having an impact on the students at the University. And, you know, Jeanine has a grandson—"

"Jake."

Snapping her fingers, Melinda had said, "Yes, now I remember she said the name Jake."

One of the most amazing events then took place: Melinda prayed, asking God to give them wisdom on how Naomi was to handle the situation with her new faith and with her husband. A moment or two after the words were out of her mouth, Melinda had simply said, "Thank You, Lord."

Naomi then felt her hand being squeezed as Melinda said, "You can open your eyes now."

"You got an answer already?"

"I believe so." She then had teasingly wagged her finger at Naomi. "Now, don't go thinking it always happens like this. Wow, I wish it did, but I guess God knew we needed immediate help. He reminded me of a place in Ecclesiastes that says, 'There's a time to be silent and a time to speak.' Naomi . . . I'm going to have to get used to not calling you Amy anymore . . . Naomi, you need to trust Jesus—that His Spirit will let you know when it is time to speak."

"So, for now, I can keep it a secret from my husband?"

"For now, just continue with your homework and. . . and . . . pray."

Upon leaving, Melinda had assured her, "Don't worry, everything will stay confidential."

How weird is it going to be when I see Sandy? What am I—? The slurping sound coming from her straw interrupted the thought. Seemed there was no more iced coffee left. Naomi pulled out money from her wallet and slid out of the booth.

She turned toward the cash register when a dazzling display of colors caught her eye. It's not like she hadn't passed this tropical nursery each time she drove to the Women's Center. Whether it was the large Spanish-designed ceramic pots, colorful enough to compete with her new bathroom, or the exotic trees and plants, something caught her eye at this time. Since today was a day of new beginnings, she would explore the Sunkissed Nursery.

She browsed the rows and rows of trees, shrubs, and flowering plants. After receiving advice from another customer, Naomi made her decision. She would keep it simple. The pots of bright yellow bush daisies, approximately two feet in height, brought a smile to her face; their cheeriness was a perfect reflection of what was effervescing inside of her. Along with the daisies, she would also purchase several pots of the buttercup groundcover. Their linen-white petals with a splash of yellow at the center should bring them all together in a wonderful cascade of color.

"This is all new to me. What kind of tools do I need?" she asked the sales clerk.

An hour later, Naomi was on her knees, rejoicing as her hands dug deep into the earth. She was also digging deep, unearthing the wisdom of Melinda's counsel.

There she was kneeling on the ground relishing her newly planted daisies when the realization struck her. Melinda's counsel reflected the journey of the Israelites when they wandered in the wilderness. They did not move until God lifted the cloud over the tabernacle. Until He did, they stayed put. In her case, her mouth would stay put.

She collected the debris from her first venture into gardening and stepped back to assess the results. She was pleased. Very pleased.

Daniel's going to love it, too. Uh, oh—Daniel. Okay, one way to relax was a hot shower, and, of course, she needed one right now. Dirt under her fingernails, on her knees, probably in her hair . . .

Waiting for the shower water to warm up, she tuned the radio to a classical music station. The strains of Beethoven's lively seventh symphony were heard and suddenly Naomi was gliding across the floor in an impromptu ballet.

That evening, Daniel pulled into their driveway and saw their beautiful new garden. He came in through the garage, a bouquet of flowers in his hand. The smell of freshly baked bread greeted him, as well as a radiant wife. It was like a dark cloud had somehow been lifted from her, a weight removed from her shoulders.

Both eyebrows arched, he extended the bouquet of red roses to her. "Seems I didn't have to bring these home, huh? You had a gardener come?"

She eagerly took the flowers, giggled, and explained, "I'm the gardener. I did it, Daniel."

He watched her joyfully placing the roses in a crystal vase. *What's different about her? Whatever she took, I want it, too.*

Daniel's first words when she arrived at the *shul* the following Friday were, "It's all set. We will be celebrating our second-year anniversary in Israel."

"You're kidding? We have enough people signed up?"

"Three more people gave their deposits today. Not only is Mark now going, but his parents will be coming with him."

The Temple was filling up and people were clamoring for his attention, and several of the women wanted hers.

Naomi made her way through the preparations for the service. These chores were no longer as tedious as before. She was now appreciating the uniqueness of each individual, including even those who in the past had been unkind to her. And when she saw her husband, love for him engulfed her. And she understood why: she now knew the Creator and His love was coursing through her.

Nonetheless, like a damaged nerve threatening to fire off painful charges, a thought continued to hang around the periphery of her consciousness. This new faith might cost her the approval of every person her eyes rested upon, and especially that of Daniel's.

Her husband's message this *Shabbat* was on Exodus 40. "As we have read regarding the travels of the Israelites, they waited for a sign from God. If the cloud did not lift from above the tabernacle, then they did not lift their feet. This speaks to me about a profound trust. And that's why we should want to obey our God. What is temptation? I define it as not trusting God and saying 'forget it, that cloud hasn't moved in days, I'm getting tired of waiting. I'm going to go out on my own.' Or maybe even thinking 'God forgot about me. Here I am waiting and hoping, but He doesn't care about me.'"

Daniel walked down from the *bimah*, made eye contact with the substantial crowd gathered, and smiled. "Let's talk about this. Do you have trouble trusting God?"

When Daniel had begun this format, Naomi had to act as a shill, encouraging others to participate in this open dialog. Now, however, this was no longer necessary as a healthy exchange of ideas and even candid-type confessions were an intrinsic aspect of a *Shabbat* service at Temple Beth Shalom.

And on this particular Friday, God, who had answered Melinda's prayer so swiftly, was now speaking directly to Naomi's heart. Only a short time ago, Naomi had been prompted to consider the very same passage Daniel was now expounding upon. How could she not trust Him? He will reveal the time for her to no longer keep silent.

But when will I be able to say the name Jesus? All my life I've been told we were never to use His name.

Her mind must have wandered because suddenly it was time for Daniel to be stepping back up to the *bimah* and give his closing remarks. "I have an exciting announcement for everyone going on the trip to Israel. We will be leaving in two months. Now if anyone was still hoping to go but didn't sign up, what can I tell you? Think of it like Noah's ark . . . you're too late. Sorry, I don't mean to be facetious, but it's the truth." He then looked into the crowd, and found his wife. "Naomi, would you tell everyone what's extra special to us about being in Israel on June fifth?"

"It's our anniversary," she shouted out to the crowd.

After all the *mazel tov's* faded out, Daniel concluded with, "*Shabbat Shalom.*"

Daniel had been so impressed with the extra sparkle the bright yellow and white flowers added to their home, that one Sunday Daniel woke Naomi up with a suggestion. "Let's go get some trees."

When asked where she had purchased the flowers, Naomi was tempted to fib, after all she had done it all her life. Yet something had restrained her. When she told him the name and address of the nursery, he asked the inevitable. "What were you doing in that part of town?"

This truth-telling had its challenges. Answering with "I don't know," "I got lost," or other cover-ups which popped into her head instantaneously, would be downright lying.

And her hesitation in answering was not missed by Daniel. "Naomi, what's going on here?" With still no response, he asked, "Did you get lost again?"

Then the phone rang. Whew! A couple wanted to talk to Daniel about their son's upcoming bar mitzvah. Daniel answered their questions, hung up the phone, and walked back to Naomi.

"My-omi, let's go to Marti's."

The issue of the nursery was dropped, but how long could she live covering up her tracks? In both her workbook and in what she had been reading in the Bible, there were promises which she was clinging to: God would never leave her; He would provide all she needed; He would give her what to say.

A block from Marti's, Daniel said, "I was thinking, rather than going out and buying stuff ourselves and then trying to figure out how to plant it . . . I mean this is all new to us . . . we'll find a landscaper. Would you like that?"

She would love it. And, most importantly, it was as if the question of why she had been in a particular area of town had disappeared into the vapor.

Over breakfast they made a final shopping list for Tuesday evening with the students. Barbecuing once a month was now a favorite attraction for all, and it would be coming up next week. Between questions regarding what kind of steak, what kind of barbecue sauce, whether baked potatoes, corn on the cob, or potato salad, Daniel kept interrupting with the same question, "What's different about you?"

At one point, after commenting, "It's like you have this special glow," he stopped, his eyes got huge, and he started to ask, "Are you—?"

Naomi shook her head and inaudibly mouthed "no."

At her next meeting with Melinda, Naomi said, "It's not that I don't still want to have a baby, but I'm not feeling like I have to. I don't have to prove something anymore. Melinda, do you have any children? I've never asked you."

"None of my own. I've been married now for three years. My husband has a daughter from a previous marriage. She's adorable. But, no, I haven't had any of my own. It's not too late though. I'm only thirty-one. You never know, maybe one day we'll be walking around the mall together pushing our baby strollers."

The hour's session now finished, Naomi admitted, "You know when I first saw all those questions in the workbook about how I felt when I walked into the clinic. . . stuff like that . . . I thought, that's it, I'm done with this study. Why should I have to relive all that again?"

"Do you still feel that way?"

Naomi shook her head vigorously. "Even though it was hard, it showed me how much I didn't want to be in that clinic. I only did it because Gary pretty much told me I had to." Burning tears now flowed. "I wanted to be loved so much and somehow I was stupid enough . . . or desperate enough . . . or both, to think if I did this, then Gary would love me."

Naomi received a box of Kleenex from Melinda. "But now, it's like that beautiful thing you told me when I first came here, about how God would give me beauty for ashes . . . that's exactly what He did. Because of the ashes, being so depressed because of my abortion, first God used that to bring Daniel into my life. And, Melinda, he is the most wonderful man . . . Thank God I didn't end up with Gary instead . . . and then over and above all that, not only do I have a beautiful husband, but now I have this relationship with God Himself."

Walking out of the counseling room together, Naomi stopped at the doorway. "Do you have another second?"

"Of course."

They walked back into the room and each took their usual positions, the couch for Naomi and the chair for Melinda.

Naomi laughed. "I always do this to you, don't I? There's always one more question. Well, here it is—I'm having a hard time saying the name of Jesus. When I'm with you I'll say God or maybe Him, something like that. And even when I'm praying, I'm having such a hard time saying that Name. Please, don't think . . ."

Melinda placed her hands on Naomi's. "Naomi, I'm not going to judge you."

"This Tuesday we had a group of students at our house for a barbecue, and I noticed how many times I heard the name of Jesus said, but it was never said in a nice way. It was like a swear word." Naomi blushed. "And in the past that's the only way I would say His name. But this Tuesday, every time I heard His name used like that, I found myself kinda cringing."

"I don't know if this will help, Naomi, but I've heard people say how His Hebrew name is Y'shua."

"Really? Wow, that means salvation."

"I once heard a Jewish woman speaking at an Easter brunch. She explained how she personally used the name Y'shua. It's too bad you can't go to church . . . I know you can't, and I'm not trying to put any pressure on you, but it would be so nice if you could be around other believers."

Naomi's eyes lit up at the prospect. "I wish I could."

As Passover approached, Naomi was finding more and more references in her New Testament regarding this Feast. She was coming to love the name Y'shua, and when she read that He was referred to as the Passover Lamb, she yearned to go running to Daniel and proclaim this truth to him. An assurance was growing in her that one day he, too, would rejoice at this good news. And each and every day she prayed, "Lord, tell me when is the time . . . the time to speak."

And it seemed each and every day, Daniel was commenting on how radiant his wife looked. "Are you sure you're not . . .?"

When Naomi's parents flew down to spend Passover with them, one of the first things out of Helen Goldblatt's mouth was, "Oooh, sugar, you're pregnant, aren't you?"

Naomi explained this was not the case and Helen apologized, but still insisted there was a definite "special glow" about her daughter. "What else can it be, sugar?"

Daniel said, "Tell me about it. I keep asking her what her secret is."

Naomi detected a hint of suspicion. *Lord, when do I speak?*

With much of the conversation around the Passover table centered on the upcoming trip to Israel, Naomi said to her parents, "I wish you could come with us. Maybe the next time we go with the *shul*, you'll come."

Saul put his napkin down and cleared his throat. "Like we told you when you were in New York, Mother and I are thinking about retiring down here. Not in this ritzy area you two live in, but maybe in the Miami area. While we're here we might look."

Later that evening, the men went to sit outside by the swimming pool at Saul's request. "Never thought my daughter would have her own pool."

In the kitchen with Naomi, Helen squeezed soap into the sink and asked, "Sugar, which one do I use?" The woman had never seen a two-bowl kitchen sink before.

"You can rinse the dishes in either of them and then we'll put them in the dishwasher."

As Naomi was arranging the plates into the dishwasher, her mother bent down, grabbed Naomi's hand, and told her, "You look so happy. Are you sure you're not pregnant?"

"Mom, let's go into the dining room for a minute." Naomi sat at the head of the table and indicated that her mother should sit right next to her. She even scooted up her chair so they were only a breath apart. "You remember how you taught me to say my prayers every night?"

"Oh, darling, of course, I do. And still, every night, when I say my prayers, I think of you."

"Mom, I found out something amazing. I haven't told Daniel yet, or anyone else even, but I want you to know."

"You want me to keep it a secret? Is that what you're telling me?"

"For now. Only for now." Naomi moved even closer to her mother. "Mom, you know, how we were told that we're waiting for the Messiah?"

"Yes, dear."

"He already came."

Helen jolted up in her seat. "Naomi, tell me you're not saying what I think you are. You know Sadie? Her son Benjamin converted. This is not what your secret is, is it?"

Naomi had promised the Lord she would never lie again. What was she to do in this dilemma? "No, I didn't convert, I'm still

Jewish, but, Mom, Jesus . . . He's our Messiah." Seeing the fear on her mother's face, Naomi stood up and said, "Let's forget about it for now, okay?"

However, it was not to be forgotten. Daniel came into the room and stood behind Helen, glaring at his wife. "Helen, please leave Naomi and I alone for a minute."

Timidly, yet quickly, Helen left the room and joined her husband outside.

Daniel demanded, "Whatever you've been keeping silent about, now is the time to speak."

Now is the time to speak? Was this how her prayer was to be answered? Not sure where to begin, the words "I call him Y'shua, and I love Him," poured from her mouth.

Daniel's face reddened and his jaw clenched.

"Daniel, I can show you—"

"Show me what? That you're a traitor? Adultery would be better than this."

"No, never, I love you so much—"

She walked towards him, but he pushed her away.

"Love me? No, I don't think so. You're no better than the Jews who collaborated with the Nazis. My parents told me about them. They sold out their own people."

He now advanced closer to her, his finger pointing at her. "I married a Jew, I expected she would have stayed a Jew."

His fists clenched, he spun around the room. He looked up and saw the picture he had once reframed when Naomi had smashed it. He pulled it down from the wall and smashed it onto the dining room table. "My-omi is now my enemy!"

Chapter 21

Who has believed ...?

*S*he's not here, Anne."

Naomi walked into their living room and corrected Daniel. "Yes, I am."

Still in his pajamas, he said into the phone, "Sorry, she's right here."

Naomi stretched out her hand to take the phone, but Daniel instead laid it down on the coffee table and walked back into the den where he had been sleeping for the past two weeks.

"Hi, Anne . . . Oh, I'm so sorry. . . When's the funeral?"

A few minutes later Naomi gently tapped on the door which separated her from her husband. "Daniel?"

Wordlessly, he opened the door, keeping his eyes downcast.

"Anne's father died. I'd like to go to his funeral. Would that be okay?"

He nodded his assent and closed the door.

By the time Naomi had made the necessary airplane reservations and packed her bags, Daniel had eaten his breakfast, showered in the guest bathroom, and vanished from their residence. Such had been the pattern since he had determined she was his enemy.

She hoped the five hours of traveling would provide a needed respite—not to be bombarded with painful reminders of the strife ripping their marriage apart. A temporary cessation of the phone calls from her parents would also provide necessary relief.

Her mother would call crying, "Sugar, please, make things right with your husband. Do it quickly, before it's too late."

Then her father would take the phone from his wife to deliver his own message, one of condemnation. "For once you had made us proud of you, but now you . . ."

Amidst the accusations and the profound sadness, every day experiencing Daniel's rejection, still there was not, even for a moment, any doubts. The presence of the One who now lived in Naomi's heart embraced her with a loving acceptance she had longed for all her life.

The One she was longing to see truly turned out to be Someone who was most certainly watching over her.

After checking her bag and receiving her boarding pass, Naomi made a quick call to Melinda to explain her sudden departure. The woman's encouragement was truly a gift from heaven.

"Naomi, I'll continue praying for you. Don't worry."

She sobbed a goodbye to Melinda. Immediately upon hanging up the phone she realized she had left her Bible on the nightstand. Her faith no longer a secret, she had become emboldened to the point of reading it inside the home. Now she would boldly walk into a bookstore within the airport and purchase a Bible. She found an exquisite leather-bound Bible. It had the special title of being a "Study Bible."

As soon as she boarded the plane and awaited take-off, she opened her new Bible. There were a number of charts, with one particularly capturing her attention: Messianic Prophecies, with Old Testament references in one column and New Testament fulfillment in another.

Most of her flight time was spent studying this information, with the remainder of time spent in prayer. *Please open the eyes of those I love. Y'shua, help Daniel to love Your Name as much as I do. No, even more. He already loves You, he just doesn't know Your Name. And my mother, too. Oh, I'm sorry, my father also.*

Reuniting with Anne at the airport was bittersweet. Naomi had resolved not to tell Anne anything about the trouble in her marriage—her friend truly didn't need to hear about anyone else's heartbreak right now.

"This was so nice of you to come. I guess Daniel couldn't make it?"

"No, afraid not."

They waited at the baggage carousel, while Anne explained, "The funeral will be first thing tomorrow. My brother Patrick will be flying in later tonight from Germany. The Air Force is giving him leave for a few days."

When Anne pulled up to her home, there was barely room for her Volkswagen. Smiling, she explained, "Mostly a lot of people from the church—they've been a real help to Mom and me. They're like family."

With Anne's help, Naomi brought in her luggage to this modest home, filled with people, flowers and casseroles. *Like family—I wonder what that's . . . ?*

Mrs. Holloway was a demure woman, but one who seemed to possess an inner strength. Naomi tried to imagine what it was like for this woman, having endured the pain of watching her husband deteriorate. According to the pictures displayed all around the house, he had been an athletic, vibrant man. Both Anne and her mother had witnessed him waste away before their eyes.

Patrick's flight was delayed and when Naomi was offered the opportunity to retire into the guest room around nine 'clock, Naomi gratefully accepted. She got into the four-poster bed and opened her new Bible to the Psalms.

But how could she not think about Daniel? Where was he right now? And what was he thinking? Was he thinking of her? A tear splashed onto the page—Psalm Twenty-seven will always now have a reminder of her heartache.

Because of Greg Holloway's funeral, Naomi for the very first time in her life entered a church. Anne, concerned with helping her mother, whispered something to her brother Patrick.

A Master Sergeant in the Air Force, he walked over to Naomi. "Please, would you sit with us up in the front? My sister considers you family."

"Thank you."

When the organ played the first few chords of "Amazing Grace," Naomi thought it sounded familiar—yes, she had heard this song before, but never before did the lyrics tell her very own story. She had been blind, but now she saw.

Only such an amazing grace could save such a mess like me. Truly amazing.

Unlike Marvin Berman's funeral, this seemed more like a celebration. And the Pastor's eulogy made it clear why the choir had also sung "Blessed Assurance." The Pastor even gave a date when Greg Holloway was born again and then baptized.

Baptized? Naomi would need to ask Melinda about this. *Baptized?*

"I've known Greg Holloway most of my life," the Pastor told those gathered in his small country church. "I had the privilege of being the best man at his wedding. It was even Greg who encouraged me to go into the pastorate." The tall gray-haired man softly chuckled. "Now, don't go blaming him if you think I never should have . . . maybe it should've been Greg, and not me. He had a pastor's heart, didn't he? Let me ask you, when you visited Greg after his accident, did you find that even though you went there to encourage him, somehow he ended up encouraging you? Whether you found him in bed or sitting in his wheelchair, his trust in Jesus never wavered. Folks, I'm looking forward to seeing our friend again when I get to heaven."

At Marvin's funeral, it was like Daniel had to beg God to let the man into heaven. And even then, one only hoped. *Amazing grace. I belong here more than I do at our Temple.*

Daniel shakily stood up. "Good discussion once again. See you next week." His knees had almost buckled under him—hopefully it went unnoticed. Maybe it was simply because he had been sitting on the floor for too long. *I'm not as young as these guys, after all.*

"Man, when are we going to talk more about going to Israel?" Mark ran to where refreshments usually were set out after their study time.

Jennifer scolded her fellow student. "Mark, you are so disrespectful. He's not 'man' but Rabbi Dan."

Mark turned around and snickered. "Ha! You're just jealous cause I'm going to Israel and you're not." He continued in pursuit of the food, but only saw an empty table. "Yo, Rabbi Dan, where's the vittles, man?"

Jennifer reached into her purse, found a pen and threw it at him, only missing him by a few inches.

Jake Marcus moved a few steps closer to Daniel. "You heard the Rabbi, his wife's visiting a friend."

"So? What's that?" Mark whined. "No wife, no food?"

Jennifer demanded, "Someone let me borrow your pen. This time, I promise not to miss him."

They were accustomed to Daniel joining in on this friendly jibing, but not tonight. Jake walked behind Daniel and placed his hand on his back. "C'mon, let the Rabbi have some peace and quiet, okay?"

Once the students were gone, the aloneness became all the more intense—more than what he had endured since Naomi's departure two days ago. Of course, her departure took place before a mere trip to Ohio. When had it all begun? When was his My-omi taken captive by the Gentiles?

Daniel sank into the couch in their conversation pit. This had been his and Naomi's favorite room. No, they loved their Florida room, too. Dropping his head to his knees, he mournfully sobbed.

How could this have happened? I never even asked her how.

An image of his wife floated before him. He saw the radiance, that special glow both he and her mother had mistakenly attributed to her being pregnant.

Was this new religion why she seemed so happy?

And even while facing his wrath for the last two weeks, she seemed to maintain an inner calm. That's not the Naomi he once knew.

Then a vicious-sounding voice whispered, "There's another man; she doesn't care about you, that's why she stayed so calm; she's in the arms of this man right now, the one who sold her a line of goods about this fake religion."

He would search their bedroom. Actually *her* bedroom now. Since learning of her betrayal, he refused to enter the room they once had shared. His clothes and toiletries were now all piled up in "his part of the house."

Rifling through her dresser drawers turned up nothing he could use to confirm his sudden suspicion of adultery. He looked toward their bed. *Her* bed now. Why did affection still linger in his heart? Whether she was a traitor or an adulteress, either way she was undeserving of his affection. Yet he found himself sitting on *her* bed and smoothing his hands across the silky comforter; this is where she slept, without him.

His eyes narrowed as he caught sight of a book placed on her nightstand. A box of tissues sat on top of it, partially concealing its front cover, but the word Bible was clearly seen. *Not our Bible, but theirs.*

He would take it to the conversation pit, turn on the gas fireplace and burn it. Just as one of his seminary professors had taught, this book is an anathema to our people.

However, once he held it in his hands, he wondered if he would find something written inside identifying who had beguiled her with this poison. Possibly there would be an inscription, but he found none.

The only thing he discovered was his wife's notes and bookmarks. The book was obviously well-worn. Never had he seen

Naomi so engrossed in anything she read. This dispelled the fears of another man—it appeared the only thing stealing Naomi from him was this book.

He walked toward the living room to carry out his book burning. But he was curious. What kind of notes had she written and why had she placed all these bookmarks in different places?

The only one he could consider a spiritual adviser would be Irwin, his old *havurah* leader. As humiliating as it would be to tell someone your wife had converted, he had to talk with someone.

Thankfully Irwin was home and after hearing Daniel's plight, he had a ready answer. "You need to debunk the lies she's been told. Don't be afraid to look through her book and check it with our Scriptures. Daniel, my friend, it's your responsibility to win her back."

While still speaking with Irwin, Daniel's call waiting came on. "Irwin, I have to go. Thank you."

On the other line was Naomi. "Daniel, can I give you the number at Anne's?"

He wordlessly wrote down the telephone number, then took a breath and asked, "Naomi, I want to know how this happened. I should have asked you before now, but now I'm asking."

His voice was distant and icy, but finally he was engaging in conversation with her. "Daniel, I had an abortion once, before I met you."

"You're just now telling me this?"

"I was so ashamed. It's hard even now telling you."

"That's why you were pushing so hard to have a baby, isn't it?"

"Yes."

"What's this have to do with your converting?"

"Since I've known you, I've been looking for forgiveness. Every Yom Kippur, I would hope I'd done enough repenting, enough of whatever that yoke of the law told me to do."

After hearing about Melinda and the Women's Center, he pleaded with her, "Naomi, they brainwashed you. You were vulnerable and they took advantage of you."

"No, Daniel, that's not true. Haven't you noticed . . . I know you have because you've asked me why . . . why I seemed happier lately. It's because I know my sins are forgiven, and a lot more than that, too. He's the Messiah, Daniel. There's all these prophecies, Psalm Sixteen and Psalm—"

"Now, you're teaching me? Excuse me, rabbi, but what seminary did you train under?" He pressed down on the off button of his phone. He must follow Irwin's advice. After all, she was not a rabbi and, as one himself, he would disprove everything she had been told by those who are the enemies of the Jewish people.

The last of the visitors having left, Mrs. Holloway told Anne, "I'm going to take a nap."

This provided Anne and Naomi their first real time alone together. "We have a lot of catching up to do," Anne said. "Let's take a walk behind the house."

Anne pointed to a place in the distance. "See that treehouse? Dad made it for Patrick and me. Can you believe it? It's still there. I've been going up there by myself lately. Even singing there. It's got great acoustics."

Naomi read her friend's mind. "Let's go." Once inside, Naomi walked over to a number of dolls stacked into the corner.

Anne explained, "I didn't have the heart to throw them away, so I just put them over there. The Raggedy Anne is still my favorite. Don't say it . . . I know you . . . she's not my namesake."

With a few large pillows spread around a tiny table, they made themselves reasonably comfortable.

"Naomi, I owe you an apology."

"For what?"

"Remember I once told you something like we had different gods?"

"I'm not sure. I think I remember that."

Anne reached over and took one of the dolls, placing it on her lap. "I was wrong. We don't."

"I know we don't."

"You do?"

"Anne, I believe in Jesus."

"You do?"

After passing the hurdle of telling her own husband about her past, Naomi now told Anne about her abortion, the yearning to find forgiveness, and how a television ad brought her to find her Savior.

"But, oh my goodness, what about Daniel? Does he believe now, too?"

This unleashed the floodgates. "He calls me his enemy now. He hates me."

There was no tissue in the treehouse and Anne improvised by removing the apron from her favorite doll and handing it to Naomi.

Choking on her tears, she told Anne, "He hates me but I still love him."

Now came the time in the Saturday *Shabbat* Service for the reciting of the Mourner's *Kaddish*. Daniel, as was the custom, asked all who were memorializing the death of a loved one to please stand as this was recited. "Glorified and sanctified be God's great name . . . Amen."

The congregation declared "Amen," as many curious eyes studied their Rabbi. He appeared to be valiantly trying to continue chanting the prayer in its entirety, but his weeping was making it impossible.

Jay Marcus stepped onto the *bimah*, placed a hand on Daniel's shoulder and leaned into the microphone, softly announcing, "*Shabbat Shalom*, everyone."

Daniel later told those who asked, "Sometimes chanting the *Kaddish* makes me think of all our people who were persecuted, from the time we were forced to convert, to the Holocaust, to who knows what may happen next."

No one brought up the fact that never before had he reacted by weeping during this part of the weekly service. And no one brought up the two-week absence of his wife.

Jay took Daniel aside. "Rabbi, I don't know what's going on with you and your wife, but you need to get her back—soon."

Mildred came to where Daniel and Jay were standing. "Rabbi, what can I do to help? With your wife gone, you must need a good supper. Please, I'd—"

"No, Mildred. Now, if you'll excuse me." Daniel turned and walked away.

Mildred and Jay exchanged glances, both unaccustomed to hearing this sharp tone coming from their Rabbi.

The walk home seemed to last an eternity for Daniel, his conscience nagging him the entire distance. *Who are you to talk to anyone in that tone of voice?* But it wasn't his fault—his wife was the one at fault, leaving him vulnerable to being unkind with others.

Jay was right, he needed to bring Naomi back, but not only from Ohio but back from whatever pit she had fallen into. His pace quickened; he must hasten his study of the false teachings she had embraced.

By the time the key unlocked the front door, he had determined where to begin. Her bookmarks would serve as a signpost. Back in the conversation pit, he opened to the first bookmark.

Genesis Fifteen. *So, they're teaching her the Torah, are they?*

Highlighted in orange was verse six. "And he believed in the Lord; and He counted it to him for righteousness." In the margin Naomi had written, "A relationship with God is to believe what He says and He will consider me righteous. I believe in You and know You love me." It was as if Daniel could hear his wife's voice speaking those very words—and it pierced something deep in his heart.

The next bookmark was placed in the seventh chapter of Isaiah, with verse fourteen highlighted. "Therefore the Lord Himself shall give you a sign; Behold, a virgin shall conceive, and bear a son, and shall call his name Immanuel." In the margin his wife had written, "A young girl—a virgin—a baby boy—God with us! I believe You!"

Now he knew—she was surely being deceived. While in seminary he learned the Hebrew word for virgin in this verse simply meant a young woman. Their professors had warned them, "Christians will try to tell you it means virgin. Don't listen to them." He did remember wondering though, "If it's just a young woman, then where's the sign—there's nothing miraculous about that?"

Next came a large laminated bookmark, also in Isaiah, in Chapter Fifty-Three. This also brought back a memory he had from seminary.

It was in Professor Silverstein's class. He had asked, "Why don't we read this chapter in synagogue? Why do we have to skip past it every year?"

All his classmates had turned to stare at Daniel while the Professor dismissively said, "It does not match any of the Torah portions or other sections of Isaiah which we read. You should know better than to ask this."

About to read the Scripture Naomi had bookmarked, his eyes went to Naomi's bold handwriting in the margin. "My Y'shua!"

Daniel slammed the Bible shut and went into his office to read from his own Holy Scriptures. He turned to Isaiah and read, "Who hath believed our report?"

Believed. It's true, God did tell Abram that because he believed, God would reckon it unto him as righteousness.

He read further along. "But he was wounded for our transgressions, he was bruised for our iniquities: the chastisement of our peace was upon him; and with his stripes we are healed. All we like sheep have gone astray; we have turned every one to his own way; and the Lord hath laid on him the iniquity of us all."

Him, it speaks of a him. Who is this man? I've always been taught it was Israel, but . . .

Leaving the Bible open, Daniel gently set it down on his desk. He wandered aimlessly around the house for a few minutes and eventually walked into the kitchen. He looked into the refrigerator and found nothing, into the pantry and still found nothing. He eventually saw a box of chocolate chip cookies he had bought for the next *havurah*. Taking the entire box with him into the Florida room, Daniel sat chewing on the cookies and staring into space.

"You know, I'm getting too comfortable here, Anne. I've appreciated you and your mother letting me stay, but it's been like two weeks already." Naomi cupped her chin with her hand and shook her head. "This is crazy. I can't run away forever."

Swinging together on a hammock on the front porch, Anne said, "You don't have to feel you need to leave right away. Mom told me to tell you, stay as long as you need to."

"But that's not fair to your Mom. I can't do that to her."

"Well, what are your plans then?"

"I don't know. And you're only asking me that because you know I don't have any. We know each other too well."

Catching sight of two women walking toward the house, each carrying a casserole dish, Anne nudged her friend. "Let's go for a walk."

"Back out to your treehouse?"

"Sure. It's beautiful at night. Dad kinda created a moon roof for my brother and me."

About to begin their hike, the phone inside the house rang. Each time Naomi heard it, her heart would leap, only to abruptly be crushed. The caller was never Daniel.

Anne's mother stuck her head out the front door, holding the phone in her hand. "Naomi, it's for you."

It was Daniel. "We leave for Israel next week. Come home."

She savored hearing his voice, but could not extend the conversation one word more than her husband would allow. "Come home," was about it. *And only for appearances—so, this is how we finally make it to Israel.*

He could not deny it was good to hear her voice, and it was obvious she was excited to hear his—she always got this breathy high-pitched thing going when she was excited—or nervous.

Hashem, may You bring my wife to her senses. She is a daughter of Abraham. Have mercy on her.

Now should he throw her Gentile Bible into the trashcan or should he place it back where he had found it? If he threw it away, she might resent him. And, more significantly, Daniel would be telling God he did not believe his prayer would be answered.

And, after all, as he had lately been reminded, believing was proof of his righteousness. He would choose to believe: Naomi would return home, see the accursed book where she had left it, and she, herself, would throw it away.

He placed it exactly where he had found it, but his eyes were drawn to her last bookmark. It was tucked into a place far enough back that he had avoided it. He knew where it would bring him— to the New Testament. Yet this would be his last chance to examine how deceived she truly was.

Daniel began reading about a member of the Jewish ruling council who came to Jesus at night.

He read that this man, Nicodemus, addressed Jesus as "Rabbi." Instead of being offended, Daniel found himself intrigued.

Well, that's not so unusual, actually. Jesus was supposed to have been a good teacher, so, sure, calling him a rabbi only makes sense.

He continued to read and discovered Nicodemus declared that he knew Jesus came from God, "for no man can do these miracles that thou doest, except God be with him."

Daniel read further into this passage until he became too offended to continue. This so-called rabbi had the nerve to tell him, a real rabbi, he would never see the kingdom of God unless he was born again.

I've dedicated my whole life to one day seeing the Kingdom of God. How dare you!

Daniel let the book drop from his hands and walked out of the room. At the threshold of the bedroom door, a voice (or was it simply a foolish thought?) halted his progress. "What if you are wrong?"

Chapter 22

Land of their Longing

I'll be in on Sunday." What if he asks why not sooner? How could she tell him that although she ached to see him, she also feared the painful sting of rejection he would inflict? "I didn't want to fly in during Shabbat, so I got the first flight they had for Sunday."

"What time? Your flight, when does it get in?"

The razor sharpness of Daniel's voice tore deep into Naomi's heart. Was returning home the right choice? Anne had said she could stay with them a while longer. However, Ginger, a Christian counselor Anne had introduced her to, advised differently.

Naomi had explained to her, "He only wants me back for appearances—he can't go to Israel without his wife. People will gossip."

She recalled Ginger's words: "I believe if you return out of consideration for your husband, God will honor that. It shows the kind of love Jesus demonstrated towards us."

Daniel exhaled heavily into the phone. "Naomi, I'm waiting. What time? And give me the flight number. I'll need that, too."

"You don't have to pick me up, Daniel. I'll take the airport shuttle bus like I did when I left." She quickly regretted hearing her own razor-sharp voice in retaliation. "Daniel, I'm sorry."

"Forget it. I'll pick you up. Just give me the flight number already."

She gave him the necessary information and received a curt goodbye.

Ginger had a group of women she called "my prayer warriors." Together they placed hands on Naomi and prayed fervently for her. Naomi also placed a call to the Women's Center in Boca, but was disappointed to learn Melinda was out with the flu.

The receptionist, Maggie, said, "Can you talk to anyone else? Jeanine is here today."

Sandy Marcus' mother? "Sure, that'll be great." Maybe this is what Ginger would call a "divine appointment." Naomi thought about Sandy's mother a number of times—how could she not? The woman had been praying for Daniel.

"This is Jeanine. How may I help you?"

"Jeanine, this is Naomi, Naomi Cantor—Rabbi Cantor's wife. Sandy's friend."

When Naomi explained how she, too, had become a believer in Jesus, Jeanine gasped. "Hold on, I have to get a Kleenex." A few sniffles later, the woman said, "My daughter and her family will be going with you and your husband to Israel this week. But . . . oh dear, how . . .?"

Naomi didn't need her to finish her question—her situation was apparent. Jeanine said, "Not only will I be praying, Naomi, but I will be fasting as well."

By this time Naomi was reaching into her box of Kleenex. "Thank you so much."

"Thank *you*. Your call is a gift from God—He has heard my prayers."

The next day, Naomi flew home comforted with the knowledge that she was not alone. God's gracious people were carrying her need—and Daniel's—to the very throne of God Almighty.

She stared out the airplane window, gazing at the panorama of clouds, sun blading through in colorful prisms. The tears burned as she recalled the first time she and Daniel had spoken about someday going to Israel. That blissful day when they shopped for Sukkah decorations at the farmers market.

Then came the time they believed the Holy Land would be the destination for their honeymoon: the Land of Milk and Honeymoon. And only recently he had announced they would be spending their second anniversary finally in the land of their longing.

Could she endure the verbal assaults she would receive from the man she loved? As she blinked away the tears, with crystal clarity a vision appeared. Y'shua Himself stood between Naomi and the one rejecting her. Her arms were wrapped tightly around Y'shua's waist and the lashes meant for her landed upon her Messiah's back.

If Naomi ran away from the one causing the hurt, she would need to take herself away from her Savior's embrace. If she chose instead to walk up to the one causing the hurt and enter into battle, she would again be separating herself from Y'shua's loving and protective embrace.

The airplane landed and Naomi prayed. *Help me, Y'shua, never ever to stop clinging to you.*

Both Daniel and Naomi needed to restrain their immediate impulse upon that moment of recognition. Daniel saw her warm and expectant face and was hit hard—he had missed her so much. He forced himself, however, to exercise control. *She is no longer . . .*

For Naomi, only caution governed her from running straight into his arms; yet she hoped. Maybe his arms would suddenly stretch out for her. If they did, she wouldn't be able to run fast enough.

The only acknowledgement of a relationship between them was when Daniel took her luggage and carried it to the car. The drive home was done in complete silence. Inside their home, he carried the luggage into *her* bedroom. In a short while, Naomi heard the front door slam. She ran out to the living room, looked out their front window and saw him drive away.

Later that evening, after having showered and prepped herself for sleep, Naomi heard Daniel moving about in the house, eventually shutting the door to the den. She had been more at home in Ohio. She buried herself under her covers and tried to sleep.

Daniel, reluctant to return home any earlier than necessary, had been strolling up and down the beach. Now home, he hoped to fall right off to sleep. First the pillows just didn't feel right. He flipped them over. Then he fidgeted with the sheets—why did they always have to end up uncovering his toes? This couch was not good for his back—and there was Naomi in their memory foam bed and . . . there was Naomi . . . there was Naomi.

He knew it wasn't the couch, nor the pillows, nor even the pizza he had eaten before coming home. It was the keen awareness that the woman he longed for was so near.

Naomi, having drifted into a shallow sleep, awoke to a familiar sound. A splash. She ventured out of the bedroom and crept toward the Florida room. Daniel was feverishly doing laps in their pool. Like gazing upon what was off-limits for her eyes, she hid behind the dining room column and continued spying on her husband. When he walked out of the pool, she saw him looking around frantically.

He must have forgotten his towel. Oh, Daniel, if only you'd let me, I'd get it for you . . . still so lean, still so handsome. Her longing for him cried out for fulfillment, but this was currently being denied to her.

While she tiptoed back to her bedroom, Daniel dripped across the living room floor and into the guest bathroom.

The next morning, Naomi tiptoed into the kitchen and brewed coffee. The den door was still shut. Walking back, mug in hand, she almost slipped on a wet spot—*Daniel must have dripped there.*

Back on the bed, she opened her Bible and closed her eyes to pray. Another very familiar sound could be heard: from the den. Daniel's chanting.

Was it her imagination, or did his morning prayer have a much more mournful resonance than when they did this together? *And he is covering himself right now in the prayer shawl we used to sit under together.*

On her knees, crying out for God's mercy, there was a tap on her door. "Are you awake?"

"Yes, I am." She quickly opened the door.

For one split second, he allowed his eyes to make contact with hers. "We need to talk about things to do with Israel. Would you want to eat breakfast together?"

"Yes," she answered tentatively. "I can make us something."

"There's not much in the way of groceries here right now. Let's go out."

"To Marti's?" Was that a smile he was trying to suppress? It was enough encouragement for her to take the plunge. "Daniel, I miss you so much. What can I do?"

"Don't do this, at least right now. I'm not up to it."

"Okay. Let me change . . . I'll be ready in fifteen minutes."

He walked away and mumbled, "Marti's will be fine."

Again they drove in silence. Yet after parking in front of Marti's Café and coming around to open her door, a look passed between them which called for an acknowledgement. In the past, when Daniel opened her door, he would reach for her hand as if she needed help getting out of the car. And they would then continue holding hands.

For a split second his hand had involuntarily reached down for hers, but quickly he pulled it away. He then turned his face from her. "Naomi, it's not that I don't still love you. I do. Very much." He turned back toward her, his eyes moist and his mouth tightened. "But I can't touch you anymore."

She fell back down into the car. With a penetrating gaze, she asked, "Why?"

Daniel opened the back door on her side and sat. Keeping his body turned toward the street, he closed the door. "You're unclean, Naomi." Hearing her agonized gasp, it was all he could do not to grab her and take her in his arms.

She now closed her door. Maybe they would continue talking without facing each other, but still it was a very private conversation. Bent over her knees, her head in her hands, she cried, "I should never have told you."

"Naomi, it's not because of what you told me . . . about the abortion. You didn't ever have to hide that from me."

She looked into the rearview mirror to see his face. "Then what do you mean I'm unclean?"

Staring back at the mirror, he said, "C'mon, you have to know. You committed blasphemy. What part of 'Thou shalt have no other gods before Me' don't you understand?" His voice grew louder and more agitated. "You're an idol worshipper now. You're unclean."

She turned full around to face him. "Then why would you want me to come with you to Israel? You're being a hypocrite, Daniel. You just want me there for appearances, don't you? I've never known you to be a hypocrite before. That's just one of the many reasons . . ." With her voice breaking, she moved to face the front of the car. ". . . why I adored you so much."

"Yes, you're right—some of it is for appearances, but that's not all of it. I'm praying that being in Israel will bring you back to your senses." His voice now broke as well. "And maybe I can't imagine being in Israel without you."

She sobbed uncontrollably. If only he could take her in his arms. "Naomi, please, I'll forgive you—and God will forgive you, too. Please, admit you were wrong and we . . ."

"I'd be lying if I did that. I could almost be tempted to do it just to have you back but, Daniel, I'd be choosing you over God."

She turned to face him and extended her hand to touch his face, but he shrunk back. "Daniel, you're the one who taught me to never choose anyone over God. Remember when you told me I was making you into a god? I still remember your words: 'don't give me credit for what God Himself is doing.' I loved when you said, 'God is the One giving meaning to you, not me.' But I never thought I'd have to choose between you and Him."

"Neither did I, Naomi."

"You want me to admit I'm wrong, but, Daniel, what if what I've found is the truth. What if *you're* wrong?"

Daniel steeled his jaw. "Look, we need to get out of the car, get in there and do some planning. Let's keep this impersonal, okay?"

She opened the door for herself this time, and over an impersonal breakfast they managed to plan a final get-together at their house with all those who would be traveling to Israel together.

Naomi thought of asking, "If I'm so unclean, why would you allow me to mingle with all the clean people?" She held her tongue. Ginger had asked her to memorize a Proverb: He who guards his mouth and his tongue, guards his soul from trouble. Ginger then would paraphrase it and say, "Zip your lips, Naomi."

Their breakfast meeting over, Daniel opened Naomi's car door and walked to the driver's side, praying, *Oh God of my fathers, please help me, the yoke of your law is sometimes more than I can bear.*

Their fellow travelers were thrilled when Naomi called and invited them to a *kumsitz* —let's all come and sit together. Jay and Sandy Marcus were, as always, a wonderful help.

To Naomi it seemed as if she were under great scrutiny. Not only by Daniel, but also by others in their congregation. It was obvious Jay and Sandy knew there was trouble between her and her husband. They had been their best friends now for over a year and would certainly be sensitive to the change in how she and Daniel were relating.

Sandy had given no indication that somehow she had learned about Naomi's new faith. Sometimes, Naomi almost wished she did. She couldn't help but wonder how Sandy would react if she told her, "I believe like your mom now."

Naomi's idea of having refreshments on this occasion included some of the Israeli food they would soon be eating. This was applauded by the students but only a smattering of the older people.

Sandy had warned her to expect this. "Our older folks are not so adventurous. Sure hope they'll have their corned beef on rye when they get to Tel Aviv."

Once the mounds of food were almost gone, Daniel made an announcement. "I thought it'd be nice if we talked about what we're hoping to get out of this trip. You can either write it on a slip of paper," at which point he gestured toward all the paper he had stationed around the tables, and then continued, "or you can share it with us. Whichever you feel more comfortable doing. So, anyone want to tell us . . . what do you hope to get out of this trip?"

Mark, predictably, was the first to jump in, and his answer was predictable as well. "Man, I hope the food over there is as good as it is here. Mrs. C, great food. Especially that hot red pepper stuff."

Smiling, Naomi told Mark, "Compliments to Mrs. M, not me. Jake's mom is a great cook, isn't she?"

Jerry, as gruff as ever, then told everyone, "Hey, let's hope we didn't get scalped. You know what I mean? This tour company is charging an arm and a leg." He looked over at Daniel and asked, "You said these hotels would all be five stars, right?"

"That's what I was told, Jerry."

Mark's mother raised her hand. "My husband and I are looking forward to a special family experience. This is the first time in a long while we've taken a family trip together."

Jay agreed. "Sandy and I are excited, too. With Jake getting older, this may be the last time we have a family trip like this. And to think it'll be in Israel. Rabbi, I appreciate so much this opportunity."

As others spoke of wanting it to be a safe and healthy trip, Mark called out, "So, what about you Rabbi Dan? You haven't told us what you're hoping for."

Taken off-guard, Daniel said, "Well, besides what I might hope for personally, let me tell you what I hope for as your Rabbi. My hope is that each of you will appreciate your Judaism more. You will come home to America having a deeper sense of what it means to be a Jew. That's what I hope." He had very pointedly avoided looking in Naomi's direction.

Mildred then asked, "Rabbi, please tell us what it is you're hoping for personally. We can hope for it with you—if you tell us what it is."

And once again Mark piped in, "Since the Rabbi doesn't want to tell us, you tell us, Mrs. C. What do you hope for?"

Daniel hastily reached for his guitar. "Before we all go home, how about we sing a song?" He tuned his guitar and placed a capo on the fret. "Let's sing *Jerusalem of Gold.*

Once everyone had left and the house contained only Daniel and Naomi, wordlessly they cleaned up, said their goodnights, and went to their separate rooms.

Alone in her bedroom, Naomi wanted to read from her new Study Bible, but realized she had left it in her car, having had a moment to go to the beach for some solitary time with the Lord. And she was too exhausted to climb out of bed and go out to the car—she also didn't want Daniel to hear something that would somehow make him suspicious—after all, she felt like she was a specimen under a microscope these days.

She would read from the hardbound Bible given to her by Melinda. The last time she had read it was before going to Ohio. She had read about a Jewish ruler who went to Jesus at night and seemed sincerely to be seeking the truth.

Why can't this be Daniel?

Determined to read this section again and then pray accordingly, she went to the one bookmark placed in the New Testament. Strange, it was in a whole other book of the New Testament. Matthew. Her eyes were particularly drawn to one section, where the letters were written in red. "Take my yoke upon you, and learn of me; for I am meek and lowly in heart: and ye shall find rest unto your souls. For my yoke is easy and my burden is light."

An hour before descending into Ben Gurion Airport, the passengers were treated to an exquisite sunset. The magnificent oranges, pinks, and golds streamed in through Naomi's closed eyelids, awakening her.

She turned to Daniel sitting next to her. His eyes were not closed, however they refused to turn toward her. *He must know I'm looking at him. That eye magnetism thing . . .*

Did others from the Temple observe the lack of interaction between the Rabbi and his wife? Once again, she blinked away stinging tears, and then was treated to a more splendid vision than the sunset. She saw Y'shua embracing her as she had seen before, but something was now added. His everlasting arms held not just her, but Daniel as well. Together they were being embraced by their Messiah.

About to make their descent, she reached into her purse and pulled out a package of chewing gum. This always helped her ears from feeling like they would burst. She extended a tinfoil wrapped stick to Daniel. "Want one?"

Without turning toward her, but actually moving his head to face the aisle, he shook his head. She popped the gum into her mouth and chose to finally ask. She touched Daniel's arm, causing him to look at her. "Daniel, are we going to be sleeping in the same room?"

"We'll have to." He gently picked up her hand resting on his arm and removed it. "We'll work it out."

"You know our anniversary will be tomorrow?"

"Actually, it's in four hours. They're eight hours ahead here."

Going through customs, getting his wife's luggage, connecting with the tour guides . . . Daniel fulfilled his responsibilities as both husband and Rabbi Cantor. After all, the tour company had billed this trip as "a chance to be personally escorted by Rabbi and Mrs. Cantor." Rabbi Cantor felt he was guilty of a charade.

With the tour bus making its way toward Jerusalem, Daniel was bombarded with questions from a host of the travelers, along with a slew of complaints. It was now nine p.m. and many were hungry, referring to the dinner served on the airplane as "chintzy."

Observing Daniel's weariness, Naomi spoke up on his behalf. "Please, we are all tired right now. Let's meet tomorrow morning for breakfast and we'll talk. The hotel has a wonderful breakfast we've been told." Even with his rejection, she would still be a helpmate.

Then there was the first sighting of the Temple Mount, glowing with lights. Naomi and Daniel gasped simultaneously. He had insisted Naomi take the window seat. While she pressed her face against the glass, Daniel impulsively leaned against her so that he, too, could see. Here they were, in the land of their longing, how could they not be experiencing this as one flesh?

They soon turned into the King David Hotel, where even Jerry was impressed. "It's a five star, all right."

Several members of the hotel staff took their luggage from the tour bus and assured each of the passengers that their belongings would make it to their room. They were told, "All you need do is go to the front desk and get your key."

Naomi followed Daniel as he walked to the concierge. "Cantor, Rabbi and Mrs." Once handed their keys, he handed one to Naomi. "I'm going to take a cab to the Wall. I can't sleep until I go there."

After her initial shock, she asked, "Can I go with you? Please?"

He nodded.

The cab ride was accomplished in silence—at least each had their own window to press their noses against. Naomi clung to the vision of Y'shua holding her and Daniel together while Daniel fervently prayed something would happen at the Wall where the Master of the Universe would speak to his wife and she would again be his My-omi.

They soon were cleared through security and approached the revered Western Wall. Daniel donned his prayer shawl and yarmulke. To their amazement, they were there alone. When they came to the partition which separated the men from the women, he nodded to Naomi and continued walking to the men's section.

Naomi moved toward the wall and placed her hand on the stone and instantly felt the presence of the Almighty pulsating within every atom; He was filling the very air with His beauty and His loving-kindness. Before the words were spoken in her spirit and before the words could be formed on her lips, Y'shua breathed, "Your prayer will be answered." At that moment, there was a soft rustling sound high above her head. She lifted her head to see a beautiful white bird soaring toward the men's section of the wall.

She felt compelled to walk to the place where she and Daniel had gone their separate ways. From that vantage point, she saw the men's section. Daniel was a precious lone figure against the wall. Why did he suddenly step back and raise his head?

Daniel had heard the fluttering of wings. He looked up and had a fleeting glimpse of a white bird. He then had the sensation that somehow the bird had touched him as it flew past. Had a feather fallen onto his tallit? He indeed did find something tangled in the fringes of his shawl.

Naomi witnessed him unloosening something from the threads, unfolding what looked like a small piece of white paper and reading whatever was written on it. If she was breathing, she was not conscious of it, but simply knew God was holding them both.

Slowly Daniel walked toward her. His eyes held glistening tears. Once alongside her, he handed her the small piece of paper and she read, "Come unto Me, My yoke is easy and My burden is light. I am your Messiah."

Daniel wrapped her in in his arms and covered her with his tallit. "Happy Anniversary, My-omi."

CONTACTING MIRIAM FINESILVER

On Facebook: MichaelandMimi Finesilver (https://www.face-book.com/ELOutreach)
Blog: https://miriamfinesilver.net
Amazon Author Page:
https://www.amazon.com/Miriam-Finesilver/e/B00WT2QGNC

CPSIA information can be obtained
at www.ICGtesting.com
Printed in the USA
LVHW011106291021
701894LV00001B/4